089438

LP   Rice, Luanne
         Blue moon.

Blue Moon

This Large Print Book carries the Seal of Approval of N.A.V.H.

Blue Moon

Luanne Rice

Thorndike Press • Thorndike, Maine

Published in 1994 by arrangement with Viking Penguin, a division of Penguin Books USA Inc.

This is a work of fiction. Names, characters, places, and incidents either are the product of the author's imagination or are used fictitiously, and any resemblance to actual persons, living or dead, events, or locales is entirely coincidental.

A condensation of this novel first appeared in *Good Housekeeping.*

Thorndike Large Print ® Basic Series.

The text of this Large Print edition is unabridged.
Other aspects of the book may vary from the original edition.

The tree indicium is a trademark of Thorndike Press.

Set in 16 pt. News Plantin by Rick Gundberg.

Printed in the United States on acid-free, high opacity paper. ∞

Library of Congress Cataloging in Publication Data

Rice, Luanne.   94B190Z
    Blue moon / Luanne Rice.
        p.   cm.
    ISBN 0-7862-0148-7 (alk. paper : lg. print)   I. Title.
    [PS3568.I289B57   1994]
    873'.54—dc20
                                              93-44120

To Derek Quigley

1

Some said Mount Hope was founded on love, and some said it was founded on war. Peter Benson, a shipbuilding English settler, gave a parcel of land on the harbor to his daughter Alice the day of her marriage, and she and her husband, William Perry, founded the town. From their wedding day forward, the Perrys built ships for the Revolution, and their descendants built ships for the War of 1812, the War Between the States, the First World War, and the Second World War.

From May until September, on certain October weekends for the foliage, and on two consecutive December Saturdays for the Christmas Strolls, Mount Hope would fill with tourists. Deluxe motorcoaches from New Jersey and Ohio brought folks hoping to breathe New England salt air, to walk the tawny dunes of Spray Cove at sunset, to gaze at sleek white yachts longer than their tour buses, to drive past the *belle époque* palaces of robber barons while over the loudspeaker the tour guide delivered salacious gossip about the barons' fortunes and depravities — and to eat Shore Dinners.

Shore Dinners were hefty meals of clear-brothed Rhode Island clam chowder, briny steamer clams, chunks of milky-white codfish dipped in succulent beer batter and deep-fried until crackling and golden, butter-broiled sea scallops, sweet corn on the cob, and lobster. Tradition had it that Shore Dinners must be eaten within sight of salt water. For the best Shore Dinners in Mount Hope, people went to Lobsterville.

With four big picture windows facing the harbor, Lobsterville had the nicest view of any restaurant in town. No one minded the hour or longer wait for a table, because the bar served the biggest drinks on the waterfront. Drinking their whiskey sours, diners loved to drift along the wharf, listening for bell buoys, halyards clanking in the wind, and the strains of the Dixieland band playing two docks away at Brick's.

The breeze turned chilly, after sunset, and people put on sweaters. They watched the harbor launch chuff from mooring to mooring, ferrying the sailors from their boats into town. Sea gulls cruised the air. Fishing boats stopped at the end of the dock, past the sign declaring the area off-limits to tourists, to unload their catches. It was exciting to know that the fish you were about to eat was *that fresh*. Women in bright cotton dresses leaned into the arms of their husbands, for warmth. Waiting to hear their names called over the Lobsterville loudspeaker, men never felt stronger.

The Keating family had owned this spot on the Mount Hope waterfront for three generations. Battered by a century of northeasters, and worse, it was a working-fishermen's wharf, glistening with fish scales, reeking of cod. The family owned a fleet of boats; tethered to the wharf, they were painted the bright primary colors of children's building blocks. Most of their daily catch went to the Boston fish auction. But the most prized fish went to Lobsterville, the family restaurant, which occupied the same wharf as the boats that caught it.

People joked that the clamming rakes crossed over the bar were the Keatings' coat of arms. Regulars knew the story of how Eddie and Sheila Keating had started the business with a bushel of clams and a case of whiskey. Lobsterville's red leather menus contained a page listing historical facts about Mount Hope, the fishing fleet, shipbuilding, Mount Hope's gilded era, the Bensons, and the Perrys. Right at the top, in old-fashioned script, as if handwritten, were the words: "Some say Mount

Hope was founded on love, and some say it was founded on war."

The Keatings considered Mount Hope's love-and-war business romantic hooey, fodder for the tour-bus drivers. The Keatings said Mount Hope was founded on cod, pollack, haddock, hake, ice to keep them fresh, and lobster. Especially lobster. The Keatings said Mount Hope was founded on fish, plain and simple.

Cass Keating Medieros, Eddie and Sheila Keating's youngest granddaughter, was keeper of the flame, guardian of the freezers. Eddie was dead. Her parents no longer spent every day tending the business. Her eldest sister, Nora, ran Lobsterville, and their middle sister, Bonnie Kenneally, filled in occasionally. At thirty-seven, Cass was still considered the baby of the family, but if you owned a fish joint and you wanted fresh sole, you talked to Cass.

Cass sat in her office on the second floor of Keating & Daughters, the fish warehouse down the dock from the restaurant, trying to concentrate on the week's accounts while listening for the sound of her husband Billy's fishing boat. Josie, their four-year-old, lay on the splintery wide-board floor, making her Barbie drive clamshells as if they were cars.

Josie made sounds. Her words. She rattled along, telling a story her mother couldn't understand. She crashed the clamshells, catching her finger, cried out.

"Be careful," Cass said, knowing Josie couldn't hear her. Josie didn't hear right.

"Ow," Josie said. She had panic in her eyes until she caught sight of Cass: it didn't matter that Cass had been sitting there all along. Josie held out her finger for Cass to kiss, which she did, still calculating on the adding machine.

Comforted, Josie went back to playing. She made a rumbling sound like cars on the highway. Cass wondered what instinct or memory made that possible; Josie's speech teacher said she couldn't hear anything too high or too low in frequency: jet planes, the vacuum cleaner, birds, cars.

Josie was born to the fish life, just as Cass and her sisters and all their children had been. She already knew the difference between sole and flounder; she wasn't afraid to pick up crabs; she could swim like a fish herself. Sometimes Cass let herself dream about what Josie's future would hold.

For fifteen-year-old T.J., Cass and Billy's only son, Cass wanted Harvard or Yale, maybe law school, more likely an oceanography program, eventually governor of Rhode Island, elected on an environmentalist platform. Right now he was having a little trouble concentrating on his schoolwork, but if there was one thing Cass remembered it was teenage hormones, and T.J. was right on the cutting edge.

Belinda, aged thirteen, wrote poetry and the previous year had won a statewide essay contest for seventh graders. She could already steer a boat by the stars. She'd grow up to be an expert boat handler, falling in love with every handsome sailor who passed by, dating guys who drove cars with disgusting bumper stickers, like "If it smells like fish, eat it." Cass imagined Belinda, after making it through adolescence, becoming a writer.

Cass's dreams for Josie were on hold. For Josie, for now, all Cass wanted was placement in normal kindergarten. To keep her out of "special" school.

One night when she was two, Josie had wakened with a fever, crying and flushed with a dewy glow in the lamplight. Cass and Billy had already paced many nights trying to comfort feverish babies, so they weren't really worried. By dawn, however, the glow had turned into a fiery red rash.

Just as Cass was dialing Dr. Malone's number, Josie let forth a shriek from her father's arms that made Cass think of the witch in the

12

Wizard of Oz crying, "Melting! I'm melting!"

It was the kind of thing she could tell Billy. Cass believed it was what set them apart from other long-married couples with kids, the way they could sweat through each of their children's crises while hanging on to their humor, to their old selves, when they were just Cass and Billy in Love, not Cass and Billy Still in Love — with Kids. Turning to tell Billy about her silly witch image, she saw something that made her drop the phone in terror: Billy fighting a wild animal, a tiger in a sack clawing to get free, snarling and writhing with such force it seemed about to fly out of his arms.

Only it was Josie in her baby blanket, having a seizure.

Roseola, Dr. Malone told them at the emergency room, instantly reassuring them it was a fairly common childhood disease. He wasn't worried; he expected her to make a full recovery, with the possibility of "some mild hearing loss."

Mild hearing loss at ninety, the age of Cass's grandmother, was one thing. But for a two-year-old child, just learning to talk, it meant a whole new world. Cass imagined it like this: Josie familiar with the sounds of her mother's and father's voices, Belinda's laughter, T.J.'s rude stereo; Josie saying new words out loud, putting those words together, beginning to make her family understand her; then suddenly having her ears stuffed with cotton so that vowels and consonants sounded the same, without edges, like mush.

Josie cried a lot.

Cass and Billy, madly in love since eighth grade and proud of it, ready for love action at any time, anywhere, hardly talked anymore. They "talked," but they stayed off the subject of Josie. And Josie affected nearly every aspect of their lives. It was as if her speech problems were contagious.

Cass, who until recently had craved hot sex with Billy the way she had twenty years ago, found herself using excuses in bed. They didn't make love as frequently as before. She no longer let him hold her all night. His arms around her felt too tight, and she had to pull away, roll over, take deep breaths.

Now she pressed her cheek against the window and watched for his boat. Wind licked the wave tops white. Summer yachts were racing the storm in from sea. The fishermen of Mount Hope wouldn't think twice about this weather; she'd been surprised to hear on the ship-to-shore radio that Billy was coming in. Any minute now she'd see him. Wind rattled the window glass, spooking her. But she didn't step back.

Mysterious to Cass was the lust she felt for Billy away from their house. Like now, at the office, she imagined them doing the wild thing the second he hit dry land, downstairs off the lobster-tank room in a dark nook furnished with two cots for exhausted fishermen who had too far to drive.

"Bob?" Josie said.

"Yes?" Cass replied instantly, facing her daughter, making sure Josie could see her lips. Josie didn't mispronounce everything, but she said "Bob" for "Mom" and "On" for "Aunt," and Cass wanted to make sure she enunciated properly when Josie was watching. "Yes?" she said again.

"I'm nnngry," Josie said darkly.

Josie could have meant either "angry" or "hungry" but, given the hour, Cass felt hopeful. "You're hungry?" Cass asked, rubbing her stomach.

"Yes," Josie said, nodding.

"Then we'll go home. We won't wait for Daddy." Cass spoke normally, the way she would with her other children, and she didn't stop to think which words Josie understood, because Dr. Parsons, Josie's ear doctor, had told them Josie was bright, that although she skipped words and missed certain sounds, she comprehended what people meant. Kindergarten would start in a year, and more and

15

more often Dr. Parsons mentioned a special school. He talked about options such as sign language. He described the deaf community, people who used sign language as their primary means of communication. To Cass it seemed as foreign as a country in Asia.

Dr. Parsons had referred them to Mrs. Kaiser, a blue-haired speech therapist with a walk-in dollhouse in her office and a wall of shelves filled with children's books. Mrs. Kaiser worked with Josie on pronunciation and concentration, and she scoffed at sign language. In spite of the fact that Josie complained that Mrs. Kaiser smelled like a geranium, Cass liked Mrs. Kaiser's approach better than Dr. Parsons's.

Cass checked Josie's hearing aids, to make sure the volume levels were set right. Then she threw her purse, the clamshells, and Barbie into a battered old sail bag. She locked the office door behind her, and she and Josie fumbled down the dark inner stairway to the vast and smelly tank room. The generator hummed, circulating seawater through the lobster tanks and running the freezers.

"Stay right here," she said to Josie, patting the top of her head. Cass opened the big walk-in freezer and turned on the light. A blast of frosty air billowed into the damp tank room. Cass selected a particularly fine frozen pollack fillet, thick and stiff as a book, wrapped it in plastic, and dropped it into her bag. Josie stood right where Cass had left her, straight and still, her back against a green wooden lobster tank. The freezers terrified her.

Josie held Cass's fingers with one hand, sucked the thumb of the other. Cass could hear her sucking noisily, still gripped by the fear that her mother could have been consumed by the deep freezer. They hurried across the cobblestoned wharf, past Lobsterville. She and Josie waved at the window, out of habit, in case Nora or Bonnie was working at the front desk and happened to look out. Cass buckled Josie into the back of their green Volvo 240 wagon. They'd be home in ten minutes, and, with a jolt, Cass realized that she'd see the sign.

They drove through town, past the boutiques and restaurants, the yacht marina and the town fish pier. Condos were going up everywhere. Builders had ripped down the sheds and docks at Dexter's Boatworks and laid the foundation for four buildings of time-share units. They'd turned Mack's Lobster Pound into a stage-set village called Puritan's Crossing. Pretty soon developers would brick up the whole waterfront.

They cut across Marcellus Boulevard, past the robber barons' glitter palaces, to Alewives

17

Park. Here the houses were cozy, ranches or Cape Cods. You could smell the salt air but couldn't see the water.

The Park, a development built in the fifties, contained dozens of dead-end streets. The developer had planned it that way to prevent drivers from speeding around, from using the Park roads as shortcuts to the waterfront or the navy base. Most of the streets were too short to work up any speed at all, but Coleridge Avenue, where the Medieroses lived, was the main thoroughfare. It was the only street that had a stoplight, and it had a posted speed limit of thirty-five miles per hour.

Last month, Dawn Sullivan, a high school senior, and a carload of friends came whipping down Coleridge just as Tally, a neighbor's dog, decided to cross the street. Josie ran after Tally.

Cass heard tires squeal. Instantly alert for Josie, she tore for the door. Brakes screamed.

There was T.J. lifting Josie off the sidewalk. Dawn ran around the front of her family's Blazer. Tally, oblivious, sniffed her way up the Camarras' driveway across the street. Time froze, and Cass's ears rang.

At first Cass thought Josie had been hit. Halfway out the door, she stopped dead and couldn't take the next step. There was Dawn crying, her round face nuzzled in Josie's neck, saying, "Why didn't you look both ways, don't you know this is a busy street?"

Then Josie lifted her head, caught sight of Cass, and let out a wail. Cass grabbed her from T.J. and held her tight, feeling for bumps or broken bones.

"She's okay, Mom," T.J. said, sounding shaken instead of sullen for a change.

"I didn't hit her; she's just scared," Dawn said. "She couldn't hear me coming. She didn't look both ways. She must have her hearing aids turned off."

"They're on, Dawn," Cass said into Josie's shiny dark hair. "She heard you, that's why she stopped."

"She's not fucking deaf, you know," T.J. said.

"Hey, I used to babysit for her, and for you, too, so don't say 'fucking' to me, T.J.," Dawn said shrilly.

Neighbors came out to see what was happening, and someone called the police. Officer Bobrowski measured the black tire marks, still reeking of rubber, a parallel smoky trail the length of three lawns, and issued Dawn a summons. An hour passed before things went back to normal, and for days afterward people talked about the teenage speeding problem and the danger it posed to the little deaf girl.

Cass believed that Josie's hearing problem

19

had nothing to do with it: Josie was just chasing a little dog, the way any child might. Cass blamed herself, for letting Josie out of her sight for that instant, and she blamed Dawn, who had babysat for all three Medieros kids and plenty of other Alewives Park families, for driving too fast.

In spite of Cass's and Billy's protestations, the property owners' association allotted money, previously earmarked for improvement of the basketball court, for two yellow signs to be posted on Coleridge Avenue, to be spaced one-eighth of a mile from the Medieroses' house in either direction.

The idea of them terrified Cass, just as the thought of a special school did. Driving home from work with her hungry daughter, knowing what she was about to see, she shouldn't have felt such shock. Shock and something else. Fear? Shame? There it was, half a block away:

DRIVE SLOWLY
DEAF CHILD

"What's that, Bob?" asked Josie, pointing. As if to compensate for the cotton in her ears, Josie had eagle eyes.

"A new sign."

"What say?"

20

Turning into their driveway, Cass navigated the wagon around T.J.'s mountain bike, the lawnmower, and Josie's Big Wheel. "It says 'Drive Slowly, Children Playing,' " Cass said, making sure Josie could see her lips.

After two weeks at sea, Billy Medieros was heading home. He usually loved this part of the trip, when the hold was full of fish and his crew was happy because they knew their share of the catch would be high, and they'd all sleep in their own beds that night. He drove the *Norboca* — the best boat in his father-in-law's fleet — around Minturn Ledge, and Mount Hope came into view.

Billy stood at the wheel. The tide had been against him, and he knew he had missed Cass. She would have left work by now, was probably already home cooking supper. He could picture her at the stove, stirring something steamy, her summer dress sticking damply to her breasts and hips. His wife had the body of a young sexpot. Other guys at sea would pray to Miss July, but Billy would look at pictures of Cass, her coppery curls falling across her face, her blue eyes sexy and mysterious, delicate fingers cupping her full breasts, offering them to the camera. She had given him a Minolta for his last birthday, but for his real present she had posed nude.

Lately, to Billy, Cass had seemed more real in his bunk at sea than she was at home. In person, Cass looked the same, she smelled the same, but she seemed absent, somehow. Raising Josie changed her every day, and Billy resisted the transformation. He missed his wife.

He was nearly home. His eyes roved the church spires, the wooden piers clawing the harbor, American flags flapping from the yacht club and every hotel roof, white yachts rocking on the waves, two trawlers heading out. He waved to the skippers, both of whom he had fished with before. Manuel Vega waved back, a beer in his hand.

Billy couldn't stand skippers who drank onboard. It set a bad example for the crew. You had to stay keen every second. Billy had seen terrible things happen to fishermen who weren't paying attention — fingers lost to a winch handle, a skull split open by a boom. On Billy's first trip out with his father-in-law, Jimmy Keating, a crewmate with both hands busy setting nets had bitten down on a skinny line to hold it in place, and a gust of wind had yanked out six of his top teeth.

Stupid. Billy had no patience for stupid crew members, and dulling your senses with alcohol, at sea on a fifty-foot boat, was stupid.

"Docking!" Billy yelled, and four guys ran up from below. John Barnard, Billy's first mate for this trip, stood with Billy at the bridge. They had gone to high school together; they'd fished as a team hundreds of times. They never confided in each other, but they had an easygoing way of passing time for long stretches.

Strange, maybe, considering that John Barnard was the only man Billy had ever felt jealous of. Cass liked him too much.

Not that anything had ever happened. But Billy knew she'd get that look in her eyes whenever she was going to see John. Before Christmas parties, Holy Ghost Society dances, even goddamn PTA meetings. Cass was a flirt, for sure; it only made Billy that much prouder she belonged to him.

Cass and John had dated a couple of times after high school, when Cass had wanted to marry Billy and Billy had been too dumb to ask. Billy, delivering scallops to Lobsterville one night, had met Cass's mother in the kitchen.

"I want to show you something," Mary Keating said. She began leading Billy into the dining room.

"I can't go in there," Billy said, sniffing his sleeve. His rubber boots tracked fragments of scallop shells.

"You'd better, if you don't want to lose her," Mary said. Five-two in her red high

23

heels, Mary Keating had a husky smoker's voice and the drive of a Detroit diesel. Standing in the kitchen doorway, blocking waiters, she pointed across the dining room. There, at a table for two, framed by a picture window overlooking a red sun setting over Mount Hope harbor, were Cass and John having dinner together. Bonnie and Nora, in their waitress uniforms, hovered nearby.

John was tall, with sandy-brown hair and a movie-hero profile, and the way he and Cass were leaning across the table, smiling into each other's blue eyes, made Billy want to vault across the bar and smash John's face into his plate. He left without a word, but the incident brought Billy to his senses; two months later, he and Cass were married.

Billy pulled back on the throttle as they passed the No Wake buoy.

"Almost there," John said.

"Can I grab a ride with you?" Billy asked. The Barnards, like most fishing families, lived in Alewives Park.

"Sure," John said. "No problem."

The deck hands checked the dock lines, then stood along the port rail, waiting to jump ashore. Billy threw the engine into reverse, then eased the boat ahead. She bumped hard once, hard again, and then settled into a gentle sway.

Billy paid out the shares, and he and John climbed into John's truck.

"You planning to talk to Big Jim?" John asked.

"What about?"

"Shit on the boat. You know."

Billy knew. His father-in-law was a skinflint, always cutting corners. Billy, the *Norboca*'s paid skipper, made excuses for him, but certain things could not be overlooked. With a crew of five, the life raft contained three survival suits. The engines needed an overhaul. Twice in two days the generator had crapped out, and Billy and John had had to start the bilge pumps by hand.

"I'll tell him, but you know what he'll say," Billy said.

" 'I'll look into it,' " John said, imitating Jimmy's heavy Mount Hope accent. "The cheap son of a bitch. I'm getting my own boat."

"You're as predictable as he is," Billy said. "You always say that."

"I'm serious. I'm working on it," John said, stopping in front of Billy's house.

"I'll beat you to it," Billy said.

"If you ever got your own boat, quit fishing for Jimmy, he'd make his daughter kick your ass out of bed," John said.

"Dream on," Billy said, laughing, grabbing

his gear out of the pickup. Waving as John drove away, Billy caught the glint of John's headlights on gray metal: the back of a sign that hadn't been there two weeks ago, when he was last home. Billy didn't have to read it; he knew what it said.

T.J. didn't expect to hear his mother run for the front door, but he listened anyway. He heard the door open, then his father's heavy boots in the front hall, then quiet voices in the kitchen. His father's homecomings never used to be quiet.

He and Belinda were in the TV room, supposedly doing their homework. Belinda Perfecto sat hunched over her math book, probably algebra or some advanced trigonometry they gave eighth-grade whiz kids. Josie had tuned in to cartoons, and until he'd seen John's headlights, T.J. had been watching Wile E. Coyote chasing Road Runner through the desert. With the sound turned off, their mother would never know.

"Dad's home," he said.

Belinda practically tripped over her books, flying out of the room. He heard her footsteps running all the way down the hall.

T.J. reached into his pocket for a pack of Lobsterville matches. He lit one and watched it burn down, a tiny blue flame, until it hit his thumb and finger. He pinched it out, feeling the pain. He lit another.

"Don't smoke," Josie said without turning around. She sat smack in front of the TV, crouched like a cat.

"Josie," he said. "C'mere."

She didn't reply.

"Josie," he said, louder. He hated that she couldn't hear right. She had to watch your mouth to understand what you were saying. She would stare so intensely, her eyebrows frowning, her mouth moving along with yours, no sound coming out, as if she were rehearsing for the day when she could talk normally.

He lit a third match, and that did the trick. Josie turned around, holding her nose. "Smoking stinks," she said. "It's gusting."

"I'm not smoking. Come here."

Josie was tiny. None of his friends had a brother or sister this little. Standing there so small and stern, she reminded him of his grandmother. "Belinda's a jerk," he said.

"No," Josie said, shaking her head sadly. "Not a germ."

"I said a *jerk*," T.J. said, emphasizing the "k."

"Okay, maybe," Josie said. She'd make fun of Perfecto just to please T.J., even though he could see she worshipped the ground

Belinda walked on. Belinda did not deserve it. She was at that age when everything embarrassed her, even Josie. T.J. had heard one of Belinda's eighth-grade asshole friends calling Josie "Earmuff Head." Belinda didn't say one thing, and she had screamed at T.J. when he called the friend "Slut Wannabe" right to her face.

His father came into the room. With his hands on his hips, he filled the doorway. Belinda was right behind him. "Hey, hey, hey," his father said. "Look who's home."

Josie squealed and climbed up his leg. Now he had Belinda on his back and Josie around his neck. People told T.J. he looked just like his father. He didn't think that was too bad. His father was tan with thick dark hair like Mel Gibson's.

"Hi, Dad," T.J. said. "Have a good trip?"

"Long and hard, and it's good to be home." He unloaded the girls onto the loveseat and took Belinda's chair.

"Did you see any whales?" Belinda asked.

"A couple."

"Certain whales are endangered. They get caught in fishermen's nets, and they could become extinct," Belinda said.

"You ought to get a medal for wonderfulness," T.J. said. "It's probably on its way right now."

"Thank you," Belinda said, and T.J. had to wonder if she thought he was serious. Belinda was living proof that being a brain had nothing to do with being smart.

"No Nukes, Save the Whales for Christ," Dad said.

Belinda laughed without understanding that their father was teasing her. T.J. could tell by that panicky look in her eye. Their mother came to the door and everyone looked up, even Josie.

"Dinner's almost ready," she said.

"We held dinner for you, Dad," Belinda said. "I told her you'd be home in time."

"She did," Mom said.

"Perfect predictions every time," T.J. said.

"Hey, I'm here, aren't I?" his father asked, oblivious to Belinda's glaring at T.J.

Their mother was looking around, trying to decide where to sit. T.J. wished she would sit on Dad's lap, the way she used to. If there were twenty empty chairs, his mother would sit on his father's lap. She was heading across the room, away from Dad, to the wing chair. T.J. couldn't figure out why, but it made him sad that his mother needed a chair now.

"Here, Mom," he said, standing, offering his mother the seat nearest to his father.

"Thanks, sweetie," his mother said, sounding surprised. She kissed the top of his head and sat down. Now that T.J. had given up his seat, he couldn't figure out what to do. He looked at his parents and sisters staring silently at the soundless cartoon, and he left the room.

2

Josie put her feet on the sand, to make sure she could stand with her head above water. Then she put the snorkel back in her mouth, bit down on the rubber, and dove under again. She blinked behind her mask. There was her mother, just a few feet away. Josie fluttered her feet, swimming forward, to take her mother's hand.

Under the sea was Josie's favorite place. Sunlight pierced the clear water and bleached her tan skin pale. Eelgrass swayed in the waves, like mysterious cartoon dancing girls. A school of minnows slashed through the grass. Delicate hermit crabs skittered along the bottom.

Cass squeezed Josie's hand. She pointed out a baby shrimp, jetting backward through the water. It seemed so funny that Josie let out a laugh that bubbled to the surface. She wondered if the air contained sound, if someone in a boat could hear laugh bubbles. Underwater, hearing didn't matter.

Josie sometimes hoped they would find a school of big fish, like the ones her father caught, the kind that had tiny teeth and ate sea plants. She wouldn't be scared. She would swim with fish as big as girls. But thinking of big fish suddenly made her stomach flip. T.J. had a shark's tooth bigger than an arrowhead. He wore it around his neck, hanging from a rawhide shoelace. Thinking of T.J.'s necklace made Josie swim closer to her mother.

They saw a lobster pot. Its buoy had broken off, and it had drifted in close to shore. Josie and her mother hovered above it. Their arms moved in slow, graceful strokes, keeping them steady. Cass glanced at Josie, then pointed. A lobster was caught in the trap.

Josie watched her mother take a deep breath, then dive down. She shimmered through the water, quick as a fish, to unlatch the trap door. Josie watched her hand reach inside, her fingers closing around the lobster's back.

Cass swam up to Josie. Josie reached out, taking the lobster from her mother. The lobster reached back, its claws clicking, trying to pinch Josie's hand. Josie smiled. She had held hundreds of lobsters. She looked at its big, round eyes, and she touched its long, skinny, green, ribbed antennae. Then she let it go.

It drifted through the water for an instant, then flapped its tail to swim backward. Josie watched it hide under a rock ledge covered with blue-black mussels. Her mother tapped her hand.

Josie knew it was time to leave, but she didn't want to. She wanted to watch the crevice, to see if the lobster would appear again. But she followed her mother anyway, into the shallow water. She touched the sand with her toes, craned her neck to breathe without the snorkel.

Her mother tossed her head from side to side, letting the water drain out of her ears. Josie copied her. Then she raced out of the water, to crouch in the damp sand below the high-tide line. Shivering in the salty breeze, she began packing sand into a sturdy castle. She knew her mother would soon join in. They always built a sand castle before leaving the beach.

When Cass and Billy first married, years after falling in love, friends of her parents would come to the restaurant and ask, "When are you two going to start a family?" Some would even add the words "of your own." The question had boggled Cass's mind. How could two grown people with parents and grandparents and brothers and sisters "start" a family? Just leave the past in a photo album, take a deep breath, and begin again? To Cass it would be like chopping down the family tree to plant a new one.

Then T.J. was born. There in the delivery room, the moment the doctor placed their son on her stomach, Cass felt the world change. Soaking wet, numb from the waist down, she held her baby. Billy tried to find a way to hold them both. Their newborn had Billy's black curls. Cass remembered looking Billy straight in the face.

"I love our family," she said, and for the first time in her life she wasn't counting the extended Keating clan. She was talking about three people — Cass, Billy, and T.J.

So why should it have surprised Cass when her son, learning to talk, had given short shrift to his ABC's and animal noises, and had seemed more interested in nailing down the intricacies of their family?

"Are you Gram's daughter?"

"Yes."

"And I'm your son," T.J. would say with satisfaction. The mother-son part he had picked up right away.

"Right," Cass would say.

"Are Aunt Bonnie and Aunt Nora your aunts?"

"No, they're my sisters."

34

"And they're my sisters, too."

"No, they're your aunts."

"Then who are my sisters?"

Cass would explain, again, that T.J. didn't have any sisters, that for the time being he was an only child, but that he had his great-grandmother Sheila, his grandparents, aunts and an uncle, and two parents who loved him very much.

Belinda had learned to talk the same way. When Billy would call, Belinda would say, "Daddy, would you like to speak to your wife?" When Nora would call, Belinda would say, "Your brother-in-law is on a fishing trip, but your sister is here," then hand the phone to Cass. It had cracked Cass and Billy up.

Cass knew that people with hearing loss often compensated in other ways: they had sharper vision, or they sensed a person's approach before anyone else in the room could actually hear it. Josie, lacking clear words, had developed superior family intuition. She loved to hug and cuddle, and she knew when T.J. needed to be left alone. Although she didn't always pronounce the names right, she knew who was who. But sometimes her thoughts would pile up, and she'd wail and rage until Cass scooped her up, patting her head and whispering into her ear, because even if Josie couldn't hear right the warm breath had to feel good.

Right now Cass and Josie were on their way back from snorkeling. They decided to stop at Lobsterville, just to say hello. Billy had taken T.J. and Belinda to a Red Sox game, and Cass needed some company.

People drinking cocktails milled about outside. The Keatings had initiated an Early Bird Special — half-price lobsters — from five o'clock to six-thirty. This was Nora's latest idea. Nora was the family moneymaker, this generation's answer to their grandmother. Sometimes Cass had the sense Nora stayed up all night thinking of the business to avoid feeling lonely. Nora was a spinster. Not just "single" or "unmarried," but somehow pinched and increasingly ungenerous. All the Keating girls had what Cass liked to call their "romantic histories," but Nora had slept with one too many womanizing yachtsmen, and she'd turned bitter.

"We're going to see the ons, we're going to see the ons," Josie said, doing a happy little high-step.

"Hello, sweethearts," Mary Keating said.

"Hi, Mom," Cass said.

Mary stood behind the reservations desk. A cigarette dangled from her mouth, and she squinted through the smoke at the thick green

36

reservations book. Mary was tiny — several inches shorter than any of her daughters. Cass saw she'd gotten a new perm. Her hair curled in tight steel-gray rings, and the red lipstick she wore made her mouth look enormous. She always matched her lipstick to warm shades in her dress, and today she wore crimson.

Josie scrambled up the tall wooden stool to see what her grandmother was doing. Waiters wearing white shirts and madras ties — a fashion innovation of Nora's; Cass liked the skinny black ties better — rushed in and out through the kitchen's swinging doors.

"Where's Bonnie, Mom?" Cass asked.

"Around. Behind the bar, last I saw."

A portly man, balding, wearing aviator sunglasses, approached the reservations desk. "Mary! How've you been? You remember me."

From her warm smile, no one but the family would know that Mary Keating had no idea who this guy was.

"Could you make me a reservation for eight people at eight o'clock?" he asked.

Mary glanced at her book. "Sorry, hon. We've got before six-thirty or after nine-thirty," she said.

The man slid a folded bill across the desk. Cass watched Josie, to see if she'd seen. Of course Josie was staring at her grandmother's closed hand. "We just cruised down from Edgartown," he said. "Would've called you from the boat, but the marine operator couldn't get a line. Everyone's going to be damned disappointed. A trip to Mount Hope wouldn't be the same without dinner at Lobsterville."

"That's right, dear," Mary said. "Okay, I'll squeeze you in. Eight o'clock sharp. In the Tap Room. No harbor view, but if you've just sailed down from the Vineyard, you've had enough of the water."

"That's great," the man said. "We'll see you then."

"Mom . . ." Cass said, nodding at Josie. She didn't approve of Josie learning graft from her own grandmother.

Mary shrugged her shoulders. "This is the restaurant business, honey," she said.

"He gave you money," Josie said.

"He was just paying for his dinner in advance," Mary said. "That way there won't be any squabbling over the check." Cass didn't consider the lie an improvement; Josie had an unnerving knack for discerning the truth. Cass watched her now, regarding her grandmother with puzzlement.

"Me have candies?" Josie asked, sensing that she had mysteriously gained the upper hand.

"No, it's too close to dinner. You can call

someone on the loudspeaker, though." Mary ran her finger down the reservations list. "You can call the Wilsons. Table for two." She handed Josie the microphone.

"That's okay," Josie said, shaking her head. Shy about speaking, she would never talk on the loudspeaker. All the other kids had loved it. Cass remembered watching Belinda lift the heavy chrome microphone, flip the red switch, and blow softly into the speaker. Then in a steady voice she'd call the party, unconsciously imitating her grandmother's Thornton accent.

Mary called the Wilson party, and they came forward: a high-school-aged couple, dressed for a prom. Mary had to smell the girl's white rose corsage, comment on the boy's pearl-gray tuxedo. Then she called Vinnie Fusaro, a waiter not many years older than the Wilsons, to lead them to their table. "Make sure they have a view," Mary commanded. "Aren't they cute?" she said to Cass.

But Cass was watching Vinnie Fusaro from behind. He had brown hair, dark and silky as a polished table. It curled over the collar of his white shirt. He didn't walk; he swaggered. He carried the leather-bound menus as if they meant nothing to him, objects that had simply materialized in his left hand. Cass thought of Billy twenty years ago: cocky in high school, carrying his schoolbooks as if they were air, as if he never planned to read them, anyway.

"Who does Vinnie Fusaro remind you of?" Cass asked her mother.

"He's the spitting image of his father, God rest his soul."

"That man looks like Daddy," Josie said, oblivious to the conversation.

Cass glanced down and wondered if Josie looked in the mirror and also saw her father. Josie had Billy's wide dark eyes, his tangled curls, a tan in June that Cass would kill to have in August.

"Well, hi," Bonnie said, untying the white apron that covered her black uniform. "What perfect timing. I'm just about to leave for the day. I have to get home and feed your cousins," she said straight to Josie, hugging her.

Bonnie weighed one eighty-three. She had always gained weight easily, but in the last few years she had piled it on steadily, as if becoming fat were her goal. She ate a handful of mints from the reservations desk.

"You shouldn't eat those," Mary said.

Bonnie ate another handful.

"Where's Nora?" Mary asked. "My feet are killing me. She's supposed to take over for me here, and I want to go home. Your father is all alone with his mother, and you *know* they're driving each other crazy."

"We'll go find Nora," Cass said. "Josie, will you be a good girl for Gram?"

Josie did not answer, and Cass, walking away with Bonnie, knew that she hadn't even heard the question.

The noise level was high tonight. A few fishermen stood along the mahogany bar, but mostly the crowd was from out of town: women wearing obvious eye makeup, men slightly overdressed in pale suits and ties. It was too early in the summer for the blue-blazer crowd.

"Hey, sailors!" Cass yelled to John Barnard and Al Sweet. They motioned her over, but she just blew them a kiss.

"You're a married woman," Bonnie said. "Good thing your husband's not here."

"I wish he were. Got to keep him on his toes," Cass said.

Nora stood between John and Al, shooting dagger looks at Cass. "My God, is she still going after Al?" Cass asked.

"She's lonely," Bonnie said. "But it turns my stomach, the way she throws herself at him. You know he couldn't care less about her."

It made Cass sad, the way Nora had no respect for herself. It showed in her face. She had pale, thin cheeks, the complexion of someone who smoked and drank too much. She had bleached the red out of her hair, and blond waves fell to her narrow shoulders. Nora was seven years older than Cass, four years older than Bonnie. As teenagers, all the Keating girls had tried to scrub away their freckles, squirt lemon juice into their hair to dull the red. Now, watching Nora talk to John and Al, Cass thought Nora looked more Nordic than Irish — someone from another family.

"Let's leave her alone," Bonnie said. "I'll take over for Mom for a while. Let the little creeps starve. This morning they missed the school bus on purpose, both of them. They're doing it to torture me. It's punishment for their father, I think. Every time he does a long trip, they act up. He's been out thirteen days, scallopping with the O'Tooles. You'd think they'd have outgrown it by now. I mean, *teenagers.*"

"A hunger strike," Cass said, glancing again at Nora. "We have to find her a boyfriend. Someone you wouldn't necessarily have to describe as 'halfway decent.' "

"All these guys talk. Gavin says you wouldn't believe the sex bragging on the boat, even about Nora. Dad's paying their wages, and they're talking about his daughter."

"They're skunks," Cass said.

"You must admit," Bonnie said, making a

matronly little clucking noise, "that she does bring it on herself."

Cass didn't reply. Bonnie was the family earth mother, everything in her life as comfortable as old clothes.

Nora needed help, not criticism. She was so lonely, she would drink too much and start making phone calls at night. She'd call her sisters, friends, people she hadn't seen in ten years. Sooner or later she'd call some horny guy just back from fifteen days at sea without a woman. Nora would tell him to come over, and things would start up.

Cass saw John Barnard watching her, his smile all crooked and sultry, wanting her to really notice him. "Come on," she said to Bonnie. "Let's get out of here."

Mary Keating turned the reservations desk over to Bonnie. Bonnie rolled her blue eyes, listening to Mary tick off familiar instructions: give the Pentwarses a good table; keep an eye on Sandy and make sure her checks match what people order; offer the lobster-stuffed sole to the best customers only, the regular seafood stuffing to everyone else.

Billy, T.J., and Belinda walked through the front door. The kids were wearing Red Sox caps.

"Will you look who's here!" Mary exclaimed.

Billy kissed Mary, Bonnie, and Josie. Cass felt a force drawing her to him. He looked her straight in the eye, but she gave him no encouragement — just to see what he would do. He pulled her close, gave her a hot kiss, didn't let her go as soon as she expected. His rough hands felt smooth running down the back of her yellow cotton sweater. Leaning back, he gave her a questioning smile; perhaps, like Cass, he was wondering why this feeling so seldom hit them at home.

"Who won?" Mary asked.

"Red Sox," Billy said.

"Oh, good. Jim should be happy. He's probably been listening on the radio."

"We brought you a cap," Belinda said to Josie.

Josie gasped with pleasure. She shimmied on the stool. "Where is it?"

Billy reached into his back pocket and fit it on her head.

"Kitty cat, kitty cat. Where is it?" Josie asked.

Bending down to Josie's level, Cass looked straight into her eyes. " 'Cap,' not 'cat.' It's on your head." Josie began slapping her own head, as if there were a live animal on it, and howling with fright and frustration.

"Oh, God," Belinda said, mortified. She escaped out the door.

Cass tried to reason with Josie for exactly thirty seconds, until she realized that Josie had worked herself into a frenzy. When Cass tried to lift her, Josie turned into rubberchild. Over and over she performed a boneless slither, slipping through her mother's arms, screaming "No, no!" as alarmed patrons glanced up from their drinks. Cass fought an urge to shake her like a dust mop. Billy stood there, motionless.

"Can't you do something?" Cass asked him. She heard the outrage in her own voice. She stood aside.

Billy put his arms around Josie — loosely at first, then more firmly. She stopped struggling. She was crying so hard, tears flew out of her eyes. "Kitty cat, kitty cat," she wept. Again, she swatted her head, slapping Billy's eye in the process. But she let him hold her.

Billy lifted Josie into his arms. "We'll be in the car," he said, leaving the restaurant.

Cass leaned against the reservations desk, watching them go.

"Special help, special help is what you need," Mary said, as if she hadn't said it too many times already.

Cass half expected her mother to whip out a brochure for North Point Academy for the Deaf. Mary would get something helpful but meddlesome in mind, then work her point home by beating aggressively around the bush, until you wanted to scream.

Cass turned her back. She started to walk out, but Bonnie caught her arm and pulled her into the corner.

"It's hard," Bonnie said, her voice older-sister confident, "but you'll figure it out."

"She acts like I don't know what's best for my own daughter." Cass paused. "Not that I do."

"Like any of us do."

"Billy handles her so easily. Did you see?" Cass asked.

"He's not with her all the time. It's the same with Gavin. They aren't around half the time, and when they come home they want to be the good guys."

"He won't talk to her," Cass said. "He's afraid to. He just hugs her and thinks everything will be fine. You have to make her understand things. He treats her like a doll, not a daughter."

"Tell him," Bonnie said.

"He knows," Cass said, looking at Bonnie straight-on. "He's heard it a hundred times."

Cass sat in Mrs. Kaiser's waiting room, watching Josie walk her Barbie doll along the sofa back. Dolls made Josie feel safe. Lately she carried this naked Barbie wherever she went. Cass couldn't convince her to put it down, even to take a bath or go to bed.

Mrs. Kaiser's door opened. A boy about Josie's age hurtled into the waiting room, his mother and Mrs. Kaiser close behind him. He stood beside Josie, saying words that sounded like "Row, row, run, row." He wore two hearing aids. Josie snatched her Barbie, as if she feared he would take it from her. She ran to Cass, and the boy ran crying to his mother.

"He's just saying hello," the boy's mother said pleasantly, making sure Josie could see her mouth.

"*My* Barbie!" Josie said, shaking the doll at the boy.

Cass shrugged at the boy's mother, and the mother shrugged back as she led her son out of the office.

Josie didn't play with children her own age. When she saw a kid, Josie would try to pretend that he wasn't there. Children her own age, even deaf children, didn't understand Josie, and they scared her.

"Hello, Josie," Mrs. Kaiser said in her melodic, singsong voice, creaking down to Josie's level. Cass could see that Mrs. Kaiser had not quite managed to zip her dress up all the way. She debated with herself whether or not to mention it, and decided not to.

"My Barbie," Josie said, still defensive.

"She is a bee-you-tee-ful doll," Mrs. Kaiser said. Cass found something fake in the way Mrs. Kaiser talked to Josie. She sounded like a kindly old grandmother with perfect pronunciation, but her expression was too crisp, vaguely critical. Cass always felt she was being judged by Mrs. Kaiser, coming up slightly short.

"I know," Josie said.

"Mrs. Kaiser, may I talk with you?" Cass asked. Usually she left Josie alone for speech therapy; Josie refused to concentrate when Cass was around.

"Of course. Please, come into the office," Mrs. Kaiser said.

Cass sat opposite Mrs. Kaiser's desk, Josie in her lap.

"Josie doesn't seem to be improving," Cass said.

"Speech therapy is a long, difficult process," Mrs. Kaiser said. "It's natural to become discouraged, but you can't give up."

"She has the most terrible tantrums. She doesn't hear clearly, we have a misunderstanding, and she . . ."

"I know. She flies into a rage. You're not the only parent to tell me that. When a child is hard of hearing, every word is a stumbling block. You must make sure she's watching you, make sure she can see your mouth."

"I try."

"Well, then," Mrs. Kaiser said positively, her chin up. "That's what you have to do, if you want Josie to be oral. You know the alternatives."

"My husband has a hard time talking to her."

"Keep after him."

"And my family," Cass said. "My mother's all for North Point."

"Heavens," Mrs. Kaiser said. "Luckily, Josie isn't her daughter. I'm sure your mother's intentions are good, but I think that is the wrong program for Josie. Josie does hear. She does talk. Communication is difficult for her, but not impossible. Not at all. We don't want her closed off in a school for the deaf. We want her to live in a hearing world."

"I know," Cass said, twirling Josie's hair while Josie walked Barbie down Cass's thigh.

"Josie has another year before kindergarten. By then she and I will make excellent progress, and she'll enter with other children her age."

"Are you sure she'll be ready?"

"She will have to be if you don't want her in North Point or Special Needs," Mrs. Kaiser said ominously.

Not for the first time, Cass thought of how

49

much Mrs. Kaiser resembled Cass's first-grade teacher, who had reminded her of a witch. An old lady who used sweet talk to hide a mean streak. What was Cass doing, leaving her daughter with a witch every week?

"Special Needs," Mrs. Kaiser said again, shaking her head.

She made the words sound like a curse — which, in a way, they were. If Josie didn't qualify for real kindergarten at Mount Hope Elementary, the school would stick her in the Special Needs class, where she and other deaf kids would share a room with Down syndrome, autistic, and emotionally disturbed children — kids with all different special needs grouped together.

"We'll make sure she's ready," Mrs. Kaiser said. "Now, why don't you leave us for half an hour, let us get some work done?"

Cass looked from Mrs. Kaiser to Josie. "I'll be back soon, sweetheart," she said, watching Josie.

"Bye, Bob," Josie said, sliding off Cass's knee. She seemed to enjoy Mrs. Kaiser, speech therapy, everything in the office; she never minded when Cass left.

"Uh, Mrs. Kaiser," Cass said, rising. "Could I help you with your zipper? It's just a little undone."

"Oh, thank you, dear," Mrs. Kaiser said

gratefully, turning slightly, throwing Cass a real smile that a true witch could never have managed.

Cass smiled back.

3

Sheila Keating wakened with the sense of falling from the sky, and she grabbed her glass locket in a panic. Holding it against her chest, she felt her heart beating. It fluttered fast and unsteadily; it made Sheila feel she had a moth inside her trying to escape. When she opened her eyes she checked her knobby hand for silvery wing dust. She stretched in the easy chair where she'd been napping and tested the feeling of her feet on the floor. She wanted something cold to drink, but she wasn't ready to move yet.

The glass locket felt warm in her hand, and she peered down at it. Nothing but a milky blur. "Goddamn it," Sheila said out loud. She hated her cataracts. She'd been thinking about having them removed until Eileen Conway had hers done. Dr. Greaves had peeled off the cataracts, and now poor Eileen wished someone would turn out the lights; brightness poured in from everywhere, Eileen said, making her eyes blink and water, and she felt like a cunner in a fishbowl, longing for deep water and nice dark rockweed.

"Goddamn it!" Sheila said louder, because no one was home. Jimmy and Mary were off to work. Sheila shook the glass locket and watched the pearl rattle around. She wouldn't want to bruise the pearl, but she liked to watch it move. When she had her hearing aid turned on, she could hear it rattle.

Eddie had given it to her the day they'd met: June 6, 1920. He'd been clamming on Easton's Beach, showing off for Sheila and her friends from Providence. After he'd filled his bushel basket full of cherrystones, he'd shucked one for a snack. Right there, in that pink clam, he'd found a pearl. He'd walked straight up to Sheila on the boardwalk and handed it to her. Placing it in her hand, his fingertips had brushed her palm. It was the first time a boy had touched her.

Just last month, lighting a candle in church, Sheila had put her palm near the flame and thought of that first touch. She had felt heat, and if she'd left her hand there, she would have burned it. What Eddie had made her feel was a surge, and Sheila should have known she couldn't recapture it with a candle in church. Sometimes, if she closed her eyes and imagined her blue straw hat, the sound of waves breaking over the Easton jetties, and the smell of clams, she could remember the surge. Not feel it, certainly, but remember it.

"Eddie, I hate it here," Sheila said out loud, but of course Eddie couldn't hear her. He'd been dead many years. She wondered what he would have thought of her freeloading with Jim. He had never approved of their friends who lived with their grown children — not because he objected to their imposing on their children, but because he couldn't understand how adults could give up their privacy.

"Well, I'm alone all day, for God's sake, that should be enough privacy for anyone," she said crossly.

"Who are you talking to, Granny?"

Sheila's eyes flew open. She'd forgotten Eddie wasn't here. Cass and Josie stood there instead, grinning at her.

"To myself," Sheila said to Josie. "Don't you ever do that?"

"Oh, yes," Josie said. She climbed onto Sheila's lap and stared at her, wide-eyed. Sheila gave her a squeeze. This was her youngest great-grandchild. She could hardly remember their names, but she knew Josie. Cass brought Josie to visit almost every day.

Sheila wished Cass wouldn't dress like a boy. Cass was her prettiest granddaughter, all pink and gold. She had the coloring of the inside of a seashell. She had a beautiful figure, but you'd never know it from the dungarees and baggy shirts she went around in.

"You're my favorite grandchild, you know," Sheila said to Cass.

"Granny!" Cass said, embarrassed.

"Well, don't worry. I won't say it in front of your sisters."

People never admitted they had favorite children or grandchildren, and Sheila didn't know why not. You wouldn't announce it to the world, but privately you had good reason for loving one more than the other. One might be sweeter, one might have the soul of Ireland, one might be a car thief. Of her two children, Sheila had loved Edward better. She loved Jim, too, but Ward was her elder, her kinder, her smarter son. From the day he was born until the day he died, a golden light had shined on him.

He had amazed his mother by never crying, by talking early, by exhibiting an interest in everything from ice-skating to clamming to watching her make pie crust. Sheila would let him flute the edges, and she would always make him a grape-jelly tart from the leftover crust. Although they'd started off calling him "Eddie, Jr.," as time went on they changed his nickname to Ward; it was the stronger, more commanding half of "Edward." Changing it was his father's idea. Ward aced anything he did. Tests in school, sports — he could have played football for the Providence Steamrollers.

Sheila couldn't see it from here, not anymore, but across the room hung a painting Ward had done in high school. It was a beautiful watercolor of two boys clamming the flats at Easton's Beach; Sheila had always assumed Ward had meant the boys to be himself and Jim. He had caught perfectly the colors of a summer day, and he'd painted the boys to be strong, with their basket nearly full of clams. That painting was Sheila's safe. Behind the painting, taped to the frame, was an envelope. In it she kept her children's birth certificates, various deeds and IOU's, and Ward's death certificate.

When Ward was sixteen, his father founded Keating & Sons Fish Company and made Ward a full partner. The plural "sons" turned out, at first, to be optimistic; Jim hadn't wanted any part of the business. Jim joined the merchant marine, and no one heard a word from him for five years.

He was gone for Ward's going-away party. That day was still Sheila's happiest memory: the day before her son left for war. In some ways, it was Sheila and Eddie's last happy day. They had never expected to outlive one of their children; by now some acceptance had seeped into Sheila's bones, and the thought of Ward dead no longer shocked her. It had been fifty years. She kept all his postcards of the Rocky Mountains in the Douay Bible; Ward had been stationed at Colorado Springs, in training for the Air Corps, before going overseas.

Sheila opened her eyes. Cass was saying something. "What?" Sheila asked, blinking to get her in focus.

Cass's mouth was moving, but all Sheila could hear were whooshing noises, like waves on the beach. "What? I can't hear you."

Josie reached up and grabbed Sheila by the left ear. The expression on the child's face was very intense, as if she were concentrating on an important job. Thumps and screeches filled Sheila's ear, and she realized that Josie was turning on her hearing aid.

"Can I get you anything?" Cass asked, the words suddenly clear enough to hear.

"A ginger ale," Sheila said. "That would be very nice."

There were ways and there were ways to catch swordfish. The method you chose depended on how much money you hoped to make selling the meat. The easiest, laziest way was longlining. You set a long line in the middle of the sea, with fifty or so baited hooks hanging down from red plastic buoys at ten-foot intervals. You checked your loran position, so you'd know where to come back to, and then you left the line overnight. When you returned at dawn you'd see a necklace of bulbous red balls bobbing in the distance. You'd pull up each red ball and its hook, one at a time. Hanging from a few of the hooks would be swordfish. Dead swordfish. Some chewed by sharks, others just dead and beginning to bloat.

Longlined swordfish didn't fetch as high a price as harpooned ones. Sharks could rip out fifty dollars' worth of swordfish meat, leaving a jagged hole. Even if you trimmed the edges, people didn't want to buy raggedy fish. Not only because it wasn't appetizing, but because something primeval in the customer twigged that the fish had died an ugly death: drowning with a hook in its mouth while sharks ate it alive. At least, that was James Keating's theory.

Today he and George Magnano wanted to harpoon a fish off the books, to cut up and store in their freezers. Christ, just for the fun of it. What a day: clear and fine, diamonds on the water. Jimmy stood beside George in the tuna tower while George drove. George owned a hell of a boat, a Grady White 25 with twin Yamaha 250s. There wasn't a ripple from here to Montauk; they were bound to spot fins. Jimmy pulled his cap down low, to keep the sun off his face. He had a skin cancer on his nose, and Mary made him wear the hat and Sea & Ski.

"What've you got there? A softball team or something?" George asked, flicking the peak of Jimmy's cap.

Jimmy took it off, handed it over. Blue mesh, it had a patch with the words "Keating & Daughters" in gold script. "Little League," Jimmy said. "Cass's and Bonnie's kids used to play. I still sponsor the team."

"They got you managing?"

"What, are you kidding? An old man like me? No, that's for the young guys. This is a smooth ride, George. This boat drives like a Cadillac when she's on her plane."

"Hell, on a day like this you could take a Boston Whaler to Block Island and you wouldn't feel a bump. Flat as glass."

"You'll pound your nuts off in a Whaler, no matter what the weather's like. Cass's boy T.J. gave me a ride in his last week, and I can still feel it." Jimmy and George laughed at the painful memories of what a Boston Whaler could do to a man.

It felt pleasant to zoom along with no particular destination. Jimmy Keating felt free

59

and young, the way he always did in sum-
mertime. Fishermen were transformed with
the summer solstice. The instant the sun
crossed the Tropic of Cancer, grown men
would skip out of work, climb tuna towers,
joke about their balls.

Throughout the dark winter and muddy
spring, Jimmy had been having deep money
troubles. He could barely keep his fleet going.
Mount Hope harbor had been iced in for the
first time in twenty-one years, and a lot of
boats were damaged. Even Lobsterville's
profits were off. It sure felt good to get away,
to stare across the waves at an empty horizon.

Back in Mount Hope, Jimmy would sneak
out of work and walk along the waterfront
until he came to old Doc Breton's pier. Doc
had run an icehouse when Jimmy was a kid,
and Jimmy had liked to hang around, listening
to Doc tell about sailing around Cape Horn
on a whaling ship and bringing ivory from
Africa to Deep River, Connecticut. Doc was
so old, he didn't have a tooth in his head.
His shipmates had called him Doc because he
had a knack for first aid. He'd known how
to apply a poultice, how to use a tourniquet,
how to brew a broth that would settle any
stomach in gale seas.

Jimmy had wondered whether Doc was a
magic man. His stories had put a spell on

60

Jimmy, made him itch to go to sea — itch so bad he'd toss all night with his skin burning. All because Doc had conjured for Jimmy the pure beauty of a ship on the sea and the peace of endless distance. Because of Doc, Jimmy joined the merchant marine.

When Jimmy Keating had told his parents he'd be leaving them for a few years, his mother had cried. But his father, Eddie, could understand Doc's power. Once, lobstering in January, Eddie had gotten frostbite in his fingers. By the time he'd made port, four of them were turning black, and he'd been sure he would lose them. But Doc had made him soak them in cold salt water, then salt water he'd heated in the kettle, then cold water again, until finally Eddie's fingers turned white. They'd never really gotten back to being normal finger-colored, but at least he hadn't lost them. And so Eddie had staked Doc some money to open an icehouse.

Now Doc's pier was tumbledown, a ramshackle mass of splinters and concrete. It was the last abandoned pier on Mount Hope's waterfront. Wind whistled through, and it sounded like a person talking. Jimmy would stand there, all alone. He could almost hear Doc's voice; it was the only place on land he could go to achieve the peace of an empty horizon.

"You and Beverly ever think of moving to Florida?" Jimmy asked.

"Never," George said. "Who needs swamps and funny red fish? Besides, we'd miss the winters up here."

"Right," Jimmy snorted.

"Seriously, Bev is a Christmas freak. She'd never leave New England. She'd miss the snow and the fireplace, all that cozy shit. She'd miss the kids."

"Same with Mary. Mary could never leave the girls."

"What about you?"

"I've thought about it," Jimmy said. "But we've got the business."

"The girls could run it, but you want to keep your hand in."

"That's right," Jimmy said. He thought he'd spied a fin up ahead, but it was just a rogue wave. A few puffy clouds were forming in the north.

They cruised along in silence, taking it easy. Sure felt good to be on the water, Jimmy thought for about the fifth time since they'd left the dock. "Sure feels . . ." he started to say.

"What?" George asked.

But Jimmy didn't answer. All of a sudden he realized that he was trying to trick himself into having a good time: the summer day, the beers, the boat. But anytime lately he wasn't actively trying to rip the head off some insurance guy, or juggle the ledgers, robbing Peter to pay Paul, he worried that he'd return to Mount Hope and find that the whole dock had washed away. Everything out to sea: his father's fish business, the restaurant, his wife and daughters, his mother, everything. Keating's Wharf would be as abandoned as Doc Breton's.

Jimmy Keating squinted at the horizon with extraordinary concentration. He refused to look down. He had the weirdest feeling that if he looked straight down into the water below, he would see his lobster tanks and his father's oak desk floating by.

"I'm thinking about selling my boat," George said.

"This one?" Jimmy asked, surprised. George had been saving for this sportfisher his whole working life; he'd just taken delivery in March.

"No, the *Rover Mar.*"

Keating wondered whether George was feeling him out. Did Keating have any use for a seventy-five-foot Desco with a six-cylinder Gardner diesel? Frankly, he had always thought the boat more suitable for southern waters.

"Billy's been talking to me. He's looking

to buy," George said.

"Holy shit. Our Billy?" Jimmy asked, bowled over.

"Yeah. But it's just talk," George said. "You know how young guys are. They're always dreaming about going off on their own."

"Billy works for me," Jimmy said, cut by the news.

Jimmy had known Billy since he was five years old and used to play with Cass after school. Billy had followed Cass around starry-eyed for years. They seemed polar opposites: Cass, fair and slender; Billy, dark and stocky. Mary used to call them "the batteries," the charge between them was so obvious. Sometimes Jimmy would watch Billy drive Cass away in his Camaro, and he would wonder how it felt to fall in love. Jimmy knew love, he knew devotion. But when he watched Billy and Cass, he knew that he had missed something in life.

Jimmy had three terrific daughters. He hated to categorize them, but he couldn't help it. Nora, his eldest, was Miss Independence, with a temper if you crossed her; Jimmy had given up hoping she'd get married. Bonnie rolled with the flow. Her life with Gavin and their kids seemed to make her happy. Keating wouldn't give two cents for Gavin's fishing talent, but he was a decent son-in-law. What more did he have a right to expect?

When Cass was little, Jimmy would have called her his most carefree daughter, his tomboy. Back then he would never have believed her to be the most complicated. He pictured Cass's life in a fast-forward blur: the braces she'd hated so much she took them off herself instead of waiting for the orthodontist (one thousand dollars down the drain); the summer she'd swum one hundred miles for charity; her eighth-grade dance with Billy, of course, the last time she ever got home before curfew; sneaking out to be with Billy; the punishments he and Mary meted out; more sneaking out; Jimmy threatening to send her to a convent; her suspension from school for stealing a marijuana cigarette during Drug Awareness Day; Billy's mother calling every night to ask if the Keatings had seen her son; Cass's graduation, thank God; six months at the University of Maine; the day she came to work for Jimmy; her wedding day; having the kids. Cass, his spark plug.

Except for the six months at Maine, Cass and Billy had been inseparable; she had quit Maine because she missed him. They'd gone through a phase of dating other people, but in truth Billy had courted Cass her whole life. It had amazed Jimmy when they'd settled down, knocked off the craziness. They had three beautiful kids. Josie had a problem, Jimmy knew. It broke his heart, the way she tried so hard to get her mouth around sounds that came automatically to everyone else. But it hurt him worse to see how it affected Cass. She hardly ever left Josie's side; she was like an interpreter assigned to a foreign princess.

"I hope to hell Billy's not having a midlife crisis or something," Jimmy said. "Buying a new boat is a major step."

"Look, I shouldn't have said anything," George said. "It's just talk. The kid has big dreams."

"Hell, that's nothing new. He married my daughter, didn't he?"

After four nights of noticing this guy come in alone and drink his Scotch at the bar instead of outside on the terrace, where the single girls hung around, Nora Keating knew he was watching her. His eyes would follow her until she looked him dead on, and then he would smile. At first her suspicious side took over. Maybe he was in the restaurant business. Maybe he planned to open a place across the bay or on one of the islands and he wanted to figure out Lobsterville's formula for success.

But on Thursday, when she finally said hello to him, his expression turned so happy and open, Nora felt herself blush. He looked about forty-five, taller than six feet, blond, with sensitive blue eyes. Very sensitive. He looked like someone whose feelings got hurt easily. She'd noticed the first night he came in that he didn't wear a wedding ring and his finger didn't have a telltale indentation or white ring line.

"Hello," Nora said, passing by.

"Hello," the man said, and he gave her such a wonderful, open smile, she had to look twice. Nora couldn't be sure, but she thought he had a southern accent.

She told the Conways, sitting on barstools, that their regular table was ready. Abe Conway struggled to his feet, then stood by for Eileen. He held his arms tense, waiting to catch her, like a fireman holding a safety net under the window of a burning house. Nora wished her mother would tell them they were too old to sit on barstools. Mary could crack a joke about it, and no one would get upset. All it would take was one fall for Eileen to break her hip and wind up in a nursing home. Not to mention the potential for a lawsuit against the restaurant. Never mind that the Conways were her grandmother's oldest friends; when medical bills started pouring in, people changed their friendly tunes fast.

Leading the Conways through the crowd, Nora did something she had never before allowed herself to do and would have fired any Lobsterville employee for doing: instead of walking the Conways to their table, she stopped short beside the bar and told them to go on ahead. "You know the way," she said to Abe. "You don't mind, do you?"

"Of course not. Thanks, darling," Abe said, palming her five dollars, as usual. Nora slipped the bill into the pocket of her tight black skirt. She did a U-turn and walked back to the blond man.

"Will you be having dinner with us tonight?" she asked.

" 'Us'?" the man said, giving her a flirtatious grin.

"Here at the restaurant," Nora said, deadpan. You can't judge a book by its cover, she thought: he looks nice, but he's just another wise guy.

"Because what I was thinking was, maybe if you haven't had your dinner, we could have it together," the man said with a definite southern accent.

"I'm working," Nora said.

"Oh, I figured that," the man said. "Four nights now I've come in here after a long day of meetings and seen you running your head off, and I've thought, that lady needs to sit down."

"Wish I could," Nora said, but she didn't

68

smile. She never minded acting friendly toward the customers; she considered it part of her job. But something about this one put her on guard. At the same time, she wished that she'd worn sheerer pantyhose and that she hadn't canceled her facial last Saturday. "Do you have business in town?" she asked.

"In Providence," he said. "But I decided to stay down here. I wanted to see a little of the New England coastline. Sure is beautiful."

"Isn't it?" Nora said. She reached into the pocket of her white linen blazer for a cigarette. He took a pack of Lobsterville matches from an ashtray on the bar and lit it for her.

"Since you let me light your cigarette, you have to tell me your name."

"Nora Keating," she said, exhaling.

"I'm Willis Randecker," he said.

"And where is Willis Randecker from?"

"From Savannah, Georgia," he replied.

"A long way from home," Nora said. Sometimes, talking to handsome men, she came out with phrases that sounded like song lyrics. She recognized this, and it embarrassed her. But Nora had a sexy voice, as throaty as Mary's had been before she'd scorched the sex appeal out of it with too many Lucky Strikes, and Nora knew she made the phrases sound inviting and suggestive.

69

"Look, Nora," Willis said. "I don't want to be too forward, but you should really consider quitting. I was a smoker myself for many years, and it took a heart attack before I wised up. I shouldn't even have lit it for you, but I'm not the type of guy who lets a lady light her own cigarette."

He'd made her feel self-conscious, but she wasn't about to let him know. She held the cigarette in the air between them, at about shoulder height. Her hands were her best feature. She thought that a cigarette between her fingers emphasized their length and elegance. Sometimes she stared at her hands because she thought they were beautiful; she knew it was vain, but they reminded her of the kind of hands Lauren Bacall must have. Nora's hands were the only part of her body she liked.

And then Willis did the strangest thing: he took the cigarette right out of Nora's hand and stubbed it out in the ashtray. Nora couldn't look at him. She knew she should be mad, but she wasn't. If she looked at him, she might start to cry.

"Gosh, I shouldn't have done that. I know how rude I must seem. Something came over me, that's all I can say." Willis was shaking his head, wiping his brow. Still, Nora didn't speak. She felt as if every hair on her body were standing on end. She glanced at her wrist, but all her wrist hairs were lying down.

"Nora?" Willis said nervously.

"When did you have your heart attack?" Nora asked. She could feel the blood pulsing at her temples.

"Two years ago last December fourteenth," Willis said. "I smoked three packs a day, I ate bacon and eggs every morning. Used to put salt on my toast in the morning. Hell, I salted everything. Apples, peanut butter and jelly, pecan pie. Everything. Then, whammo. I knew what was happening to me the minute I felt the pain. Unbelievable pain, Nora, up and down my arm."

"But you . . ." But you survived? was what Nora had been about to ask.

"I changed my life," Willis said. "First thing I did was quit smoking. That was so strange. All my life, since I was twelve, I'd lived for cigarettes, one after the other. It got so I wouldn't go to a movie because they wouldn't let you smoke in the theater."

"What else did you do?" Nora asked. She wasn't used to talking to strange men without holding a cigarette in her hand; she couldn't believe it, but for the moment, the desire to smoke had left her. She felt light as a feather, ethereal. She imagined she was hovering above the bar, like someone having an out-of-body experience.

"I changed my diet entirely, lost twenty pounds. Now I season my food with lemon juice instead of salt." He grinned suddenly, and Nora noticed a wide space between his two front teeth. He pulled from his pocket a yellow plastic squeeze lemon.

Nora laughed. "You don't need that here. We serve all our fish with fresh lemon."

"Not every place does," Willis said.

A comfortable silence unfolded between them. They might have been sitting alone on the balcony of Nora's condo instead of here in the crowded bar. Nora knew she should relieve her mother at the reservations desk; the sauce chef had to leave early tonight, and Nora had to smooth things over in the kitchen. But she couldn't move. She felt at peace, staring into Willis's blue eyes. She caught a glimpse of Bonnie coming toward her. *Leave me alone,* she wished. And when she turned to say she'd be with her in a minute, Bonnie had gone.

"That girl a friend of yours?" Willis asked.

"My sister," Nora said.

"She works here, too?" Willis asked.

"Yes."

"Nice," Willis said, nodding. "It's nice when a family can be together. That's the way it should be." He paused, cleared his throat. "Boy, you sure make it easy to talk. This isn't the kind of thing you tell someone you've just met, but you want to know the biggest change I made after my heart attack?"

Nora wasn't sure exactly how, but she knew what he was about to say. "You got divorced," she said.

"But how did you guess? That's what happened!" Willis exclaimed. "This is amazing, you and me being on the same wavelength like that."

"I guess you seem like the married type," Nora said. "I know the difference. I don't know why . . . I guess I meet a lot of people here. Some are the married type, some aren't. So I took you for married, and then I didn't see a wedding ring."

"I wore one for sixteen years," Willis said. "And the first thing I thought after they took the tubes out of my nose was, I'm not happy. Not a bit happy, and lying there in the hospital, I had plenty of opportunity to figure out why. And so I got a divorce. How long'd you wear yours?"

"My what?" Nora asked.

"Your wedding band."

"I've never been married," Nora said.

"That surprises me," Willis said. "That really surprises me."

Suddenly the silence turned awkward. Nora remembered that her mother was going to

Providence that night to meet her father. "I have to get back to work," she said.

"I figured. You sure you can't get your sister to fill in for you and join me for dinner instead?"

Of all the nights for this to happen, Nora thought. She meets a man she likes, and her mother has the night off. Bonnie hardly ever worked at night, because of her kids. Nora didn't exactly blame her, but it was moments like this that she felt different from her sisters. Cass and Bonnie were wives and mothers, and Nora was not — simple as that.

"I can't," Nora said. "It just won't work out tonight. Maybe . . ." She wanted to ask him if he was free tomorrow night; that would give her time to work things out.

"That's a rotten shame," Willis said. "I was really hoping. I knew I should've asked you last night for dinner tonight, but the way you looked, I didn't think you'd give me the time of day."

"There's always tomorrow," Nora said in her torch-song lyric voice.

"Tomorrow I fly home to Savannah," Willis said.

Nora felt her heartbeat flatten out. Her breath came steady once again. Things were back to normal. Even her eyes, which hadn't left Willis's face, went back to work. They began to scan the room for regular customers, for deadbeats, for drunks, for sailors. Nora wanted a cigarette.

"Would you like a table anyway?" Nora asked. "We're booked, but I could squeeze you in."

"Nah. If I have to eat alone, I'm going back to the hotel. I'll call room service. I've got my lemon. They never serve lemons with room service," he said, squeezing his lemon. "I come back on business from time to time. Maybe we could have dinner then."

"That would be fine," Nora said.

"Don't you smoke," Willis said. "I mean it. You've gone fifteen minutes without one, and you know you don't need it."

"I'll try," Nora said.

They said goodbye, and she started to shoulder her way through the crowd. Someone had plugged elevator music into the tape deck. Probably that sap in the kitchen, the oyster shucker her mother had hired. Nora's hand slid into her pocket and closed around a cigarette.

"Hey, pretty Nora," Al Sweet said as she passed by.

Her spine stiffened as she remembered their last time, facedown on his bed, his weight on her back, his voice insistent and deliberately little-boyish, begging her to let him try it a

75

new way, a slash of pain, Nora's quick scream. She hurried her pace, jostling a crowd of college kids. Maybe her mother hadn't left yet. Maybe if Nora explained about Willis, her mother would stay.

"Where's Mother?" Nora said to Bonnie. Bonnie, with a pile of menus and a wine list in her hand, was leading a group of six into the dining room.

"On her way home."

"Can you work tonight?" Nora asked right in front of the party of six. "Can you take over for me?"

Bonnie shook her head. "I can't. Sean is putting together his science project tonight, and I've got to be there."

Nora stood still, slightly disoriented. "What's his project? I'm a science teacher," she heard one of the customers ask Bonnie.

"A papier-mâché ocean basin," Bonnie explained, leading them to their table. "Seamounts, guyots, and the continental shelf."

Standing at the reservations desk, Nora raised the cigarette to her lips. She flicked her lighter and stared at the flame for a few seconds. Glancing at the barroom door, she half expected to see Willis watching her with reproach. She lit the cigarette, took a long drag. She held it between her long fingers, and she stood perfectly still, gazing at her hand for one minute, until Joe Kenneally, Bonnie's father-in-law, came forward to ask if his table was ready.

4

Josie's sister, Belinda, and her cousin Emma
Kenneally wanted her to climb out onto the
roof with them, but Josie didn't want to. She
stood in Belinda's bedroom, turning the
Snoopy lamp off and on. Belinda reached
through the open window for her. Belinda's
fingers wiggled, and Josie gave her a low-five,
laughing.

Belinda was trying to talk her into it, but
Josie kept her head down so she wouldn't hear
her.

"It's high up," Josie said, even though it
was only the second story. She remembered
once she had followed Belinda to the top of
Granddad's pine tree. She hated when Belinda
dared her to do something scary, because Josie
didn't like to disappoint her. She acted very
busy, frowning at the Snoopy lamp as if it
were broken and her frown could fix it. She
held it steady with both hands. After a while
Belinda got the message, and her face disappeared from the window.

Belinda was babysitting for Josie while Cass went grocery shopping. Darcy, Josie's regular daytime babysitter, never came anymore, because she had to take care of her old mother. Darcy's mother had been in a nursing home, but she wasn't happy there. Josie's own mother had explained this to her. Josie didn't understand what was so hard about taking care of your mother. But she felt very embarrassed to imagine Darcy's mother, whom she had met once, in a *nursing* home, sucking on a plastic bottle or someone's bosom. Darcy's mother had gray hair and smoked cigarettes, and Josie would have said she was much too old to be nursing.

Belinda had her own telephone. It was made of clear plastic, and when it rang or you called someone, all the bells and wires inside would light up. Some were hot pink, some were bright blue, like the lights on the police car that had come the time Josie had run into the street.

Josie poked her head out the window to see what her sister and cousin were doing. They had forgotten about her; they were putting dark red polish on their fingernails. It smelled evil and poisonous. Josie pulled her head inside.

She lifted the telephone receiver and dialed some numbers. She waited for a long time.

She wondered what it would be like to talk on the telephone. Her mother had told her in case of emergency to dial 911 and start saying her name and address over and over, even if she couldn't hear the other person, until someone came to help.

Having the receiver against her ear reminded Josie of hearing tests. Those headphones were always hard and cool, just like this phone. Nothing like the earphones on Belinda's Walkman, which were too small to completely cover her ears. The scratchy black fabric on them made Josie's ears itch.

Sometimes Belinda let Josie try her Walkman, and even though no music came through, Josie wanted one of her own, to wear to school when she was old enough. Speaking into the phone, she pretended she was calling the Walkman place. "I want a red one with blue earphones. I hate black, don't you? I don't want the scratchy kind. The smooth kind. Okay? Okay. We have to wear them to school. Don't forget. Call me back."

Cass parked her car in front of the Star Market and waited for Billy. She had planned this carefully. She had asked him to call her at home before heading out to the hardware store, so that she could give him a list of things to pick up at the market. He'd called at four, said he was leaving, and she'd asked him to get milk and bread. Then she had immediately jumped into her car to intercept him.

But now it was four-thirty, there was no sign of Billy, she had grocery shopping to do, and she had to head home soon. He had taught her to drive in this exact spot. Back then, the parking-lot lights were on a timer. They'd switch off at ten. All their friends would meet up here, then fan out to parties, the beach, the highway to Providence. Then, when they were alone, Billy would slide under Cass into the passenger seat and she would climb behind the wheel.

With his arm around her, she would circumnavigate the dark lot. Every night the landmarks changed: a lone grocery cart, a discarded tire, the occasional parked Chevy. Vacant cars seemed mysterious and sexy, hinting of married lovers coming to meet in separate cars and going off together in one of them.

Some nights, when the tar was slick, she would drive in wide circles without braking, rings spiraling smaller as she increased her speed. Holding the wheel hard to the right, she would lean into Billy, her shoulder touching his, and he'd be laughing in her ear.

Then she'd tap the brake, tap it again easy, and pull the car into the darkest corner of the lot. She'd turn off the headlights. Billy would slide down in the seat. Cass would lie half on top of him, her lips kissing his, her back arched forward, leaving just enough room between their bodies to unbuckle his belt while he undid her buttons.

She sat still, watching the entrance where Billy would drive in. She checked her watch: four-forty-five. She thought of Josie, at home alone with Belinda and Emma. A chain of worship: Josie worshipped Belinda, Belinda worshipped Emma, and Emma worshipped herself. By now Emma would have finished teaching Belinda beauty secrets of the universe. In fifteen minutes Emma would ride her bike home, and Belinda would be itching to start her homework. With regret, Cass realized she had just enough time to buy the groceries.

Climbing out of the Volvo, she spied Billy driving in. Since he hadn't known she had been planning to seduce him, she couldn't justify the anger she felt at his being late.

"Groceries?" he asked, kissing her.

"Yes," she said.

He caught her tone. "What?" he asked. "What did I do?"

Explaining it would sound so stupid: Well, I got Belinda to babysit so I could fuck your brains out. . . .

"You followed me here, didn't you?" he

asked, grabbing her bottom.

"Yes, let's have sex right . . ." She kicked away a piece of glass. "Here. Right on the tar," she said, as if she were joking.

"Too hot, Cass. You'd melt it." He mouthed the word *"Later."*

"What do you want for dinner?" Cass asked.

"I'll come in with you," Billy said, surprising her. About to head offshore again, he had work to do on the *Norboca.*

"Good," she said. "We'll get done faster."

"That anxious? Don't worry — it'll keep." He brushed his crotch with a funny, crass gesture, but Cass didn't smile. He grimaced, holding his index fingers twelve inches apart.

"Great timing," she said.

"What do you mean?"

She shook her head, starting to walk toward the Star Market.

"Knock off the silent treatment, okay?"

"Let's just say I had plans," Cass said. "You, me . . ." She glanced at his crotch. "You."

"Oh, yeah? So what happened?" Billy asked, smiling.

"The time clock," Cass said. "I have to get home. Belinda has homework to do, and Josie can't stand being by herself."

"Let Josie handle it for once. It's good for her."

"You're full of shit," Cass said. They walked

together into the store. As a father, Billy was entitled to his theories. The problem was, he was hardly ever around to try them out. All the lust Cass had been feeling ebbed away.

"What would happen?" Billy asked. "What would be the big deal if Belinda ignored her?"

"Screaming fit," Cass said, easing into the numb zone she inhabited when Billy didn't grasp one of the most rudimentary facts of her daily existence.

While Cass pushed the cart, Billy threw things in. He knew what everyone liked as well as she did. He pawed through a bin of oranges, choosing six with the right color.

"These come from Florida, right?" he asked, reading the box.

"I guess so."

"It says right here: 'Packed in Orlando, Florida.' "

"That's that," Cass said, still distant. Her eyes roved the fruits and vegetables while her mind composed balanced meals for a family of five.

"I always think of coral snakes when I buy oranges," Billy said. "Here's this box straight from Florida. Probably packed at the groves and shipped straight to the airport. What's to prevent a coral snake from slithering into the box while the worker's not looking?"

"What a horrible idea," Cass said, leaning

forward to look into the box. "Could that happen?"

"Why not? When I fill a box with cod it doesn't guarantee that a crab won't crawl in."

"Aren't coral snakes poisonous?"

"The most poisonous, I'd say," Billy replied. Cass moved the cart forward.

"Well, think of something else crawling in. Something harmless. Some nonlethal southern reptile."

"I was thinking danger, baby. Where were you planning to seduce me, anyway?"

Cass ignored him. She knew Billy thought he was being cute, but she wasn't ready to give in.

"Your father told George Magnano he's thinking of retiring to Florida," Billy said.

"Oh, were you talking to George about his boat again?" Cass asked.

"Feeling him out."

"I don't know," Cass said. "I don't see you on a Gulf shrimper."

"A chump boat, right?" Billy said. "Better suited for John Barnard."

Cass reached for the Pop-Tarts. Her husband was flirting, teasing her about John. They cruised into the frozen-food aisle. Billy touched the small of her back. She felt him getting to her.

"They must keep these freezers at twenty

degrees," Cass said. During the winter she never registered temperature at the grocery store. She would be bundled in a scarf, hat, and parka, so the chill never got to her. But shopping during the summer, in a jean skirt without tights and a sleeveless shirt without a sweater, she'd be shivering halfway down this aisle. Her nipples were standing straight out under the thin cotton. She wanted Billy's hands on her breasts, she wanted to run her tongue down the long red ridge of his penis.

"Maybe we should have ice cream for dessert," she said.

"What kind?"

Delilah Pentwarse hurried past the aisle, waving hello; Cass waved back. "Chocolate-almond," she said to Billy.

"Coming up," he said.

Billy rummaged through the waist-high freezer. He came toward her, a devilish grin on his face.

"What?" she asked.

He held out a pint of ice cream to her.

"That's too small," she said. "T.J. would polish that off in ten seconds."

"This isn't for T.J.," he said.

Cass watched fuzzy circles of frost melt around his fingertips. He let the cold transfer to his fingers. She shivered as they trailed across her collarbone. She thought of his fingers beneath her, lifting her hips.

"Leave the cart," he said.

They moved toward the door. For a moment Cass thought he was going to walk out without paying, but he handed the checkout clerk some money.

"Hurry," Billy said, his hand under her elbow.

"Not now," Cass said. "I don't have time. I have to get home. . . ."

"Get in," he said, opening the door to his truck.

Cass wanted to protest, but she didn't. Now that she was inside, she could only think of what would happen next. Cass hoped he wouldn't turn left out of the parking lot, toward Alewives Park. She didn't want to go home. They could stick to her original plan: the boat. It would take too long, the girls would be fighting, Cass hadn't even bought the groceries, she would be late — but she didn't care.

Billy started the engine, shifted into first, and slid forward twenty yards, into the spot where they used to park. "Oh," she said, smiling as if he'd tickled her.

He opened the pint of ice cream.

"Oh," she repeated, now disappointed.

"What did you expect?" he asked.

"Not exactly this."

"I want to eat ice cream."

"We don't have spoons," Cass said.

"We don't need them," Billy said.

Swirling his index finger, he made an *S* in the soft, melted top. He licked off his finger, then dipped it again, holding it out to Cass. At first she thought he was joking. Was this his way of getting back at her for teasing him before? But his finger was right there, ice cream dripping onto the seat between them. She lapped the chocolate off his finger.

Studded throughout the ice cream were dark-chocolate-covered almonds. This was Cass's favorite treat. She loved to hold an almond in her mouth, sucking lightly until the chocolate melted off. Sometimes Billy teased her about how long she could make one almond last. His finger explored the ice cream now, searching for almonds. When he found one, he worked it to the surface.

"Spoons would be easier," Cass said. She opened her mouth, waiting.

"Unzip your skirt," Billy said.

"What?"

He didn't reply. He slipped the almond into her mouth. "Take your time with that," he said.

Cass said nothing. She curled her tongue around the cold almond, watching him.

He eased her jean skirt down over her hips.

She hadn't been out in the sun yet this summer; her unexposed skin was white. Billy wedged the container between the dashboard and the windshield and ran his cool hands between her thighs. He pulled her panties down.

Cass glanced around the parking lot. A boy collecting grocery carts roamed the lot; two girls on bikes stopped to talk to him. Their voices drifted out on the hot breeze. People hurried in and out of the market. A car passed by. But Billy's truck was alone in this shady corner.

The dark chocolate tasted delicious, bittersweet on the back of her tongue. Intent on finding her another, Billy had the container in his hands, mining it with his finger. He pulled one out before Cass had finished savoring the first. He eased open her thighs. He placed this second frozen almond against her clitoris.

"Ah!" she exclaimed. Radiant ice; it felt so good, it hurt.

"Close your eyes," he commanded.

Cass couldn't believe what was happening. She lay across the seat her eyes closed, tasting the rich, intense chocolate in her mouth while Billy's fingers massaged her, enclosing the almond in her warmth, sending exquisite icy spurts all through her groin.

Then he opened her up, let the almond

drop. She felt it slide beneath her, falling through the crack between the seats. She didn't care. His tongue found her clitoris; she imagined him tasting the same deep chocolate she did.

He licked her, played with the soft nut. Long, broad tongue strokes concentrating into the smallest circles. Tighter and tighter circles, everything focused on that one spot. Grocery-cart wheels clattered across the hot pavement outside; she knew that they were close, and that made it more exciting, other people, and Cass came.

"Oh," she said after a while, pushing herself up on her elbows.

"I've always wanted to do that," Billy said.

"Which part?"

"Give you a real one."

Cass smiled. On Valentine's Day at Lobsterville, diners received complimentary strawberries dipped in chocolate. Mary called them "strawberry kisses," but their underground name, coined by Bonnie and Cass, was "chocolate orgasms."

"Hey, Billy," she said. "It's your turn."

He said nothing, but smiled and raised his left eyebrow.

"You know it is," she said. Her thoughts turned to giving Billy oral sex; she envisioned her head moving up and down as she tried to take all of Billy's penis in her mouth, and she wondered how much attention she would attract. A man could stay very still, his head steady, his tongue doing all the work. But for Cass to give him the same sort of pleasure at the Star Market in broad daylight might be to invite arrest. The idea excited her more.

With one yank she undid his five-button Levi jeans. He moaned as she reached into the fly of his blue-striped boxers and grabbed his dick. It was already stiff against her hand as she pulled it free. Cass gave the very tip a quick lick, and Billy moaned again. She glanced around.

Here came Delilah Pentwarse, carrying her grocery bag. She seemed to be on a direct course for the truck.

"Shit," Billy said, hiking himself up.

Lying halfway across the seat, her bare ass gleaming in the sunlight, Cass hit the floor, crouching under the dash before Delilah could see her.

"Hi, again!" Delilah called.

"Hi," Billy called back.

"Some women have all the luck," Cass heard Delilah say. "Billy, how does Cass get you to go grocery shopping with her?"

"I blow him in the parking lot," Cass said in a low voice.

"She begs," Billy said.

"You men," Delilah said. "I'd have to beg pretty damn hard to get Joe to the Star Market."

Cass reached for the ice cream container. She dipped her finger in to make it cold. She could almost feel Billy glancing down to see what she was doing. She felt his thighs tense up, anticipating her next move. At her icy touch, he let out a sharp breath.

"Are you okay?" came Delilah's voice.

"Never better," Billy said.

"Glad to hear it," Delilah said, her voice moving away. "Take care."

Billy didn't reply. He slouched down in the seat. Cass's tongue traced his penis from bottom to top, making slow circles around the head while she cupped his small, perfect balls with one hand. She loved to lick his balls, even though he had told her it didn't cause the same wild sensation as when she licked his penis.

The pressure of Billy's hand on the back of her head, the way he arched his spine, told Cass to take him in her mouth. No matter how many times she did this, Cass never believed she could. She had often wondered about the fineness of his balls, hanging at the base of his cock, which was massive.

She mouthed the head, kissing it at first, then surrounding it with her lips. With her tongue she traced its ridge, just the base, where it overhung the shaft. She moved slowly down his penis, taking it deeper and deeper. All the way.

She licked upward, freeing him, starting all over again. Even slower. He grabbed the back of her neck. He wanted speed, so Cass slowed down. So slow. She imagined someone approaching the truck, standing even closer than Delilah, beginning a conversation with Billy, Billy talking about the weather, the fleet, anything, while Cass sucked him off.

A tug on her shoulders, impatient now. Cass was tempted to ignore it. She felt she could go on all day. She clasped the base of his dick while concentrating on the tip, moving her mouth faster; she had barely started when Billy began to shudder. He squeezed her shoulders. She felt it with her tongue and lips: that electric sizzle along the base of his cock that always preceded his orgasms. It blasted through his body as he came.

Cass wiped her mouth with the back of her hand. Billy was sitting with his head back, his eyes closed. "Wow," he said.

"Yeah," she said. She hitched up her bottom, wiggled into her panties, pulled on her jean skirt.

"Chocolate spots," Billy said, touching where he'd dropped an almond. "Sorry."

"You're forgiven."

Cass gave his penis one last lick. She eased it back into his boxer shorts.

Billy glanced around the parking lot, barely seeming to register where he was.

"It was all a dream," Cass said. "We didn't just go down on each other in the middle of the parking lot. The Star Market parking lot. Did we?"

"Did we?" Billy asked.

Cass gave him a long, soft kiss, full of lust and tenderness. The back of his neck felt hot and sticky in the summer heat, and she blew a cool stream of air across it.

"See you at home?" he asked.

"After I get the groceries," she said.

5

Bonnie loved to invent recipes. Today she had asked her sisters over, and she was baking a new creation: fudge brownies laced with fresh-brewed coffee, drizzled with thin butterscotch sauce halfway through the baking process. She would cut them into squares before they cooled, and when you bit into one, the lacy butterscotch would crunch into the mocha brownie.

Occasionally she entered bake-offs, but mainly she baked for her family and fundraising bake sales for school and Little League. She considered herself an innovator in the traditional mode. Pies, cakes, brownies; Shore Dinners — but with a twist.

And who would expect such a big woman to wear gorgeous underwear? Most men would look at a Playboy bunny–type woman and instantly think of crotchless panties, when for all they knew she bought her underwear at Sears, simple white cotton briefs — the better in which to play racquetball and do high-impact aerobics. The same men would look at Bonnie and picture the large white cotton briefs. Little did they know.

Bonnie had found an outlet in Mystic that sold large-sized lingerie, and she had bought satin bras, lacy pink panties, and a startling lavender garment that felt soft as a teddy but actually lifted her magnificent bosom right up to where it belonged. She believed a touch of the unexpected was always in order. She never wore cotton.

Bending to check on her brownies through the oven's glass door, Bonnie heard someone in the kitchen behind her.

"That smells fantastic," Cass said, standing there with Josie and Belinda.

"I thought they'd be ready by the time you got here," Bonnie said. "Why don't you girls run upstairs and find Emma? She just got home from school. See if you can get her off the phone."

"Okay, Aunt Bonnie," Belinda said, already gone.

Josie stood still, one arm linked around her mother's left leg.

"Hi, Josie," Bonnie said, stooping down. "Can I have my hug?"

"Hi, On Bon," Josie said loudly, clutching Bonnie's neck. Bonnie hung on as long as Josie would let her. It had been years since her own kids had let her hug them.

Sometimes, on his way to bed, when he was too sleepy to protest, fifteen-year-old Sean would let her get away with it. He would stand totally inert, as if he had fallen asleep standing up, while Bonnie leaned forward to kiss his cheek. Then he would somnambulate out the kitchen, up the stairs, and into his bedroom, where the last thing he would do before crashing into a deep sleep would be to don headphones and crank his stereo up to maximum volume.

Emma wouldn't even give Bonnie that much. Bonnie was lucky to kiss the air, redolent with Liz Claiborne perfume, when Emma rushed by. Emma, her thirteen-year-old swan, was ashamed, possibly even revulsed, by Bonnie's weight. As a child she had settled into her mother's lap as comfortably as if it had been a featherbed. But when her own baby fat began to disappear, Emma stopped cuddling with Bonnie. As her cheekbones emerged and she discovered her hipbones, Emma had stopped going places with her mother, stopped confiding in her; lately, it sometimes seemed to Bonnie, had stopped looking at her.

"Sweetheart," Cass said, crouching down to Josie's level. "Would you like to go upstairs with the other girls?"

"Yes," Josie said. Taking Cass's hand, she followed her out the room.

Bonnie could hear their footsteps on the stairs. She could already see Belinda beginning to separate from Cass, but she wondered whether Josie ever would. Bonnie thought Cass mothered Josie too much. Just now Cass had looked Josie straight in the eye, enunciated like a speech therapist, and gotten her message through. Then, instead of letting Josie run upstairs like a normal four-year-old, Cass had led her by the hand.

The brownies and a pot of tea were ready when Cass came back.

"I love the way you have your kitchen," Cass said. "We have the exact same floor plan, but mine looks nothing like yours."

"That's because you don't go to every single craft fair from here to Westerly. I'm into quaint."

"It's not quaint," Cass said. "Why do you put yourself down? It's cozy. That basket over there —"

Bonnie had baskets everywhere. Filled with peaches, beach stones, scallop shells, pencils, zucchini from the garden. "This one?" she asked, tapping one with her finger.

"No, the one filled with marsh grass. It looks like an antique. Who'd you inherit that from?"

"I bought it brand-new. The dog chewed it up."

Cass bit into a brownie. "Delicious," she said with her mouth full. "What is it? Toffee?"

"Butterscotch Drizzle," Bonnie said.

"Even the names you give them make my mouth water," Cass said. "I'm telling you, you should start a business. Take them to the craft fairs and set up a stand."

"I just bake for fun," Bonnie said. "You know my great idea, how that went over."

"Mail-order Shore Dinners," Cass said. "I know, that idea never got off the ground. That's because you had too many people to convince. Mom, Dad . . . we're not exactly talking avant-garde. I still think it would be great. We could all use the money."

"You're the only one who thinks it could work."

"I think selling your brownies could work better. But you know how I feel about chocolate," Cass said. "Mind if I have one more?"

"It'd kill me if you didn't."

The doorbell rang.

"Can you believe that?" Bonnie asked. "She goes to the front door and rings the doorbell. It's Nora, you know."

"I figured. She does that at my house, too."

"So formal, so . . . how do you say? Genteel." Bonnie chuckled. "Hey, it's the way we were raised, Bon. The back door is for servants. How did you and I ever sink this low?"

The sisters smiled.

"The front door is wide open, by the way. Feel that breeze?"

"Let's ignore her. We'll force her to walk in," Cass said. "It's for her own good. She needs to loosen up."

The bell rang again.

"We're in the kitchen!" Cass yelled.

High heels clicked on the hall tiles. Nora, dressed for work, entered the room. She stood back from her sisters, her lips tight, as if she knew they had been making fun of her.

"How did you wind up with all the class?" Cass asked, throwing her arms around Nora.

"What are you talking about?" Nora asked briskly. She's hurt, Bonnie thought.

"We're family, sistah."

"She means you don't have to ring the doorbell," Bonnie said, kissing Nora. "Here, have a brownie."

"Maybe a glass of white wine instead?" Nora asked.

"Oh, make it martinis," Cass said. "You know how clever we get when we drink martinis. Noël Coward should write a play about us. We could also star in it."

"Isn't Noël Coward dead, dear?" Nora asked.

"Yes. Before he gave us our big break, the bastard," Cass said. "A talk show, then. A roundtable discussion group with a pitcher of martinis in the middle and us discussing teenage sex."

"Pertinent issues," Bonnie said.

"No, I mean our *own* teenage sex," Cass said.

"Like how we lost our virginity . . ."

"And how often," Cass said.

"I thought you hated martinis," Nora said.

"I do. Give me a Diet Coke. Never mind, Bon — I'll get it myself."

"This is a subject I can't relate to," Nora said. "I was a twenty-four-year-old virgin."

"Well, Mom and Dad were so strict with you," Bonnie said. "They lightened up with me, and they gave up on Cass."

"I wouldn't be a teenager again for anything," Nora said. She sipped the wine Bonnie had set in front of her. "So polite, such a good girl."

"At least we haven't turned Belinda and Emma into good girls," Cass said. "They're great girls."

"I know," Bonnie said. "Mom and Dad were so high on good manners, I was afraid to say no. I thought it was impolite."

Nora sipped her wine, blushing, as if Bonnie had hit a nerve. Bonnie wondered when had been the last time Nora had said no to any man. She needed a real man who would love her right, not another local playboy.

"I never wanted to say no," Cass said.

"Well, you were always with Billy," Nora said.

"True," she said, nodding. She seemed about to say more, but upstairs something thumped and Josie screamed. Cass flew out the door. Bonnie and Nora stared at each other. They heard Cass taking the stairs two at a time.

"They shut me owwwwwww!" howled Josie, her words mushing together in that pitiful, familiar way.

"Then we'll knock on the door and ask them why," came Cass's voice, loud and calm.

Josie screamed louder.

"That poor little thing," Nora said.

Bonnie said nothing. Her view of the situation was unpopular. She thought the family blamed all of Josie's difficulties on her handicap, when at least half of them could be chalked up to the simple fact that she was a four-year-old. Josie had begun to catch on, too. She knew exactly how to get her mother's attention.

"It must be so frustrating for her, not hearing right. Imagine what will happen when she gets to school. The other kids will be brutal."

Bonnie shook her head. "Don't fall into that trap. Do you think that" — she pointed upstairs — "is only about deafness?"

Nora shrugged. "Doesn't Cass like us to say 'hearing-impaired'? Or whatever. I just know she hates 'deaf.' "

"Belinda and Emma are thirteen. Remember being their age? Would you have wanted Cass around then? They're not being mean to Josie because of her hearing problem. She's too little to play with them."

"That's not what I meant, exactly. I understand the girls' kicking Josie out. But just listen to her."

Josie was screaming louder; it sounded as if she were kicking her heels on the bare wood floor. As Josie's volume increased, so did Cass's. But the steadiness of her voice did not change.

"I don't know how Cass does it," Nora said. "I'd go insane."

"I know," Bonnie said. The longer the racket continued, the less certain she felt of her theory. Those shrieks weren't coming from a manipulative toddler.

"It's awful," Nora said. "I wish we could do something to help."

"What can we do?"

"Nothing at all. I just wish we could." She wondered how Cass kept herself from shaking

103

Josie to make her stop. She remembered taking the Block Island ferry, one time when Emma was about Josie's age. Standing at the rail, waving to a fishing boat, Emma had accidentally dropped her favorite doll overboard. Out of control with crying, she couldn't be consoled, and after fifteen solid minutes of trying to calm her down, Bonnie remembered feeling an overwhelming impulse to slap her.

"This reminds me of hearing Mother and Daddy fight," Nora said.

"Mom and Dad fought?" Bonnie asked, searching her memory. "I don't remember that."

"They fought all the time. I remember sitting on the stairs, listening to them fight in the dining room. Nothing violent or anything," Nora said, seeing Bonnie's expression. "Usually about money, the business, one of us. They didn't know I was listening. I felt like I ought to be able to make them stop, but there was nothing I could do."

"I never knew they fought," Bonnie said. She was stunned by Josie's fit, which was louder than ever. If she heard those screams coming from a neighbor's house, she would call the police.

She remembered that when her kids were little, when one of them would skin a knee, or have a temper tantrum, everyone would want to help. Her mother would make funny faces, her father would hold out a nickel, her sisters would hover close, making soothing sounds. But all her children ever wanted was Bonnie. She'd hold them and rock them and kiss their scrapes.

Bonnie and Nora sat silently at the kitchen table while the voices of their niece and sister rang through the house. The pitch grew higher, more frantic; Josie was clearly hysterical.

"So mean," Josie cried. "They hate me. They hate me."

"No they don't, they love you," Cass said.

"They hate me."

"Big kids like to play alone sometimes." Cass's voice, though still steady, was full of tears and frustration.

Josie wept, her cries still punishingly angry, as if she hadn't heard a word her mother said.

Bonnie yearned to stand up, grab Josie and Cass, and shake both of them. Instead, she reached for Nora's hand. Nora gave it a squeeze, and Cass's two older sisters sat together, holding hands, as they listened.

6

Nora hardly ever felt like smoking anymore. She still carried her cigarettes with her, and occasionally she would reach for one, from habit. She would get as far as placing it between her lips before discovering she didn't want it at all. The other day at Bonnie's, when Cass had finally gotten Josie to calm down, Nora had lifted the child into her arms for a hug. Although she had stopped crying, Josie's chest heaved in big, shuddering breaths. "Your hair smells pretty, like shampoo," Josie had said, with difficulty, into Nora's ear.

It had amazed Nora that after crying so hard for so long, Josie had any breath left to talk.

"Thank you," Nora had said. While Bonnie sat Cass down and poured her a cup of tea, Nora had played with Josie, letting her try on her silver bracelets and jade beads, until her breathing returned almost to normal. It was the first time Nora could remember anyone telling her that her hair smelled pretty.

Nora had conditioned her hair and decided to persuade it back to its natural auburn color. She had stripped off her bright-red fingernail polish and applied shell pink. Standing before her refrigerator, looking into its open door, she felt dismayed to discover it contained only two open bottles of white wine, a six-pack of Narragansett beer, a container of clam chowder so old it was tinged blue, and the unopened currant preserves Bonnie had given her for May Day two years ago.

On her day off, Nora went grocery shopping at Almacs. She filled her cart with whole-wheat bread, boneless chicken breasts, mineral water, cranberry juice, broccoli, carrots, one baking potato, and a lemon-scented air freshener. Grocery shopping was new for Nora; in the past, she had been known to run into a store for some peanuts, olives, or pickled onions, but she always ate her meals at Lobsterville. She wheeled her cart slowly, as if she were taking her first steps.

For a long time — years, actually — Nora had thought of herself as someone with hair of straw, a washed-out face, the body of a cornhusk doll. Bonnie had turned forty blooming like a rose, treating herself to a fabulous masquerade party to which people brought presents. That everyone loved Bonnie was obvious to Nora, who had sat in the

Kenneallys' TV room in a rented flapper costume, remembering her own fortieth birthday.

Her sisters had wanted to give her a party, but Nora had said no, that turning forty was nothing to celebrate. Instead, she and Tony Domingus had gotten drunk on his boat. They'd started on tequila, then changed to vodka. They'd ripped off their clothes — literally torn Nora's black blouse — and tried but failed to fuck on a berth that smelled of herring. Too far gone to maneuver, Nora had spent the night onboard and had to walk down the dock the next morning, past Mount Hope's entire jeering fishing fleet.

Now, after grocery shopping, Nora drove home. She lived at Bensons' Mill, a condominium complex several piers down from Keating's Wharf. Pulling her 280Z into the carport, she smiled hello at some neighbors and carried her two brown bags upstairs.

Unlocking her condo door, Nora felt a tingle of anticipation. It started on the top of her head, where she parted her hair, and shivered down the backs of her thighs. "Hello?" she called, though she didn't actually expect anyone to be there. She had left the air conditioning on low; it hummed reassuringly. In spite of the fact that she hadn't had a cigarette in several days, the room smelled like smoke. The first thing Nora did, even before unpacking her food, was to unwrap the air freshener and place it smack on her black marble coffee table. Breathing in the lemony scent, she sank onto her overstuffed white leather sofa and closed her eyes.

Every time Nora stopped moving, she thought of Willis Randecker. He swirled through her mind, making her head swim. In a way, it seemed as if their time together had been much longer than simply part of one evening. She remembered the vulnerable angle of his eyebrows, his gentle southern drawl, the way he had put out her cigarette, his words when she had told him she'd never been married: "That surprises me."

Nora remembered feeling that he wanted something from her. Her first impression of Willis had put her on guard. Now that she'd had time to consider it, she thought she knew why: because Willis had seemed to like her right off the bat. She wasn't used to men simply liking her.

That night, after a dinner of sautéed chicken and broccoli, she wrapped herself in her peach silk robe. She stood on her balcony, facing out to sea. Across a dimly lit asphalt parking lot and the tall silhouettes of construction cranes lay Mount Hope harbor. A summer breeze fluttered Nora's robe against her legs; it carried northward the scents of Spanish moss, azaleas, black-bean soup laced with sherry, and mud flats in the Savannah River. Halyards clanked against flagpoles and the wire stays of sailboats on their moorings; the bell buoy at Minturn Ledge Light groaned.

The sea sounds filled Nora with longing. She gazed at the sky, a blanket of gray flannel, and knew that beyond the loom of harbor lights were constellations full of bright stars. In the middle of the North Atlantic, men had filled their holds and were charting courses home by those stars. Billy, Gavin. Al, Tony, John, all the others. She wondered whether Willis Randecker knew anything about celestial navigation. She wondered whether the night sky over Willis was hazy with the lights of Savannah, or whether he had a clear view of the stars.

Independence Day always brought out the patriot in Mary Keating. Summer was the Keating family's season, and Independence Day was summer's best holiday. All three of her daughters worked at the restaurant that day. Every Fourth, Mary played show tunes — her idea of patriotic music — over the Lobsterville loudspeaker. All day long, the cast recordings of "The Music Man," "South Pacific," and "Oklahoma!" would alternate with songs by George M. Cohan, a born-and-bred Rhode Islander — "Over There," "You're a Grand Old Flag," and "Yankee Doodle Boy." Mary would wear a red dress with a blue-and-white sailor collar; when folks ordered twin lobsters, they were served with little American flags on toothpicks clutched in their claws. After sunset she would set out complimentary fried scallops and hot cheese puffs, and people along the wharf would jockey for the best spots from which to view the fireworks.

Midway through the afternoon lull, Mary left Vinnie Fusaro in charge of the reservations phone and stole out to meet Jim and have a smoke. Walking down the dock, she peered at the sky. It had the weight and color of an old pot, mottled gray and heavy in a way that made it hard to breathe. She felt sorry for people who couldn't be at the shore; the smog in Providence must be terrible.

She found Jim leaning on a piling, watching Tony Domingus load empty fish barrels onto the *Aphrodite*. Just seeing her husband made her feel happier. His hair had turned gray, but it was full and wavy, and he still had the posture of a young fellow. A few of their friends had started to stoop and thicken, but not Jim; watching him straighten to face her, Mary believed she could see him grow even leaner before her very eyes.

"Hey, sweetheart," she said.

"Lousy weather for fireworks," Jim said, glancing at the sky.

"Maybe we'll have a nice afternoon thunderstorm to clear things up," Mary said soothingly. Jim had invested plenty in this year's display — had even hired a pyrotechnic expert from Providence's Federal Hill.

"After all those clear days last week, we wind up with a mucky sky on the Fourth."

"Are you interested in the governor's speech?" Mary asked. "He's going on the air at three."

"Nah," Jim said. "It'll just be more bullshit about pulling together during tough times, more layoffs, more cutbacks."

"Well, aren't you a bundle of cheer!"

"Just because I don't like the governor?"

"He's having dinner at the restaurant tonight," Mary said. Occasionally celebrities came to Mount Hope on their boats, and it usually thrilled Mary and Nora when they'd dine at Lobsterville. But Governor Malloy did nothing for her, not a damn thing. In the first place, she and Jim had known Mike Malloy forever. They only called him "Governor" out of respect for the office.

It frightened Mary to admit this, but Ronald Reagan had been the last politician to move her. She disliked his politics — Mary was a dyed-in-the-wool Democrat. But his warmth, the twinkle in his eye, his obvious love for Nancy had endeared him to her.

"That should be good for a plug in the papers tomorrow," Jim said glumly. "The governor eating Fourth of July dinner at Lobsterville."

"Now snap out of it, Jim," Mary said. "Quit feeling sorry for yourself just because we don't have a clear sky. There's hours yet before the fireworks, and the weather could break."

"I know," Jim said. As if he were sick and tired of indulging a bad mood, a slow smile started. It tugged the left corner of his mouth in a way Mary had always found sexy as hell.

She couldn't in a million years have predicted this, but Mary suddenly thought of Jim's brother, Ward. She had dated him once before she even met Jim. Right now, beguiled by Jim's smile, she saw Ward's easy grin, his bright hazel eyes, his handsome nose. It took a long look at Ward's Air Corps photo, or moments such as this, when a certain expression flashed across Jim's face, for Mary to imagine how Ward would look now, as a senior citizen. But she'd conjured him up; he stood before her here, right in Jim's spot. Mary gasped and thumped her heart.

"Mary, darling," Jim said, wrapping one

arm around her shoulder. "What is it? Do you have a pain?"

"It's nothing, I'm fine," Mary said.

"It was a chest pain, don't lie to me."

"It was not a chest pain, for God's sake! You make me feel so old. I just had a fright, that's all."

Even so, Jim forced her to sit on one of Tony's upside-down fish barrels. "Right there," he commanded, sitting beside her.

"Oh, Jim, watch the dress," Mary said crossly. "I'm going to have fish scales all across my behind." She tapped out a cigarette to stop her hands from shaking. "I thought I saw Ward, that's all," she said.

"I've thought of him all day," Jim said.

"I suppose it's natural to be thinking of him on a national holiday."

Usually Ward was frozen in time: a young hero shot down over the German island of Helgoland. But Mary liked to think of him aging along with everyone else. She believed he was as much a part of the family as when he'd been alive, hovering just out of sight; she believed that even death couldn't tear a family apart.

"Ward wouldn't be in deep shit with the insurance police, that's for sure," Jim said.

"What are you talking about, 'police'?"

"I mean the pinstripes whose job it is to

114

keep from insuring you after you've been a policy holder for fifty years."

Mary, who thought it odd and slightly alarming that Jim would say "police," as if he had the real police on his mind, tried to sort things out. "Are you in trouble?" she asked finally.

"No, dear. Not trouble. But my main trucker's going out of business, I can't afford to insure my fleet, I've got captains shopping around for their own boats. And you've just reminded me that if Ward were still alive, we'd all be sitting pretty; we'd be running in the black every month of the year."

Mary climbed off the fish barrel. Standing, she was barely taller than her seated husband. "I don't know what's gotten into you today, Jim, but I don't like it one little bit."

"Neither do I, my darling. Neither do I."

Mary, in her red Independence Day dress, marched back to the restaurant, and she had a crazy picture of Nancy mad at Ron, leaving the big man at the end of some dock. Mary wondered whether Jim could tell by the way she walked that she was furious with him. Usually, Jim could charm you out of staying mad at him. Jim had charm, all right, but frankly, he'd been too damned stingy with it lately.

★ ★ ★

Nora had been working the reservations desk all day. Time flew; it felt like they'd never been so busy. Six o'clock, seven o'clock. Soon it would be time for the fireworks, if the rain didn't spoil things. "Pentwarse, party of two," she called over the loudspeaker. "Hartunian, party of four." Her throat felt dry from speaking and from others' cigarette smoke. A lot of the regulars complimented her on her new hair color. Nora even managed a civilized smile and a thank-you when Al Sweet told her she looked like a college girl.

"Have they been in?" Cass asked, looking harried, stopping by with a tray laden with drinks.

"No. I'm sure they're fine," Nora said. Cass had left T.J. in charge of the girls, as they waited for the show to start outside.

"Dad's going to get me when the fireworks are about to start," Cass said. "I promised Josie I'd watch with her. She's so excited."

"No problem. I'll have someone cover your tables."

Vinnie Fusaro swaggered over, picked up a wine list, and smiled at Cass and Nora as he walked away.

"Vinnie," Cass said, smiling at Nora. "Boy, he's cute. If he weren't so young, and I weren't so married . . ."

"He's twenty," Nora said, then wished she hadn't spoken. She wondered what Cass would think if she knew Nora had slept with him. It had happened only once. The strange thing was, in spite of his being so young, he had treated her better than men twice his age. Although they never directly acknowledged what had happened between them, Vinnie always seemed to twinkle in her presence. It was very flattering.

"What's wrong with Mom and Dad?" Cass asked.

"They do seem a little tense," Nora said. She lifted the microphone: "Connors, party of two; Burns, party of six."

"They're in a mood," Cass said. "The same mood: bad."

"His Excellency," Nora said, standing tall and facing the door.

"What, no honor guard?" Cass asked, hurrying into the bar.

"Good evening, Governor, Mrs. Malloy," Nora said, grabbing menus for them. "Happy Fourth."

"Happy Fourth, Nora," Governor Malloy said, pulling her against him in a backslapping hug. He smelled of cigars and whiskey. As the menus dug into her breast, Nora noticed that the governor had freckled, whiskery ears just like her father. He had a paunch and a dwindling voter base, and so Nora let him hug her like an uncle.

"What a lovely dress, dear," Mrs. Malloy said, nodding at Nora's blue knit. "It's so patriotic, and it looks lovely with your hair."

"Thank you." Nora had bought it just this week, for the Fourth. She'd gotten it at the Eastport Shop in Providence's Wayland Square, and she liked the way it hugged her figure but managed to look sophisticated instead of cheap.

"Let me show you to your table," she said.

"Oh, is that Sheila over there?" Governor Malloy asked.

"Yes," Nora said, glancing around for her grandmother. It was family tradition to have everyone together at Lobsterville on the Fourth.

"Hello, dear," the Governor said, bending to take Sheila's hand, but she walked right by without acknowledging him.

"A bit deaf, is she?" the governor asked.

"Well, it happens to us all," his wife said.

"This way, please," Nora said.

After Nora had seated the Malloys, she discovered her grandmother leaning on the customers' side of the reservations desk.

"But I *have* a reservation!" a burly man was insisting. He wore a New York Yacht Club blazer, and he jabbed his finger at the book

118

with undue vigor. "It's right *there*."

"Smada?" Sheila asked, frowning at the book. "What an unusual name. Where are your people from?"

"My name is *Adams*," the man said. "*Adams*. I can't believe this."

"You're reading it upside down, Granny," Nora whispered in her grandmother's ear. In the circle of Nora's embrace, her grandmother felt insubstantial, about to blow away.

"Oh, Adams. I'm sorry, Mr. Adams," Sheila said, tugging on the collar of her beaded pink silk dress. She blushed with embarrassment.

Without even greeting Mr. Adams, Nora asked Vinnie Fusaro to show him to table thirteen, right between the kitchen door and the bus table.

"You want to help me tonight, Granny?" Nora asked, leading her around the desk, pushing the stool beneath her rump. Sheila leaned precariously against it.

"He really gets my goat, that *big shot*. His mother would turn in her grave if she could hear him talk. You'd think he was king instead of just governor."

"Oh, he's not that bad."

"He was in Ward's class at school, and he couldn't hold a candle to him. Ward would have made a wonderful governor. Too bad you never knew him."

"I know."

"They should have named the highway after him, for that matter."

Nora smiled, patting Sheila's shoulder to console her. Sheila was about to launch into her Casey Memorial Highway tirade. At groundbreaking in 1950 for a swath of road intended to connect Mount Hope with the main drag to Providence, the town council had announced plans to name the new highway for Timothy Casey, the first Mount Hope boy to die in World War II. Tim and Ward had gone through St. Vincent's High together. Although Sheila had been fond of Tim Casey and still prayed for him and his parents, it pierced her to think the town could mourn any Mount Hope boy more than her son Ward.

"Well, hello again," Willis Randecker said. He stood before Nora, looking exactly as she had remembered.

"Aren't you tall!" Sheila exclaimed. "Do you have a reservation?"

Nora couldn't look away from his eyes. People waiting for tables had piled up behind him, but she just stood there.

"So, you're back," she said finally.

"Yes, I surely am," he said. "More business up this way. I thought I'd come up a day early and see what the Fourth of July is like in New England."

"Go on," Sheila said, poking Nora. "Go off with him. I mean it, now. I'll take care of the restaurant. It's not as if I haven't done it before." She laughed, flirting with Willis. "I'm the old grandmother. I started this place."

"Best seafood place I've ever been to," he said.

"We're so busy tonight," Nora said, nodding at the line.

"I'll just go have a drink at the bar," he said.

After Nora had seated seven tables and brought the checks to three others, the first firework went off. Swizzles of red fire reflected in the picture windows. Nora turned down the restaurant's globe lights.

"There you are," Mary said, standing between her eldest daughter and her mother-in-law. "Like old times, seeing Sheila at this desk, isn't it, Nora?"

"It's great," Nora said, listening to the explosions. Nora wondered whether Willis was watching from the bar's porch.

Sheila chucked Mary under the chin. "Be a good girl and take over for Nora, will you? She's got a man on hold."

"A man?" Mary said, raising her eyebrows. "Go ahead, dear."

Nora struggled through the crowded bar, past tables of sailors, friends, regulars, and a few fishermen. For the third time since she'd come to work, Nora heard "You're a Grand Old Flag" coming from the speakers.

Nora found him, towering above the others, on the bar porch. He stood at the rail, his head tilted back, watching the fireworks. Nora stood aside for a moment, taking in the flat plane of his tan cheeks, the sweep of his jaw line, the strength with which he gripped the porch rail. Nora eased closer. She stood beside him, and he smiled down.

An umbrella of blue and gold sparkles lit the sky, followed by a red lobster, its claws clicking. In the firelit glare, Nora looked across the small channel that separated Lobsterville's porch and Keating's Wharf. There, standing between two sturdy pilings, were her father, Cass, T.J., Belinda, Josie, Bonnie, Gavin, Emma, and Sean. As the red lobster flashed and disappeared, Nora saw Cass and Bonnie watching her.

"That's my family over there," she said.

"Wow, you've got a lot of them. A whole bunch of nieces and nephews?"

"Five altogether."

"Will you look at that little one? She's having herself a great old time."

Nora looked at Josie, spellbound by the fireworks. "She can't even hear the explosions, really," Nora said, but her words were muffled by the next bang.

"What?" Willis asked, but Nora didn't repeat herself.

She blinked at the momentary darkness. She felt Willis take her hand and hold it. "You folks sure put on a beautiful show," Willis said.

"We do it every year," Nora said with shy pride.

"And what a gorgeous place to watch from. One heck of a nice piece of property." He slid a glance at Nora. "Did I tell you I'm in the real estate business?"

"I don't think so," Nora said.

"Have you kept to your plan, Nora?" Willis asked. "To quit smoking?"

"I have," she said, amazement coming through in her voice.

Willis squeezed her hand, as if to direct her attention back to the fireworks. It didn't matter why he had returned to Mount Hope; it only mattered that he had. A light breeze picked up. Nora shivered under her blue dress. Waiting for the pyrotechnics expert from Providence to set off his next charge, Nora leaned closer to Willis.

She watched her sisters across the narrow channel, surrounded by their families. For once, Nora didn't feel so different. Blue streamers popped overhead. A silver cascade. Purple starbursts. The grand finale: jewels of azure, gold, scarlet, and emerald scattering into the harbor. Josie spun around, her arms waving as if she were a baton twirler leading the parade, to make sure Cass was watching. Sean jostled T.J., pointing up; Nora loved how fireworks could make her teenage nephews lose their cool. She wished she could catch her sisters' eyes, but Cass and Bonnie had their heads tilted back, watching for the last silvery streaks to fade away.

Now Nora saw Cass kiss Josie, then run with Bonnie back to work. Nora turned to Willis, to tell him she had to go, too, when she noticed his gaze. He was staring at her with the sweetest expression. Then he brushed her throat, his touch tender as a feather.

"I hope you don't mind," he said.

"I don't," said Nora, because she knew what was happening, and she let him kiss her.

7

"Aunt Nora is a slut, you know."

Emma had said it the other night, when everyone was together watching the fireworks. Aunt Nora was across the channel, leaning against some stranger with her eyes closed. Belinda hadn't even noticed her. She had her head back, watching colors exploding everywhere, when Emma put her mouth against her ear: "Aunt Nora is a slut, you know."

Now Belinda sat under a beech tree, shredding grass while she waited for Emma to come out of summer school. It felt dangerous, illicit, to be on school grounds instead of at the beach on such a hot July day. Everything looked different from the way it did during the school year. The parking lot, usually full of teachers' cars, was empty except for five or six spots. The rolling green lawn had dried in patches to scorched brown straw. All the folding chairs lay stacked on the sidewalk as the custodian waxed the auditorium floor. There weren't any kids around.

When Emma had said that Aunt Nora was a slut, Belinda had laughed and said, "I know what you mean." Actually, she had been totally shocked to hear it. She had always thought of Aunt Nora as the old-fashioned type — very tightlaced, like an old lady's shoe. Not at all fun-loving like her mother and Aunt Bonnie. She never brought men to family gatherings; in fact, Belinda couldn't remember ever seeing Nora with a man. She used to dye her hair blond, and she smoked cigarettes like a movie star. Maybe that was why Emma had called her a slut.

Belinda had the idea she had to act dumb in order for Emma to like her. Emma had failed math and gotten a D in science, and Belinda had gotten straight A's. But the fact was, Belinda felt dumb around Emma. Emma was beautiful, funny, and wicked, and she was always surprising Belinda. Her latest shocker was having her hair cut like a boy's. Belinda couldn't imagine doing it, but on Emma it looked great.

Here she came now, across the schoolyard. All the other summer-school kids hung around the bike rack, laughing and talking loud, as if it were recess. Emma took long strides, but she didn't seem in a hurry. She wore a dark-yellow sundress and black sunglasses; she had gelled her spiky hair. Emma was thirteen, same as Belinda, but she seemed so much cooler.

"You look fabulous," Emma said theatrically, bending under the low branches to join Belinda.

"Are you serious?" Belinda said. But she posed anyway, elbow crooked, hand behind her head, like Marilyn Monroe. Belinda wore torn Guess? jean shorts, a flimsy cotton peasant blouse she'd borrowed from her mother, and flip-flops.

"It's knowing how to sit," Emma said. "You're lying under this gorgeous tree, very mysterious in the shade. All those juvenile delinquents are wondering what the smartest kid in school is doing hanging around outside summer school."

"I'm not the smartest kid."

"Don't be embarrassed."

Belinda didn't say anything. She didn't want Emma thinking of her that way: Belinda, the smartest kid.

"Don't look now, but you-know-who is watching you."

"He is?" Belinda peeked from under her bangs. She was smiling like a maniac in spite of herself. Todd Evans was talking to kids at the bike rack, but he was definitely looking their way.

"He wants you," Emma said.

"He's probably looking at you."

"No. He told me. He wanted me to ask you if you'll go out with him."

"Are you kidding?"

"No, but I'm not going to do it. He's a jerk. You can do a lot better."

Belinda felt flattered, but Emma didn't know what she was talking about. Belinda had liked Todd since April. "What did he say?"

"He said . . ." Emma took off her sunglasses, raked some hair into her eyes, and let her lower lip protrude. She cleared her throat. "He said, 'I wanta go out wit huh.' "

"He's nice, Emma," Belinda said, laughing but stung.

"He used to go out with Lisa Larrabee, and she is the biggest slut. Just like . . ." Emma's eyes flicked to Belinda. "Aunt Nora. I know you don't believe me about her."

"Well, how do you know she's a slut?"

"Two ways. I can see with my own eyes, and I heard our mothers talking."

"Mom said that? About her sister?" Belinda couldn't believe it. Her mother was so loyal, sometimes so annoyingly devoted to her family, she would never say anything bad about any of them. "I'm sorry, but she would never rag on Aunt Nora like that."

"You poor baby," Emma said, touching Belinda's ear. "If it's the truth, it's not a

128

putdown, no matter what. You know how you can tell a slut?"

Belinda waited for one of Emma's wicked punch lines.

"Sluts are sad," Emma said. "They think there's only one way to get people to love them. You know that purple eyeshadow Lisa wears? And the big dangly earrings and the bleached-blond hair? You have to think of it as a costume. It's exactly like a clown suit. When you see a clown, you laugh just because it's a clown, whether you think it's funny or not. When you see a slut, you fuck her just because she's a slut, whether you really like her or not."

"Just because Aunt Nora bleaches her hair does not mean she's a slut."

"Of course it doesn't. But have you ever seen her happy? No, because she's not. She is incredibly sad. Just like Lisa, if you think about it. They both sleep around."

"What do you mean, 'sleep around'?" Belinda asked, concentrating on a thick blade of grass. She had already shredded it into four pieces, and now she was shredding those four into eight. Talking with Emma about sluts and sleeping around felt more delicious than talking about Todd.

"I mean going to bed with more than one guy. One after the other. Whoever wants you,

you do it with him."

"Like you actually sleep," Belinda said, thinking of how weird it was to use such little-kid words — 'sleep' and 'bed' — to describe something as exotic as sex.

"Why do they say 'going to bed'?" Belinda screwed up one of the grass shreds, tearing it unevenly. She threw out all the pieces and began fringing a new blade.

"It's just a bullshit way of saying you go someplace alone together, take off all your clothes, and play with each other's body. Some prude probably thought it up."

"Have you ever done that?"

"Maybe."

Belinda's head jerked up. "You have?"

Emma shrugged, a little smirk on her lips. She pulled a lipstick out of her pocket, swished on some glittery red, and handed the tube to Belinda. Belinda's hand closed around it; her palm felt sweaty. "I have never slept around," Emma said.

"What about the other?"

"No. But I've had the chance. I don't want to."

Belinda wondered who Emma had had the chance with. You heard so much about boys being sex-starved, always ready to take advantage of you, but that had not been Belinda's experience. She could lie awake for hours at night, stiff as a board with the tension of desiring Todd, and before him Paul, and before him Jeremy; she'd feel it so powerfully that she was sure the next day that, sensing her love, he would pull her into the coatroom and cover her face with kisses.

But nothing would ever happen. The boys would hardly even look at her. Sometimes she would get a message, like the one she had just gotten from Todd, delivered by one of her friends or her brother or her cousin, that someone liked her. Wanted to go out with her. Big deal. Even when she said yes, like she had with Paul, the message came back, "I can't go out with you. Now I like Colleen."

"Did Todd really tell you he wants to ask me out?"

"Yes."

"What else did he say?"

Emma started to take off her dark glasses again, stick out her lower lip, rearrange her hair. "He said . . ."

"Okay, never mind," Belinda said, laughing.

"Would you want his grubby hands all over your beautiful bod?"

"Beautiful? Hah." Now Belinda could never go out with Todd, knowing how Emma felt about him.

"In case you haven't noticed, Bel, you're

one of the only girls in school with tits."

Belinda had, in fact, noticed. She blushed.

"Of course, I'm one of the others," Emma went on. "Small tits do not run in our family. Just look at our mothers. God, I hope I look more like your mother when I'm old than mine."

"Your mother's so nice," Belinda said.

"She's a cow. An entire herd. She let herself go. But let's get back to the subject."

"What subject?" Belinda asked, shredding grass again. She knew exactly what subject, but the whole thing was making her feel hot in the face and funny between the legs.

"The subject of bodies. Do you want Todd's grubby hands on yours?"

"Not particularly."

"Then whose hands do you want?"

"Whose do you want?"

"Keanu Reeves's," Emma said. She lay on her back, one arm under her head, and arched her spine. "Oh, Keanu baby."

"I mean someone real."

"He's real," Emma replied. "I can have him whenever I want him."

"Oh, right. He just flies in from Hollywood?"

"No," Emma said. "But if I feel like it, I can think of him when I masturbate."

Belinda had never heard someone her own

age say that word. Her mouth felt too dry to talk.

"Don't you ever?" Emma asked, raising herself up on one elbow.

Belinda shrugged.

"Don't you know how?"

Belinda shrugged again.

"It's nothing to be ashamed of. Come on. No one's home at my house. I'll show you."

Emma's garage felt cool after their long bike ride. The girls parked their bikes, and Emma used her key to let them into the kitchen. She poured them glasses of lemonade. Belinda was glad to have something to drink, because she didn't know what to say. She felt as though she were on a train heading for somewhere scary, somewhere she knew she shouldn't go. The train kept stopping at safe stations, places with familiar faces on the platform, but she didn't get off. She felt too thrilled to be on the train.

They went upstairs. Emma, for once, was as quiet as Belinda. She poked her head into her parents' room, then Sean's.

"They're all out," Emma said, as if she were surprised by this. She closed her bedroom door. Belinda stood in the middle of the room, pretending to be interested in Emma's bookshelf. Usually she'd just flop on the bed without being asked, but now she felt too nervous.

"Let's put on some makeup," Emma said. She stood in front of her mirror, applying brown eyeliner to her lower lid. Belinda stood beside her, brushing on mascara.

"First of all, you have to make yourself feel sexy," Emma said. She dipped her pinky into a pot of red lip gloss and smeared it on her lips.

Belinda tried to listen to her, but all she could think about was what they were going to do. Her mother had explained masturbation to her, and Belinda had read about it in the blue book her mother had given her: *A Doctor Talks to Nine- to Twelve-Year-Olds.*

She had tried it a couple of times, but nothing had happened. It had embarrassed her, touching her own bottom. Because no matter what the diagrams showed, no matter how the books explained about the "clitoris" and "vulva" and "labia majora," it was all the same to Belinda. Her bottom.

Emma was getting undressed, so Belinda did, too. Naturally, Emma had on a filmy pink bra, straight out of Victoria's Secret or somewhere. Also some kind of string underpants.

"Those are nice," Belinda said. "Mine look like rejects from a gym suit." She stood there in her plain white bra and plain white panties that Emma had seen a million times. But it had never counted before. Just last week they had given each other fake tattoos. Josie had been sitting right there, at Emma's dressing table, drawing all over Emma's schoolbook with a lipstick. That's when Belinda had kicked Josie out, causing the war to erupt.

"They're very refugee," Emma said, laughing. "Okay, you sit at that end of the bed. There. I'll take this end."

"Then what?"

Emma giggled. "God, I really do have to teach you, don't I? You take off your undies, you lie back, and you touch yourself." Belinda watched her strip off her bra and panties. Emma's breasts were round and pale, compared with the rest of her tan body. Her nipples, which were sort of brownish, stuck way out, like flower buds. Only Belinda had never seen a pinkish-brown flower. She took off her own underwear, embarrassed but slightly proud that her breasts were bigger than Emma's.

They sat at opposite ends of the bed, nude.

"You know the spot, right?" Emma asked.

"Not exactly."

Emma looked skeptical. "It's very specific. You have to know how to find it." She spread her own legs, revealing a dark, moist crack. "Here."

Belinda pretended to see what Emma was pointing at.

135

"You didn't see, did you?"

"Not exactly."

"Okay." Emma pushed Belinda onto her back. Instinctively, Belinda let her legs fall apart. Emma took the middle finger of Belinda's right hand and placed it on a particular spot on the front part of Belinda's bottom. "That little bump. You rub it."

Belinda couldn't, not with Emma watching. "Okay," Belinda said. "What else?"

"Well, you lick your finger first, to make it slippery. You do that whenever it gets dry. Think of something that turns you on. Like Todd. Or Keanu Reeves. Or some sexy scene from a movie. And just keep touching that spot, light or hard, even with your fingernail, and keep your finger slippery, until you come."

Belinda wanted to ask what "come" meant, but Emma had already gone to the other end of the bed. Emma stretched, then lay on her back. Her eyes closed, her hand traveled down her body to the spot she had shown Belinda. Her hand stayed still, but her finger seemed to move. Belinda tried to locate the place Emma had told her to touch. Now, with Emma not watching, Belinda definitely found it.

"Uh," she gasped before she could help herself. She glanced over, to see if Emma was looking.

Emma had one eye open, smiling, her finger still going. "Uh," Emma said back, teasing. Then Emma licked her finger and turned her head away again. With her other hand she plucked at one breast, then the other.

Just watching Emma while she touched herself made Belinda feel so hot and sexy, she didn't know if she could stand it. She didn't know if Emma would mind that she was watching, but Belinda couldn't turn away. She licked her middle finger, and the salty taste made her even crazier. She played with the spot. There it was. There. There. She felt like she was in danger. She was standing on a cliff. The bottom was going to fall out. She was going to crash. She stopped.

Something was happening to Emma. Emma's back was arched and her thighs were shaking. "Oh," Emma moaned. "Uh." Her legs shook, her hips wiggled around, and she pinched her bark-brown nipple over and over.

"Did you come?" Emma asked in a funny voice, without looking.

"I don't think so," Belinda said.

"Keep touching yourself," Emma said, still lying back.

Belinda licked her finger again. She reached down. The first touch, she felt a jolt. Her clitoris was sore. She started to pull her hand back, but Emma's hand on her wrist stopped her.

"Make it more slippery," Emma said. She held out a pot of lip gloss and dipped Belinda's finger in it. Now Emma was watching, but Belinda didn't care. She rubbed the glossy pink goo into the hard little bump. She closed her eyes, to block out Emma.

"Here's a sure way," Emma said. Belinda was going to open her eyes, but suddenly she felt something hot and wet on her left nipple. It was Emma's mouth. Emma sucked and nibbled, flicking it with her tongue. Belinda watched, her own finger still going, she had to tell Emma to stop, but she couldn't. Belinda was on fire between her legs and in her nipples. She wanted to slow down, even stop, because she wanted the feeling to go on forever.

Forever. There. There. But it didn't go on forever. Something wilder than Belinda had ever imagined swept over her, knocked her down, so that she saw stars behind her closed eyes and thought she might be blind when she opened them.

She wasn't blind. There was Emma, laughing, the first thing she saw.

"Now, that wasn't so bad, was it?" Emma asked.

★ ★ ★

Josie sat on the front step with her mother. They were watching for her father's truck. Tomorrow he'd be leaving on a fishing trip, so tonight he'd be home early for dinner. Josie and her mother were playing a game, counting all the blue cars that drove by. Every time you saw one, you had to say, *"Blue car."*

Josie leaned on her mother's leg, watching the street. "Blue" was one of her favorite words. It was easy to say. Josie could say anything in front of her mother, and it didn't matter if she made mistakes. The same with T.J. But some words she would say to her father or Belinda, and they'd frown or look everywhere except at her face, and Josie would know they thought she was stupid.

"Blue car," Josie said, squeezing her mother's knee. Belinda and T.J. were somewhere with their friends; Josie wished her father would get home before they did. She had more fun playing with him when they weren't around. He always paid lots of attention to her then.

Her mother tapped Josie, so that she would look up. "Let's start counting them," her mother said. Josie held up four fingers on her left hand: she'd been counting all along. It made her laugh, and her mother gave her a big hug.

Josie's shoulder rested against her mother's side, and suddenly she felt her mother talking. She looked at her mother's face, to hear what she was saying.

"Here comes Sean."

"Oh," Josie said, disappointed. Instead of her father, Sean was walking down the sidewalk.

If Sean weren't fat, he would look scary. Josie knew he was her cousin and that he would never hurt her, but he had four earrings in one ear and black polish on his fingernails. His jeans had the knees ripped out, like T.J.'s. He usually wore sunglasses, even in the house. But he had a friendly plumpness that made the other things seem silly.

He came down the front walk. He said, "Hi, Josie. Hi, Aunt Cass," but then he started talking too fast for Josie to understand.

"T.J. is at the beach," her mother said.

Sean nodded. He was about to walk away, but suddenly he stopped short. Josie looked from him to her mother, who was standing up.

"Can you watch her while I answer the phone?"

"Okay," Sean said.

Josie watched the screen door slam shut behind her mother. She looked up at Sean. She felt a little afraid, but he was smiling. She smiled back. She looked at the living-room window and saw her mother standing there, watching Sean and Josie while she talked on the telephone.

Sean said something and pointed down the street. Josie followed his gaze. About three driveways away, some kids had made a ramp, and they were flying off it on skateboards. Sean started walking toward them. Josie didn't want to go, but she knew Sean was supposed to be watching her. She followed behind.

The kids were big. Older than Josie, but not as old as Sean. Josie didn't like them. She knew they would be mean if she had to talk to them. T.J. said they were jerks, babies. She looked down, watching for ants on the sidewalk.

They stopped what they were doing to talk to Sean. They stood back, listening to what he was saying. Josie moved closer to him. She could see they thought he was cool. T.J. never talked to them, so they seemed surprised when Sean did.

Sean wanted to try the ramp. He got on the skateboard. He looked too big and wobbly to stay on right, like a human Weeble. He pushed off with his foot, but before he even hit the ramp, he tipped forward. He tried to get his balance. His arms flapped, and he fell.

His sunglasses flew off and smashed on the sidewalk.

He jumped up almost before he hit the ground. His face was red. The other kids were laughing. One of them swung his arms, imitating Sean falling. Josie couldn't understand all the words, but she knew the kids were making fun of Sean. Someone kicked his sunglasses into the gutter.

Then they started pointing at Josie.

She stepped closer to her cousin, just behind his leg. She didn't think they would hit her; she just didn't want to see them saying mean things. They pointed at the sign in the street, laughing. Now Sean was laughing, too.

Josie felt relieved, but still nervous. They weren't making fun of her. They were laughing at the big yellow sign that said "Drive Slowly, Children Playing." Josie laughed too. She didn't think it was funny, but she liked fooling around with the big kids. The more she laughed, the more everyone else did.

One of the girls leaned down so Josie could see her mouth. She had braces on her teeth and beautiful bead earrings. She was smiling; Josie watched her mouth, but the girl was making funny noises that Josie couldn't understand. Josie kept smiling, but suddenly the noises gave her a bad feeling. She felt scared, like something terrible was going to happen.

Then another girl leaned down. She had curly blond hair like Barbie. "Why are you laughing?" she asked.

"At the sign," Josie said.

"It's *your* sign," the girl said.

"No, it's not," Josie said. She didn't understand. Suddenly she felt even more scared. She looked toward her house. She didn't see her mother. The girl was laughing, but Josie knew it wasn't happy laughing. All of a sudden she knew they were making fun of her.

"It says 'Drive Slow, Deaf Kid,'" the girl said. "That's you."

Josie glanced wildly at Sean. He had a sorry look on his face; Josie knew the girl was telling the truth. Josie felt her lower lip pushing forward, and tears spilled out of her eyes.

Sean pushed the girl, and she pushed him back. "Fat kid, fat kid," the girl said.

Josie started to walk, then run, toward her house. Sean caught up to her. She didn't want to look at him. He touched her shoulder at first, then held it tight, to make her stop. She kept her head down; she didn't want him to see her crying. But Sean crouched down low, so she had to look at him.

"I'm sorry, Josie," he said. "I didn't mean it."

Right now she hated Sean. She wanted to tell him, but she was afraid he'd make fun of her, too. From now on, no matter how nice he pretended to be, she would know how he really felt. She wanted to punch him in the nose.

She was walking fast toward her house when she saw her father's truck turn into the driveway. Her mother stepped outside to meet him. Josie couldn't hold her feet down; she ran as fast as she could.

Her parents stood there, saying hello to each other, not even seeing Josie. As she ran, she saw her mother turn slowly, see her, and say something to her father. Both her parents were smiling. They thought she was happy, excited to see them; Josie didn't want them smiling. She wanted them to know how mean Sean, and the kids, had been to her; her feelings were a furious, wordless tangle. A sob tore out of her throat.

Now her parents frowned. They stepped forward together, but Josie was past seeing. She ran blindly, her arms held open. She flew straight at her parents and hit one of them with full force. She wasn't sure which one caught her, and she didn't care.

"If he weren't my nephew . . ." Cass said.

"It's not his fault," Billy said. "He's a teenager. He's fat, and he wants to be popular. He's a teenager."

144

"He made fun of Josie just like those other creeps."

"He said he was sorry. You could see how bad he felt about it."

Cass didn't reply. They were sitting outside, drinking iced tea, listening to the crickets. All three kids were supposedly in bed, but Billy heard different rock beats coming from both Belinda's and T.J.'s windows.

"You going to hold it against Sean his entire life? Remember the time T.J. poured ketchup all over Emma at her birthday party?"

"I'll get over it," Cass said. "Anyway, Sean's not the point."

"Do you know what actually happened?" Billy asked. Sean at the scene was so flustered, so apologetic, they hadn't been able to get much out of him.

"He told Bonnie some kids down the street were laughing at the sign and making fun of the way Josie talks."

"Nice kids."

"I'd love to know exactly who was there. Joyce Barnard was the only one I saw for sure. I feel like calling John and Rachel."

"What good would that do? Kids are mean to each other. It's one big, endless chain reaction. Joyce'll get hers."

"She has braces," Cass said.

"So, call her 'tinsel teeth' next time you see her."

Cass actually seemed to be mulling that over.

"You can't shield Josie from every little thing," Billy said. "You always let T.J. and Belinda handle their own scrapes."

"It's different with Josie."

"I know it is. Kids are going to pick on her. That's why she has to be tough."

"You make it sound easy."

Billy knew it wasn't easy. Seeing Josie so upset today, crying so hard you couldn't understand a word she said, had made him crazy. She kept trying to talk, her tears making the words broad and shapeless.

"What?" Billy had asked, making her try again. Then again. Cass, realizing Josie was past reasoning with, had signaled him to be quiet. Billy had pretended to understand Josie's babbling while patting her head, kissing her damp cheeks, rocking her in his arms. Figuring out how to deal with this daughter of his bewildered him.

When he didn't talk to Josie, Cass would give him hell. Now she was upset because he'd tried to make Josie talk at the wrong time. Billy knew he did a good job with the other two kids, but it seemed he did nothing right with Josie. Tomorrow he'd leave for a short summer fishing run, and he was actually looking forward to getting away. He glanced at Cass; she had a far-off look in her eyes.

"Whose?" he asked.

"What do you mean?"

"Whose blood are you after? You look like you want revenge."

She shook her head. "I don't."

He waited for her to go on, but she didn't. She stared at the sky. She always used to watch for shooting stars. They could lie on their backs for hours at a time, counting meteors and making out. He moved closer to Cass; it almost surprised him when she rested her head on his shoulder.

"I'm scared," she said in a low voice.

"Why?" he asked.

"That we can't protect her enough."

"We can't protect any of them enough," Billy said. He knew what Cass was going to say, and he waited.

"But Josie's different."

Billy couldn't talk her out of that. He wished he could talk Cass herself out of being different from how she used to be. Out of losing herself along the way.

T.J. prowled his parents' bedroom when no one was home. He opened their drawers and stared at what was in them. He pawed through

his father's sock drawer, his mother's underwear drawer. He looked through the desk
where they kept the bills. He checked under
the mattress on his mother's side of the bed,
then his father's.

He walked along the upstairs hall, looking
at all the pictures. Nearly every inch of wall
space upstairs was covered with framed pho-
tographs of the family. His great-grandparents
in old-fashioned outfits on Easton's Beach;
Gram in her wedding dress; his mother in her
wedding dress; his father (with a mustache
back then) holding two gigantic lobsters toward the camera; Aunt Bonnie in her wedding
dress; everyone's first communion, school,
and baby pictures; Belinda holding Josie right
after Josie was born and not looking very
happy about it; T.J. sledding down the golf-
course hill, his mouth wide open in a shout.
He stared at that picture for a long time, trying
to read his own lips or remember what he
was yelling.

They didn't have an attic. They stored their
winter coats and special-occasion tablecloths
in trunks and big cardboard boxes printed to
look like wood grain; his mother would shove
them into the crawl space over Belinda's and
Josie's bedrooms. T.J. hoisted himself up.
Wasps swarmed in and out of a small louver
at the north end. The roof slanted just above

his head. Beads of amber sap glittered along the two-by-fours that formed the eaves. Sweat dripped down T.J.'s back as he went through the boxes.

Next he took a shower. He turned the water on as hot as he could stand it. He scrubbed himself clean and washed his hair, then leaned against the tile until the water went from scalding to warm to lukewarm to freezing cold. He felt sad; he didn't know exactly why. He didn't understand why he was snooping through his own house.

He went down to the basement. His father had put a Ping-Pong table and dartboard down there, and his parents were always encouraging Belinda and him to have their friends over. Nothing depressed T.J. more than the idea of his parents fixing up the basement so he and Belinda could have parties there. Maybe his parents thought it would keep them off the street, out of parking lots, away from fast cars. The only kids who had parties in their parents' basements were stone-cold drags.

On the other hand, a Ping-Pong party right here with chips and soda and ice-cream sundaes and spin-the-bottle while his parents were out of the room would be just the thing for Belinda. Perfecto. T.J. would have to suggest it to her. She'd be the hit of study hall.

He heard the back door close and his mother's and Josie's footsteps in the kitchen.

"T.J., are you home?" his mother's voice called.

"Down here," he yelled.

"Dinner in half an hour. What are you doing in the basement?"

"Playing darts," he called, just to see if she'd come to investigate. He leaned against the Ping-Pong table, waiting. When she didn't appear on the basement stairs, he went back to snooping. He'd always thought his mom was pretty cool, definitely smart, but she was losing it. Playing *darts?* If she'd fall for that, she'd fall for any wimp excuse. The next time he felt like taking off for Fall River with Chris and Sean, he'd tell his mom he and the boys were washing cars for charity.

Six unvarnished pine cupboards stretched the length of the room. Their fake Colonial wrought-iron hinges and door handles were black, arrow-shaped. He remembered being scared of them when he was little. They had the same evil shape as Satan's spear-point tail, the one pictured in his prayer book.

He could still see that picture of Satan: pointy red face, sharp beard, glittery black eyes, hooves instead of feet, a loincloth that had reminded T.J. of a diaper, that long red whip of a tail with a barbed arrow at the end.

In the picture, the tail seemed to be snaking out of the diaper, and T.J. had thought Satan had a monster cock, red and dangerous, ready to jab any innocent girl who walked by.

The devil's-tail door hinges had kept T.J. out of these cupboards; right now, about to explore something totally unfamiliar in his own house, T.J. felt strange and wild. He stared at the hinges. Satan, guardian of the basement cupboards. T.J. opened the first one: a stash of booze.

His parents hardly ever drank, except at Christmas. Not like at his grandparents' house, where the bottles were in plain sight, full today, empty tomorrow. Of course, his grandparents never seemed affected by liquor. They were always the same: kind of grumpy in a nice way, always trying to joke, laid-back old people. They were more likely to have a shelf full of liquor than his parents. T.J., who had already drunk from a keg and bought beer on his own, felt a little shocked.

Next cupboard: a pile of records. He read some titles: *Super Session, Concert for Bangladesh, Sweet Baby James, Bridge over Troubled Waters, Tapestry, Imagine.* Nothing too unfamiliar; his parents had pretty much the same goofy shit on CDs now. He stared at Carole King's album cover. Ugly hair, pretty tits.

Looking through these cupboards made T.J.

feel like a detective. What if his parents secretly smoked pot, kept their goods down here? His parents weren't that old; they had told him they'd tried it once in high school.

Maybe the hinges were no accident, maybe his parents were Satanists, like his cousin Sean. Sean said Satan gave you whatever you wanted, but you had to give something to him first. Sean had sacrificed his sister's baby pictures and an entire side of beef his parents had bought at the food co-op. Steaks, roasts, ribs, chopped beef: half a cow. He'd hauled the packages out of the freezer in the middle of the night, borrowed his father's truck to cart them to the harbor, and fed them to the black water. He had taken Emma's baby pictures to Minturn Ledge Light and set them afire. In return, Satan was going to get Sean his own Harley and get him laid.

"Yeah, right," T.J. said out loud. T.J. had never gone for the Satan shit; he thought it was totally bogus. Sean was a fat kid, and Satan worship was the only way he could feel tough. In real life he was a spineless dweeb: he had made fun of the Deaf Child sign right in front of Josie, just so T.J.'s asshole neighbors would stop laughing at him.

But here, opening the basement cupboards, T.J. felt totally, one-hundred-percent convinced his parents were Satan worshippers.

It would explain everything: that distant look in his mother's eyes, the way she never seemed to be all there anymore — nothing ever made her really happy, the way she used to get. Now his father always itched to go fishing, just to get away from home, and T.J. couldn't entirely blame him, considering how miserable everyone was all the time. Maybe Satan had the family in his clutches, was dragging them all down to hell.

Ready to open the third cupboard, T.J. would not have been surprised to find dead babies, boiled kittens in jars, chopped-off fingers and toes. He yanked open the door.

"Holy shit," T.J. said. Boxes of bullets. Sunny yellow boxes stacked one on top of another filled with hundreds and hundreds of bullets. T.J. opened one box, and then another. He put a bullet in his pocket. He knew his father had a rifle and a handgun. He had seen the rifle onboard the *Norboca* in April, and his father had told him it was there in case of emergency.

What the hell kind of emergency could a rifle solve one hundred miles at sea? Maybe his father was expecting a deranged whale. Or maybe he was afraid the men would mutiny, seize the helm, hijack the boat to the Bahamas.

His father had given him a man-versus-nature lecture, about sharks and hurricanes and the Bermuda Triangle, then he'd eased into a man-versus-man lecture, about drug smugglers and gunrunners and modern-day pirates. T.J. had listened without saying one word, because he'd figured the real reason his father had a rifle onboard was that if the day arrived when he couldn't take it anymore, he'd have the means to blow himself away. None of the other reasons made any sense. Fucking pirates.

Then, arranging the bullet boxes the way he'd found them, T.J. saw the snake. He jumped about a mile. "Hey!"

He was going to call his mother, but then he changed his mind. His mom had enough to handle. T.J. would scope out the snake himself. Coiled up, it was hiding at the back of the cupboard, in the shadows. T.J. grabbed a Ping-Pong paddle, pushed some boxes aside.

"Jesus," he said. It was his father's handgun, not a snake. "You big asshole," he said to himself, reaching for the gun.

He wondered whether it was loaded. He didn't know how to tell. He held it in his right hand, pointed it at the floor. Then, he couldn't in a million years have explained why, except maybe from some macho instinct he'd picked up from cop shows or Nintendo, he pulled the trigger. Click.

"Idiot!" he said out loud, but inside he felt

charged up, thrilled, because he had known — really known for sure — that the thing wasn't loaded. He'd just known.

"What doing, T.J.?"

He spun around.

"Hey, Josie," he said, hiding the gun behind him.

"What doing?" She had the cutest little smile on her face; she ran toward him, trying to look behind his back, like she thought he was playing a game. T.J. pivoted, rooted to that one spot, while she grabbed at his arm. They circled around in a crazy dance. "What have? What have?"

He held the gun in his left hand and gave her a push with his right. She stopped still, like he'd slapped her. Her mouth dropped open. T.J. hadn't pushed her hard, but he knew he'd hurt her feelings really bad. She looked more surprised than anything. She'd expect Belinda to treat her like dirt, but she trusted T.J.

"Shit," T.J. said. He used his body to shield Josie from seeing him slide the gun back into the cupboard. He slammed the door, then turned back to Josie. Her mouth was just starting to quiver, betrayal written all over her wide eyes.

"I'm sorry, Josie," he said. "C'mere."

She just stood there, looking at the floor.

He sat on the floor, patted his knee. "C'mere."

She wouldn't budge. He knew she wouldn't start to howl, the way she did when Belinda was mean or when she couldn't make people understand her. Everyone thought Josie was a little weakling, a spoiled-brat crybaby, but T.J. knew that wasn't true.

Her bad screams were how she communicated at certain times. With T.J., she didn't need them. T.J. could always get through to her. Right now, though, her feelings were hurt, and he knew he couldn't rush her. She'd come through when she damn well felt like it.

"Danger," T.J. said, pointing at the third cupboard. He reached out to touch the handle and slapped his own hand hard.

"Ouch!" Josie said.

"Yes, ouch if you go near that door. You got that, Josie? Danger."

"Danger in there," Josie said. Suddenly she looked psyched, like she'd forgotten T.J.'s rebuke, and because she could sense he was asking her to keep a secret.

"Dinner, you guys!" their mom called from upstairs.

"Come on," T.J. said. Josie clasped her arms around his neck, and he carried her up to the kitchen. He put one finger to his lips. "Ssssh," he reminded Josie.

She nodded her head.

"Any bull's-eyes?" his mom asked as soon as he walked through the door.

"Huh?"

"I thought you were playing darts."

"Oh. Yeah, a couple."

"A couple is pretty good. Be careful playing darts with your sister around."

Was she kidding? God, he didn't want to believe his mother really thought he'd been playing darts. It was every teenage boy's dream to put things over on his mom, but this was radical. It only made it worse, her telling him to be extra careful around Josie.

His mom dished out helpings of baked sole for him, Josie, Belinda, and herself. She had a frown in her eyes, as if she were thinking of something nasty. Belinda was babbling about some great song she heard on the radio today.

"Ever thought of having a Ping-Pong party?" T.J. asked her. "Downstairs would be perfect."

"Why haven't you ever had one?" Belinda asked suspiciously.

"I'm planning a dart party. If it's okay with Mom."

"A dart party?" his mother asked, raising her eyebrows. "Is that what you said? A dart party?" She was beginning to get it.

"Yeah."

"I wouldn't mind a Ping-Pong party," Belinda said carefully, warming to the idea. God, you could put anything over on her.

"They're really fun," T.J. said. "You could make it even a little more special by telling everyone to wear polka dots. Kind of a Ping-Pong theme."

"And for your dart party," his mom said, "you could have everyone wear pointy little hats and pointy shoes, and you could tell everyone they needed a password to get by the front door, like 'What's the point?' They'd have to say it to me or I wouldn't let them in."

"Awesome," T.J. said. His mother had this wise-guy smile on her face, like she wasn't quite having fun, but for the moment, at least, she wasn't miserable.

"I don't even know how to play Ping-Pong," Belinda said.

"Hey, I'll teach you," T.J. said. "If you'll let me come to your party."

"Are you faking me out? Mom, is he?" Belinda asked.

"Yes," Mom said.

T.J. and his friends always joked about "Fantasy Moms," the kind of moms who still looked young, dressed in jeans and T-shirts instead of teacher-style stuff, wore their hair loose instead of done up, were cool. You never thought of your own mom as a Fantasy Mom, but you didn't mind if your friends did. And T.J. knew that a lot of his friends thought of his mom that way.

Josie had stopped eating. She pulled out her right hearing aid, fiddled with the control.

"What's wrong?" their mother asked, dropping her fork to lean clear across the table.

"It's broken," Josie said. Only the words came out sounding like, "Eh bwokah."

"Here," Cass said. She wiped her hands on her napkin, then took the hearing aid out of Josie's hand. To T.J., Josie's hearing aids had always looked disgusting, like blobs of shapeless flesh. He didn't know how Josie could stand them. The sight of one out of her ear made him gag. He put down his fork and concentrated on not throwing up.

Josie, tapping her left ear, started to whimper. "Eh, eh, eh," she said urgently, like a hurt puppy. "Eh, eh, eh."

"Oh, please!" Belinda said.

"Eh, eh, eh, eh . . ."

"Hang on, Josie," their mom said. "Please don't start that. I'm trying as hard as I can. Just a sec . . . Jesus, just hold on a minute."

T.J. had the feeling their mother felt she was alone at the table, under her own pressure to fix the hearing aid before Josie launched into a bad fit. The realization filled him with

159

rage. He felt tempted to bolt, leave them all alone, let Josie throw one of her super whoppers.

"Eh, eh, eh," Josie went, getting louder, screwing her face into a knot. "Want it back! Want it back!" She clapped her left ear over and over, as if trying to clear it, like a diver who'd gone too deep.

"Please, Josie!" his mother said, a horrible pleading tone in her voice. "You'll hurt your ear. Stop!"

T.J. still felt like splitting, but instead he took Josie's left hand. "Hey," he said sharply. "Cut it out."

"Eh, eh, eh . . ."

"I said *cut it out*. Mom'll fix it."

Josie's face stayed twisted and scared, but she stopped her whimpering. He stared at her for a minute, until her face relaxed. Then he stuck out his tongue, making her laugh.

"Battery," his mom said, dashing to her desk and back. She unscrewed a piece of the hearing aid with a miniature screwdriver, inserted a tiny silver battery, and wiggled the hearing aid back into Josie's ear.

Josie nodded without speaking and resumed eating.

Cass smiled at T.J. "Thanks, buddy," she said. "You saved the day."

"No big deal."

"I mean it. I think I'd have flipped out if we really got going here." She nodded at Josie.

"No sweat."

"I noticed that, actually. How do you and your father do it? I have to talk till I'm blue in the face."

"Hey, Mom," T.J. said. "Lighten up, will you?"

She nodded. But instead of lightening up, her face got all cloudy again, and she went back to what she'd been thinking. "Shit," T.J. said under his breath. No one seemed to hear him. At least, no one said anything.

8

One night in August, when the kids were in bed and Billy was at sea, Cass left the house. She thought she was simply taking out the garbage, but after she'd dropped the plastic bag into the trash can, she just kept walking. The whole neighborhood was asleep. Streetlights hummed overhead. She passed from one circle of light into the next, listening to the electric buzz. It reminded her of someone blowing low into a pitch pipe.

She passed Bonnie's dark house, the Sullivans', the O'Tooles', the Barnards'. John's truck was parked in the driveway. He hadn't gone fishing with Billy this trip; he was sleeping in his own bed. Cass sneaked down the driveway and peeked in his truck window. Cassette tapes, coiled line, empty soda cans, marine-supply catalogues covered the seat. She remembered dating John in a truck like this about twenty years ago.

She wondered what life was like in the Barnard home. Rachel lived the fishwife life, just

162

like Cass. She rode out John's absences, probably as lonely for him as Cass was for Billy. Unlike Cass, though, Rachel did aerobics. Cass had seen her coming out of the High Step Fitness Studio in turquoise spandex tights and hundred-dollar aerobic shoes. To Cass, Rachel seemed as if she didn't have a care in the world beyond keeping her butt tight. Cass and Rachel kept their distance from each other. Being married to fishermen was all they had in common.

Cass had never told Rachel about her daughter Joyce's making fun of Josie. Bill was right: What good would it have done? Joyce was just another kid. Before having Josie, Cass had always laughed at overprotective mothers. She remembered Carol O'Toole calling up, miffed because Belinda, in first grade, had told Tanya her winter coat was ugly.

"It's a very *expensive* coat," Carol had said. "From Lord & Taylor. And Tanya feels very hurt, because she picked it out herself. We want Belinda to apologize." Of course, Cass made Belinda say she was sorry. But she remembered laughing with Billy for a month at the way Carol had sniffed, "It's a very *expensive* coat." At Carol, for making a mountain out of a first-grade molehill.

Cass continued down the street. It flashed through her mind that one of her kids might wake up and need her. That Josie would. But it felt so good to walk, to enjoy the summer night while everyone else slept, that she just kept going.

Cass didn't understand what was coming over her. She was turning into one of those women she despised — an overprotective mother. She had known a hundred of them, and she could see them now: armed with Kleenex, extra sweaters, galoshes, batting helmets. Fretting that their children would want to play contact sports, try mountain climbing, cross the highway, swim out too far.

Cass and Billy had never planned on having a third child. Life with their first two had been a dream. T.J. and Belinda were the easiest, happiest babies imaginable. Any fears Cass had had about losing herself in the process of raising children had flown out the window. She couldn't imagine not being a mother.

Then Josie, her third baby, arrived. Cass and Billy had played sex roulette. She couldn't say they'd taken a trip, forgotten her birth control. Or that they had misread the calendar, misjudged her cycle. No, Josie had been conceived out of sheer passion, Cass's and Billy's inability to stop their lovemaking long enough to open the drawer, squirt on the jelly, insert the diaphragm. Lust.

It had come over them a thousand times

— a lust so strong they would tempt fate, lock legs, French-kiss, rub bodies, whisper love stories, touch, tease, fuck wildly without a thought for opening the drawer.

Cass knew her parents and sisters felt sorry for her, thought her life was difficult. They knew she had to cope with Josie's acting up, her misunderstandings, her frustration. When Josie threw a tantrum in public, they admired Cass's patience and determination. Her firm grip in those public situations lessened their own embarrassment. "I don't know how you do it," they all said to her.

Well, Cass didn't know, either. She just did it. Here came another parade of women from her childhood: the women with burdens, the ones you'd feel sorry for. Mrs. Muldowney, who had to push her husband around in a wheelchair, wiping the drool off his chin; Mrs. Vetrano, who used to bring her middle-aged son everywhere she went, a gray-haired man who wet his pants and read comics all through Mass; Mrs. Cray, whose only child, a girl Cass's age, had been born blind.

"Poor Mae Muldowney," "Poor Ginger Cray," everyone would say. Cass figured people probably looked at Josie and said, "Poor Cass Medieros." That made her more furious than anything. Cass loved Josie with a passion. Josie felt terrors Cass couldn't imagine. Cass could see it in her eyes, the panic of not being able to hear right. She'd give anything to take away her deafness, but she didn't love her less for it.

When she reached the Alewives Park playground, Cass walked across the grass. There was the sandbox where her children had played. She could practically see Belinda building sandcastles. There was the swing set T.J. once toppled over, he'd gotten himself swinging so high. The tall shiny slide.

This playground scared Josie. Other little kids moved too fast, seeming to come out of nowhere, because she couldn't hear them. Sometimes they did it on purpose. She didn't like to swing because she didn't trust what was behind her. Being so high in the air and falling back into the unknown was too frightening. Once Cass, pushing Josie, stepped back for one beat in midswing to tie her shoe. Josie, expecting to feel her mother's hand, instead felt nothing. The sound Josie made was inhuman, and now it echoed in Cass's mind.

Life without Josie. Cass imagined what it would be like. The thought sneaked up on her, out of nowhere: What if she'd never been born? She pictured this playground, T.J. and Belinda playing, surrounded by an aura of contentment. The way things had been. She tried to remember what Josie had been like

166

before her hearing loss, but she could not. The hearing Josie did not exist.

At that exact moment — she couldn't have said why — Cass looked up. She saw a shooting star, and then another. Her head tipped back, she reached behind her for the dangling metal chain, pulled the swing underneath her. She sat down, her feet in the scuffed, sandy path, and pushed off. She swung gently, in a slow rhythm. One more, she said to herself, watching the sky. One more star, and then I'll go home.

Her heart pounded at first as she waited. Summer meteor showers always excited her, made her feel that anything was possible. Looking up, she hardly blinked. As a kid, keeping count, she would beat Nora and Bonnie every time.

"One more," she said out loud, and then she saw it: a star trail blazing straight from Arcturus to the Pleiades — bright white fire through the night. She swung a few seconds more, letting the motion calm her heart.

Cass headed home. Because she had been gone for so long, she cut through yards, passing directly beneath her neighbors' bedroom windows. She heard men snoring, a couple fighting, a radio playing low. Coleridge Avenue was silent, empty of traffic. Cass crossed without looking both ways, then entered her house. She climbed the stairs. Outside each bedroom door she stood still, listening to the steady breathing of each sleeping child, and then she went to bed.

Meteorologists called the summer the hottest in years. Going into Providence was like stepping into a clay oven. A mysterious sandstorm whirled through Hartford, depositing a massive sand dune just behind the Wadsworth Atheneum; local car dealers sold more dune buggies and dirt bikes than ever before. After dark each night, kids came from all over to leave their tire tracks on the dune. People trying to sleep complained that the engines sounded like giant chain saws, so police imposed a curfew on the city until enough steam shovels could be commandeered to clear the dune away.

By some thermal fluke, a shift in the winds, or a combination of the two, Mount Hope was experiencing slightly cooler temperatures than the surrounding areas. People came from as far away as Newark, just to spend the day at Spray Cove. The ferry from Block Island carried islanders to Mount Hope, hoping for relief from the airless heat.

In Little League, Keating & Daughters won game after game. Driving by the field one day, Bonnie Keating Kenneally stopped to watch and reminisce about the days when her kids had played; it almost seemed unfair to Bonnie, watching her team slug triples and homers into a field full of tired players whose home fields were too hot for batting practice. She missed Gavin, but he was making them a fortune scallopping. He and the O'Tooles had tapped into a rich bed on Georges Bank where you'd trawl and trawl and never come up empty.

Lobsterville sold so many frozen daiquiris during the last Saturday in July, the blender broke. People slept with their windows open, lightweight blankets pulled to their chins. Sheila Keating, grandmother of Cass, Bonnie, and Nora, wore a flannel nightgown all day long, if she wasn't going out; she tried to sleep as much as possible, because Eddie visited her dreams more and more. One night, when Cass Keating Medieros fell asleep on the living-room floor, Josie snuggled close for warmth, talking in her sleep about her father coming home from sea.

Mary pressed close to Jim every night. Snoring, she slept like a log. She never heard Sheila yelling, "Oh, shut up," from down the hall. She dreamed of herself as a young bigamist, a pretty girl married to both Jim and Ward, and she never knew that Jim lay awake beside her, counting the times the beam from Minturn Ledge Light passed across the ceiling.

★ ★ ★

Billy Medieros returned from his brief fishing trip. He came in late from longlining off Block Island, hot and sweating, and felt the air turn cool just as he passed Minturn Ledge Light. He'd missed fishing with John this trip. His crew hadn't gotten along, and the heat didn't help. Pulling into port, he couldn't wait to get home.

Driving up the hill, he checked his watch. It was nearly eleven, and there was a good chance all three kids would be asleep. He wondered if he'd find Cass in bed, naked and waiting. Not that she knew for sure when he was coming home. In their early days, at least, that element of surprise would add to the anticipation, would drive them crazy waiting to be together.

Now he felt a different anticipation. He never knew what to expect with Cass. Would she be too drained to talk? Angry because her mother had suggested North Point again? Thrilled to see him, ready to seduce him anywhere but in their own bed?

Tonight he didn't care. He wanted to drink a beer with Cass in the back yard, then go upstairs and fall asleep together, nude.

Driving down Coleridge with the truck windows open, he felt himself starting to relax. But then he heard it: Josie screaming. Her voice pierced the muggy air, though Billy couldn't make out one word she was saying. He thought of Cass, of how tired she must be, dealing with Josie so late. It could be anything, he thought. Maybe she'd had a nightmare, maybe she had a heat rash. He tried to tune in, to tell from her pitch how serious it was.

He parked across the street, where tall pines in the Camarras' yard blocked the yellow streetlight. Billy climbed out of his truck. He stood hidden, his arms folded across his chest, watching his own house. He imagined going home, trying to sort out the problem, saying the wrong thing or not saying enough.

He found he couldn't make himself go inside.

Split down the middle by love and shame, he climbed back in his truck and yanked the wheel around. He sped down the hill, toward the harbor. For the first time in his life, he was going to sleep onboard the boat instead of going home to his wife.

Willis Randecker gave up his room at the Ramada Inn and rented an apartment on Abalone Street. His real estate venture in Providence kept him busy all day, but every night he'd wait for Nora to finish work at Lobsterville and dine with her at her Benson's Mill condo. He would tell her about the properties he'd been looking at, and he'd tell her his ideas for development. Half the contractors in Rhode Island ate at Lobsterville, so Nora would set him straight on who had a good reputation and who didn't.

Nora had cooked every chicken recipe in her *Dining for Lovers* cookbook, and still Willis hadn't taken her to bed. They would kiss for hours — sometimes on her balcony, sometimes on her leather sofa — but that was it. He never even tried to touch her breasts.

It was two o'clock one Wednesday morning, with the harbor lights slanting in the condo windows. They had been kissing since midnight. Her mouth bruised and a fire between her legs, Nora pulled back from him. They gazed, panting, into each other's eyes. She guided his big hand to her hip, pushed it up her silky caftan to her breasts. No man had ever made her feel this way; she didn't want to beg, but she would if she had to.

"Willis . . ."

As if mesmerized, he stared at his hand caressing her breast. Cupping its full curve, rolling the nipple between his fingers right through the caftan. Suddenly he stopped. "It isn't right, Nora," he said.

"It is, Willis. You have no idea how right this is. . . ." Nora rubbed against him.

"Please," she said, her eyes closed.

He stroked her cheek, passed his smooth fingers over her lips. When she opened her eyes she found him watching her with such tenderness that she momentarily forgot her lust. She couldn't remember ever seeing such a loving expression on any man's face before.

"You see, I don't believe in it," Willis said.

"In what?" Nora's sex still felt hot and liquid; her nipples tingled. If anything, what he was saying excited her more.

"Sex outside of marriage. I've only been with one woman my whole life, Nora — my ex-wife. I can't explain this to you; it's how I was raised." His eyes looked troubled; he touched his temple.

Nora had been rejected before. She had come on too strong with guys who were married, guys who didn't want her; it had always hurt her to the quick when a man said no. But this was different. Willis looked so unhappy about what he was saying, Nora cared only about comforting him. She took his head in her hands, kissed his forehead, his cheeks, the tip of his nose.

"It's okay," she whispered.

"It's not okay," he said. "I want you so much. I'd give anything if I didn't have this problem with my conscience."

"Don't worry, Willis," Nora said.

"Nora, I care about you very much."

"But why?" Nora asked the question she'd been wondering about all summer, when Willis had first appeared at Lobsterville.

Willis gave a little laugh, held her hands between his. "Who can explain chemistry? I felt it the first time I laid eyes on you. There you were, marching back and forth through the restaurant with a cross little frown on your face, and I said to myself, 'I would like to cheer that girl up.' "

Nora laughed nervously. Was that it? He wanted to cheer her up? She straightened her caftan.

"I've been lonely, Nora, and I'll bet you have, too. I can see it in your eyes. You act like a tough lady running a famous restaurant, but you're just a little girl. You've been lonely inside. Am I right?"

Two tears squeezed out of Nora's eyes. She wiped them away, but more followed. To finally be understood!

"There, there," Willis whispered, pressing her head against his shoulder. "What silky hair you have. And the color . . . it's the exact shade of a very rare azalea, the Savannah Russet, that used to bloom in a square outside my grandmother's house."

"I've always wanted this," Nora said, thinking of all the time she'd lost with men who didn't like her.

"So have I," Willis said. "We both have, but we've found each other, Nora. It doesn't matter how long it took."

"Your business up here can't last forever," Nora said. "After a while you'll go back to Georgia."

"Once you've found someone you love, it doesn't matter if events force you apart for a little while."

Had he really said "love"? Nora had to remind herself to breathe.

"I'm an entrepreneur, Nora," Willis said. "I have an office in Savannah, but I don't see why I couldn't open one up here. There's plenty of opportunity for development in the Northeast. I've been looking at parcels of land in Seekonk, Pawcatuck, Warwick. I put together a condo project just up Narragansett Bay from here. This condo complex you're living in? Nora, I've been involved with ten just like it, from Atlantic City clear down to Key West. No reason I couldn't open up a northern office."

"You're really thinking of it?" Nora asked.

"Why do you think I rented an apartment instead of staying in that hotel room? I'm thinking long-term. I thought you might have figured that out on your own." His tone was teasing, fond, and he continued to touch her hair.

"I guess it occurred to me, but . . ." Honesty didn't come naturally to Nora. Not that she would lie, but she found it excruciating to tell a man her deepest, truest feelings. "I didn't dare to hope. I thought we'd get . . . close. And then you'd leave."

"You mean you thought I'd go to bed with you, then dump you."

"Yes."

"That could never happen," Willis said. He touched, then kissed the rim of her left ear. She saw by the lighted dial of his gold watch that it was 2:55 A.M. on August 15. At 2:57 he proposed to her. "I want to marry you. I want to take you as my wife, Nora. Please say yes."

"Yes," Nora said.

9

Sheila Keating stood ankle-deep in sea mud, feeling around with her toes for clams. When she felt one, she'd flip it up with her foot and wash the sand off it. Eddie said she had a gift for clamming the way some people could play the piano or tell fortunes. He had no sensitivity in his feet, so he had to make do with a wood-handled fork with long, curved tines. The sun baked down. The clam basket, kept afloat by an inner tube, bobbed between them. Pretty soon the basket would be full, and they could go home to their cottage and lie down for a nap.

Someone came in the front door, awakening Sheila. She hugged herself, savoring the dream. "That was a good one," she said, nodding with satisfaction. Pretty soon she'd be able to fall asleep again and pick up the dream where she'd left off. She was getting better and better at it. Sheila couldn't wait to get rid of this visitor so she could dream about taking a nap with Eddie after clamming, cuddling under their white cotton sheet on a hot summer day.

"Hi, Granny," Cass said.

"Cass!" Sheila exclaimed. She'd rather talk with Cass than almost anything — even dream about Eddie.

Cass sat on the edge of the sofa. She looked so lovely, as delicate as a rose. Peering up at her, Sheila tried to tell what was different about her.

"Are you pregnant?" Sheila asked.

Cass shook her head and let out a hard little laugh.

Sheila's feelings were hurt. "I don't know what's so funny," Sheila said. "Babies are wonderful."

"I can't have any more babies," Cass said. "I had an operation."

Sheila tilted her head. She knew this must have to do with Josie. None of the women in her family had ever had a problem baby before Cass. But Cass didn't seem like the mother of a problem baby. Generally the experience hardened such mothers. They grew thick skin, like armor, but what they passed on to their children was the opposite: skin so thin you could see through it. Sometimes the children were given away for adoption, but you could always tell. The children who cried in kindergarten, who gave away their lunches, who carved their initials in their desks when no one was watching, who wanted to make friends with every older person they passed on the street: these were the children who had been problem babies.

"Where is Josie?" Sheila asked.

"At speech class. I'm going to send her for three hours a day while Belinda and T.J. are in school. They go back next week."

"That will help her, dear."

"I hope so," Cass said. But she didn't sound very hopeful. She was looking a little droopy, like a dust mop.

"It will help you, too. To have her off your hands part of the time."

Cass said nothing.

"Where's Billy?" Sheila asked.

"Fishing."

"Always fishing. Well, they have to do it while the weather holds. Pretty soon the winter will be here, and he'll be home when it storms."

"Yes."

Sheila looked at Cass long and hard, a small smile touching her dry lips. Her granddaughter had something big on her mind, and she was afraid to say it. "Spit it out," Sheila said. "Right now."

"Billy stayed on his boat instead of coming home." Cass looked fierce, but like she might cry at any second, too.

"Did you have a fight?"

Cass shook her head. "He said he couldn't take Josie crying all night. He'd been up thirty-six hours straight, so he fell asleep on the boat." She paused. "It was only one night."

"And you're mad at him?"

"Well, of course I am. He told me last night, like it was no big deal, and he left this morning for two weeks. Out to Georges Bank and back."

"Fishermen have the life, don't they? You're ready for a nice big fight, and he's out to sea."

"Lucky for him."

Sheila was thinking about happiness, about how Cass had laughed and shivered all through her own babyhood, as though she couldn't wait for the next adventure. But Sheila knew that one place you didn't want too much adventure was your marriage. Spice was one thing, but you didn't want to wait and wonder.

"Men can never roll with the punches," Sheila said. "You have to coddle them every second."

"I'm not the coddling type," Cass said. "I don't have the patience. I'm thinking about bagging this, joining the Peace Corps. Me and Josie. We'll go to India."

"That sounds nice. Will you send me a post-card?"

"No, Granny. You're coming with us."

"I used to want to be a missionary, you know," Sheila said.

"I didn't," Cass said, her adorable, wicked smile back in place.

"Your hand is so warm," Sheila said after a while. "I'm *freezing*. Your mother won't turn on the heat."

"It's barely Labor Day!" Cass said. "We're just in the middle of a cool spell. Can I get you another blanket?"

Sheila stared into Cass's face. "With all you have to do, why do you waste your time with me?"

"Waste my time? I came because I needed to talk to you."

"Do you ever count your blessings?"

"Not exactly."

"Well, count them."

"Okay, I will."

"I mean right now."

Cass sat there, a drifty look on her face.

"Come on. Out loud," Sheila said.

"Well, I have my kids. Billy. You. The family . . . let's see . . . I love the water, and it's everywhere I look. The wharf. The business. I like my job," she said, but she didn't sound convinced. She sounded more like she was pacifying Sheila. Sheila patted her hand.

Cass tilted her head questioningly.

"See, dear? You're really very happy. Don't think quite so hard all the time. You'll make yourself old."

"How about I make us some tea?"

"What a good idea," Sheila said. While Cass walked into the kitchen, Sheila leaned back and concentrated on sleep. If she hurried, she had time for a quick dream before the kettle whistled.

Dropping off a season's worth of *Penny-savers* at the recycling bin, Bonnie found a stack of French magazines. She'd taken French in high school; out of curiosity, she opened the journal on top, *Les Femmes d'amour*. Instead of text, she found sharp-focus pictures of two naked couples playing on a bed together. Bonnie instantly shoved the magazine into her purse.

The women in the picture were older, heavier, realer-looking than the women in *Playboy* or *Penthouse*. The photos did not appear staged — everything set up and retouched like a bland teenage fantasy. The foursome might have been caught in the act, unaware of the photographer. Both women had stretch marks, just like Bonnie.

At home, she hid the magazine in her bedside cabinet, right under *The Joy of Sex*.

When Gavin got home from scallopping four days later, Bonnie decided to show him the French pictures. The kids were at the beach; it seemed like a perfect time. But she couldn't find the magazine. It had disappeared.

After a long trip to the scallop beds, Gavin liked nothing more than to stand in the shower until the hot water ran out. Bonnie had been ransacking the room for fifteen minutes and still couldn't find it.

She threw her terrycloth robe over her new lavender teddy and walked barefoot into Sean's room. Clothes he'd worn days ago were strewn across the floor. Absently, Bonnie gathered up dirty socks and underwear, jammed them into his hamper. She got to her knees, peered under his unmade bed, pulled out more clothes. She found an assortment of earrings. Ten minutes ago she'd had thoughts only of sex with Gavin, and here she was cleaning her son's room.

Bonnie hated the thought of invading this place, but something told her to keep looking. The place was awash with hormones, and Sean wasn't even in the house. Posters of *Sports Illustrated* swimsuit models hung over his bed. He'd left the radio on, and some singer was rapping about "the pleasing curves and jiggles of a teenage girl."

"Jesus," Bonnie said, snapping off the radio. Staring at Sean's desk, she hesitated for one instant, until she heard the shower stop. She yanked open the drawer. A small notebook, covered with slogans, lay inside. Bonnie leaned over to read her son's writing: "Satan Rules, Pentangle Controls." "If Someone Goes Against You, You Must Kill: The Seventeenth Commandment." "666." "Lucifer is Lord."

Bonnie felt the blood drain out of her face. She carried the notebook back to her and Gavin's room. Gavin lay naked on the bed, his hands folded behind his head, with a devilish grin on his face and an enormous purple erection. "What a nice outfit," he said, nodding at her teddy. "How about taking it off?"

Sitting beside him on the bed, she handed him the notebook.

"This is Sean's?" he asked, reading.

"It's his handwriting."

Gavin let out a big sigh. "Satan worship. Well, that explains the earrings."

Bonnie stared at him. Usually she felt wildly attracted to her husband: to his bearded face, his curly brown hair, his taut arms, his not-so-taut belly. But right now she saw his redneck side showing through, and she didn't like it.

"What do earrings have to do with Satan

worship?" she asked.

"Seven earrings in one ear, all daggers and skulls and pistols? That's what."

Bonnie now felt obliged to defend her son. "That's the style," she said. "All the kids have their ears pierced now, not just the girls. And Emma wears just as many daggers as Sean."

"Maybe I don't get it."

"He just wants to be popular. It's natural," she said doubtfully. Bonnie understood that chubby Sean needed to fit in. She glanced at the notebook and shivered.

"Didn't you tell me you used to pretend you were a witch?" he asked.

"Yeah, but trying to get eggs to stand up on the summer solstice seems less, I don't know, sinister than this."

"Get over here, you beautiful bombshell. You're making me crazy." Gavin opened his arms. "Ask the kid about it when he gets home."

"I will," Bonnie said. She could practically predict what would happen. Her son would look her in the eye, all sweet and dopey, and she would have to believe every word he said. He had such an open face. Like last month, when he had denied stealing the meat. If he and his friends wanted to throw a barbecue, all they had to do was ask. He dressed like a Hell's Angel. But just last week he'd stood in the kitchen after Bonnie had confronted him, gulping back tears as he told her how he'd been mean to Josie, and how bad those other kids had made him feel.

Gavin pulled Bonnie into his arms, giving her a deep kiss. "Enough about the kid, okay?" he said.

"Okay." She snuggled into his arms. "I miss you when you're gone. Don't ever go fishing again."

"Chain me to the bed, Bonnie. I'm your love slave, and you know it."

"Damn straight," Bonnie said, watching him slide the strap of her new teddy off her shoulder.

But she felt too preoccupied to really concentrate on making love. Her body went through the motions, but some part of her brain was engaged in listening for the door, for Sean's footsteps in the hall. Later, while Gavin slept, she dressed and slipped out of the bedroom.

In the kitchen, she poured a glass of milk. She grabbed a bar of baking chocolate from the cupboard. She felt frantic for the sugar, for the feeling of fullness it would give her. Nibbling the hard chocolate, she flipped through a cookbook for the dessert section. Reading about food while eating gave her double the feeling.

Emma walked in, her wet bikini showing through her yellow sundress. Bonnie wanted to hide the chocolate from her, but Emma had seen it.

"How was the beach, Em?" Bonnie asked.

"Raw chocolate?" Emma asked. "Gross. Isn't that the stuff you bake with?"

"Yes. Want some?"

Emma shook her head. "The beach was fun. We had a wicked wet-towel fight."

"Sounds great. Did you see Sean?"

"He's on his way. Huffing and puffing, as usual. What's for dinner?"

"Scallops," Bonnie said.

"Figures. Can I eat at Belinda's?"

"If Cass says it's okay."

Bonnie rewrapped the chocolate and settled back to wait. Five minutes later, Sean came through the door. He wore his customary earrings and new shades, cutoff jeans, a plaid shirt with the sleeves torn off, and motorcycle boots. He gave her a sweet smile.

"Hi, honey," Bonnie said.

"Hi, Mom."

"Sit down a minute," Bonnie said. "We have to talk."

Sean flopped onto a kitchen chair, his arm slung across the rail back. He had the guileless expression of someone with a clean conscience. Bonnie slid his notebook out from under a copy of *Gourmet* magazine.

"You looked in my drawers," Sean said accusingly.

Bonnie tapped the notebook's cover. "This caught my attention," she said.

Sean shrugged. "I'm not the only one. A lot of kids are into it."

" 'Into' it? You mean devil worship?"

"Whatever you want to call it. You know, séances and shit. Magic. Satanism. It's no big deal."

Bonnie studied his face. Was he kidding? She could still picture him making his first communion. As the shortest boy, he had led the procession. In his white suit with matching white belt and shoes, his face glowing, his blond hair slicked back, he had resembled a miniature Florida insurance salesman. He had looked so dopey and uncool, Bonnie had wondered whether he would ever outgrow it.

"I'm serious, Mom," he said. "Don't worry, I don't worship or anything, I'm just doing it for fun."

"Uh-huh," Bonnie said. Last year it had been Dungeons and Dragons.

"Don't worry," Sean repeated.

"If you say so," Bonnie said. She watched Sean rummage in the refrigerator, grab some slices of American cheese, and head for his room. She sipped her milk thoughtfully. For now she'd follow her usual mode of dealing with her kids: sit back and wait while keeping her eyes open. Wide open.

10

School had started, the summer people had left Mount Hope, and woodbine, always the first leaves to change, wove vines of scarlet through trees along the New England coast. Billy was just back from his longest trip of the season. Now he sat across the office from Cass, staring her down. But she wouldn't blink.

"You planning to hold it against me from now till the end of time that I spent one night on the boat?" Billy asked.

"Yes," Cass said.

Billy leaned back. The night before he'd left on this last trip, sixteen days ago, they'd been fooling around, talking in bed after the kids were asleep. Billy was giving Cass a back rub, and out of the blue she said, "Tell me something you've never told me before."

"Like what?"

"Like something you've done. Something I don't know about."

It had felt conspiratorial, like the early days, when they would tell each other everything.

So Billy had told her about the night he'd driven home, heard Josie crying, and gone back to the boat. The minute the words were out, he'd known it was a mistake. She'd rolled out from under his hand, given him a cold stare, and said, "Bastard."

Now, sitting in her office, Billy was trying to make up.

"I wouldn't have told you if I'd known it was going to upset you this much," he said.

"Well, it does," she said.

"You asked me to tell you something you didn't know about. It was just one night."

"Oh, you're away plenty of nights." Cass rose from her desk, kicked off her sneakers, and stepped into work boots. Big, battered clodhoppers, the leather uppers all scuffed and scarred, they looked so big that Billy imagined Cass could fit both her feet in one.

"I was tired that night," Billy said. "I'm sorry."

"I was tired that night, too. I'm tired every night. Sometimes I think of you out there, far, far out, and I feel like I'd trade everything to be there instead of home."

"You don't mean that."

"Yes, I do," she said, dead serious. "Sometimes." She stood close to the window, to get a good view of the harbor. "I have to check the mooring floats," she said.

"I'll come with you."

Keating's Wharf could accommodate four trawlers. Dock space was reserved, mainly, for loading gear onboard the boats before a trip and loading the catch off at trip's end. Sometimes you'd chug into the harbor and find all the dock space taken. For those occasions, Keating kept ten moorings in the harbor. You identified Keating moorings by the big orange balls floating on the water.

Billy watched Cass pull on a heavy sweater, her big dark glasses, and a Red Sox cap. She tried to tuck all her hair up, but she missed a piece.

"Hold it," Billy said. He twisted the strands around his index finger, wedged it under the cap. Her neck, beneath that snaggle of red-gold hair, looked so pale, curved like a ballerina's. Billy couldn't stop himself from kissing it.

Cass stood still, allowed his lips to trace the curve, but did not encourage him to continue. She tromped down the interior stairs, through the lobster-tank room, out into the bright cool sunshine. This was goldenrod weather: the end of summer, when the days were clear and fine and the sky shimmered with particles of gold.

Billy hung back for a moment and rummaged through a bin for some extra work gloves. When he started out again, he saw Jimmy Keating leaning against the warehouse, talking to John Barnard. They were both watching Cass, but she didn't see them.

"Hey, Medieros," John yelled. At first Billy thought John was talking to him. He had one foot out the door before Cass answered.

"Hiya, Barnard," Cass called.

"What about me?" Jimmy called.

Cass gave her father a long indulgent look, then went over to kiss him. The three of them stood there — Cass, Jimmy, and John — a tight little knot. Seeing them like that, so comfortable together, Billy had a flash: what if I don't make it home some trip? We sink, I drown. Would John be the one to console Cass? Would she fall in love with him again?

Halfway through Billy's last trip out, fishing Georges Bank one hundred fifty miles into the North Atlantic, he rode straight into a major storm. Waves breaking over the wheelhouse, wind shifting direction every gust. It wasn't the first time, or the worst storm, but Billy saw everything pass before his eyes. Cass, their kids, their life in Mount Hope; Billy believed he was about to lose it all. His ship groaned and chattered, bolts beneath the decks vibrating under the stress.

When the worst passed, Billy checked the ship to make sure she was sound. He went directly to the life raft to force himself to face what he already knew he would find: three survival suits; five men on board.

"Jimmy," Billy said now, driven by the memory. He walked over.

"Billy!" Jimmy said, clapping Billy on the back. With both of Billy's parents dead, years now, Jim and Mary had been more to him than standard parents-in-law. On the other hand, in his capacity as Billy's boss, Jimmy was a businessman first, and Billy always kept his guard up.

"We need to update some equipment on the *Norboca*."

"Like what?" Jimmy asked.

"Like two survival suits, for starters."

"Oh, you're short two?" Jimmy asked, all surprised, as if Billy hadn't mentioned it last month, and two months before that. "Well, we'll order them today. We'll have them in time for the cold weather, that's for sure."

"We'll get them overnight," Cass said. "Why didn't you tell me right away?"

"Actually, Jimmy," John said, "I have a list of stuff we need on the *Aurora*. The more I take her out, the more I get to know her."

"Just like dating a girl," Jimmy joked. "You boys are putting me out of business. But that's what I get, I hire the best captains. Safety first."

"What else are you missing?" Cass asked Billy, her tone unamused. Jimmy Keating could charm a smile out of anyone; he could sell a lobsterman a barrel of lobsters. But his youngest daughter saw right through him.

"That's about it. She needs an overhaul, but Jimmy knows about that."

"The way I figure it," Jimmy said, "we do our best fishing in the warm weather. Let's fill our holds now, yank the boats for a week or so first of November. Good for me, good for you. I make money so I can pay you a decent cut. Plus, of course, we'll get those safety rigs on board. Thanks for bringing it up."

Jimmy would use his gift of gab to cheap out, stall for time, hoping all along that Billy and John would forget in the meanwhile. Billy knew that survival suits didn't come cheap. Most fishermen believed they were useless, anyway. If you went down in a bad storm offshore, a few hundred dollars' worth of rubberized plastic wasn't going to save you.

"That's not good enough, Dad," Cass said.

Billy put his hand on Cass's arm. Family was one thing, but you didn't criticize Jimmy Keating in front of an outsider. And John Barnard, for as long as the family had known him, still wasn't family.

"It'll have to be good enough," Jimmy said, standing tall.

"What if it's not?" Cass asked.

"I'll sell this damn place," Jimmy said angrily. "I'll sell it tomorrow. My boats are safer, better equipped than any fleet in town. I look after my captains, and you know it."

"That's right," Billy said. "You're the best, Jimmy."

"Relax, Cass," John said.

"I've got three kids," she said. "I want to go to bed at night and know their father is going to come home."

"It's okay, Cass," Billy said, sliding his arm around her waist. She tried to squirm away, but he held on. "It's okay."

"I'll sell, so help me God," Jimmy said bitterly, shaking his head. "Second-guessed by my own daughter."

Cass opened her mouth, anger flashing in her eyes, then thought better of it. She calmed herself down. Billy could practically feel the anger shuddering through her. "Dad?" she said finally.

Proud James Keating squinted over Cass's head, right out to sea. She stood on tiptoe, her hands on his shoulders, forcing him to look at her. Billy thought she was going to kiss her father, but she didn't. She stayed on her toes for one long minute, then gave his shoulders a shake, and smiled. You could tell he didn't want to smile back, but he couldn't help himself.

"Maybe this is the time for some good news," Jimmy said. "I've just made John captain of his own boat."

"Wow," Cass said. "Congratulations, John."

"Congratulations," Billy said, shaking John's hand. "Which boat?"

"The *Aurora*," John said, grinning.

Billy nodded, impressed. The second-best boat in the Keating fleet.

"I can't have my two best men fishing on the same boat," Keating said. "That's no way to make money. Find another first mate, Billy."

"Maybe I can get Cass to sign on," Billy said, thinking of his own boat, the one he'd buy as soon as he had enough money.

"If you could get her to take orders," Jimmy said. "Good luck."

"Congratulations again," Cass said, kissing John.

Billy felt a hot flush in his neck. Cass and John were smiling into each other's eyes. Billy stepped forward, clapped John's shoulder. "Yeah, it's great," Billy said. "What do you say, Cass? Want to get moving here?"

Cass nodded, waving goodbye to her father and John. She walked down the dock, ahead of Billy; she threw her tool bucket into the twenty-four-foot work boat, which was tied to a piling. Watching it rock and pitch in a light chop, she waited for her moment and jumped in. Billy followed. They had taken a million boat rides together. Cass loosened the stern and spring lines while Billy undid the bow line. Then she fired up the engine and they chuffed into the harbor.

This was Cass's show. Billy sat in the bow, watching her do the work. He had the feeling she'd whale him good if he offered to help. She yanked on big rubber work gloves. With expert timing she'd pull close to each mooring, shift the engine into idle, grab the mooring line with a long wood-handled boat hook, and check the shackle connecting it with the float.

By this time in the season, a hundred things could have fouled a mooring; connections were the first to go. To secure a big trawler, you needed the float, fifteen fathoms of nylon hawser, forty feet of chain, a three-ton anchor, and plenty of room to swing.

Cass yanked in the first line. Seaweed, algae, mussel colonies, and black harbor muck covered every inch of the line. Oily gunk clung to her gloves, but she seemed oblivious, a real pro. By the fourth mooring she had worked up a sweat. She threw her sweater onto the seat, and she didn't object when Billy started to help.

"Why didn't you tell me about the survival suits?" she asked, pulling close to the tenth mooring.

"It's not that important. They're bogus, anyway."

"Till you need one."

"A little orange suit? It keeps you from freezing to death the first hour, but by then you're shark meat anyway."

"If you feel that way, why did you bother mentioning it at all?"

Billy shrugged. He didn't want to tell her about the storm, about his vision of Cass being consoled by John Barnard.

"Did you tell my father about the survival suits? Before, I mean."

"I don't remember. Forget it, Cass."

"He never told me, if you did. I would have ordered them right away."

"I know."

"They'll be here tomorrow. I'll order them as soon as we get in, for overnight delivery."

They took care of the last mooring, then swished their filthy gloves in the salt water.

Billy was about to say, "Let's take a ride," when Cass turned the boat around, heading out toward Minturn Ledge. The boat bucked across the waves, past the other fish piers, the condo piers: the old Blue Moon section.

When Billy and Cass were kids, only sailors

and drunks came to this part of town. Driving past with car windows down, you could hear music blaring from the dance halls, women laughing, people fighting, sometimes even gunshots. Parents warned their kids to stay away from there. It was a place where people shot heroin, sold their bodies, and murdered for love.

The Blue Moon faded from sight as they passed the row of mansions, the yacht club, the playground. Billy rode in the bow, the sun in his eyes, facing backward, enjoying a boat ride with someone else driving. Watching Cass.

At Minturn Ledge, she gunned the engine and headed into open water. They turned southeast, and Billy could tell she was steering for the Trench, a stretch of extremely deep water. After twenty minutes, she pulled back on the throttle. Billy looked overboard and saw an army of sleek shapes, tapered as missiles, passing under the boat. Bluefish were running.

"Are you going to make me catch our dinner?" Billy asked when Cass handed him a rod.

"Let's try," she said, excited.

Cass reached for another rod. She rigged it with a big Kastmaster, striped silver and metallic blue to trick the fish. She threw the line — a perfect over-the-head cast — into the school.

"I haven't caught a blue all summer," she said. "T.J. brought home a beauty last week."

Billy pretended to fish, but he was actually studying his wife. Some hair had slipped out from under her hat, and it glinted in the sun. He felt like taking off her hat, seeing the rest of her hair tumble to her shoulders, tangling it in his fingers. But he held back.

She reeled in her line, then cast again. Her shoulders seemed to relax before his eyes, and it made Billy sad to think fishing for blues could soothe Cass when he could not.

"Any bites?" he asked.

She seemed not to hear him for a moment, then said, "What?"

"Have you had any bites?"

She shook her head. Something was going on behind her eyes. Cass and Billy were in the same boat, but Billy could swear Cass wasn't there at all. Hadn't she told him she wanted to get far, far away? Was she dreaming of Europe, California, Borneo, the North Atlantic? Suddenly she reeled in her line, stuck the rod in its holder.

"We haven't caught anything," Billy said.

She flashed her watch at him. "No time. I have to get Josie in forty minutes."

"Wouldn't you rather be going to Borneo?" Billy asked.

She chuckled lightly, her eyes softening.

Billy crossed the boat to stand behind her. He placed one hand over hers on the throttle, the other over hers on the wheel. She leaned back, into his body. His chin rested on the top of her head, the button on her Red Sox cap digging in.

"What do you really think about John?" she asked.

"He deserves it. He'll make Jimmy a good captain."

"You'll miss fishing with him," Cass said.

"Nah, he's a bum," Billy joked. But he couldn't make himself laugh. He saw his life flying by. He and John had been competing forever, but Billy had always stayed a little ahead. He had Cass; Jimmy had made him captain first. Now here was John catching up. Maybe that was fair, Billy thought, but he felt his throat tighten. He wondered how Cass really saw him.

"What do *you* really think about John?" Billy asked.

"He's a good fisherman," Cass said. "My father wants to keep him in the fleet."

"He's one of the best," Billy agreed. "One of the best."

"But not *the* best," Cass said, teasing.

"Maybe not," Billy said, holding her from behind. Being the best, staying on top: it didn't just happen. It took some proving. You had to work your ass off to get there, and you had to fight like hell to stay. Billy squeezed Cass's hand on the throttle, and the boat kicked forward. They opened the engine, and together they drove home.

11

Belinda and Emma sat side by side in fourth-period study hall. Kids from all different sections took study hall together. You could be in the 8-A group and wind up next to someone in 8-D. Which is how Belinda wound up next to Emma. Todd sat two benches away. Now Belinda was going out with him, but they never talked in school. He'd get embarrassed if she even said hi. But he didn't mind when she called him after school.

"Your brother is really strange," Emma said.

"No kidding," Belinda said. She had the conjugations of twenty irregular verbs to memorize for French, and she wished Emma would stop talking so she could concentrate.

"I'm serious," Emma said. She had her math book open, but under the table she was putting apricot polish on her nails. As if the teacher wouldn't smell it! "He's been telling people he has a gun."

"He's lying," Belinda said, but she was

shocked all the same. Why would T.J. lie about having a gun?

"He ought to wash his hair more often, like once a day. He could probably have anyone he wants, if he took better care of himself. The clothes he wears! Doesn't your mom ever do laundry?"

"He likes the messy look. He thinks it makes him look like a rebel."

"Yeah, him and Sean. Rebels without a clue. Someone forgot to tell Sean there are no fat rebels. Don't you get sick of girls trying to get close to you just so you'll put in a good word with T.J.? It's so hypocritical."

"They don't even bother," Belinda said. "They go straight to him. Our phone is ringing all the time."

"Did you really make fun of Alison when she called?"

"No! That was Josie," Belinda said.

"Alison is telling everyone it was you."

Belinda loved Josie; she tried to be patient with her. But sometimes it seemed Josie was ruining her life without even trying. Stupid slutface Alison McCabe called T.J. last week and got Josie. Josie had picked up Belinda's extension to play phone call, and naturally she couldn't hear Alison on the other end. Alison, who didn't know Josie, had thought it was Belinda making fun of her. And now Alison was spreading it all over school that Belinda was an immature jerk.

"Bel, you should see the incredible magazine I found in my parents' room," Emma said. "Like, superhot."

"Really?" Belinda asked, blushing. Since she and Emma had spent the afternoon in Emma's room, she'd played with herself a few times. But the funny thing was, the more she did it, the more embarrassed she felt when Emma talked about it.

Belinda tried to block out Emma's voice. She had all honors courses this year, and the work was killing her. If she didn't get at least some of her homework done in study hall, she'd be up past midnight again. Emma just wanted to waste time till the bell rang, then get through the next period, then the next, until the end of the day.

Emma tried a different tack. "I think it's really funny, Sean wanting people to think he has a dark side. Talking about Satan — give me a break! He's nothing but a nerd. He's saving up to buy a black leather jacket."

"I think T.J. should get one."

"T.J. could get away with it. But Sean? Forget it. He's too fat and blond. You'd look great in a black leather skirt."

"I would?"

"Yeah. A real tight French one. You could

wear it to Aunt Nora's wedding."

Belinda hunched over her paper. *Offrir, maigrir* . . .

"Didn't you hear me? Black leather at Aunt Nora's wedding. I'm looking forward to meeting the dude this weekend. Any excuse for a family bash. Once he meets all of us, he'll probably take the next plane back to Florida, or wherever he comes from."

"Georgia, I think."

"Forget about Alison," Emma said. "Is that what's bothering you? You're so quiet."

Mr. Sheehan, the study-hall teacher, walked down the aisle and stood right in front of Belinda and Emma. He spread his feet and folded his arms across his chest, to let them know this was serious. Mr. Sheehan was the type of teacher who wanted everyone to think he was cool and tough.

To prove he was cool, he wore gaudy ties and saddle shoes with argyle socks. He taught history, and he'd talk about historical figures as if they were his personal friends. Like "Tombo" for Thomas Jefferson, "Big Al" for Alexander Hamilton, and "Benny and the boys" for Benjamin Franklin and the delegates to the 1787 Constitutional Convention. He'd drop a few "damns" and "hells" into his lectures, then say, "Excuse my French," as if he'd just said the worst profanity ever invented.

To seem tough, he'd act just like he was acting now. He'd give you this very long, head-shaking, disappointed look, say nothing until you started to squirm, and then give you detention. Belinda didn't plan to give him the satisfaction of looking up. Finally it was quiet enough to concentrate. Mr. Sheehan cleared his throat. She just kept working. His shadow fell across her paper.

"He's looking down our shirts," Emma whispered.

"What was that, Ms. Kenneally?" Mr. Sheehan asked.

"I said, 'My finger hurts.'"

"I'm glad you're so far ahead in your classwork that you feel you can spend study hall painting your nails."

Belinda hadn't looked up, but she could just picture him shaking his head, a big droopy frown on his face.

"Ms. Medieros, what is so fascinating?"

"My homework," Belinda said, still not looking up.

"Are you and Ms. Kenneally collaborating on it? Is that why you've spent the whole study hall talking?"

"She's teaching me French," Emma said.

"I thought you took Spanish."

"I do, but I'd rather speak French. I'm going to live in Paris."

"If you ever make it out of eighth grade," Mr. Sheehan said coldly. Emma acted as if she didn't care about school or grades, but Belinda knew she felt ashamed when she failed subjects. "Detention for both of you. After school, today," he said.

Belinda still hadn't looked up. She heard Emma sniffle twice, very quietly. Belinda slid her hand onto Emma's chair. She linked Emma's little finger with her own. The cousins sat that way for just a few moments, until Belinda needed her hand to write again.

All four Keating cousins were on the detention bus. T.J., Sean, Emma, even Perfecto. T.J. knew their mothers would be pissed. Of course, half the school had detention. The teachers liked to start the school year off extra nasty, so you'd think twice before you acted up the next time. They believed in setting an example right off the bat. T.J. had gotten his for skipping science, when actually he'd just mixed up his schedule and gone to the music room instead. It wasn't his fault that Mr. Amato and the jazz band were jamming, but it was his fault that he'd stayed to listen.

The bus made six stops in Alewives Park. Emma got off a stop before her normal one, probably so she wouldn't have to walk home with Sean. She and Belinda had to have one of their major farewells; the bus driver, a new one this year, told them to move it. Little did she realize what she was in for. Knowing his sister and cousin, they'd be on the phone together in twenty minutes, so why bother with a big, dramatic bus goodbye?

"Let her go, Belinda," T.J. called. "She's going home, not to the morgue. You'll see her again."

Belinda shot him a very gratifying furious look. Good. Didn't she think everyone else wanted to get home?

"See ya, bro," Sean said when they got to his stop. "The morgue — that was good. How'd you think of that?"

"I don't know."

"Okay. Later." Sean made a circle with his fingers that had something to do with the devil. He'd explained the signs to T.J., but T.J. hadn't been paying attention.

"Yeah," T.J. said. He wondered whether there'd been a teenage trend invented anywhere that Sean hadn't picked up on. The Satan stuff, calling people "bro," wanting a leather jacket. T.J. hated himself for thinking this way. He felt like something must be wrong with him to be so critical of everyone, even people he liked, all the time.

"Hey T.J., do you have our history assignment?" Alison asked him from across the aisle.

"Uh, yeah. In here somewhere," he said, riffling through his notebook. She was wearing a T-shirt stretched really tight across her chest. Not that she had much to show, but just the thought of it was giving T.J. a boner.

"Here's your stop," Alison said. "Maybe you could call me later? To give it to me? I mean, I'd call you, but I might get your monster sister. Didn't she tell you I called last Friday?"

"I don't think so," he said, thinking he'd nail Belinda later. He wondered what Alison meant by "monster sister." Belinda and Alison would never be best friends, that was for sure, but Belinda was too perfect to be a monster.

"Give me forty-five minutes to get home," Alison said. "I live out Marcellus."

That figured; the rich neighborhood. Alison looked expensive, with her gold bracelets, model-style hair, that certain kind of handbag that Belinda was always begging for. Passing by, he smelled her perfume. He didn't know what it was called, but it was the kind Aunt Nora wore. Expensive-sexy.

When he got off the bus, Belinda was waiting for him. She acted like she wasn't. She was pretending she had a pebble in her shoe, leaning on the mailbox. But when T.J. walked past, she caught right up with him.

"Thanks for giving me my phone messages," T.J. said. "Alison called last Friday?"

"I'm sorry, I forgot to tell you. I was too mad. Was she talking about me?"

"Long enough to call you a monster. What'd you do to her, anyway?"

"That's *Josie* she's calling a monster. Josie picked up the phone to play one of her phone games, and Alison just happened to be calling. I'm surprised you didn't hear about it. She's telling everyone it was me making fun of her. I hate her."

"What did Josie say, anyway?"

"What's the difference? She's just a little girl."

"I'll tell Alison it wasn't you. That make you feel better?"

They walked half a block without saying anything. From here T.J. could see his mom's Volvo in the driveway.

"Can I ask you something?" Belinda sounded really nervous.

"What?"

"Someone told me . . . someone said you're saying that you have . . . that you borrowed, or you own, or something . . . a gun."

"I don't."

"Then why are they saying that?"

"Who's saying it?"

"Everyone."

"I don't know what they're talking about."

"I mean, I could sort of understand you saying you had one, even if you really didn't. You did say you have one, right?"

"No. Did Sean tell you that?"

They had stopped in the street, right at the end of their driveway. Sean was the only person T.J. had told about the gun. If there was one person T.J. had thought he could trust, it was his cousin — especially after all that bullshit about the Brotherhood.

"It wasn't Sean. All I mean is, saying you have a gun would be one thing, but actually having one would be another. You don't, do you?"

"Belinda, I don't have a gun."

Belinda nodded. "Good," she said.

T.J. should never have told Sean. But he'd needed to tell someone. Just knowing about that gun in the cupboard made his brain burn. It occupied one spot in his mind. He kept going back to the cupboard, again and again, just to see if the gun was still there.

Sometimes it gave off heat — a constant, steady warmth that reassured T.J. Other times it blazed out of control, searing his nerves and making him crazy. It made him feel powerful. He had liked holding it in his hands. He would never use it, but it was something no one else had. Playing at devil worship and wanting black leather was one thing. Having a gun was another.

12

The Captain Ed Room, upstairs at Lobster-ville, was normally reserved for private par-ties. The Frostbite Club held its annual awards ceremony there; local companies vied to re-serve it for their Christmas parties. Rehearsal dinners, fiftieth-anniversary parties, bar mitz-vahs, bashes to herald the Blessing of the Fleet were regular occurrences.

Everyone knew it grieved Mary to have turned away the two large groups who both wanted the room that Saturday night: the Sylvester-Drake rehearsal dinner and Pat McAllister's eightieth-birthday party. On the other hand, Nora wanted to introduce Willis to the family at large, and for that Mary said she was willing to lose good business. She made sure everyone knew how happy she felt to be hosting this party.

"She's laying it on a little thick, isn't she?" Cass asked Bonnie. "Willis will think she's overjoyed to be marrying Nora off."

"Face it," Bonnie said. "She is. Where are

Nora and the lucky man?"

"They stopped to pick up Granny," Cass said. Usually her parents drove Sheila to family parties, but tonight the honor went to Nora. Josie kept running to the window to watch for their arrival.

T.J., Belinda, Emma, and Sean stood by the dessert table. Bonnie had baked brownies, and the kids were sampling them. Both boys had their hair slicked back; Belinda wore a pink ribbon in hers. Emma's chic crewcut looked shorter than ever.

"There's trouble cubed," Bonnie said, pointing to them. "Four teenage cousins dressed like they're ready for church. Look at Mom and Dad watching them. So proud of their model grandchildren."

"They probably think the kids are having a very responsible discussion about the third world or safe sex. All these terrible issues kids today have to face," Cass said.

"Unlike us," Bonnie said.

"Very unlike us." Cass smiled and sipped her white wine.

They all wore their best clothes, as if this were the actual wedding, not just a chance to get to know Willis better. Cass watched her father in the blue suit he wore to weddings, funerals, and special family parties.

Billy wore the blue blazer he'd owned since

215

before Cass married him; T.J. was wearing a black-and-navy-striped tie over a blue denim shirt. Belinda and Josie wore flowered dresses. Cass felt so proud of her kids. T.J. hadn't wanted to come, but he'd been very polite, kissing his grandmother and Bonnie; talking about the Red Sox with his grandfather, he'd actually seemed enthusiastic.

Mary had set out bowls of shrimp and spicy cocktail sauce, clams on the half shell, and miniature crab quiches. There were smoked mussels, scallops skewered with roasted red peppers, new potatoes hollowed out and filled with salmon mousse, a tureen of buttery lobster stew, tidbits of ginger-lime swordfish. Everything but Bonnie's brownies was restaurant-made.

Their father came over to stand with Cass and Bonnie. His eyes were liquid, but not from the whiskey he was drinking. He was very sentimental where his family was concerned; Cass doubted he would get through the night without crying.

"I gave you two away; it's about time Nora had her turn," he said, his arm around Cass's waist.

"Oh, I remember that day," Bonnie said. "You were so nervous I didn't know if we'd make it."

"I only hope her marriage is as blessed as

216

you two girls' have been. Good husbands; nice, smart, good-looking kids. Beautiful girls, Emma, Bel, and Josie. You've made me a happy grandfather."

"Oh, Dad, it's too early to start crying," Cass said. "God, they say women are sentimental."

"Don't you start in on me, Cassandra," he said. "I still haven't forgotten your display in front of John Barnard."

"Do you want to get into that now?" Cass asked. "Or should we try to have a nice time?"

"Knock it off," Bonnie said. "Billy! Get over here and keep your wife out of trouble."

At that, everyone — especially T.J. and Belinda — glanced over. Cass thought her teenagers looked hopeful, as if they thought she might fly off the handle and cause the party to break up.

"It's under control," she called to the kids. They went back to picking at the desserts. "Look at that. All your brownies are going to have little finger holes in them."

"Oh, they're just nibbling the corners," Bonnie said. "It'll keep them occupied. When it's time for dessert we'll make them eat the ones they've claimed."

"You really need to start a brownie business," Cass said.

"Will you give up on that?" Bonnie said.

Billy and Gavin strolled over with Mary. "I hope my new son-in-law treats me as well as you two," Mary said. To link arms with the two tall men, she had to hold her arms akimbo at shoulder level.

"Where is he, anyway?" Billy asked. "Gavin and I have to welcome him into the family, do the obligatory arm wrestle. See what he's made of. I mean, he's marrying a Keating girl."

"Dear, he's a man of high class," Mary said. "He might not appreciate our humor right away. We'll have to bring him along slow."

"Are you saying I'm a classless fisherman?" Billy asked.

"Yes, dear," Mary said, dimpling. "That's exactly what I'm saying."

Josie, standing guard at the window, squealed to let everyone know Sheila had arrived. She scurried happily to her parents, words and sentences tripping over each other. Not understanding a word she said, her parents, grandparents, aunt, and uncle just smiled back.

Nora and Willis walked into the room behind Sheila, who set the pace.

"Hi, Willis," Bonnie said, reaching up to embrace him. The rest of the family surrounded him.

"This is such a pleasure," Willis said. He

had a broad forehead that gave him what people like to call "an open face."

Nora kissed her sisters and parents. "How's
the party going so far?" she whispered to Cass.

"It's terrific."

Her mother lit a cigarette.

"Mother, you don't need those things,"
Nora said. Cass watched her mother light the
match, touch it to the cigarette's filter end.

"Oh, Nora. You made me do it wrong,"
Mary said. "There's nothing worse than a
reformed smoker." She laughed out loud, lit
another one.

"Mrs. Keating, I smoked for many years
myself," Willis said.

"Please call me Mary. I was just thinking
how old I feel."

"Okay, Mary."

"Nora tells me you're going to settle up
here?" Mary's voice rose questioningly.

"That's right," Willis said. "No reason I
can't run my business from Rhode Island. An
office is an office as long as you've got a telephone and a fax machine."

"But won't you miss Savannah?" Bonnie
asked. "You haven't lived through a Mount
Hope winter yet."

"Don't scare him off!" Jimmy said.

Nora's head snapped toward him. "Why?
Are you afraid he'll change his mind?" Her

eyes blazed, and it hurt Cass to see her father duck his head. Nora was still so sensitive. He had just been trying to joke. When he raised his eyes, Cass saw they were bruised with shame.

"I'm sorry," Jimmy said.

"Scare me off?" Willis boomed with good humor, hugging Nora hard. "You'd have to come at me with bazookas and pitchforks, and even then you couldn't scare me off. No, the day Nora came into my life was the day I became a happy man. I'm never letting her get away."

"That's what a father wants to hear," Jimmy said.

"Thanks, Daddy," Nora said, smiling. Funny, Cass thought, how Nora called him "Daddy" and their mother "Mother," while Cass and Bonnie called them "Dad" and "Mom."

"So, you're in the real estate game," Jimmy said.

"That's right."

"There's plenty for sale here in the Northeast," Jimmy said. "If you've got money to spend, you can make a killing. Buy up property, hang on to it until the market turns around."

"I'm mainly into development," Willis said. "We buy a parcel, make some improvements, and sell it off real quick."

"That's what happened right here," Jimmy said. "People buying up the waterfront. Just look at Nora's place. That used to be a fish wharf, if you can believe it."

"Places change," Willis said.

"That's the wrong kind of change," Cass said. "Condos on the waterfront."

"It takes a lot of opinions to make the world go round, Cassandra," her father said.

"Hey, this town needed some change," Gavin said. "When I was a kid, no one with a sane mind would set foot in this part of town after dark. The old Blue Moon. My uncle lost an eye in a fight down here."

"I didn't know that," Jimmy said. "That's how Harp lost his eye? I'll be damned."

"Yep," Gavin said.

"Of course, our warehouse was always here," Jimmy said. "But this building, the restaurant, used to be an icehouse. What's wrong with progress? If Ma hadn't gotten the idea to turn the place into Lobsterville, what the hell? Customers had to walk right past the tarts and drunks, but they came anyway. Nothing wrong with moving ahead."

"All I'm saying is, I hate condos," Cass said.

"Headstrong girls, Willis," her father said. "You're marrying into a family of headstrong girls."

"That's 'women,' Granddad," Emma called.

"Oh, right. I mean, 'headstrong *dames*,' " he called back.

"*Granddad!*" Belinda and Emma yelled, running over to attack him.

"You should have put on a dress for the party," Sheila said, eyeing Cass's black velour pants and goldenrod sweater.

"This town is just peachy as it is," Willis said, gesturing toward the window. "You can't improve on harbor views like this."

"Isn't it?" Sheila asked. "You're going to be very happy here. Let me show you some old pictures," she said, tugging Willis's arm. "Nora named this the Captain Ed Room, after my husband, Eddie. No one ever called him that, but everyone expects nautical stuff at the shore."

Josie held her mother's hand, following her around the room. This was a standup party, with all the relatives leaning on walls, clustered around the food table, moving from one group to another. Josie's neck ached from tilting back. She tugged her mother's pants leg.

Cass leaned down, so Josie could grab onto her neck, and suddenly Josie was lifted to eye level. Her mother's neck and hair smelled cool and sweet, like honeysuckle at night. Josie sniffed it while her mother talked to Aunt Nora. Their voices blurred together, one word splashing into the next. Josie tried to understand the conversation by watching their faces, the way they smiled, their eyes following Nora's boyfriend and their old grandmother.

Now Cass and Josie moved to the food table, where they ducked down to admire the tray of shrimp and clams. The last time Josie and her mother had gone snorkeling, they had seen a tiny clam zipping along the sand. Just like a girl skipping. Josie had picked it up, wanting to take it home. But when they were on the sand, her mother had said to throw the clam back. She had said it would die out of the water. Josie stared at the clams on the tray.

"Let's see them," Josie said, reaching down.

Her mother's hand closed around Josie's. "They're to eat, not play with."

"But I want to play!" Josie said, squirming. "Let's be mermaids. Let's play . . ."

"Sssh," Cass said. "Calm down. I know you're having fun, it's a party, but don't get too excited."

Her grandmother walked over. She held out her arms, wanting to take Josie. But Josie held her mother's neck tighter. She loved her grandmother, but she didn't like the way she smelled: a mixture of cigarettes and fried fish. Her grandmother didn't seem to mind; she wanted to talk to Cass about lobsters.

"We don't need that," Cass said. "There's enough here."

Even though she was talking to someone else, Cass made sure to speak clearly, so Josie could understand. Josie watched her mouth, catching every word, while her grandmother's words were mush. But her grandmother had a funny look in her eyes that made Josie think she was worried. She fiddled with the parsley on the shrimp tray, rearranged the lemon slices.

"Okay, okay," Cass said. She rolled her eyes, to show Josie she thought something was ridiculous. Now Cass hurried across the room, toward Billy.

"You stay with Daddy," she said to Josie. "I have to help Gram."

Instinctively, Josie clung to her mother's neck. Cass had to pry her arms loose. Josie didn't want her father right now. He always played with her extra hard, and it made her feel bad, that she never seemed to have enough fun for him. But her mother kissed her cheek, handing her over.

"Josie's all wound up," Cass said. "See if you can calm her down while I run to the kitchen. Help your dad, T.J."

Her father took Josie and immediately began joking, pushing Josie's nose and saying "beep-beep." Now he was telling her a story, or maybe he was talking to T.J. and Sean. Josie couldn't tell; her brother and cousin were right there, laughing at something. Knowing Sean, he was probably laughing at her. Josie wiggled like a fish, until her father put her down.

Standing on the floor, Josie looked around for her mother. She started to walk away, but her father pulled her back. He plunked her onto his foot and moved it up and down like a horse. She climbed off. T.J. leaned over.

"What's wrong?" he asked.

"Want Mommy," Josie said.

"She'll be right back. She's getting a lobster for Willis."

Josie nodded. Her brother stood up, went straight back to talking to Daddy and Sean. She stared at her black patent-leather shoes, glinting in the lamplight. She was starting to get a bad feeling. The comforting hum of her relatives' voices now seemed mean. People were talking, and Josie couldn't hear. Everyone was included but her. They were leaving her out.

She started to whimper. She felt it in her throat, a lump that made her want to scream. Her father, brother, and cousin were standing right there, not caring about her. She wanted to bite their knees. The lump grew bigger.

T.J. bent down again, an angry look in his eyes.

"Stop that," he said.

"Eh, eh, eh," Josie said, feeling tears burn her eyes.

"This is a *party*," he said. "Be a good girl."

Josie stared at T.J.'s flashing eyes. If he would rather talk to Sean, if he wasn't going to pay attention to her, she hated him. She pushed his chin.

"Don't do that," he said, touching her chin with his finger.

She slapped out with both hands, flailing like a windmill. Then she jumped back, running away from him.

He went straight back to their father and Sean. They were all talking as if she didn't even exist. Josie could see them laughing about something, not watching her.

She saw her mother coming through the door. There were people in the way, but Josie tore across the room toward her. She flew around Belinda, and she brushed Aunt Nora's skirt. Josie's voice tore out of her chest, calling her mother's name.

Her mother stopped still, her mouth open. She held up her hands, motioning Josie to stop. Confused, Josie tried to slow down, but her legs kept moving. Suddenly she saw. She knew what was going to happen, but she couldn't make her feet stop. She felt frozen, even as she flew.

"Josie!" T.J. yelled, diving across the room.

Josie charged into the waiter with such force, she fell down, flat on her back. The waiter wobbled; for one instant Josie thought he was going to keep his balance. But the tray jiggled on his hand like a live thing. Plates and lobsters shuddered like a cartoon earthquake. The tray hovered, wanting to right itself, and then Josie watched it come crashing down.

13

Billy sped them to the hospital. Cass held Josie, unconscious, wrapped in a tablecloth. She knew that when someone's been hurt, you're supposed to wait for trained emergency people to arrive, to check for neck or spine injuries. But as soon as the tray fell, Cass had flung broken plates out of the way, scooped up Josie, and carried her to their car.

"Your hands are cut," Billy said.

"Drive, Billy," Cass said, intently watching the road, as if by concentrating she could get them there faster.

T.J. sat silently in back, holding a handful of napkins against a deep cut on his forehead.

Cass felt afraid to look down. Josie had so many cuts from shards of china, the white tablecloth was soaked with blood. Cass had lifted her from the floor as if she were a cloth doll. In the car, Cass held her in her arms like a baby, making her as small as possible, compressing her, and she realized that she believed every bone in Josie's body was broken and she was trying to hold Josie together.

"Bonnie was going to call ahead. They're waiting for us," Billy said.

Cass bent low, whispered in Josie's ear. "Mommy's here, sweetheart. Mommy's right here."

"Mom, is she going to be okay?" T.J. asked.

"We're doing our best," Billy answered.

Their car sped up Vincent Street, screeched into the hospital's emergency entrance. Cass remembered coming here the night of Josie's fever, after her seizure. She had wrapped Josie in a blanket that night, too, held her tight, whispered in her ear. She had believed Josie could hear her, but she was wrong. The damage had already been done.

Two men in white took Josie from Cass. They strapped her to a stretcher and rushed her inside, through the waiting room, behind a curtain. Cass tried to run after her, but Billy made her stop.

"Let the doctor look at her," he said.

"I need to be with her," Cass wailed.

"Don't yell, Mom!" T.J. said, alarmed.

"You two let this happen to her! I should never have left her with you. I was only gone a minute . . . oh, God, if she's not okay . . ."

"Mom, I didn't mean to," T.J. said with anguish.

"What could have been so important? What were you thinking?"

"Mom!"

A nurse hurried over from behind the desk. "Please, Mrs. Medieros, try to calm down. Tell me what happened."

"Do I have to admit her?" Cass asked numbly while a secretary led Billy and T.J. to the desk.

"No. Your husband can take care of that." The nurse had straight brown hair pulled into a ponytail, freckles across her cheeks, wire-rimmed glasses, a steady voice. "Sit down. Tell me what happened. What's her name?"

"Josie. Her name is Josie," Cass said, and for the first time since the accident, she started to cry.

"How old is she?"

"Four."

"I have a four-year-old."

Cass stopped listening. Her pants were stained with Josie's blood. She leaned over, her face very close to her thighs. Her pants smelled like lobster.

T.J. had walked over. He stood in front of the nurse. "Will my sister be okay?" he asked, his voice still shaking. "The tray knocked her out."

"Let the doctor look at her. I want someone to check your head — and your mother's hands. What happened?"

"A bunch of plates crashed. Right on top of Josie," T.J. said. He had slid across the floor to protect her just a moment too late. He'd slashed his forehead, just above his eye. Cass glanced at his face, then away. She already regretted her outburst, but now found she couldn't speak.

"If it knocked her out, she probably didn't realize what was happening," the nurse said. "That's a blessing." Then she took T.J. away for stitches and a head X-ray.

But Cass kept seeing the look in Josie's eyes, just before the tray crashed down on her. She was lying on her back, looking almost comfortable, her fine black hair splayed around her head. Amid the furor, her dark eyes searched for Cass. Finding her mother, she gazed at her with apology and a question: Are you mad at me?

Now Billy sat beside her. He tried to take her hands, to check her cuts. She started to pull back, but stopped herself and let him look at them.

Thirty minutes passed, but it seemed like hours. A doctor came into the waiting room. Cass recognized her; she came into Lobsterville now and then with her husband and young kids.

"Josie will need to be watched here," the

doctor said, "but she will be fine. She has a concussion, a broken wrist, and some bad cuts, especially on her arm. You're very lucky it wasn't much worse."

"She's alive?" Cass asked. Only when she heard the words come out of her mouth did she realize what she had been thinking.

"Oh, yes," the doctor said.

Cass felt the tension break. She burst into tears of relief. Billy touched her shaking shoulders, then withdrew his hand when she didn't lean into him. The doctor stood by patiently, waiting for Cass to stop. She must see this all the time, Cass thought. Little children covered in blood.

"Is she awake?" Cass asked, sniffling.

"No. She regained consciousness, but we sedated her. She's had some stitches, and we had to set her wrist."

"All that blood . . ." Cass said, feeling that she might start to cry again.

"The chin bleeds heavily, and the tongue. She broke a tooth, and it cut her tongue."

"They're just baby teeth," Cass said. "She's never lost one before."

"But she'll be okay?" Billy asked.

"Yes," the doctor said. "She'll be fine. Still, we'll need to keep her for a few days. I've reviewed her chart, and we want to watch for any change in her hearing."

"Could it get worse?" Cass asked.

"That's a possibility. But let's just watch and see."

Watch her hearing, Cass thought incongruously.

"Can we see her?" Billy asked.

"Of course," the doctor said.

They tiptoed into a curtained cubicle. Bluish light filtered in from the central section. Josie lay on a stretcher, the sides up like a crib, a white sheet tucked around her. They had washed away all the blood. She had some fierce black stitches on her chin and over her left eyebrow. Cass peeled back the sheet. Josie wore a white hospital gown with blue stars on it. Both her arms were bandaged, and her left wrist was in a cast.

Cass let Billy hug her, rock her at Josie's bedside.

"It's my fault," he said quietly, his eyes wide. "Oh, Cass. I'm so sorry."

Cass, who to a large degree believed that it *was* Billy's fault, remained silent for a moment. She wanted to reassure him, but her anger choked her. "The doctor said she'll be fine," she said after a moment.

She stared at Billy, feeling cold. At the same time, she wanted to relent, to make everything okay, to pull her family together. Yet she felt that familiar numbness seeping in, keeping her still.

"Say something," he said.

"Why did you turn away? Why didn't you watch her when I'd asked you to?" Cass asked calmly, turning the questions over in her mind, like two shells she'd picked up on the beach.

"It was just for a second," Billy said miserably.

"Yes," Cass said, nodding. Nothing was getting through to her. Suddenly she thought of Josie's death: she'd half expected it, before the doctor had come to tell them Josie was alive. The thought was so real and powerful, it hit her like a truck. She covered her eyes, heard herself moan out loud.

"Oh, Cass," Billy said again. "Cass."

Pressing against his chest, she felt him shaking as hard as she was.

The nurse brought T.J. to find them. He hung back, as if he didn't want to get too near to Josie. Cass turned to look at him, shocked by the long gash in his forehead, frighteningly close to his eye, a mirror image of Josie's cut. Until now, Cass hadn't realized her son had been hurt, too.

She stood on her toes, pulled T.J. down so she could kiss him. "I'm sorry for what I said before," she said.

"Shhh," T.J. said. "You'll wake Josie."

"Come on," Billy said. "We've done all we can tonight. Let's get a doctor to look at your hands." He lightly touched Cass's cut fingers. "Then get Teej home and into bed. Come on."

"I'm going to stay," Cass said. "I want her to see me when she wakes up."

Billy stared, shaking his head. "I'm not letting you. You shouldn't be alone here. Come on."

"I won't be alone. I'll be with Josie." Her voice was soft, to let Billy know she would be okay if he left. He gave her a long, questioning gaze, then shrugged, as if he knew he'd never win this argument.

Cass kissed her husband and son goodnight and settled down in a chair next to Josie's bed. The hospital seemed mysterious, full of magical sounds. Strange gongs rang; nurses whisper-called each other on hidden intercoms; someone in pain howled. Cass watched dreams flicker across Josie's face.

Cass tried to imagine what her dreams could be. Josie had one long, placid stage of sleep, no movement whatsoever, and Cass envisioned her dreaming of them rocking in a boat together on gentle waves in a peaceful cove. A warm breeze stirred the water's surface; they watched cunners and minnows dart through the shallows. Sea birds were singing, and Josie could hear their calls. They dove from the boat and swam underwater.

Josie's face twitched; she called out in pain. "Oh!" she cried without waking up.

"I'm here, Josie. I'll be right here when you need me," Cass said against Josie's cheek.

She sat back, exhausted. Staring at Josie, she thought of T.J. She had the feeling that if she could see into his deepest heart, she would discover that she had hurt him worse than he had ever been hurt before. Worse than the leg he'd broken skateboarding; worse than the shoulder he'd dislocated windsurfing; worse than the time he'd taken a blood oath with Sean and his finger had gotten infected; worse than the cut for which he had just gotten stitches.

Cass had wounded T.J. in the worst way. Sitting there in the hospital, she had no real idea how badly. But if she was lucky, if she opened her eyes, if she started to listen as hard as Josie did, she might find out.

14

The same day Josie had her accident, Billy Medieros had bought his boat. First thing that morning he'd gone down to Mount Hope Savings Bank and withdrawn five thousand dollars for a down payment; George Magnano, the seller, had agreed to hold a fifteen-year note for the rest.

Billy had planned to cap off the family party with an announcement. He had dreamed, in a vague, unformed way, of toasting Cass, then his new boat, which he'd been planning to name *Cassandra*. He had imagined congratulations, toasts all around, the pleasure he would take in Cass's pride. He had dreamed of sneaking away from the party with Cass, leaving the kids with their grandparents, while he showed her the boat, her namesake.

He had been dreaming of his own boat forever. Before he and Cass had ever talked about having kids, they'd imagined the day he would get his own boat. Weeks ago, when he'd first started considering George's boat as a real possibility, right after Keating had named John a captain, Billy had bought a can of red paint. Right then he'd envisioned the boat's new name and home port painted on the transom:

CASSANDRA
MOUNT HOPE, R.I.

He had a bottle of champagne under the seat in his truck, ready for Cass to smash across the bow at the christening. But now any celebrating would have to wait. Cass spent every day at the hospital. Today Josie's doctor had given them the test results: it looked as if Josie's accident had caused her hearing to get worse. Maybe the problem would disappear when the swelling went down, but the doctor wasn't sure.

Cass didn't even know he'd bought the boat, and the longer Billy waited to tell her, the more guilty he felt: for not looking after Josie right, for buying the boat without telling Cass, for how happy the boat made him.

Billy knew it exhausted Cass, seeing their daughter hurt, unable to bring her home. At night she would crane her neck, rub her tired muscles. Full of plans for his new boat, Billy would feel ashamed. After all, Cass was blameless, while he had failed to protect Josie. Sometimes he felt himself start to turn on Cass.

She'd begin to seem saintly and dutiful, suffering while he had all the fun. The crazy part was, it was supposed to be fun for her, too. Buying a boat was supposed to have been a high point of their life together.

"I bought George's boat," he said bluntly on Josie's third night in the hospital, when he and Cass were finally in bed.

Cass didn't say anything right away. She fiddled with the top button of her cotton nightgown. At night Cass wore fabrics that left little to Billy's imagination, that clung to her body and left him crazy to see what was underneath.

"You signed the papers? It's yours?" she asked.

"All mine," Billy said.

"Wow," she said.

A lifetime of knowing Cass warned Billy that this "wow" did not indicate excitement.

"Your own boat," she said. "You could have let me in on it."

He exhaled. "I knew you'd say that."

"What am I supposed to say?" she asked, sparks crackling just under the cool surface.

Billy shook his head. He wasn't going to write the script for her. He watched her remove her watch. She fidgeted with it for a minute, twisting the metal band, then flung it on the bedside table.

"You asshole," she said.

"Hey!" Billy said.

"God, your timing is lousy, Billy."

"That's the point," Billy said, trying to stay calm. "I couldn't predict Josie was going to get hurt. You've had so much on your mind."

"Too much to let me in on the boat?"

"I didn't plan it this way."

"It feels exactly as if you went out and bought a house without me," Cass said, a trace of bewilderment in her voice. "We've been talking about your boat since we were kids."

Billy felt like he'd been punched in the mouth, and deserved it. "This sounds lame, I know, but I thought I'd surprise you."

"You're right. It sounds lame."

"You knew I was looking at George's boat. You told me it was a chump Southern shrimper."

"I would've changed my mind," Cass said.

Billy knew that. He shrugged.

"I thought looking for a boat would be half the fun," Cass said. "Maybe more fun, for me, than owning one. I'm not even sure this is a good time . . ."

"It's the *only* time for George's boat," Billy said, riding over what she'd been about to say. "Look, some fisherman in Newport wants to go independent, and he made George an offer. George feels loyal to Mount Hope guys, so

240

he gave me a chance to beat the offer."

Cass's expression said she didn't want to believe him, but she knew Billy didn't lie.

"He pulled that on you?" Cass asked.

"It's legit," Billy said. "There are lots of guys in Newport who want to go independent. Hell, there are plenty around here. Just look at John — he wants his own boat. We all do."

"Still, George shouldn't have played you against someone else. It's not right."

"He wanted his price, and he was tired of me stalling for time."

"Why were you stalling?"

Billy couldn't tell her that he had been ready to make this move for a long time but that, deep down, he'd figured Cass wouldn't approve. She would listen to his late-night boat fantasies, and even encourage him. But buying his own boat meant that Billy would leave the Keating fishing fleet, and Cass would see that as disloyal. No matter what, Cass believed in keeping the family together.

"I didn't think you'd like it," Billy said after a long silence.

"Well, I have mixed feelings about you going solo," she said. "It's what I meant before when I said I'm not sure this is the best time."

"You mean money?" Billy asked.

Cass flexed her shoulders. She reached behind her neck to rub a spot, but Billy took over. He worked the muscle steadily, waiting for her to answer. "The chair I sit in at the hospital," she said. "It's too high. I have to bend way down to talk to Josie."

"Is it money?" Billy asked. "You think I won't make a good enough living on my own?"

"Oh, Billy," she said, sounding discouraged. "You're the best there is. If there are fish, you'll catch them. But when you add up insurance, dockage, fuel . . . you'll have to spend more time out than you already do. You'll never be home."

"I've totaled it up. We can swing it."

"Dad gets a pretty good group rate for health insurance. And it's a good plan. Finding a company to cover Josie will be impossible."

"Not impossible. Besides, you're the Keating bookkeeper. You know I'll be making a lot more when I sell the fish on my own."

"Exactly, Billy. But you'll be it. There won't be anyone else to fall back on. If you come back dry one trip, what about the bills that month? I'm just part-time. I'll help, but I can't carry us."

"We'll manage. You know we will."

"When did you make the deal?"

"The morning of the party."

"Before Josie had her accident," Cass said, sadly. "You could have told me before we left the house. You could have, but you didn't want to."

Now Billy saw how bad an idea it had been. How could he actually have planned to announce his big news at Nora's party? Seeing the hurt in his wife's eyes, he realized how she would have felt, hearing about the boat at the same time as the rest of her family.

"I have to get some sleep," she said, then added pointedly, "I want to get to the hospital early. She's having tests in the morning, and I should be with her."

Billy wondered why Cass deliberately tried to make him feel guilty. Didn't she know he loved Josie? He would give anything to call back the moment when he'd looked away.

But he and T.J. and Sean had been having a rare talk, and Billy hadn't wanted it to end. It wasn't the sort of heavy-duty conversation parents always think they should be having with their teenagers, about sex, drugs, drinking, and report cards. No, the night of Nora's party, Billy, T.J., and Sean had been talking about cars. How T.J. wanted a Jeep when he got his license. How much fun it would be to drive through the dunes at Spray Cove.

Cass rolled over so that her back was to Billy. He wanted to touch her shoulder, run his hand down her silky side, make her want to twist around, kiss him goodnight. He stared at her shoulder, at the spot he wanted to touch, for a long time. After a while, he didn't want to touch it anymore.

Tomorrow, on the noon tide, he'd take the *Norboca* out for a quick, seven-day trip. Before leaving, he'd give Jimmy notice. Jimmy wouldn't be thrilled, but he wouldn't hold Billy back; he had known that this day was coming. Fishing-fleet owners could bank on the fact that fishermen — even sons-in-law — would go solo the first chance they got.

Billy lay on his back, dreaming of his new boat. While he was gone, he would have the boatyard haul her, make her ready for winter. Billy would give them the paint he'd bought, the soft red color he'd chosen because it reminded him of his wife's hair, and he'd have them paint his boat's new name on the transom.

The next morning, Cass set out orange juice, boxes of cereal, and a half gallon of milk. Billy sat at the table, reading the paper. Belinda and T.J. wandered sleepily into the kitchen, said good morning, and ate their breakfast. Usually Billy joked with the kids, tried to pump them up for the school day. But today, angry at Cass, he didn't speak. He stared at the local-news page, occasionally checking his watch. Belinda noticed.

"What time are you leaving, Daddy?" she asked.

"About noon," he said.

Cass knew Billy liked to sail with the tide, as early as possible, so he would waste as little of the day as possible. She watched him, his shoulders tight, a tense frown on his lips, and she imagined him trapped at the breakfast table. Maybe he felt nervous about meeting her father. Or maybe he just wanted to escape the whole family.

"Have a good trip," Belinda said, giving Billy a kiss before easing out the door.

"Yeah," T.J. said, trudging after her.

When they had gone, Cass waited for Billy to start talking. He didn't; she reached across the table and jostled the paper.

"What?" he asked, finally looking up.

"You still upset about last night?"

"Thinking about the trip."

"Nervous about my father?"

"Not really."

Cass knew they were just filling the air with words. "You're mad at me," she said.

"If you have something to say," Billy replied, "you should say it."

Cass fiddled with her coffee spoon. She knew she had something to say; she just didn't know what it was.

"It's just . . ." she began. "You're about

to leave for a week, and we're both mad. As soon as you walk out that door, I'll probably think of ten things to say to you."

"They'll still be there when I get back."

Cass gave him a long stare, to see if he was teasing her. But there didn't seem to be any humor in his expression. "Nothing ever changes?" she asked. "Is that it? Things are so difficult, so unpleasant?"

He shook his head. "Cass, don't put words in my mouth."

"Then say something."

"I love you. How's that?"

Strange, but Cass already knew that Billy loved her, and his saying so only made her feel worse. Love wasn't their problem; it never had been. But Cass wanted to ride through the hard times together, learning to tell each other everything.

"Look," Billy said, rising, pulling her to her feet. "Don't be mad at me. I don't want to leave like that."

"I know," Cass said, shaking her head, trying to convince herself. "We can't say goodbye mad."

Billy began kissing her. He kissed her eyebrows, her cheeks, the tip of her nose, her lips. Her eyes closed, Cass let her fingers trace his hair curling at the nape of his neck. They stood there for a long time. Then it was time for Billy to go.

"Better?" he asked.

Cass nodded, smiling.

"Kiss Josie for me." He exhaled, gave an oddly violent shake of his head. "I want to be here when you bring her home."

Cass touched his hand to comfort him, knowing he meant it. Sometimes she envied him, being able to leave. But right now he seemed to wish just as passionately that he could stay.

Then Billy gathered his things, slipped on his jacket, and kissed her again. Cass stood at the back door, waving as he backed his truck out of the driveway. She watched him drive down the street. Whether he wanted to or not, he drove away. And by the time he turned the corner, the anger his kisses had soothed out of her had started to smolder again, and then burn.

As soon as T.J. came home from school, he went straight upstairs. He lay on his bed, waiting for the house to clear out. These family visits to the hospital reminded him of when he was little, back when everyone would go to church on Sunday. His mother would wake up Belinda and him, help them pick out their clothes, make sure their shoes were shined. If his father wasn't out fishing, he'd warm up the car. No matter how early they got up, they always left the house with just enough time to spare. That made going to church a race, kind of exciting.

At the doors to the church, T.J. always felt nervous. Maybe because the doors were so big, or because they were almost late, or maybe because the smell of incense was leaking out, and incense smelled so mysterious. That was before Josie got sick. At first, only their mother had stopped going to church — because, she said, Josie was too much of a handful during Mass. But gradually the rest of them had stopped, too.

"T.J., hurry up," his mother called. "We're leaving for the hospital." The hospital: like church, another family outing from which they'd all return better people.

"I'm not going," he said. He heard her footsteps coming down the hall. She stood in the doorway of his room with a look that said he'd better have a good reason. Maybe he should tell her he wanted to play darts.

"You haven't once come to visit Josie," his mom said.

"She'll be home soon, won't she? What's the big deal?"

"The big deal is that she's alone and scared in the hospital, and seeing us makes her feel better."

"You go every day."

"And so does Belinda, and so did your dad until he had to leave. Now get ready."

"I'm not going. I'm studying with someone."

"You just got home from school. Take a break and study later."

"I already made plans."

"Josie's worried about you. She can't understand why you haven't visited her."

"And of course that's more important than me!" The words spewed out before T.J. could stop them. "I just have to study, that's all."

His mother gave him a long, cool stare. He knew she could get very intense in these situations. He could see she realized that a split-second decision was called for, and she was weighing all the factors. This could go either way. She might yank him by the hair and scream at him to get moving; even though she had never before yanked him by the hair, T.J.'s guilty conscience could picture her doing it now. On the other hand, she might believe his study story, kiss him goodbye, and leave. Or she might not believe him, kiss him goodbye, and leave anyway.

"What subject?" she asked.

"History."

She nodded hard, so her chin just about bumped her chest. T.J. could tell that she didn't buy it, but she'd decided not to argue. "Okay, then," she said. "Anything you want me to tell your sister?"

"Nothing special. Just 'hi.' "

His mother kissed him and left. The funny thing was, T.J. sort of wished she had yanked him by the hair. The second he heard her and Belinda leave the house and start up the Volvo, T.J. grabbed the spare truck keys and headed out.

The October air felt chilly. He rode his bike into the wind, weaving down the long hill toward the wharf. He sped through red lights, bounced over cobbles, dodged slow-moving tourists. You needed a mountain bike in Mount Hope just to avoid hazardous old people. Pedaling onto Keating's Wharf, he tried to act nonchalant. He parked his bike beside a few others locked to the chainlink fence.

His father had left just yesterday morning, which meant he would be gone for a week. There was the truck, parked in a lot his grandfather reserved for fishermen. T.J. glanced around; you didn't really have a clear view of this spot from either Lobsterville or the warehouse, but you never knew who might be on the prowl. He wished his father hadn't parked right here in the middle of the lot, but what was T.J. going to do? Ask his father to leave the truck in a nice dark alley so T.J.

could steal it easier?

The engine fired up. His heart pounding, T.J. hunched low in the seat, so no one would see him. He stepped on the brake, the clutch, the gas, getting a feel for the pedals. Without moving, he shifted through all the gears. Then he backed out of the parking spot, shifted into first, and pulled carefully into the traffic cruising down Memorial Highway.

T.J. had known how to drive for two years. His mother had taught him one summer afternoon when he was thirteen. She'd let him drive up and down a dead-end street in the industrial park for an hour. "This'll be our secret," she'd said, letting him know he shouldn't tell Belinda or his father. T.J. had kept his word; he had already promised his father he wouldn't tell anyone *he'd* taught T.J. to drive two months earlier.

Until now, he'd never driven without one of his parents in the front seat. He hadn't even planned to take the truck until last night. He'd been lying awake, thinking about stuff, when suddenly the idea hit him: the truck's just sitting there, no one will ever know. And once the idea took hold, he couldn't shake it. The details just burned in his mind: wait till they leave for the hospital, get the keys, ride your bike down to the wharf, get in the truck, and take off.

He wanted to take off from Belinda, dressed for the hospital in her church clothes. It bugged the shit out of him that she was visiting Josie every day. Like she even cared. She probably had a crush on some young doctor; she was probably just hanging around Josie's room hoping Dr. Wonderful would drop by. When Belinda came home, she'd talk on and on about how tiny Josie looked in her hospital bed, how brave she was, and Belinda would have a worried, reverent look in her eyes, like she considered Josie a saint.

But what really got T.J. was seeing his mother so freaked out. His aunts didn't even want her driving to the hospital alone, that's how upset she was. Now that his dad was away, Aunt Bonnie took her in the mornings and Aunt Nora at night, but his mother insisted on driving in the afternoon, because she thought it was important "the other kids" — meaning Belinda and him — see their little sister.

T.J. had heard all this last night, when Aunt Nora came for a cup of tea. His mother had thought he and Belinda were asleep, but she kept her voice low, anyway. Then he heard Aunt Nora say, "That's okay, let it out," and his mother said in an icy voice, "Sometimes I hate it so much, I want to leave. Just leave."

After that, only Aunt Nora talked, and T.J.

figured his mom was crying. From then on T.J. kept thinking about the plates crashing on Josie, how it was his fault she'd almost died. That was when he decided to take a long ride.

So it actually amazed him when he found himself driving past the Slow — Hospital Zone signs. He drove once around the zone's outer block, then slowly past the hospital itself. There was his mother's car, parked on the street. He searched the hospital windows, hundreds of them, as if he might actually see Josie, and he nearly ran a stop sign.

"Whoa!" he said out loud, coming to a complete stop. Then he peeled out the way his father used to, laying rubber like Mario Andretti. His father never drove wild with T.J. anymore, and he talked about "responsible driving" — probably because T.J. would be getting his license next year, driving for real, and his father wanted to set the right kind of example. T.J. thought it would be neat if Josie had been looking out the window at the exact moment of his burnout, but that would mean that his mom was looking, too.

Since he was in the neighborhood, he cruised down Marcellus Boulevard. He could hardly believe people lived in these mansions. They were castle-sized, with stone towers, statues in the yard, and turnaround driveways.

Some of them were open to the public, like museums. T.J. was looking around, wondering which one Alison lived in, when he saw her riding her bike. He did a wicked U-turn.

"Hey," he said, stopping across the street from her. She sped up; she probably thought he was a gross old horny guy trying to flash her. "Alison!" he shouted.

She slammed on her brakes. "T.J.?" she said, her mouth dropping open. "What are you doing driving?"

"I felt like going for a ride. Want to hop in?"

"You drive?" she asked, just standing there. "You have your license?"

"Yeah," T.J. said, thinking she looked gorgeous in her tight white sweater and white jeans. No one but Alison wore white jeans during the school year.

"You're not old enough," she said.

"I stayed back," T.J. lied. "In first grade. Come on."

"Okay. Wow," Alison said.

T.J. stuck her bike in the truck bed. Then he got in the cab. Alison was looking around, dazed, as if she'd just agreed to take a ride in the space shuttle.

"I've never been in a truck before," she said.

No kidding, T.J. thought. Her parents probably had a Mercedes. "I could have brought the Volvo," he said awkwardly. Never mind that it was the family tank, fifteen years old — the same age as T.J.

"No, this is awesome," she said. "I can't believe you drive."

They cruised along without saying anything. T.J. was in shock that his first time alone behind the wheel, he'd picked up Alison McCabe. It seemed like this was meant to be. He glanced sideways at her. She had such a beautiful athletic body, clean swishy hair, and the cutest profile. Everything turned up: her thick eyelashes (from this angle T.J. could see she wore violet mascara), her nose, the corners of her mouth, even her chin.

"You have dimples," he said.

They deepened, her smile growing wide. "When I smile."

"You're always smiling," T.J. said.

"You don't know me very well," she said. "I have my moments."

"Oh, you mean a deep, dark secret?" he teased.

"Yes, I guess it is."

She sounded serious. T.J. shifted down, so he could look right at her. She wasn't smiling.

"What do you mean?" he asked.

"Oh," she said. "I have problems."

"Like what?" More than anything, T.J. wanted Alison to tell him her problems.

Maybe she had a split personality. Maybe no one in her family understood her. T.J. pictured them taking the truck to California, right now. Two misunderstood kids escaping their families — the kind of kids River Phoenix and Winona Ryder always played in the movies. They could pretend to be from the same troubled family, a brother and sister in need of lodging. They could call teenage hotlines, stay in runaway shelters. Late at night, when all the other runaways were asleep, they could hold each other under the blankets.

"Like what problems?" T.J. didn't want to press her to tell him painful things, but he thought he'd explode if he couldn't know. "I have problems, too."

"What, like your parents are too strict?"

Suddenly her voice had a mean, bitter edge that T.J. had never heard before.

"No. Like my sister almost died because of me," T.J. said.

"Really? How?" Alison asked. She sounded suspicious, like she didn't really believe him.

"She's only four, and she can't hear. The one who answered the phone when you thought Belinda was ragging on you."

T.J. hadn't told this story to any of his friends — even Sean, who was there the night of Josie's accident. T.J. had only said he felt bad for Josie. He'd left out the part that it was his fault. Right now, he didn't know whether Alison was going to be nice about it or jump out of the truck. He just didn't want her thinking he was a run-of-the-mill kid with wimp teenage problems, like acne or strict parents.

"Oh, T.J.," Alison said. "That must be so awful for her."

"Yeah."

"She's still in the hospital?"

"Uh-huh." T.J. had thought that telling the story would make him feel better, but instead he felt more depressed.

"I don't think it's your fault. You didn't know the waiter was coming that exact minute. I think it's really horrible of your mom to make you feel so bad."

"She took it back."

"Look, you still feel it, right? It's written all over your face."

T.J. tried to laugh, wondering what she meant. Did he look ugly? Was he going around with a frown all the time? He knew how quickly a frown could turn a person ugly.

Alison undid her seat belt and slid across the seat toward him. She brushed her fingertips across his forehead, just above his stitches. "How did that happen?"

"Trying to get to Josie."

"Your mom sounds really sick," Alison said. "Blaming you when you got hurt trying to help."

"Aren't you going to tell me?" T.J. asked, really wanting her to get off the subject of his mom.

"Tell you what?"

T.J. didn't like being played with, and he knew that was what Alison was doing. So he kept his mouth shut and drove along, like he didn't care.

"Oh, you mean about my problems?" she finally asked.

"Yeah."

Alison exhaled, as if she were trying to get up the courage to tell him.

"What?" he asked.

"I started off kidding, saying I have problems. I mean, people always say that, but the problems turn out to be something stupid, like their parents are getting divorced. You know?"

"That's stupid?" T.J. asked, thinking that someone's parents getting divorced counted as a pretty big problem.

"But then you told me about Josie. So maybe I can tell you."

"You can."

"Okay," Alison said. "My parents are getting divorced."

Billy drove the *Norboca* across the waves, through the night, into the North Atlantic. The two guys on watch, Cliff Sherman and Joe Markopolous, stood on deck talking. Their voices drifted back to Billy in the wheelhouse; he saw their cigarettes glowing in the dark. He steered out to sea, but his thoughts turned back to home. To Cass.

This morning, he'd seen her emotions veering out of control. He'd felt it at the breakfast table. Leaving her now, with Josie still in the hospital, had been one of the hardest things he'd ever done. When he'd looked at her eyes, at the face he loved more than any in the world, he'd seen her hiding some terrifying fear. As if she hadn't expected her life to turn out to be so difficult; as if, somewhere along the line, their lives had gotten too complicated for her to handle, and she didn't know what to do. It killed Billy, because he didn't know what to do, either.

He hadn't wanted to leave, but now it felt good to be away. He breathed the cold air, so dry it made his throat ache. Overhead, the stars blazed. Billy knew these northern stars; he followed them to the fishing grounds. Even with all the electronic equipment on-board, Billy still would rather steer by the stars. The Milky Way swept across the sky, filmy as a woman's scarf.

"Pretty night," Cliff said, coming into the wheelhouse. "We're making good time."

"We'll be fishing before dawn," Billy said.

"Maybe I'll sleep a little," Cliff said. "If you can spare me."

"No problem."

"Hey, it's great, you buying your own boat. If you need crew . . ." Cliff left the offer hanging.

It seemed strange to be fishing without John Barnard; they'd been together on over a hundred trips, and they knew each other's style and pattern of fishing. Billy glanced at Cliff, wondering if he — or any of this crew — would ever fit in the way John had.

"Thanks," Billy said. "I'll let you know."

"Hey, how's your little girl?" Cliff asked. "Joanie said she was in the hospital."

"She's doing better," Billy said, turning his attention back to the helm. "She'll be fine."

The silence stretched out. Cliff arched his back and yawned. "Well, I guess I'll turn in. See you at four."

"Good night," Billy said.

He checked his course, adjusted the wheel. He stared at the stars, tried to conjure their magic again. But it wasn't there. His emotions were pushing it away: feelings for Josie and

Cass. Thoughts of his wife, seventy-five miles behind him, and her desperation, overshadowed the magic of the stars.

15

When Cass arrived at the hospital on Josie's fifth morning there, the doctor gave her good news.

"The swelling's gone down," she said. "So I'm sending Josie home."

"Today?" Cass asked, feeling her heart leap.

The doctor gave her a bright smile. "Tomorrow," she said. "We'll watch her one more night to be absolutely sure."

"Thank you," Cass said.

Cass poked her head into Josie's room. Josie held her new doll, a gift from her grandparents, between her stomach and the cast on her left wrist.

"Guess what?" Cass asked, kissing her. "The doctor says you can come home tomorrow!"

"Yay!" Josie bounced in her bed. But she seemed to have something else, equally exciting, in mind. She wedged her doll under her left arm. With her free, right hand, she saluted Cass. Then she tapped her chin with her thumb and wiggled her four fingers.

"Are you playing?" Cass asked.

"No, talking," Josie said. "I'm saying, 'Hi, Bob.' "

"With your hands?" Cass said, feeling a sinking in the pit of her stomach. Josie didn't answer, but continued making the same gestures over and over, smiling as though she were enormously pleased with herself.

"Who showed you that, sweetheart?"

"Zach," Josie said.

Cass wandered out to the nurses' station. The nurses were huddled together, preparing to change shifts, briefing one another on the previous night's developments. A few doctors sat at a long Formica counter, writing notes for patients' charts. Cass leaned against the desk, waiting for someone to look up.

"May I help you?" Josie's nurse asked.

"Who's Zach?" Cass asked.

The nurse pointed at a young man dressed like T.J., and not much older. He sat among the doctors, writing furiously. Cass approached him. He looked up, a friendly, inquisitive expression in his eyes. He had springy red hair and professor-style horn-rimmed glasses that did not succeed in making him look any older than twenty; he arched an eyebrow flirtatiously.

"I'm Josie's mother," Cass said.

"Great to meet you! I'm Zach Butler," he said, pumping her hand. "Boy, do you have a terrific kid! Learns just like that." Letting go of her hand to snap his fingers seemed to require a degree of concentration.

"Thank you. Could we talk, um, privately?" Cass asked. Zach's powerful enthusiasm had all the doctors and nurses gazing in their direction. Cass felt like she'd just entered a crowded elevator with someone wearing too much aftershave.

"Sure! Let's step in here," Zach said, ushering her into a conference room. "First off, you're wondering who I am, what business I have interviewing Josie. I'm a speech pathologist, certified" — he handed Cass his card — "and the hospital called me in to consult."

"No one told me," Cass said.

"That's called bureaucracy," Zach said.

Cass didn't like this cavalier attitude. Did Zach know how it felt to have a four-year-old daughter in the hospital for five days, with people Cass didn't even know going in and out of her room? "I'll speak to the nurse," Cass said.

"Good idea," Zach said jovially.

"Let me get to the point," Cass said. "Josie told me you taught her some signs."

"She picks up right off the bat. Smart kid."

"Josie's not deaf," Cass said.

"That's absolutely true."

"Signing will set her apart."

"I only taught her one phrase: 'Hi, Mommy.' "

"Still," Cass said stubbornly, determined to explain her position to Zach. "I don't like it. Josie's been tested since she was two. Every step of the way, Dr. Parsons has told me she'll need extra help, but she doesn't need a different education than my other kids."

"What if a different education would help her?"

"I'll do anything to help Josie, but I don't want her set apart. I don't want her in the deaf community." To Cass, that wasn't Josie, a person who had to communicate in silence, with her hands.

"Everyone's scared of the idea."

"I'm not scared."

"Look, Mrs. Medieros, I'm not trying to talk you into anything. I only taught her a couple of words."

"And I'm not trying to put down your life's work," Cass said. "But I know how I want to raise my daughter."

"She seemed excited to learn the signs," Zach said, still smiling.

"Yes," Cass said, seeing Josie's face lit up, wreathed in pleasure.

"The hearing tests are necessary," Zach

said. "And they may seem to point you in the direction of a standard public-school education. But there's a more important indicator."

Cass hated how speech therapists, social workers, doctors, and school personnel spoke, using jargon like "indicator" instead of "hearing test." But, politely, she went along with it. "Which indicator?" she asked.

"Josie," Zach said.

Cass left the hospital early and stopped by the wharf on her way home. Bonnie had been filling in as part-time bookkeeper, and Cass hoped she hadn't left yet. But when she climbed the rickety old stairs, she found the office nearly dark. Her father sat by the window with a single light burning.

"Dad, do you need help closing up?" Cass asked, alarmed by how lonely he seemed.

"No, Cass. I think I'll just sit here a while. What are you doing here? How's our baby?"

For a second, Cass didn't know whether he meant Josie or Cass herself, and she felt a rush of affection for her father. She loved this wharf; coming here always made her feel steady and secure, part of something that went on forever, even in bad times.

"Josie's coming home tomorrow," Cass said. "All the swelling's down."

"She's sure had us scared. You hate seeing a little kid all alone in the hospital. Your grandmother couldn't stand it the night we visited. She gave Josie the doll, and then we had to leave."

"Josie loves the doll." In two days it had become her new favorite toy. Josie, never fickle about her dolls, had abandoned her old faithful Barbie in favor of this new one, a pucker-faced baby that looked to Cass like it belonged in an incubator. Maybe Josie had somehow sensed it needed more care than she did, and giving it made Josie feel stronger.

"I wanted to keep this place going strong for my grandchildren," her father said. "It's going, but not strong."

"My taking so much time off hasn't helped."

"Bonnie's been handling it. Hard to get used to having her here afternoons, I was so used to having you here all morning. But I hear Bonnie on the phone just like you, discounting scallops, discounting lobsters just to move them out of our tanks. That's not even breaking even."

"We have to discount just to keep our customers," Cass said, reminding her father of what he had taught her. "Joe at the Edgemont Inn said he'd just as soon buy shark, make cookie-cutter scallops. Cheapskate."

"Hell, what are business problems compared with having a kid in the hospital? Don't think about this place till you have Josie squared away."

Growing up, Cass had turned more to her older sisters than to her parents. But suddenly she wanted to talk to her father.

"Some guy at the hospital taught Josie sign language," Cass said. "Just a couple of words."

Her father shook his head. "She doesn't need that."

"That's what I say!" Cass said, patting his shoulder.

"She does just fine with what she has."

"Sometimes kids make fun of the way she talks. Even I can't always understand her."

"That's the hell of it. She does sound funny."

"You think so?" Cass asked defensively.

"It's a fact, Cass."

"She misses certain sounds, but we work on it all the time. I'd rather have her in the mainstream than using signs," Cass said, slipping into the jargon.

"Is that what they call that sign language — signs? Well, I don't see our Josie doing that. You see people in the restaurant once in a while, gabbing away with their hands so they can barely eat their meal. It's bizarre, their hands moving a mile a minute."

"What do you mean?" Cass asked, shocked.

"There's something freakish about them, handicapped people," he said. "It's right there, for everyone to see. The white canes, leg braces, whatever. You can see they're different."

"They're not freaks, Dad," Cass said, becoming furious. Her father had an underground streak of bigotry that surfaced occasionally, proving to Cass that she didn't really know her father.

"Maybe not," James Keating said. "But their handicaps set them apart. So does talking with their hands."

"It's how some people communicate," Cass said stonily, feeling sick. She had used those same words to Zach: "Signing will set her apart."

Her father looked around the room, as if searching for a new topic. His expression flickered from neutral to cloudy as something apparently occurred to him.

"So, we're losing Billy," her father said.

"The company is," Cass said coldly. "We're not."

"The other captains look to Billy. Doesn't speak well for the Keating fleet when my own son-in-law leaves."

"You know that all the guys want their own boat."

"I can't afford to run this place the way I used to. Got a new tax bill today. The state's trying to drive me out of business. I'm charged the same rate as all those real estate holdings around the harbor, and I'm not making anywhere near the income they are. And I can't stand disloyalty."

"Disloyalty?" Cass exploded. "Are you talking about Billy? Isn't it disloyal to call your own granddaughter a freak?"

"I did not," her father said. But he stayed in his chair, seeming to stare out the window at the harbor lights. Cass saw that his eyes were fixed on his own morose reflection in the amber glass. She stood still, wanting to say something more, to leave on a better note. But when her father refused to look her way, she took her things and slipped quietly out the door.

T.J. and Belinda would be waiting at home, but Cass walked the waterfront from Keating's Wharf to Doc Breton's. The October evening was frosty. In the ugliest way possible, her father had mirrored Cass's own fear: that the outward signs of Josie's hearing loss would alienate her from the world. She shook her head to dislodge the thought and hurried along, feeling the chill.

Except for a ghostly wind and the skittery sound of a hundred water rats, Doc's pier was silent. Cass knew that her father sometimes came here for solitude, and she could understand why. She tried to shake free of the fear and anger that gripped her. With her back to the town, facing out to sea, she could pretend it was an earlier time, the dawn of the twentieth century, when rules were a rich man's racket and smuggling a way of life.

This was Cass's territory, the waterfront. Breathing the sea air, Cass felt how closed off she had become. Wrapped tight as twine, she couldn't draw a deep breath at home. Since Josie's fever, Cass had lived small, in the interior, watching for little signs and missing the big ones.

She headed back toward Keating's Wharf. The cold night was clear, full of star trails. Venus hung just above the harbor; Cass believed she could chart its iridescent progress through the night. She headed past Lobsterville and the warehouse, now totally dark. Her father had gone home.

Up ahead, Cass saw lights on the *Aurora*. She wondered whether John Barnard was aboard, getting ready for a long trip. Approaching the big stern dragger, Cass saw him coiling lines on deck. For a minute, she hung back in the shadows. She heard music coming from speakers onboard.

"Hi, John," she said.

"That you, Cass?" he asked, peering up. "It's me."

He hesitated, and suddenly Cass felt shy.

"Come down here where I can see you."

When Cass didn't move, he offered his hand. She took it, jumping onto the deck.

"Are you heading out to Georges Bank?" she asked.

"Later tonight. I gave the crew shore time till midnight."

"Oh. Leaving on the old tide, huh?"

"Middle of the night, yeah," John said. "Convenient." He and Cass had been standing close since she'd jumped aboard. Now he raised his hand, moved it so close to her face that she wondered if he was going to brush back her hair.

She felt her heart skittering in her throat, waiting for his touch. But then, as if he had just realized what he was doing, he stepped back.

"Great news about Billy's new boat," he said.

"Thanks."

"I'll be right behind him," John said. "Next year at this time, I'll have my own ship."

"I don't doubt it," Cass said. "Not that we want you to go."

There had been something awkward in the air, something dangerous and romantic, but it had passed, and they leapt at the chance to talk business. Cass pitched in, helping him coil lines on deck.

"Cass, your father needs to put some serious money into his boats or he won't have any captains left. He keeps up the fishing equipment, because that's where the money is. But everything down below is bad. The bunks are mildewed; that might sound petty, but when you're out for fourteen days straight . . ."

"It doesn't sound petty," Cass said.

"Jimmy's heart is not in it anymore," John said.

"No, you're right about that. How's your life raft?" Cass asked.

John grinned. "Old Jimmy stocked up on survival suits after you lit into him. So we're all set if we sink. But we won't."

"It's getting cold. You can't have many trips left to make this year."

"We'll be fishing till January," John said. "She may need some work, but this boat rides through storms like you wouldn't believe." The way he scoffed at weather reminded Cass of her husband. In their world, waves couldn't rock you, boats didn't capsize, fog didn't matter as long as you had loran and a radar reflector.

"I wish I could go," Cass blurted out. She meant it: she had a vision of herself hauling nets full of herring, breathing the cold, fishy air, free from worries about Josie and the business, free from herself.

"You want to come fishing with me?" John asked, standing close again. She felt his breath on the top of her head. If she tilted her face up, he would kiss her. Cass felt the kiss before it started, warming her from the balls of her feet straight into her shoulders. Cass closed her eyes and melted against John's body.

"Cassie," John whispered, using the name he used to call her.

Cass tried to say his name, but she couldn't speak.

"I'm sorry. I shouldn't have done that," John said, but didn't let her go. Outside her jacket, he traced up her backbone with one finger. He reached beneath her hair, held the back of her neck. He was waiting to see if she would push him away; she didn't. She leaned back, pulling his head down to kiss him again.

John's hands slid under her jacket, untucking her shirt; they felt rough and cold against her smooth skin. Shivering against him, she felt her whole body shaking, and she knew it wasn't from the cold.

"I want to make love," he whispered against her mouth. "I still want you, Cass."

"John. . . ." she said, confused by how good

it felt to hold him, by how much she wanted to go below and lie with him in his bunk.

He stopped kissing her. He held her very tightly, full of tension, waiting for her to make some move. She leaned her head against his chest, trying to catch her breath.

"What is this?" he asked. "Why now?"

Cass shook her head. "It's not —"

"It is," he said, touching her face with both hands, drawing her close in a long kiss.

After a moment, reluctantly, she eased back, but he didn't let go. He gave her a slight shake, as if he knew she had already made up her mind and hoped she would change it.

"I can't," she said.

He said nothing, but held her tightly. They hugged for a long time, and Cass didn't want to let go. She pressed her face into his shoulder, so he couldn't see her eyes. Then she kissed him again, on the cheek.

"Cass —" he said again, helplessly.

"Have a good trip, John," she said, pulling away, climbing onto the dock. She hurried down the wharf, into the darkness.

"Cass!" John called out, just as she was about to turn the corner to the parking lot. He waved, and she waved back, then turned away.

She leaned against her car, her eyes closed. Her heart had started to pound again, and she knew it wasn't because of John. Slowly, she opened her eyes and looked at the sky full of stars. Picking one, she made a wish.

"Make things better," she said out loud. Then she added on her standard wish suffix, the one that had come automatically since before her wedding day: "Billy, come home safe."

Josie knew it was late because Barbara, the pretty nurse with glasses, came in with her flashlight. She covered the light with her hand so it wouldn't wake Josie up. But Josie was lying there with her eyes open, so it didn't matter. Barbara held Josie's hand, and from her nice eyes and the way her mouth hardly moved, Josie knew she was saying lullaby things. But Josie didn't sleep with her hearing aids, so she could only hear "night" . . . "sleep" . . . "night."

"T.J.," Josie said sadly.

Barbara patted Josie's head, and then she left.

Josie was going home tomorrow. She knew that should make her happy, but it also gave her a stomachache. T.J. must be very angry with her. He hadn't come to the hospital once, and Josie had been there for a long time.

Maybe he didn't like her anymore. Maybe he was saying bad things about her, the way he did about Belinda. When Josie smashed into the man, she must have looked stupid. Belinda said the lobster had fallen all over her. Josie couldn't remember, but when she got up she must have looked like a TV cartoon: with lobster claws for hands, and skinny feelers on her head, and red fanned tails instead of her skirt.

Josie liked the hospital. Everything was supposed to be quiet here. You could tell, because people did their jobs without moving their mouths. Nurses looked serious, reading the cardboard at the end of Josie's bed. Then they would look at her and smile, and still their mouths wouldn't move. When people asked her questions, they waited for as long as it took her to answer them.

Josie liked Zach. He was funny and nice, and she wondered why her mother didn't like him. As soon as Josie had told her mother his name, her mother had run out of the room with that busy look on her face. And Zach didn't come back until after her mother left.

He told her there were lots of things she could say with her hands. He showed Josie some things she already knew: waving hello and goodbye, rubbing her tummy when she felt hungry, blowing kisses to someone she loved. Then he asked her if there was anything special she wanted to learn how to say.

"T.J.," Josie said.

Both letters began with a fist. Zach showed her how to make a fist with her right hand. For *T* she poked her thumb between her index and middle fingers, the exact thing her father did when he pretended to steal her nose. For *J* she kept the fist, then stuck out her pinky finger and made a "J" in the air with it.

Lying in her hospital bed with the lights out, Josie called her brother. "T.J., T.J., T.J., T.J.!" She made the letters with her hand faster and faster, so it felt like she was yelling. No one in the hospital heard her, and no one came, and Josie was glad. The only one she wanted to hear her was T.J.

Alone in her bed, days after she brought Josie home, Cass tossed through a night of dreams. In one she held Josie in her lap, telling her stories. The feeling was so true, she might have been awake. The weight of Josie on her knee, the scent of Josie's hair, the noise Josie made sucking her thumb. Cass told her the same stories she'd told T.J. and Belinda, the old family tales about fairies at Spray Cove, the good witch who watches over Minturn Ledge Light, the wicked lobster boys. Josie asked to hear the stories over and over, and then she climbed off Cass's lap.

"I will remember them," Josie said in a solemn, clear voice, "but I have to leave now." She walked through a dream-door, into a playground filled with children. The door became glass, a picture window overlooking the scene, and it blocked all sound. Cass could see Josie playing, and Josie smiled at Cass over her shoulder. Then Josie waved and turned away.

Cass wakened with tears on her pillow. She felt as if she had just lost Josie forever. If Josie started to rely on sign language, Josie would move outside Cass's world.

But since Josie had come home, she'd been asking to see Zach again. Her eyes sparkled when she signed, "Hi, Mommy," "Hi, T.J." She'd promised Belinda she would learn how to sign "Belinda" and "Daddy," too.

Downstairs, a door closed softly. Cass raised herself up on her elbow, listening to footsteps on the stairs. Belinda said T.J. had a girlfriend; remembering herself at his age, she bet he was starting to sneak out late at night. Cass listened, vigilant, ready to pounce. But her door creaked open, and Billy entered the room, moving wearily. He had been gone for six days.

"Hi," she said.

He jumped. "I didn't think you'd be awake," he said

"I didn't think you'd be home till tomorrow."

"We got lucky and filled up early."

Cass lay on her back, watching him stuff his dirty clothes in the hamper. He'd left his boots downstairs, but he sat on the edge of the bed to take off his socks. He rubbed his feet.

"How's Josie?" he asked.

"Sleeping in her own bed," Cass said.

Billy walked barefoot out of the room. After a minute, Cass put on her robe and followed him down the hall. Josie's door stood ajar. Cass slipped inside, found Billy standing at the foot of Josie's bed. They stood side by side, their shoulders touching, watching Josie sleep by the glow of her Minnie Mouse night-light.

Billy slid his arm around Cass's waist. At first his grip was light. But the longer he stared at Josie, the tighter his arm felt around Cass's waist; suddenly he pulled her all the way around, hugging her hard.

He led her from the room. Instead of going back to bed, they headed for the kitchen. Cass poured two glasses of milk, while Billy pulled out a bag of ginger cookies.

"She looks good," he said, a little shakily. "Is she okay?"

"Her wrist itches under the cast. This morning I was washing her hair, and some water got inside. So it feels clammy, and she says it smells like a wet sweater."

Billy shrugged. "Were the other kids so sensitive to smell?" he asked.

"Belinda, when she was little," Cass said, smiling, watching Billy's face. He had gotten tan and windburned these last six days, in spite of the chilly fall weather.

"Nothing more serious than her wrist? Her hearing's the same?"

"As far as we can tell. Oh, there is one new development. Zach."

"Zach?"

"A speech therapist."

"Another one? What about Mrs. Kaiser?"

Cass sipped her milk. Her chin tucked down, she watched Billy through her bangs. "He has a different approach. I'm not really sure what I think. He says Josie should learn signs."

"Major shift here," Billy said. He ate half a cookie, then polished off the rest. "I thought you were against sign language."

"I am, I think," Cass said. "But you should see her signing our names, concentrating on each letter, doing it over and over. I don't know."

"She can hear some," Billy said.

They finished their milk; the lights of a car speeding down Coleridge Avenue played across the ceiling. Billy reached across the table; Cass felt his fingers tracing the back of her hand. She let him continue, trying not to think about kissing John Barnard.

"You could hardly look at me before I left," Billy said. "I thought about you the whole time."

"And still came home?" Cass asked, laughing.

"Yeah. I missed you a lot."

"Me, too." She always missed him, even when she knew they'd probably be fighting if he were home.

"Want to go back to bed?" he asked, reading her mind.

Cass rose. She reached up to brush a dark curl out of Billy's eyes. He looked sleepy and full of desire. He took her in his arms, smiling back. They walked out of the kitchen together, up to bed, putting the mysteries of their house down to rest for the night.

16

"Thank you for coming," Cass said, leading Zach to the kitchen table. "We could have come to you."

"I generally work at hospitals and in people's homes. I think learning in a familiar environment puts people, especially children, at ease," Zach said. Then he broke into a wide grin. "Besides, I don't have an office yet."

"Did you just graduate?"

"I finished my master's last summer."

Cass poured two cups of tea and set out milk, sugar, and a plate of Bonnie's brownies. Zach sat across the table. He looked so eager, ready to dive right into the tea, or anything else she put in front of him.

"Josie's been seeing a speech therapist for a while now," Cass said. "An older woman. She doesn't encourage using sign language."

"Conformity is a standard goal of the old school," Zach said. " 'Don't stand out, be just like everyone else.' Like the old days, when they used to train lefties to write with their right hands."

"I want my kids to stand out, but I don't want them to feel uncomfortable. Or to feel set apart," she said, thinking how "set apart" and "freakish" meant the same thing to her father. And maybe even to her.

"That's how Josie feels now: set apart. Our goal is to reverse that."

"She's in her room," Cass said, rising.

"I'd like to work alone with Josie today, if you don't mind," Zach said. "It's very helpful for the family to become involved, but first Josie and I have to get comfortable with each other."

"I want to learn the gestures, so I can know what she's saying."

"They're not gestures, Mrs. Medieros. What Josie is about to learn is a language. A complicated language, like English or French."

"I never got past French two in high school," Cass said, leading Zach upstairs to Josie.

"Neither did I," Zach said.

With his father back in town and the truck parked out front in the driveway, T.J. was back on two wheels. He and Alison would sit together on the school bus home, and the second T.J. got off, he'd hop on his bike and ride up Marcellus to meet her again. All T.J. could think of was Alison.

Today some strange car was parked on the street in front of his house. He walked inside and found his mother standing at the foot of the stairs, looking up.

"Hi, honey," she said. She seemed really happy to see him. The nicer his mother was to him lately, the more uncomfortable T.J. felt. What he and Alison shared was their miserable families, and the last few days his mother had been messing it up.

"Hey," T.J. said, heading for the kitchen. She followed him.

"I am so glad you're home. Zach's upstairs with Josie, and I'm dying to horn in. But I'm supposed to give them a little time alone. How was school?"

"Crappy. Who's Zach?"

"The new speech therapist."

"Oh, yeah. The sign-language dude."

"Why was school bad? Did something go wrong?"

"Nothing particular." T.J. dumped his books on the table and grabbed a brownie. He munched it as he looked in the refrigerator. He wished his mom would leave him alone, or, better yet, rag on him, so he wouldn't have to feel guilty telling Alison that his family sucked.

"How's your scar?" his mother asked, peering at him across the refrigerator door. She tried to touch it, but he pulled back.

"It's fine."

"It gives you that dangerous look, you know? Like you got knifed on your cross-country motorcycle trip," his mother teased. He could tell she was in a good mood; she was really trying to pump him up.

"No, I got it trying to get my sister killed."

His mother pulled back, her eyes all hurt. "Oh, T.J.," she said.

"That's what happened, isn't it?"

"That is *not* what happened. Josie's accident was not your fault — not one bit. It was terrible of me to say what I did; I still feel so bad about it. You got hurt trying to save Josie."

T.J. just stared into the refrigerator. He didn't even feel like finishing the brownie.

"T.J.?" she asked.

"What."

"Listen to me. T.J.?"

He looked up, extra defiant. "What."

"You aren't to blame for what happened to Josie. I don't blame you, and you shouldn't blame yourself. You got that?" she asked, a little desperately, trying to make him understand.

"If you say so."

"Do *you* say so?" his mom asked. "I want it to come from you. Please, T.J.?"

"Yeah. Okay," T.J. said. But even as he pretended to go along with his mom, he could see that she didn't believe him.

"You're a wonderful brother, and Josie is lucky to have you. Belinda, too, but I know how you feel about Josie. She's sad because she thinks you're mad at her."

"I'm just busy."

"I wish you'd tell me about your new girlfriend," she said, that teasing tone in her voice again. T.J. had the kind of mom he could talk to about girls if he felt like it, but he would never tell her about Alison. That would be a betrayal. He looked down at his feet.

"I'm taking Josie over to visit Granny later. Want to come with us?"

"No thanks. I'm going out."

"To see Alison?"

"Will you *lay off* me?" T.J. said.

"Okay, okay. Jeepers!"

T.J. pulled on his wool jacket. He and Alison would probably take a long bike ride, then head for Cathedral Woods. He wanted something nice and soft for her to lie down on.

"Teej," his mother said, then stopped. He could tell she knew she wasn't getting through to him; you could see how helpless she felt, and T.J. felt sorry for her. "You know I wish I could take back that stuff I said that night. I'm really sorry."

"Okay."

"I love you."

"Okay."

"Will you take out the garbage every night for the rest of your life and get straight A's in school and always be a good boy and never forget to call your mother on Mother's Day?"

"Okay." T.J.'s mouth twitched into a smile against his will.

"Okay," his mom said.

T.J. walked out the kitchen door, jumped on his bike. Riding to meet Alison, he concentrated like mad to wipe his mother's words out of his mind.

Billy came home from the boatyard in time for dinner. He didn't want to get too used to this new routine: working days on his boat, home every night for dinner. He'd be sanding a rail, or building the chart table, and suddenly he'd feel hungry. He'd look at the clock, and it would be five-thirty, and he'd lock up the boat and head home. He was never away from Cass for more than ten hours at a stretch. If he let himself get too comfortable at home, he might never go back to sea again.

Life at home was sweet now. Sleeping till six felt luxurious, especially with Cass warm and close, her body right there, pressed against him. At sea he had to make do with her pictures and his imagination.

Last night, he'd imagined a permanent life on shore. He could help Cass and Jimmy run Keating & Daughters. He could run the fleet from dry land. Cass was right, although he wouldn't admit it, about the difficulties of owning his own boat. He had so many extras to worry about: the high insurance premiums, the fines he'd be charged if he got caught fishing a species with the wrong nets (something fishermen did all the time — he'd done it), the maintenance costs.

Laws of the land didn't account for the vagaries of water and ice, fish populations, and Japanese factory ships. Let them police the stock market, the automobile industry, slaughterhouses, real estate brokers. How could you regulate the fishing business, the dangers of deep water, ice in the rigging, magnetic anomalies that could screw up a compass?

At the end of the day, Billy came through the back door into the kitchen. He walked over to Cass, standing at the stove, and kissed the back of her neck. "I'm home," he said.

"Hi," she said, leaning back, her head

against his chest. When she turned to hug him, he lifted her off the ground, onto the counter.

"See?" she said. "If you'd quit fishing and become an insurance salesman, we could do this every night. We'd have you in traction in no time."

"You're light as a feather," he said.

She slung her legs around his waist, kissing him. Something in a skillet on the stove beside them sizzled. She reached around him to turn down the heat.

"What's that?"

"Caper butter. For the haddock." She nuzzled his neck. "I'm making Potatoes Dauphine. You eat like that at sea?"

"If I ever served fish, my crew would throw me overboard. Meat and potatoes, all the way. The kids home?"

Cass stopped kissing him. "Belinda and Josie are," she said, hopping down. "T.J. went to visit his girlfriend. Does he seem okay to you?"

"Moody," Billy said.

"I'm hoping it's because he's in love," Cass said. "Or because he's fifteen."

"She's making him crazy," Billy said, hooking his thumbs through Cass's belt loops. "Every second. She's all he can think about."

"How do you know?"

"I was there," he said, pulling her pelvis

against his. "I remember fifteen."

Cass gave him a wide, sexy grin. "So do I."

"Hmmm." Billy's eyes roved the stove, wondering whether the dinner preparations were at a crucial point or whether he could carry Cass up to bed.

Belinda scooted through the kitchen, calling, "Hi, Daddy," over her shoulder. He caught Cass laughing to herself as she slowly stirred something.

"What's so funny?" he asked into her neck.

"I'm remembering being fifteen."

"Hi again," Belinda said, racing past.

Cass grabbed her hair in mock frustration — or maybe it wasn't mock at all. Billy kissed her right hand, clenched against her head.

"How was Josie's speech lesson?" he asked. He tasted the butter sauce. He felt starving, it smelled so good.

"I think it went well," she said, sighing. "Zach didn't let me sit in. But I think I can next time. From now on, I guess."

"It went well? Really?" Billy asked. It amazed him that Cass would have this reaction. He had expected her to say there wouldn't be another lesson.

"You look surprised," she said.

"I guess I am. You really think she needs it?"

"Now you sound like my father," Cass said. She seemed hurt, but then she laughed. "I take that back. You don't sound like him."

"Thanks," Billy said.

She stirred the sauce, thinking. "I don't know if she needs it, but she does seem . . . easier, doesn't she?"

"She hasn't flown off the handle the last couple of days," Billy said, feeling uneasy. "Maybe it's her medication."

"She's not on any medication, Billy. That stopped at the hospital. My God."

"Sorry!"

"Anyway, we can sit in at her next session with Zach."

"Yeah, maybe," Billy said. "I'm trying to get the boat ready. Get out there and make some money." The truth was, the idea of watching Josie learn sign language made him feel squeamish. He didn't know exactly why, but it reminded him of something both clinical and too personal. He hadn't minded watching Dr. Parsons fit her with hearing aids, and he had met with Mrs. Kaiser more than once. He'd never minded taking his kids to the pediatrician, so he didn't understand his discomfort now.

"After you get the boat ready, then," Cass said, briskly. She checked the potatoes, then started setting the table, clearly dismissing him. He knew he'd disappointed her, and now she was pushing him away.

He went to the refrigerator and took out a beer. "Want one?" he asked Cass.

She shook her head.

"Another difference between fishing and home," he said, opening the bottle. "I never have beer out there." He waited for Cass to say something, but she just kept setting the table.

"It's called denial," Zach said. "It's really common."

"He's never denied Josie's hearing problem," Cass said. They leaned against the kitchen counter. If she craned her neck, she could see Josie playing down the hall. Josie had made a nest of dishtowels, pretending to be a mother duck. She kept shifting on her haunches to see whether Barbie and her new doll had hatched yet. Cass felt like jabbing Zach, so he'd see how cute Josie looked. But he was intent on what he was saying.

"He didn't have to deny it before, because your goal was for Josie to hear. All your efforts went into that: the best hearing aids, Mrs. Kaiser for speech therapy . . ."

"Billy's not like that," Cass said stubbornly. "He doesn't expect her to be perfect."

"Mrs. Medieros, many parents of deaf kids

don't expect anything at all."

Now Cass felt glad Billy was working on his boat, and wasn't here to hear this. Since Zach had started working with Josie, it was like Josie had opened a door, stepped into someplace wonderful. For that, Cass felt grateful. But Zach had an overenthusiastic manner that bordered on rudeness, as if he liked to play out of bounds.

"You know, sometimes you don't know what you're talking about," Cass said coolly. "We expect plenty for Josie."

"Like what?"

"Kindergarten, for starters."

Zach shook his head. He took off his glasses, held them to the light, cleaned them with his shirttail. "Josie doesn't belong in kindergarten."

Now that Josie was making some progress, holding her temper in check more and more, Cass had let herself look forward to Josie starting kindergarten at Mount Hope Elementary next September. It would be the same classroom where Cass, her sisters, T.J., Belinda, and their cousins had gone: finger-paintings on the wall, the bathtub-sized stone turtle well in the middle of the floor, the story corner.

"She has ten months to get ready," Cass said.

Zach didn't say anything. He leaned forward

to watch Josie playing in the hall. Now she was pretending her dolls had hatched, transforming themselves from duck eggs into ducklings; she duck-walked down the hall, dragging the dolls along.

"You think she should be in that special class?" Cass asked. "I've seen it. It's actually a warehouse where they throw in every little kid who has a problem. One teacher and ten kids with birth defects, autism, Down syndrome, hyperactivity. What kind of help will Josie get there? How's she going to think of herself? She's been eligible for a year, but I've kept her out, getting her ready for kindergarten."

"You're right about that special class," Zach said. "But kindergarten in Mount Hope would be just as bad. Kids will make fun of her — you know they will. Do you want that?"

"Of course I don't want kids to make fun of her. But I want her educated."

"She needs a total communication program."

"Oh, you mean deaf school?"

"It's not . . ."

"What's wrong with kindergarten in Mount Hope?"

"She won't learn. She won't develop a" — Zach waved expressively, painting the air — "a richness of language."

"Dry up, buddy," Cass said. "She's going to kindergarten."

T.J. and Belinda walked in, single file, and T.J. continued up the stairs without saying hello to anyone.

"Hi, T.J.," Cass called after him.

"Hi, Mom. Hi, Zach," Belinda said, twinkling. Her crush couldn't have been more obvious if she had had a big *Z* emblazoned across her chest. Cass fought back a smile.

"Hi, Belinda," Zach said. "I'm arguing with your mom."

"You'll never win," Belinda said. "No one ever does." She stood with her feet apart, as if she were straddling a line. Cass could actually see her swaying back and forth, a worried frown on her face, trying to make up her mind about something. At thirteen, Belinda was beautifully transparent; Cass would bet anything Belinda had promised someone she would do something after school, but now she'd rather stay here with Zach.

"I'm supposed to help Emma study," Belinda said. "But it's really cold out. I'd freeze riding to her house."

"Have her come here," Cass said. "I'll bet Bonnie would drive her over."

"Thanks, Mom," Belinda said, tearing upstairs to use the phone.

"A little word like 'freeze,' " Zach said. "If

Josie goes to Mount Hope Elementary, 'freeze' probably won't find its way into Josie's vocabulary. She'll have one word for 'cold,' one word for 'hot,' one word for 'fast.' She won't have words to draw from."

"Won't you keep working with her, Zach? That'll help her."

"Mrs. Medieros, things will get harder for Josie. Even at home, where people accept her, it's hard for her to learn. She doesn't like to play with children — that's because they make fun of her, don't understand what she's saying. Kids are mean to kids outside their peer group."

"So what wonderful place would you like me to send her?"

"It's called North Point Academy."

"You're kidding," Cass said, shocked because it was the place her mother was always mentioning.

"Why? You've heard of it?"

"Only a little."

"It's an incredible place," Zach said.

"My mother's been mentioning that place for two years," Cass said.

"And it scares you," Zach said. "That's natural."

It seemed odd to Cass — vaguely amusing — that such a young guy would be reassuring her that her feeling was "natural." "Wait till you have kids, Zach," she said.

Suddenly, Josie screamed. Her arms flailed above her head, and she flung Barbie against the wall. Cass started down the hall, but Zach held her elbow to stop her.

"What are you doing?" he asked.

Cass threw him an impatient glance and hurried to Josie.

"What happened?" she asked.

"Head, head, head, head, head!" Josie screeched.

Cass tried to hold Josie still, to examine her head. Her scar, her ears looked okay. Cass reached out, feeling Josie's head for bumps, but Josie slapped Cass's hand away.

"Barbie," she cried. "Head, head."

Now Cass saw the problem. Josie had removed Barbie's head and gotten it stuck in the new doll's hand.

"Give me the new doll," Cass said clearly, trying to hold Josie still.

"Eh, eh, eh," Josie began.

"What are you doing?" Zach asked, standing over them.

"What does it look like?" Cass snapped. Then, to Josie, "I said, give me your doll." She acted out fixing Barbie's head, wondering whether Zach would be impressed with her improvised sign language.

"Eeeeeh!" Josie screeched, her face beet-red.

"Leave her alone," Zach said.

Cass snapped around to look at him. "She's frustrated."

"Would you let Belinda and T.J. get away with behaving like this?" Zach asked. "You're singling her out because she's deaf."

Cass yanked Barbie's head out of the new doll's hand, started to repair Barbie, but it was too late. Josie was ripping her own hair, yelling at the top of her lungs.

"No head, no head!" Josie cried. *"Fix, fix!"*

When Cass finally calmed Josie down, rocking her in her arms, she turned to Zach, to tell him he was out of line. But he was gone. She heard his car start up in the driveway, then pull away.

17

"What do you think of eloping?" Nora asked Willis one late-October night. Frost was forecast; they huddled under her down comforter on her balcony loveseat, shivering together as they watched the lighthouse beacon traverse the sky.

"For a couple of runaway kids, it's fine. For us, I think it's a terrible idea."

"Why?"

"Because you have a wonderful family that loves you, Nora. They'd be devastated."

"They would not," Nora said, knowing they would.

"Your sisters would never speak to me again."

"Oh, Willis." Nora tingled as he played with the hair on the nape of her neck. If only he wasn't so old-fashioned, she wouldn't feel in such a hurry.

"We have to put on a beautiful wedding, to make up for what happened to Josie at our engagement party. The accident's what they'll think of when they think of us together unless we block it out with something beautiful."

"You're a real romantic."

"Do you ever think about having kids, Nora?"

Nora closed her eyes, feeling him tickle her neck. A long time ago she had wanted children. When Cass and Bonnie were both pregnant for the first time, Nora had felt so jealous she couldn't stand to see them. They'd be comparing notes on maternity clothes, nursery color schemes, whether or not to breast-feed, and Nora would have to leave the room so she wouldn't cry.

But watching her sisters raise their kids, seeing how devoted they had to be, at the mercy of their children's schedules, Nora had realized she liked her life. She liked working late at night and waking at noon; she loved doting on her nieces — taking them to Providence or Boston shopping — then dropping them off at their own homes.

"I'm lucky," Nora said. "I have five nieces and nephews. I guess I put my maternal energies into them."

"I think you'd make a great mother."

Nora's eyes flew open. "You do?"

"If you ever decide you want to be one."

Even when she had lusted for a baby sixteen years ago, she had doubted whether she would be a good mother. She was too insecure, too selfish. She didn't have Bonnie's earth-mother warmth or Cass's spice, and she didn't have patience.

"I'm forty-four. My clock's about run out."

"We could always adopt."

Nora squeezed Willis's hand. "Sounds like you want a baby."

"Oh, I'm probably too old to start being a father," Willis said. "I'm just talking. But I'll tell you, Nora: I won't let you out of being a bride."

"White dress, veil, the whole bit?"

"You got it."

The last time Nora had visited her grandmother, Sheila had offered Nora her wedding dress. She sent Nora to the attic to find it. The dress was stored in an enormous box from a shop that no longer existed. Nora lifted the lid, and inside she found a yellowing antique of a garment, with crumbling lace and net, seed pearls dangling from broken threads. As small children, Nora and her sisters had played bride in that dress; Bonnie had torn the train, stepping on it with high heels. Knowing it would break Sheila's heart to see her dress in that condition, Nora had simply thanked her grandmother, saying that the dress was still beautiful, but too small.

"You haven't talked me out of eloping,"

Nora said. "By the time we get everyone in one place, it could be Christmas. I think a nice Halloween elopement, right here on this balcony, would be divine."

"You'll have to get your family's blessing."

"My grandmother gave us hers. Yesterday, after telling me wedding stories of every person she ever knew, she told me that at my age, elopement would be wise."

"Don't you want a nice wedding story to tell your grandnieces?" Willis asked.

"Not every wedding story is nice," Nora said, hearing her voice echo over the water, cuddling closer to Willis in the frozen night air, coughing once before she began to speak.

In the summer of 1920, just before Sheila Hannigan married Eddie Keating, a terrible thing happened. Men from an asylum had to take Doreen Murphy, who was to have been Sheila's bridesmaid, away in a straitjacket.

It happened like this: One muggy July morning, Doreen, who was Sheila's roommate, wakened with a pimple. Just a little thing, really. You'd hardly notice it.

"Does it hurt?" Sheila asked, only because Doreen was making such a fuss when they were dressing for work.

"Yes, and it's enormous." Doreen stood before the mirror, poking at it. It was pink, just below her right cheekbone, the size of a pin-point. Doreen, a fiery girl with chestnut hair and snapping blue eyes, was known for being fun, as well as somewhat vain and dramatic. She had that perfect poreless skin of girls born in the west of Ireland.

"Leave it alone, or you'll make it worse," Sheila said. "It's tiny."

They rode the trolley from Thornton to Providence's Market Square. They stopped to eat johnnycake, then walked to the hosiery mill on India Street. The next morning they were going to take the ferry to Mount Hope to meet their fiancés. Sheila was marrying Eddie Keating in a month, before Doreen would marry Patrick Barnard, and that was all Sheila could think about. Walking along, she daydreamed about the white lace dress she would wear, while Doreen kept touching her face.

The next morning, Doreen's pimple was larger, but not by much.

"I can't let Patrick see me like this," she said. "You take the ferry without me."

Sheila pretended to examine Doreen's cheek as a doctor would. "It doesn't look infected or anything. The salt water will do it some good, and Pat will be so disappointed if you don't come."

"No," Doreen said, staring into the mirror.

That was the way Doreen was: if she didn't feel she looked her best, nothing could convince her to join the party, go to the dance, or walk down the beach to neck with Patrick.

Sheila and Eddie took Patrick under their wing that hot July Saturday. The instant Sheila stepped off the Mount Hope steam ferry without Doreen, she caught sight of Patrick's lovesick face. Sheila and Eddie held hands down the ferry dock while Patrick shambled behind them.

Sheila changed her clothes at Mrs. Richardson's boardinghouse, where instead of Doreen she had a roommate she'd never met before. Sheila, Eddie, and Patrick walked down to the beach and took seats on the boardwalk. While Eddie went swimming, Patrick turned his back to the water and lowered his voice so only Sheila could hear.

"Does she still love me?" he asked.

"Of course she does. She just has a summer cold," Sheila said, lying as she'd been instructed.

"She must know that I still love her. In fact, I love her even more than before we . . . She was afraid that wouldn't be so, but it is."

Could Patrick be telling Sheila what she thought he was? All those nights when Sheila and Eddie finished necking and had to wait by the car for Doreen and Patrick to return from the dunes, Sheila had had her own private ideas about what was going on.

"Even more than before what?" Sheila asked, both eager and afraid to hear.

"She'll know what I mean. Please tell her." Patrick had red hair and high coloring that responded to his every emotion; at that moment, his face was scarlet.

Eddie came back wet from swimming, and when he kissed Sheila — in broad daylight, right on the boardwalk — she forgot about Patrick's near-confession. She felt charged that weekend, wanting Eddie to be touching her all the time. But it wasn't until Sunday night, when she was alone on the steamer and had time to think, that she consciously remembered what Patrick had said.

When Sheila walked into the room she shared with Doreen, she had the shock of her life. Doreen's pimple was bright red, the size of a cherry pit.

"Doreen, you have a boil," Sheila said, taking Doreen's hand. "Have you tried a warm washcloth?"

Doreen nodded. She could barely meet Sheila's eyes, for the shame of it.

"Should we call a doctor?"

"I will tomorrow," Doreen whispered.

"Patrick wanted me to give you a message: He loves you. Even more than before." Although Sheila put a question mark in her voice, Doreen made no response.

Sheila closed the curtains to keep out the night air, but she hardly slept. All night long Doreen knelt beside their bed, saying the rosary. She prayed silently, but simply knowing Doreen was on her knees, that she was troubled, kept Sheila awake. She wondered what terrible sin could keep her friend up all night, praying to the Blessed Mother. Unable to sleep, Sheila prayed that God take care of Doreen.

On Monday, the doctor gave Doreen a salve and told her to apply it hourly. For a while it seemed to work. Although the boil did not shrink, it did not grow. Doreen and Sheila worked side by side at the hosiery mill, spinning strands of silk into high-fashion stockings, daydreaming of their fiancés clamming in Mount Hope. Two nights passed.

After one o'clock Thursday morning, Doreen wakened moaning. Sheila stared in horror. The pimple had grown to the size and color of a red grape. It looked obscene, rising from the field of Doreen's pure-white skin.

"Mother of God," Doreen said, gasping at the sight of Sheila's expression. "What is it? What's happening to me?"

Sheila did not want to admit that she felt afraid. In the middle of the night, this monstrous thing on her friend's face looked purely evil.

"Will you say the rosary with me?" Doreen asked, her voice shaking.

The girls knelt beside their bed, holding hands, sharing the crystal rosary beads Doreen's mother had held on her deathbed. They prayed until they couldn't keep their eyes open. That was how they fell asleep: kneeling at their bedside, holding hands, and they stayed there till dawn. Already the day felt humid. Doreen touched her face, cupped the boil.

"It's moving," she said, clammy with fear.

Sheila peeled back Doreen's fingers and peered at the boil, which seemed somehow even more malevolent in daylight. It seemed to seethe beneath the skin. Like a volcano, a tiny opening formed at its peak.

"I think it's going to burst," Sheila said. She put the kettle on the stove and soaked a washcloth in steaming water. Again, she peered at Doreen's face. A silvery molecule of dust puffed out of the boil, then another and another. Sheila couldn't believe her eyes: the molecules had legs.

"Pray," Sheila said to Doreen, and Doreen began saying the Hail Mary out loud. Sheila pressed the hot washcloth to Doreen's face with both hands. The boil opened up, only it wasn't a boil at all.

It was a nest of spiders. Thousands of tiny, just-hatched spiders spinning silk parachutes drifted into the air, crawling all over Doreen. Doreen screamed. Sheila leapt back, watching Doreen swipe her face and body with frantic hands.

Not knowing what else to do, Sheila soaked the washcloth in scalding water and slapped it over Doreen's skin, trying to chase the baby spiders. Doreen's hysterical cries brought neighbors, then the police. Sheila tried to explain what had happened, but no one believed her. If only Sheila could contact Patrick — but neither they nor Patrick had a telephone.

After everyone left, Sheila bandaged Doreen's cheek. Doreen calmed down enough to talk. She told Sheila the spiders had been the devil's work. She was no longer a virgin. She and Patrick had fornicated one night on the beach, and the devil had entered her at the same time. Sheila had said that was nonsense, that a spider had just laid its eggs in a pore.

But even so, Sheila had had her doubts: Doreen was from Galway, and she had poreless skin.

In the middle of the night, Doreen started screaming, and wouldn't stop. Horrible, bloodcurdling screams, calling for her dead mother. Men from the asylum came for her. Strapping her into the straitjacket, one man got his nose broken. Doreen flailed at the men and at invisible demons, screaming, "Holy Mary, Mother of God!"

And Sheila never saw her again.

"What happened to her?" Willis asked.

Nora shivered, pressing closer to him. It felt as if it might snow at any moment. "Granny didn't say. But, like I told you, there's more than one kind of wedding story."

Willis smiled down, an indulgent sparkle in his eyes. He stared as if he were under her spell, and it made her neck tingle.

"If that's your way of telling me you really want to elope, you know I'll say yes," he said after a while. "Anything for you, Nora."

"Thank you, Willis."

"Only, you'll have to be the one to break this news to your family."

"I know," Nora said.

Jim and Mary Keating were playing Scrabble by the fire while Sheila dozed in her chair. Mary had put on an old Dean Martin record, Jim had mixed two big Manhattans, and the fire warmed Mary's feet.

"Doesn't it seem colder than usual for October?" she asked.

"There was frost on the docks this morning," Jim said. "It's your turn." When he was concentrating extra hard, he had the nervous habit of twirling the hair above his left ear. Watching him do it now, Mary knew he had a good word ready. She laid down her pieces, spelling out "chimp."

"That's an abbreviation," Jim said, frowning.

"I didn't say anything when you used 'Rome' before, and that's not allowed."

"You're right," Jim agreed, taking his turn. He spelled "quack" on a triple-word score.

"How about that," Mary said, admiringly.

Jim nodded, pleased. Sheila let out a loud snore. Mary watched while Jim leaned over to pull Sheila's blanket back up her chin. "Frost on the docks in October," he said again. "Maybe we should move to Florida."

"And retire," Mary said, thinking the idea sounded best on a chilly night, that it would seem daunting in the light of day: to leave all the people they loved just for the sake of warm weather and workless days.

"It's a dilemma, all right," he said, seeming to read her mind.

At the sound of the front bell, they looked at each other. It was past nine o'clock at night. "Who could that be?" Mary asked, starting to rise. But Jim motioned her to stay put.

He returned a moment later with Nora. When she saw Nora's nervous expression, Mary felt her heart quicken. It had to be bad news.

"Is it Willis?" Mary asked, touching her chest. "Has he . . ." *Left you?* would have completed the sentence.

"He's fine," Nora said, leaning over to kiss Mary. She moved toward Sheila, but she was asleep. "Everything is great. I just have something to tell you."

"Here, darling," Jim said, pushing Nora into his chair by the fire. He settled on the sofa, his drink in hand, as if he sensed he was going to need it. Mary sipped her own Manhattan. Nora took a deep breath.

"Willis and I are going to elope," she said.

Mary stared at her. "Don't you want a wedding?"

"We think it makes more sense, at our age, to do it small."

"Elope? You mean cross the state line?" Jim asked, trying to get it through his head. "That's what teenagers do."

Nora laughed. "No. In our own apartment, with just us and a judge."

Mary caught the look on Jim's face. Nora had just cut him to the quick. He had been looking forward to the ceremony, to walking Nora down the aisle, ever since she'd told him there would be a wedding.

"Aren't you stealing your own thunder?" he asked thickly. "Announcing your secret wedding to your parents?"

"Try to understand," Nora said. "Maybe I used to care about a big wedding, but I don't now. You gave Cass and Bonnie beautiful big weddings, and that was perfect for them. Please, let me do this my way. All I want is to be with Willis."

"Sweetheart, whatever makes you happy," Mary said. The truth was, she felt choked up herself. Nora's decision disappointed her, but the main thing was for Nora and Willis to be together.

"Thank you, Mother," Nora said, reaching for Mary's hand. Mary squeezed back, holding on a few seconds longer.

Jim nodded grudgingly. "I don't understand it, but I'll go along with what you want."

"Is it Willis's idea, dear?" Mary asked. "Is he uncomfortable around us?"

"Nope," Jim said, before Nora could answer. "It's Nora's. Am I right?"

"Yes," Nora said, amazing Mary. Now, how had Jim known that? A long look of affection passed between Nora and her father, proving to Mary, once again, that she shouldn't try predicting anything Jim might do.

"He's a family man, Willis," Jim said. "I'll bet he tried talking you out of this."

"He did," Nora said.

Jim nodded, smiling that handsome crooked smile of his. "I could tell right off the bat. He's a good man."

"Takes one to know one," Nora said.

"Well," Jim said, seeming to make up his mind. "You have my blessing. I'm not happy about it, but I'll go along with you."

"You will?" Mary asked, frowning.

"Mary, she's a grown woman," he said crossly. The smile disappeared for a minute, then came back. He shined it straight on Mary, and she felt the heat rise in her neck. "Give her your blessing," he urged.

"If your father can give you his, I can give you mine," Mary said.

"Thanks, Mother," Nora said, a sentimental smile on her face.

Mary wondered how Cass and Bonnie would take this news. She wouldn't want to be the one to break it to them. Or to Sheila. Mary glanced at Jim's mother, sleeping with her mouth open, emitting little snores.

"Granny might feel bad about this," Mary said.

"I think it's for the best," Sheila said, opening her eyes for just a moment. Mary, Jim, and Nora watched as she pulled the blanket higher, wriggled into a more comfortable position, looked them each in the eye, and went back to sleep.

"Well," Mary said, "I guess that's that."

18

T.J. was hot and heavy with Alison, that was for sure, and it made Belinda sick to see how he treated her, like she was a poor, fragile waif. Alison would put on a big act, whispering to T.J. in school and on the bus, with fawn eyes. If Alison could fake crying, Belinda would bet she'd do it.

"What is Alison's problem?" Belinda exploded to Emma one afternoon. They were slouched on the couch in Emma's rec room, watching "Another World." This was Aunt Bonnie's favorite soap, and now it was Emma's. Belinda couldn't get into it, but she didn't feel like starting her homework yet.

"Alison McCabe? Your future sister-in-law? Maybe they can have a double wedding with Aunt Nora and Willis."

"Don't even joke, Emma."

"Do we get to call him 'Uncle Willis' after they get married? I like him, don't you?"

"I'm serious. What is Alison's problem?"

"I'd say she has chronic VR. On the rag

every day of the month."

Belinda chuckled. VR was their mothers', and now their, secret word for "period." Translation: Virginia River. Secret translation: Vagina River.

"You're supposed to be happy when you're in love, like Willis and Aunt Nora," Belinda said, "but T.J. isn't. He and Alison always look so tragic."

"Maybe they think that's romantic, like Romeo and Juliet. What's the word? You know the one I mean."

"Star-crossed?"

"God, I love that word," Emma said. "Star-crossed. I only hope I'll be it someday."

"Alison's cross-eyed, not star-crossed," Belinda said.

"Actually, she's gorgeous. Hate to tell you, Bel. T.J.'s got the horntoads for her. That's all the explanation you need."

"He never says anything at home except 'Is it for me?' when the phone rings. He hardly gives Josie the time of day anymore."

"Hero worship deluxe," Emma said flatly. "Well, Josie can kiss him goodbye. He's got himself a real woman now, and she will just have to adjust."

"I feel bad for her."

"Yeah, sure," Emma said, punching Belinda's arm. "You're just hot for her speech teacher. Sock it to me, Zacharoonie."

Belinda blushed, because Emma was absolutely, one-hundred-percent, nail-on-the-head right. Zach was totally cute, and he actually wanted Belinda there when he taught Josie. He said they could practice on each other. "I just want to learn to sign so I won't get caught talking in study hall. I'll teach you when I learn more."

"I want *Zach* to teach me," Emma said, kissing the air. "Oh, Zach, baby, teach me how to use my hands."

"It's not like that," Belinda said, blushing harder.

Sean rushed in, all out of breath. He stood in the doorway looking worse than Alison and T.J.

"Look who's here, straight from the altar of Satan," Emma said. "The Bridegroom of Cruella. Sacrificed any kittens today?"

"Shut up, scuzface," Sean said. "Where's Mom?"

"Having an orgy," Emma said. "She invited about a thousand peanut M&M's over, and she's having her way with them. Eating them out."

"I was at the arcade, and I just saw Willis, all dressed in a fucking tuxedo. He says he and Aunt Nora are getting married today. He was on his way to pick up their rings."

"You're kidding! Mom!" Emma yelled. She tore out of the room, and Belinda followed her. They found Aunt Bonnie in the kitchen, ironing and watching "Another World."

"Mom, did you know Aunt Nora and Willis are getting married today?" Emma asked accusatorily, her hands on her hips.

"Yes, honey. Aunt Nora wanted a very small wedding, just her and Willis and a justice of the peace at Nora's apartment." She shrugged, shaking her head. "Belinda, your mom knows about it, too. We think it rots, but what can we do?"

"This is outrageous!" Emma yelled. "A family wedding, and we're not even invited?"

"Remember, sweetheart — Nora and Willis are in their forties, and it's Willis's second marriage. Aunt Nora just felt this would be more . . . appropriate."

"Fuck appropriate," Emma said, storming from the kitchen. As soon as she was out of Aunt Bonnie's sight, Belinda clutched Emma's forearm.

"We're crashing the wedding," Belinda said.

"Yes!" Emma said.

They raced upstairs to Emma's room. Emma pawed through her closet, throwing clothes all over. She emerged with last year's spring-dance dress and her standard family-party red satin skirt.

"Pick," Emma said.

"This one," Belinda said, reaching for the strapless lavender dress.

"Ravishing."

They packed the dresses and Emma's best shoes in a grocery bag and left the house, telling Bonnie that they were going to ride over to Belinda's on their bikes. Then they took off down the long hill to the harbor. Icy wind stung Belinda's cheeks, and it wasn't even winter yet. She could practically feel her nose turning red. She'd look really great in Emma's sexy dress with a bright Rudolph nose.

Now that she was halfway to Aunt Nora's, riding as fast as she could, Belinda had second thoughts. If Aunt Nora had wanted them there, she would have invited them. She wondered if her mother's feelings were hurt. Everyone in the family had liked Willis right away, and Belinda had heard her parents talking about how good he was for Nora. But what kind of man would want to marry her and not invite the rest of the family?

Belinda passed Emma on the straightaway. She wanted to see if Emma's nose was red, but she was moving too fast. She wheeled into the Benson's Mill parking lot and pedaled into a deserted carport.

"What a perfect dressing room," Emma said, looking around approvingly. Naturally, *her* nose was only a little pink, not flaming. She whipped the clothes out of the bag, and she and Belinda stripped.

"This is colder than the girls' locker room," Belinda said, her teeth chattering.

"I know! What kind of luxury condo doesn't heat its garages?" Emma said. "Chintzy."

Belinda turned so that Emma could zip her up. She had goosebumps across her shoulders, and she couldn't stop shivering. "What time do you think the wedding is?"

"I don't know," Emma said. "I didn't see Willis's car when we came in."

Belinda pulled on her jacket. She ran to Aunt Nora's carport and back. "Just one car. That gives us time to get a wedding present." Her eyes roved the garage area.

"I didn't bring any money," Emma said. "Besides, we don't know when Willis might get here."

"We have to find something. Something right around here should be perfect." Her eyes down, Belinda covered the pavement. Some pennies, a few flip-tops, a battered hubcap. In the corner of the parking lot, someone had abandoned a lobster pot.

"Oh, look, a lovely coffee table," Emma said, doing her New York summer-person imitation. "Such a nice reminder of our New England vacation."

"Kindling," Belinda said. She dragged it into the carport/dressing room and used a rock to break the brittle wood slats into small pieces. Lots of Benson's Mill residents had firewood piled in their carports, but Aunt Nora never remembered to buy any. Belinda and Emma darted in and out of the neighbors' carports, swiping a log from each pile.

"Six logs and a bag of kindling," Belinda said.

"They can have their first married fuck in front of a roaring fire. You're so romantic, Bel."

"Thanks, Em."

They rang Aunt Nora's buzzer.

"What if she doesn't let us in?" Belinda asked, balancing three big logs under her chin.

"Leave it to me."

"Yes? Who is it?" crackled Aunt Nora's voice over the intercom.

"Flowers," Emma said, disguising her voice like a delivery boy.

The buzzer sounded, and the cousins pushed open the door. They climbed the five flights, bowing under the weight of the firewood.

"I can't believe we're doing this," Belinda said. She felt lightheaded, as though she might start laughing and not be able to stop. She had the terrible feeling they were making a mistake, that Aunt Nora was going to be furious at them.

They got to her floor, opened the fire door, and there she was in the hallway, her red hair curled and tumbling onto the shoulders of a gorgeous low-cut white lace gown.

"Oh, my God," Aunt Nora said.

"Aunt Nora, you look so beautiful," Emma said. "Doesn't she, Bel?"

"You do, you look incredible," Belinda said, afraid she would drop the wood.

"I'm sorry we faked being florists. Can we put this wood in your apartment before we die?" Emma staggered through the door and laid the logs on the raised brick hearth. Belinda stacked the wood in the fireplace.

"We wanted to give you a fire for your wedding," Belinda said. "May your love always burn bright."

"And may your heart always burn whenever you think of Willis," Emma said.

Aunt Nora laughed, and so did Belinda, but Emma didn't quite get what she'd said. "Willis told Sean you're getting married, and Sean told us, and we had to come," Emma said. "You can kick us out if you want."

"God, I'm glad you're here," Aunt Nora said, holding her arms open so they'd give her a hug. "I am so nervous, I'm about to start smoking again. Eloping sounds romantic, but it's been terrible so far. I'm all alone, and I can't even call your mothers because I'm ashamed of uninviting them. I was bridesmaid at both their weddings, and I didn't even invite them to mine."

"We're here now," Emma said, patting Aunt Nora's hand, beautifully manicured with shell-pink nail extensions. "We'll be your bridesmaids."

The three of them sat on the sofa, leafing through bridal magazines. Belinda saw about fifty dresses she'd like to wear to her wedding. Every picture of a groom wearing glasses made her think of Zach.

The doorbell rang, and Aunt Nora jumped. "They're here, Willis and Judge Garrity."

"Take a deep breath," Emma advised. "Pinch your cheeks — you're a little pale."

Nora went to the kitchen. Her satin-toed shoe snagged on the carpet, and she nearly tripped. Belinda caught her elbow.

"Thank you, Belinda. Thank heavens you're here."

"We're your family," Belinda said.

Aunt Nora opened the refrigerator door. Her hands shook as she removed a pristine white box. She opened the lid, ruffled back the green tissue paper, and took out a bouquet of white roses. Aunt Nora pressed them to her nose, and then, almost as an afterthought, offered them to Belinda to smell. Thinking of Aunt Nora buying her own bouquet all by herself, storing it in her refrigerator, alongside the orange juice and coffee beans, made Belinda's throat tighten up.

"I should have flowers for you and Emma," Aunt Nora said absently, examining her bouquet, as if she were considering splitting it into three.

"That's okay, Aunt Nora," Belinda said quietly, to calm her down. You could see she wasn't getting nearly enough air.

Emma answered the door. Willis's face lit up when he saw Belinda and Emma. He didn't say, but suddenly Belinda knew it had been Aunt Nora's idea, not Willis's, to elope. Belinda stood extra close to Aunt Nora, because Aunt Nora had a long way to go in the love department, and she needed support. Belinda beckoned Emma to stand on Nora's other side.

Willis looked tall and elegant in his tux. Aunt Nora walked toward him, taking small steps, the way a bride walks down the aisle. She and Willis stood perfectly still, staring into each other's eyes. Belinda and Emma moved to one side, watching.

"My Nora," Willis said.

Then, as if she had just remembered, Aunt Nora fumbled her bouquet, freeing up one rose. She took a hat pin out of her sleeve and started to pin the rose on Willis's lapel, but Emma tapped her back.

"That's a job for the best man," Emma said. Belinda doubted Emma had ever pinned a flower on a man before, but she managed to do it without sticking Willis.

Judge Garrity, a white-haired friend of her grandparents, cleared his throat. "Where would you like to stand, Nora?" he asked.

"By the window," she said.

Everyone moved across the living room to the big picture window overlooking Mount Hope harbor. It was dark out, and the living-room lamps cast cloudy brown reflections on the glass.

"We need candlelight," Belinda whispered in Aunt Nora's ear, and Aunt Nora nodded.

"It gets dark so early now," Emma said, to make conversation.

Belinda found matches on the mantelpiece, and she lit two tall white candles in crystal candlesticks. She handed one to Emma, and they moved around the room lighting all the candles.

Through the window, you could see all the harbor lights. There was Lobsterville and the wharf twinkling at the right, and Minturn

Ledge Light, its beam piercing the sky, at the left. Except for the chapel where her parents had gotten married, Belinda thought this was the best place anyone could have a wedding.

Judge Garrity began the ceremony with the old words, "We are gathered here to celebrate . . ."

Belinda tried to listen, but she was too busy gathering everyone together in her mind, all the people who should have been there to celebrate Aunt Nora's wedding: her parents, T.J., Josie, Emma's parents, Sean, their grandparents, and Great-granny Sheila.

Belinda had just about finished in time to hear Judge Garrity say, "I now pronounce you husband and wife. You may kiss the bride."

Willis took Aunt Nora's head in his hands, tilted her face so it glowed in the candlelight and from all the love Aunt Nora had inside, and he kissed her. Belinda had never been to a wedding before, and she didn't understand why such a happy occasion would make her feel so choked up.

Then Aunt Nora and Willis turned to face Belinda, Emma, and the judge, and from their great smiles and the way they opened their arms, you'd think they were ready to greet a hundred people.

"Can we call you 'Uncle Willis' now?" Emma asked.

"I'd love that," he said.

"Oh, you girls," Aunt Nora said. "Surprising me like this. You're exactly like your mothers."

"We know," Belinda and Emma said at the exact same time.

19

"Don't you wish we'd thought of it?" Bonnie asked, the day after Nora's wedding. Reaching into the tank, she grabbed a small lobster. She weighed it on the overhead scale, then threw it into a crate full of seaweed with fourteen other lobsters.

"Our own sister gets married," Cass said, "and it takes our daughters to crash the wedding. God, I'm proud of them."

"If you start thinking about it, it's depressing," Bonnie said, holding her hand over the tank's circulation jet. Cold salt water bubbled through her fingers. She watched Cass, dressed in yellow oilskin overalls, a red plaid jacket, and her Red Sox cap, throw lobsters into a crate marked "Wickenden Tavern."

"What's depressing? They're thirteen, and they're wild. We couldn't hold them back if we tried. So let's just be glad they decided to crash their aunt's wedding instead of hitch-hiking to Seattle."

"I'm talking about *us*. Middle-aged suburbanites."

Cass squealed. She dropped the lobster she was holding and made an exorcism cross with her index fingers. "Say you're sorry!" she said. "It's a well-known fact that once you start thinking you are something, you become it."

"Alewives Park, Cass. Forty years old."

"State of mind, Bonnie. Once you start thinking of yourself as a middle-aged suburbanite, you wind up spending entire days going to grocery stores in search of the best buy on coffee filters."

"It did cross my mind to crash Nora's wedding," Bonnie said. "But I didn't feel like stopping what I was doing."

"Oh, dear. Do I want to know what that was?" Cass asked, her voice sinking.

"Ironing. While watching a soap opera."

Cass resumed weighing lobsters. "That's just considerate," she said. "We were specifically uninvited to Nora's wedding. First of all, I wouldn't have given her the satisfaction of crashing her wedding."

"Are you mad at her?"

"Furious. But still. It not only crossed my mind to crash it, I couldn't think of anything else all day: the fact that she was getting married and no one from the family would be there. I planned what I was going to wear to crash it, what clever reason I was going to give for showing up. Luckily, I had to work, then Zach came over."

"That makes me feel a little better," Bonnie said, but it didn't. She watched Cass sort the lobsters. Cass in her oversized work clothes managed somehow to look more feminine and vulnerable than she did in a dress. Yet Bonnie was sure that that morning Cass had just thrown on whatever was most practical and comfortable. Bonnie, who spent an hour every morning dressing and making up, saw Cass's careless style as a metaphor for why Cass didn't feel like a suburban matron and Bonnie did.

"No, it doesn't make me feel better," Bonnie blurted out.

Cass looked up, surprised. "What's wrong?"

"You don't see the difference between you not crashing Nora's wedding because of work and waiting for Josie's speech teacher, and me not crashing because of ironing and a soap opera?"

"Look, we weren't invited. Let it go."

"I am in a rut," Bonnie said.

"I think you have a nice life."

"It's *very* nice. But all of a sudden it's scaring me."

"Just because you didn't crash Nora's wedding?"

Josie had been talking to Barbie, walking her up and down the wooden stairs. Now she dropped the doll and started making hand signs in the air. Cass stopped working for a minute to watch.

"What's she saying?" Bonnie asked.

"I have no idea. So far I know about ten words," Cass said. "All our names, 'I love you,' 'good night,' 'tell me what happened,' 'stop that.' The basics."

"I'm impressed," Bonnie said, watching Josie resume playing, totally involved with her doll.

"She's doing better," Cass said, watching Josie. "I'm terrified, of course, because she's way ahead of me. Zach says she picks up quickly because the signs fill a void. I don't need it, so I don't learn as fast."

"But you'll learn, right?"

"Zach says it doesn't work that way. I'll learn the rudiments, but Josie will be fluent. It'll be the difference between learning French in high school and being born in Paris."

"Does it help with her tantrums?"

"She has rough spells. It's a bad combination, a temper and a speech problem."

"Temper runs in the family," Bonnie said. "Have you and Dad made up?"

Cass shook her head, not taking her eyes off Josie. "I know he's old-fashioned, set in his ways, all that. But you didn't hear him call handicapped people freakish right in the middle of a conversation about Josie."

"Every time I think I'm having a bad day, I should come see you," Bonnie said. She pretended to dry her hands, head for the door. "Will you excuse me while I go home to my lovely suburban rut?"

Cass laughed. She sealed the Wickenden crate and kicked it toward the door. Then she started counting a new batch of lobsters, for the Wellsweep Restaurant.

"I've done some research," Bonnie said, trying to sound nonchalant.

"Oh?"

"That brownie idea you had."

"Good!" Cass said. She opened her mouth to say more, but she must have sensed Bonnie's hesitancy.

"Well, lots of places have baskets by their cash registers, full of individually wrapped brownies, cookies, stuff like that."

"I know, a dollar twenty-five for a cranberry muffin," Cass said. "I'm telling you, you'll rake it in."

"Christmas craft shows are coming up," Bonnie said. "I'm thinking about bringing a basket to one in Peacedale."

The telephone rang twice — a signal from upstairs to pick up in the tank room. Cass answered. She whooped once, then stayed on another minute.

"Billy," she said when she came back. "He's been at the boatyard all week, getting the boat ready. He wants to launch her this afternoon."

"Great!" Bonnie said, oddly let down. She was so used to helping Cass: soothing her, giving her support, listening to her talk about Josie. Sometimes Bonnie thought that she gave so smoothly, her sisters didn't realize how much she needed back.

But Cass came around the tank, shook the water off her hands, and gave Bonnie a bone-squeezing handshake. "Sure, a boat launch is exciting," Cass said, shaking Bonnie's whole arm. "But we're talking business launch here. I can say I was there on the ground floor."

"Thanks, Cass," Bonnie said, genuinely touched.

"And there's nowhere to go but up, sistah. Stah. *Star*." Cass stopped midway. "Well, look who's here! Speak of the bride . . . What's this? No honeymoon?"

Nora stepped into the tank room, sheepish, gazing at her sisters through newly feathered bangs. "We're going to Savannah for two weeks in the spring; neither one of us could really get away from work now. Are you two mad?"

"Mad? Just because you didn't invite us to

your wedding? Are we mad, Cass?"

"Oh, nothing the ritual dunking of the bride won't cure." Cass swept magnanimously toward Nora, her arms extended.

"What ritual?" Nora asked, pulling back as first Cass, then Bonnie hugged her.

"It's a little tradition, dates back to the early days of Mount Hope, sort of a play on the love-and-war theme." Bonnie pulled her toward the lobster tank. Nora, elegant in cranberry cashmere, dug in her heels.

"Yeah, we love you, but this is war. You don't ask your sisters to your wedding, you get dunked," Cass said.

"Please, guys," Nora said, laughing, then moving forward, as if she'd decided to give in. "Let me take off this sweater, will you? It cost a fortune. God, I just had my hair done yesterday . . ."

Suddenly, Cass stopped fooling around. She reached for Nora, pulled her close in a big hug. Bonnie looked on, surprised to feel tears in her eyes.

"I'm so happy for you," Cass said.

"Thank you, both of you," Nora said, as Bonnie moved forward.

"Tell us about it," Cass said. "Belinda said you were beautiful."

"They are so terrific, those girls," Nora said. "They made me realize how much I wish you two had been there."

"We wish that, too," Cass said. "But . . ."

"But . . ." Bonnie said. She started to cry, realizing how hurt she had felt. Wiping away tears, she caught Cass doing the same thing. Looking into each other's eyes, they started to laugh. Nora joined in, sounding sheepish.

"I was a jerk," Nora said.

Instead of contradicting her, Cass and Bonnie hugged her harder. Then Cass found herself checking her watch. "I'd better go. Billy's waiting."

"Who's going to the boat?" Bonnie asked Cass.

"Me and Josie, I guess. There's no way I'd ever drag T.J. away from the phone this time of day, and Belinda's studying for a test."

"Leave Josie with me," Bonnie offered.

"Are you sure?" Josie was playing quietly on the stairs, trying to get Barbie to surf on the back of a sand crab that had escaped from a tank.

Bonnie closed one eye as she figured out her schedule. "Sure. I have to pick up the kids at six. Does that give you enough time?"

"Definitely. I have to be home to feed mine before then."

"Go launch."

"Launch?" Nora asked.

"Billy's boat," Cass said, and Bonnie saw

she could barely hold in her pride. "Today's the day."

"Wow," Nora said, shaking her head. "I was so wrapped up in me and Willis, I had no idea Billy was even close. I thought maybe next season . . ."

"See?" Cass said, edging for the door. "That's the thing about eloping. You miss all those family-get-together news highlights like boat launches, speech therapists, Mom's sore back, Dad's retirement plans . . ."

"Stop," Nora said, holding up her hand. "You'll make me feel worse."

"Worse? I was trying to make you feel better," Cass said, blowing a kiss, disappearing out the door.

20

Cass walked along the waterfront from Keating's Wharf to the Mount Hope Boatyard. She knew Billy had a surprise planned because he'd kept her from visiting the boat the last few times she'd asked. Cass had seen her three weeks ago: out of the water, in the cradle, patchy below the water line, the bottom paint scraped off. Billy had had a long way to go to make her seaworthy.

She saw the boatyard two piers away, the black spars of a windjammer silhouetted by the tawny sunset. Her pace increased as she got closer. The cradle where Billy's boat had been was empty: two weathered wooden supports standing bare in the yard. Then, hearing a whistle, she looked toward the water. Billy waved to her from the dock. "Over here," he called.

Cass ducked her head against the bitter cold and ran over. The bib of her oilskin overalls scooped the wind inside; with both hands she held it close against her chest. She caught sight of Billy's face: he had that look he'd get on her birthday and Christmas, when he knew in advance she was going to love her present. So she kept her eyes from the boat, suspended by webbing from the Travelift fifteen feet away. She made a show of holding her right hand like a blinder to her face.

"Don't look," Billy said.

"I have to." Cass sneaked a peek; she spied a white hull and cabin, red trim, glistening brass. "Wow," she said, covering her eyes again. Billy came over to her. His dark curls tossed in the wind, and his eyes held hers.

"This is it, eh?" Cass asked. "Billy Medieros's boat." She felt herself grinning so wide she thought her face would crack. From the minute she'd met him, she had thought of Billy as a sailor, and now she was going to help him launch his own boat. He slid his hand between her overalls and the wool plaid jacket; he tugged the small of her back, and she bumped his pelvis.

"Hey, Billy," she said. She had never seen him like this, so totally confident in his own power. Their marriage, the children's births . . . When the babies were born he had held them for the camera, paraded them before the relatives, but there had been a tentativeness that bordered on reserve, as if he were overwhelmed, a little unsure of himself.

No reserve here. Billy held Cass close, looked her straight on, couldn't stop smiling. Finally, he held his hand over her eyes like a blindfold. "Watch it . . . I have you . . . there's a rock," he said, leading her across the gravel-strewn yard.

He let Cass's own excitement carry her body forward, then he stopped her momentum, one hand gripping her shoulder, with a flourish. She swayed, but he held her. He took his other hand away from her eyes.

CASSANDRA
MOUNT HOPE, R.I.

"Oh, my God," she said.

"What do you think?" Billy asked.

"I can't believe it," Cass said, thinking how every girl in Mount Hope grows up wishing her sweetheart would name a boat after her, and now it had happened.

"Take her down!" Billy yelled to Pete Turner, the old guy operating the boat lift. The machinery creaked, and wind zinged through the elaborate webbing as Pete lowered the swinging boat into the choppy water. She rocked at her berth as the webbing was disengaged and the yard guys made her fast to the dock.

"Who are those men on our boat?" she

340

asked proprietarily.

"Hang on," Billy said. "I'll be right back."

Cass watched him run across the yard to his truck. He opened the driver's door and disappeared inside, searching for something on the floor.

"A big day for Billy," Pete Turner said, climbing down from the lift. "He's been like a little kid, waiting for this."

"You're a boat owner, Pete," Cass said. "You know how it feels."

"I sure do. They say the two happiest days in a man's life are the day he buys his boat and the day he sells it," Pete said. Pete was a grizzle-faced codger not much younger than Cass's father, and he played the role of Yankee cynic to perfection. When he retired, the Mount Hope chamber of commerce would have to train someone to take his place.

"What about the day he launches it?" Cass asked.

"That's the best of all," Pete said. "Billy stood over my shoulder, watching me paint your name on the transom. I told him I've painted ten boat names this year alone, and if he didn't like the job I was doing, here's the paintbrush."

"You did a great job."

"Well thanks, Cass," Pete said, heading into the boat shed.

Billy hurried over, a bottle of champagne in his hand.

"To break over the bow?" Cass asked.

"I thought we'd drink it first and smash the empty bottle, but someone beat us to it." He turned the uncorked bottle upside down. Bits of gold foil fell out.

"Uh-oh," Cass said. T.J. Somehow she knew, with unfailing clairvoyant certainty, that T.J. had crossed a new and extravagantly forbidden teenage threshold: drinking his father's champagne in his father's truck.

"I've been noticing all the gum wrappers," Billy said, "but I didn't think much of it. I'm going to kill the little shit. I buy champagne and it isn't even New Year's Eve, and my goddamn son drinks it."

"I don't like this," Cass said. "Stealing your truck *and* drinking? I don't like it at all."

"That's the last time I leave my keys home."

"Let me see the label," Cass said, grabbing the bottle.

"Perrier-Jouët," Billy said.

"We'll kill him," Cass said, nodding. She tapped Billy's wrist. "But we'll get him later, okay?"

Billy shrugged, his eyes sullen until he looked at his boat.

"Take me onboard?" Cass asked.

This boat had been known around Mount

Hope as a tub. George Magnano had bought her cheap in Louisiana and converted her on his own for the North Atlantic. Her steam-bent ribs gave her a round belly, and broadside waves could roll her the way they never would a deep-keeled dragger.

Cass walked through the wheelhouse, which was filled with electronic navigation equipment, a digital fishfinder, his rifle for shooting sharks, a chart table, and a framed photo of Cass and the kids.

Touched, Cass climbed down the companion ladder and crossed the compact galley. The main saloon, where the crew would eat meals and relax off-watch, had a wooden table gimbaled to stay level during the worst storms, and benches covered with scratchy brown-plaid covers.

"George left those," Billy said.

"I would never have guessed!" Cass responded.

"You don't like them?"

"Aren't they a little brown?"

"I like brown," Billy said. He sounded slightly brisk, and Cass realized that he felt so proud of every aspect of this boat, he couldn't even admit George had stuck him with some ugly seat covers.

She walked through the crew's quarters and looked into the head, and then she came to

Billy's cabin. He had hung jackets and foul-weather gear from hooks, put paperbacks and tide tables in the hanging net shelf and bedding on the bunk.

"You're ready to go?" she asked, surprised.

"I want to get fishing right away," he said. "It's been a few weeks since I've been out, and I'm afraid of falling behind. It's already November. There's not much fishing weather left."

"We have enough in the bank. I just didn't expect . . . I didn't know you were this close to launching," Cass said.

"I've been riding hard on Pete to get her in," Billy said. "Now that she's launched, I don't want her sitting idle. She's costing me too much money."

"I've gotten used to having you home at night," Cass said, moving into Billy's arms.

"It's like another life," Billy said, stroking her hair. "I don't want to get too used to it."

"No, we might never give it up."

Billy stretched out on his bunk, one arm bent behind his head. The reading light cast a warm cone of light on the pillow. "Let's break this boat in right," he said, the corners of his lips turning up.

"I only get crazy in our own bed now," Cass said, lying beside him. "No more funny stuff. Bonnie says we're middle-aged suburbanites."

"Yeah?" Billy asked, unhooking her overalls.

"Middle-aged," Cass said, kissing him. "Suburbanites."

"You on your back, me on top?" Billy asked, his tongue tracing her earlobe.

"Twice a month."

"Once in February, cause it's short."

"Like I said, no more kinky stuff," Cass said.

"And only in the dark with our socks on," Billy said, reaching up to switch off the light.

"I want to see you," Cass said, turning it back on.

With Billy unzipping her fly, Cass wriggled out of her shirt. She lay on her back, her arms folded beneath her head. Billy lowered his head to her breasts; one flick of his tongue, and she felt her nipples harden.

She reached around his back to untuck his shirt. Then she began unbuttoning it — one button at a time, taking her time, sliding her cool hands up his narrow waist, across his belly, into his dark tangle of chest hair.

Their mouths found each other, their kisses familiar and wild all at once. The bed, though large for a bunk, was cramped. A small heater blew warm air that was instantly consumed by the musty chill; Cass snuggled against Billy as he pulled both their pants down to their knees. Cass's boots kept hers from sliding off. Billy leaned down, to ease her boots off, but Cass stopped him.

"Let's not get all the way undressed," Cass said, breathless.

"You cold?" Billy asked.

"Yes, but that's not why. It's more exciting, like we're in a hurry this way."

"Yeah," Billy said, his hand closing over Cass's wrist as she freed his hard dick, pushed it into the purple wetness between her legs.

"Cause we are," Cass said. "In a hurry."

Now he tried to touch her, to rub her with his fingers, but she pushed his hand away, behind her, so it rested on her back. She wanted to lie smack against his body, with no space between them. He understood; with one hand on the small of her back, the other between her shoulder blades, he held her close.

"Like that?"

"Tighter," she said.

They were breathing hard now, lying sideways, her leg slung over his hips, the toe of her boot wedged under his ass. They thrust in a rough rhythm, their pelvises slapping, like water hitting the hull.

She hung on to her husband, feeling him hard against and inside her; when he started to hold his breath, his movements became

346

more urgent, and she knew he was about to come. When he was very close, when she felt the rhythm change, she reached down between their legs, to touch the spot where his penis entered her body.

She grasped him for one final, shuddering second. Then, when he lay still, she brought her fingers, salty with their juices, to his mouth, and trailed them across his lips.

"You," Billy said.

"No, us."

"I mean, it's your turn." Still breathing hard, he reached down, to touch her. Again, she pushed his hand away.

"That's not what I want right now," she said, gazing into his eyes.

"Then what? What do you want?"

"I have it." With her arms around his neck, she gave him a long kiss, tasting the salt on his tongue. "What I want. Right here. I want you."

"I think he's going to marry her," came Alison's whispery voice over the phone.

"Really? Shit," T.J. said, lying in his bed, the receiver clamped to his ear.

"He hasn't exactly said so, but when he took me out to dinner, he was telling me how much I'm going to like her, how much we have in common. He said she can't wait to play me in tennis. Can you believe that?"

"He's gotta be kidding."

"There is no way I'll ever visit him if she's there."

"No way. He's crazy."

"His condo is actually pretty nice. The bathroom's black marble, and it has a TV and a sound system. And a Jacuzzi."

"He has his own Jacuzzi?" T.J. said. He imagined sitting in a black marble Jacuzzi with Alison.

"It's big enough for two," she said.

"Yeah?"

"He says he's taking me to Florida for Christmas, but there's no way if she's going."

"Florida for Christmas?" T.J. asked, sitting a little straighter. This was the first he'd heard of it.

"Yeah. My parents own a condo in Florida. They're going to have to sell it, but until the divorce my father gets it for Christmas and my mother and I get it for February vacation."

"You think he's probably going to take her to Florida for Christmas? His girlfriend, I mean?"

"I wouldn't be surprised. I think she actually lives with him up here, there's so much of her stuff around. She probably just gets out when I come over."

"Then I definitely wouldn't go to Florida,"

T.J. said. The idea of being apart from Alison for as long as she would be in Florida was too terrible to imagine. "I think it would be a lousy idea, you going to Florida. He'd probably expect you to play tennis with her and all."

Alison didn't reply. "Alison?" he said.

He heard the sharp breath, and he knew she was crying. "Alison? Alison, don't cry."

"We used to go," she whispered. "All of us, every Christmas."

"You did?" T.J. couldn't imagine spending Christmas in Florida — sand instead of snow, the water summer-blue instead of choppy gunmetal-gray.

"Yeah." She couldn't talk. T.J. hated it when she cried on the phone. He wanted to hold her, to kiss her tears away. But it made him feel bad, that she was crying so hard about not going to Florida this year. He knew she hated her parents' divorce, that she wanted them all together, especially at Christmas. But how could she stand the idea of spending so much time away from him?

"I'm coming over," he said. "Just hang on. Look out your window in twenty minutes. Fifteen."

"Okay," she whispered through her tears.

T.J. ran down the stairs, grabbed his coat. Belinda sat at the kitchen table, books and

349

papers all over the place. "Where are you going?" she asked.

"Nowhere," he said, pulling on his gloves.

Just then, the back door opened and Josie raced in. Shit, that meant his mother was home. Now he'd have to invent some bogus emergency-study story. Josie stood in front of him, saying his name over and over in sign language.

"Not now, okay Joze?" he asked.

His parents walked in together, their faces solemn.

"Daddy, you're home early!" Belinda said.

"Sweetheart, will you take Josie upstairs for a few minutes?" his father asked.

"Sure," Belinda said. Her face lit up as she glanced from her father to T.J., smelling blood. T.J. wondered what he was about to be busted for; all he could think of was getting to Alison.

Josie stood right in front of T.J., moving her hands insistently, and Belinda had to practically drag her away, making signs of her own.

"Do we all have to learn that?" T.J. asked, pointing after his sisters.

"Sit down," his father said.

T.J. sat at the table. His mother had been standing by the door, her back to the wall, but now she came forward. She had a very serious look on her face as she brought something from behind her back.

"What's that?" T.J. asked, face-to-face with the champagne bottle he and Alison had drained the last time he'd taken the truck. Shit! He'd meant to throw it into the state park Dumpster, but Alison had said she wanted it for a souvenir.

"What does it look like?" his father asked.

"Like a wine bottle."

"Yeah, how was it?" his father asked.

"What do you mean?" T.J.'s heart was pounding. He didn't care about the inquisition. He'd deny he drank it, and what were they going to do? Fingerprint the bottle? But he couldn't stand thinking of Alison crying at her window, imagining he'd forgotten about her.

His father slammed the bottle down so hard, Belinda's history book bounced off the table. "You've been driving around in my truck, haven't you?" he yelled. "You drank this whole bottle of champagne, and then you got behind the wheel?"

"I did not!" T.J. slapped his hands on the table. He knew he sounded frantic. He hoped his parents took it for being wrongly accused. He could just see Alison, her face pressed against the glass, looking down the dark driveway.

"Don't lie, T.J.," his mother said. She was trying to sound calm, but she had a little shake in her voice.

"I don't even have my license! How could I drive your truck?" He looked back and forth between his parents, realizing how stupid he sounded. They'd both taught him to drive.

"I wouldn't drive alone without a license," he said. "And I definitely wouldn't drink if I did. Drunk driving is totally wrong."

"That's true," Cass said. "I'm glad to hear you say that."

"You know how many kids get killed every year drinking and driving?" his father asked, a little less insane.

"A lot," T.J. said, nodding vigorously. "They show us movies at school, worse than horror movies, with smashed cars and kids all decapitated and mangled. Believe me, I would *never* drink and drive," he said, remembering how he'd felt after the champagne, how he'd had to close one eye just to drive straight. How he'd pulled over to the side for Alison to throw up, and then, while he was helping her back into the truck, how he'd thrown up all over his own shoes. Thank God Alison didn't even remember.

"We saw it happen," his mother said. "Remember Mark Costello, Billy?"

"Mark Costello was in our class," his father

said, as if T.J. hadn't heard the story ten times before. But T.J. knew he had to listen patiently if he was ever going to convince his parents he was innocent and make it over to Alison's before she did something desperate.

"Mark and his girlfriend Sally," his dad started.

"Sally Sheffield," his mom supplied.

"Right. Mark and Sally came to our senior prom in his new Chevy Nova. Graduation present from his parents. Mark was going to go to Notre Dame, football scholarship. He was a big guy, thought he could hold his liquor. He had a bottle with him, offered it to all his friends."

"Sally had one, too," his mom said. "Vodka. She said no one would ever know we were drinking because it didn't have any smell. I took a sip."

"You did?" T.J. asked, wondering if it would be too much to add "Gee."

"Anyway, Mark kept drinking all through the prom," his dad said. "No one thought he was drunk. He and Sally danced every dance, they stopped at every table and talked to their friends. After graduation a lot of us were going to work, others to college, so we wouldn't be seeing each other so much anymore. He offered everyone hits from his bottle."

"What happened?" T.J. asked.

"We all decided to head for the lighthouse, to look at the stars," his dad said.

"To park," his mom said.

"Anyway, Mark and Sally took off in the Nova, and your mom and I were right behind them in my Camaro. Mark's car was weaving down the road, and I said to your mom, 'They're going to crash.' And they did. We were at the stoplight at Memorial Highway and Overlook Road, and they went straight through the red light into a truck."

"They died?" T.J. asked.

"Yeah," his dad said. "They died."

"It was the worst thing I ever saw," his mom said. "You know that movie you've seen at school? It was worse than that. We were right behind them, we tried to help them . . ."

"What did you see?" T.J. asked, both curious and squeamish.

His mom just shook her head.

"That sounds awful," T.J. said. "Wow. That's horrible. You must have hated seeing that — no wonder you never drink and drive." He hoped his parents didn't know exactly to the ounce what they had in the cupboards downstairs.

"Glad you see it that way, Teej," his dad said.

"I'm sorry about your wine getting stolen,"

he said. "But can I go now? I have a wicked important math test tomorrow, and I have to study with Alison."

"No, you're grounded," his mom said.

"*What!* You can't be *serious*, I didn't *do* anything! She's expecting me, you have to let me *go*."

"You're grounded," his dad said.

T.J. thought his head was going to explode. Alison . . .

"Call Alison and tell her you can't make it," his mom said, and at that moment T.J. hated her so much, he couldn't stand it. "Make it quick, though. No phone, no going out, no *nothing* for two weeks. Got that, T.J.?"

T.J. couldn't open his mouth, he felt so furious.

"Just *think* about that, grounded for *two weeks*, the next time you feel the urge to drink a little champagne and take a spin. No *way* are you getting killed like Mark and Sally. I don't care if you hate me, but that's not going to happen," his mom yelled, working herself up. "And if you had Alison in that truck with you, you'd better have been wearing a condom."

T.J. had never seen her so mad. He left the kitchen, stomped upstairs. His hand shook, lifting the receiver to call Alison. You could tell, when his parents told the story of

Mark and Sally, that they'd been his age once. They kept giving each other love looks that they'd tried to disguise with super-stern lecture frowns. T.J. thought of that as he dialed Alison's number.

"Hello?" she answered, her voice so small and trembly T.J. thought his heart would break.

"My parents are such assholes," he said. "I'm grounded."

"*Why?*" she asked.

"Some stupid reason," he said. "It doesn't matter. They hate me."

"It all goes back to your sister's accident," Alison said.

"I know. I can't even stay on now. I can't use the phone."

"Oh, T.J.," Alison said.

"I know," T.J. said.

"They're so unfair," she whispered hotly.

"My father'll be gone in a few days," T.J. whispered back. "Maybe even tomorrow. I'll be able to sneak out then."

"And there's always school."

"I never thought I'd look forward to school," T.J. said.

"I knew something had happened. I was watching for you out my window, and more than twenty minutes went by."

"You know I want to be there."

"Did they look in your wallet?" Alison whispered. "Did they find your condoms?"

"No, it wasn't that," T.J. said.

"Good," Alison said.

"I need you, Alison," he said. "I need you so much."

She giggled suddenly, a nervous burst that surprised him. "You just think you do," she said.

T.J. held the receiver, listening to her breathe, wondering if she could hear his heart pounding through the phone line. Sometimes when Alison snapped right out of her blues, went from sounding sweet to tough, T.J. would feel all turned around. He wondered if he'd ever understand what made her tick. He just sat there, listening to her breathe, until his mother knocked softly on the door, told him to hang up and get ready for dinner.

As if he could eat.

Belinda thought the lasagna was delicious, but she didn't know if she should say anything. It was as if someone had cast a spell of silence over the table. Her parents sat opposite each other, giving each other "we're doing the right thing" looks. Belinda knew her parents weren't the punishing types, that when they said "It's going to hurt me more than it hurts you," they probably meant it.

"How's school, Bel?" her father asked.

"Great, Daddy."

He winked at her. She loved having her father home. Both her parents were fun, but her mother could get pretty serious when she was home alone with Josie for too long.

"T.J., eat your dinner," her mother said.

"Not hungry."

"It's delicious," Belinda said.

"I'm not *hungry!*" T.J. said. Belinda wondered what he'd done to get grounded. She figured it had something to do with his tragic life with Alison.

"Can I be excused?" T.J. asked.

"Okay. Do your homework," Mom said.

Everyone relaxed when he left. They heard him stomping up the stairs. If Belinda had been in charge, she would have given him exactly fifteen seconds, then picked up the kitchen extension to see if he was calling Alison.

"Hang in there," her father said.

"It ain't easy," her mom said.

"Whatever he did, he deserves it," Belinda said.

"Hey, you'll be fifteen someday," her father said.

Josie banged her cast on the table. She had an angry frown on her face, and she had her new doll in a headlock.

"What?" Mom asked, crouching down to Josie's level.

"Daddy!" Josie said. Only she pronounced it "Dah-*dee*," the way people did when they were babies.

"What?" her dad asked, cutting another piece of lasagna.

"Daddy, I'm talking!" Josie was signing, "Hi, Daddy."

"Pretty dolly," her dad said. "That's a very pretty dolly."

Josie looked blank.

"Billy . . ." her mother said.

"What?" he asked, surprised.

"Listen."

"Hey, Joze," he said. "Josie-Posie. Your brother T.J. thought that up."

"Better than what he used to call *me*," Belinda said. "Bel from hell."

"That's right." Her father laughed. He cut a tiny piece of lasagna and tried to feed it to Josie.

Josie looked insulted. "*Big* girl!" she said. She was still signing "Hi, Daddy." When he didn't reply, she started with her little tantrum drumroll, "Eh, eh, eh. . . ."

"Oh, God," Belinda said. "Daddy, just say, 'Hi, Josie.' "

"You can't just have a generic conversation with her," Mom said. "She's trying to tell you something. She's not asking for lasagna."

"Sorry," her dad said, looking as if he'd been beaten.

"Give me your hand," Belinda said. Her father's palm felt like leather. She tried to form it into the signs Zach had taught her. " 'Hi, Josie.' Like that," Belinda said.

But her father pulled his hand back and began eating again. "I'm too old to learn mumbo jumbo," he said.

Her mom pushed back her chair so hard, Belinda thought it might fall over. She scraped her plate into the garbage.

"Eh, eh, eh! Eh, eh, eh!" Josie said, louder.

"Dad, it's easy," Belinda said. But she was afraid if she took his hand, he'd pull it back again.

"Easy for you, maybe," her dad said. He bent down now like her mom, something he hardly ever did, and looked Josie in the eye. "Hi, Josie. Hi, Josie," he said.

But Josie was shaking her head back and forth. "Eeeeeeeh" she screamed. *"Eeeeeeh!"*

Belinda pushed her plate away. She felt bad, but she couldn't stand when Josie got like this. She bet her mom wished they hadn't grounded T.J.; he was the only one who could get to Josie when she was this upset. Belinda looked at her mother, standing at the sink with her back to them, and her father, sitting at his place, staring at his plate, and Josie, waving her arms all over like a tiny maniacal red-faced dictator.

Belinda would have thrown her parents an apologetic glance if they'd looked at her, but they didn't. She pushed in her chair, gathered up her schoolbooks, and headed upstairs. She'd give herself half an hour break, call Emma and Todd before she started studying again. At least she wouldn't have to fight T.J. for the phone.

"You were awful to her," Cass said, staring at the bedroom ceiling.

"Cass . . ." Billy flipped onto his stomach, rustling the covers. He made a big deal of inching toward the clock, to see the dial: just past midnight. "I said I was sorry. Now let's get some sleep."

"I can't," she said, facing him.

"I shouldn't have called her sign language mumbo jumbo. Okay?"

"Why does it scare you to talk to her?"

"Don't be ridiculous," Billy said, rolling over, scrunching his pillow.

"You don't treat her like a person. You treat her like a little deaf puppy."

"What do you mean?" he asked, lifting his head to look at her.

"It's terrible for her, when she tries to tell

you something very specific, and you just ignore it. She wants to show you a sign, and you try to feed her lasagna?"

"I didn't understand."

"No kidding," Cass said. "You don't even try."

"That's bullshit, Cass. I love her."

Cass knew he loved their daughter. But she felt he was in over his head. They both were, and had been for a long time. "I think we should look into North Point," she said.

"I thought everything between you and me was great," Billy said sadly. "You seemed so happy on the boat."

Suddenly Cass felt like Josie, trying to make a point as clearly as possible, Billy seeming to listen but then replying as if he were in a different conversation. And it made her feel crazy: how could she and Billy go from being so close on the boat to this?

"You're shifting all over the place. Listen . . ." Cass began.

"*You're* the one who's shifting," Billy said. "North Point? What happened to kindergarten at Mount Hope? Ever since she lost her hearing, you've been against sign language. You didn't want her set apart from the other little kids. Now you're talking about a deaf school."

"Zach thinks she would do badly at Mount Hope."

"Some textbook expert, great. He knows better than we do?"

"I'm beginning to agree with him," Cass said.

"Her signs mean nothing to me," Billy said. "I can't understand what she's saying. How am I supposed to talk to her if I can't understand?"

Cass reached for him, hearing the fear in his voice. "I know," she said, her arms around his neck. She felt afraid of the same thing.

The next morning, Josie sat in her chair, paying careful attention to Zach. He had a big cardboard square covered with rows of circles, each a different color. She had already learned to sign "red," her favorite color, and "green," the color of her overalls.

"Very good, Josie," Zach said. "You learn fast."

Josie smiled. She liked when Zach said she learned fast. Yesterday he had said she was smart. Usually Josie felt stupid. Everyone thought she didn't understand things because she couldn't hear them, but Josie knew that wasn't always true. Sometimes she would hear words and not know what they meant.

"Now let's learn 'blue,' " Zach said.

"Blue car," Josie said, remembering the game she played with her mother.

"Blue," Zach said, signing the word. Then he said "car," signing it at the same time.

Josie tried hard to copy the way Zach moved his hands. He reached out and changed the way she was holding her thumb.

"Like that," he said, and Josie tried it his way.

"Very good!" Zach said, making Josie feel proud.

"Blue car, blue car," Josie signed over and over. She glanced at him, and then she signed "red car."

He laughed, his eyes big, as if he thought she had done something wonderful. Now he signed "green car."

Josie wished her father would realize she was smart. He talked to her like she was a baby. He didn't believe she could learn. Josie knew that, because he always said the same things to her. Like last night: he would ask about her doll, or about the food on her plate, questions he already knew the answers to. He would never try different things with her.

"Something new?" Josie said to Zach.

"You want to learn something new? Let's see. . . ."

Josie's mother would invent games like "blue car," games that felt scary at first because Josie was afraid she might make a mistake, say the words wrong, and look stupid. But no matter how bad Josie's mistakes were, her mother would keep playing the game, and the next day she'd invent another one. Zach was like that, too.

"Here's something new," Zach said. "It's a song."

"A song?" Josie asked, frowning. Belinda and T.J. played songs on their stereos. They each had favorite songs, and it made Josie feel left out. Music, when she could hear it at all, sounded harsh and tuneless to Josie. She didn't like that Zach was about to teach her something she wouldn't understand. She felt afraid she would feel stupid, and she ducked her head. Her chin began to wobble; she didn't want to cry.

Zach tapped her hand, making her look at him.

"It's fun," he said. "Don't be afraid."

Josie wanted to look away, but she didn't.

"Will you try?" he asked.

She hesitated. She didn't want to.

"Please? Just try?"

"Okay," she said in a small voice.

"Twinkle, twinkle, little star," he said out loud.

Josie understood the words "little" and "star." She sat very still, feeling dumb for knowing only two words. She could never learn a song.

Now Zach signed, "Twinkle, twinkle, little star."

Though she didn't understand the word "twinkle," Josie tried to form all the words with her hands. Each time she made a mistake, Zach would correct her. She moved her fingers slowly, with precision, wanting to get every word right. After the second time she got all the way through, she started to feel excited.

"Twinkle, twinkle, little star," she signed.

"Excellent, Josie!" Zach signed back.

She kept signing the words. After a while, she could do it on her own. It felt different from anything she had ever learned. The words were pretty, and she liked the way they went together. She pictured the sky at night, and she began to imagine what the word "twinkle" meant.

"Would you like to try some more?" Zach asked.

Josie nodded, and then she signed, "Yes."

"Okay," Zach signed. "Here we go."

The night before Billy was to leave for his first trip on his new boat, Cass slept badly. At one point she dreamed of having two husbands. One was her lover — Billy as he had been on the boat, as close to Cass as a husband could be. The other was an unbending Billy with thick, cloudy glasses, who refused to see,

366

who thought all change was bad. When she woke up, sweating, Billy had already gotten out of bed.

Hearing the shower run, she drifted in and out of sleep. The clock said four-fifteen; it was pitch-dark outside. She tried to wake up, to go downstairs and make coffee, but bed felt too delicious. Just another five minutes, she told herself, snuggling under the comforter. Her feet found the warm spot Billy had vacated.

Now he came into their room, a towel around his waist. He moved silently, dressing in jeans, a black T-shirt, and a red-plaid flannel shirt. While Cass was watching, he didn't look at her. She knew he had a mental checklist, things he had to do before heading offshore. But she worried a little; he had seemed distant since their argument a few nights earlier.

"Are you still mad?" she asked from under the covers.

"You're awake?" he said, sounding surprised.

"Slightly."

He sat on the edge of the bed, his weight making the mattress bend. "I'm not mad," he said.

"Disappointed?"

"In what?" he asked, frowning.

367

"I don't know," Cass said, thinking of her own disappointments. "In me. In our life."

He sat still for a long moment, saying nothing. "Maybe I'm disappointed in myself," he said. "For not rolling with it."

"With what?"

"Everything. Being a father. I don't know." He chuckled, making light of what he'd just said, but Cass didn't think he was kidding. He checked his watch: time to make his getaway. "Got to leave," he said, bending over to kiss her. He stroked her bed-tangled hair, kissed her ear, the warm curve of her neck, and finally her mouth.

"Have a good trip," she said, hating to have him go. She wanted to pull him under the covers, feel their bodies moving together.

"Me, too," he said, even though she hadn't said a word. Then he pulled a heavy wool sweater over his head, stepped into his shoes, and left for sea.

21

Cass worked at her desk, figuring the accounts for the early part of November while Josie stood behind her, playing hairdresser. She brushed Cass's hair with slow, gentle strokes.

"Call me Deb," Josie said.

"Okay, Deb," Cass said, knowing that Josie was making a leap of faith. Since Josie couldn't see her lips, she could only assume that Cass was playing along.

"You pretend to be Mrs. Clay."

"I will."

"Mrs. Clay, you have pretty hair."

"Thank you, Deb."

A few fishing boats tossed on their moorings. The November wind whistled through their rigging; halyards clanked, and the Minturn Ledge foghorn rumbled down the bay. She glanced out the window, wondering when Billy would get back. So far he'd been out three days on *Cassandra*'s maiden voyage. She had made an appointment for the Monday before Thanksgiving to visit North Point. She wondered how he would react.

"Two of my favorite girls." Cass looked up to see her father entering the office.

"Call me Deb," Josie said.

"Hi, Deb," he said. Cass smiled; you could tell he'd raised three daughters. He began rummaging through a file drawer. His posture was stooped as if with defeat, and he moved slowly, as if he ached.

"What are you looking for?" she asked.

"Old property-tax forms," he said.

"In the bottom drawer."

"Thank you," he said without looking up.

Cass felt frozen to her seat, lulled by Josie's playing with her hair. She stared at the window as if by sheer will she could make Billy's boat appear.

"What do you need with the property-tax forms?" Cass asked, slowly turning to watch her father.

He riffled through files, sighed, leaned on the sturdy oak drawer. "Thinking of making some changes," he said.

"Changes? Like what?"

"Thinking of retiring." He grabbed a handful of manila folders and brought them to the desk.

"Yeah, sure," she said, smiling.

"Bet you won't even miss me," he said.

"You'll still be around, Dad," Cass said.

"This'll always be your business."

"The funny thing is, Cass," he said, settling across the desk from her, "I never really felt this was my business. My father meant for my brother to run it. And if he'd lived through the war, he would be here now."

"You really think so?"

"I know it. I came home on leave from the merchant marine, and this place was going to hell. My father never got over Ward dying in action. So I stepped in."

"And never left."

"No, never did."

"What would you have done?" Cass asked curiously, noting the cold, far-off look in his eyes.

"I wanted to run cargo and salvage wrecks." He flashed a smile — the old Keating charm. "I'd have been a sea bum."

"Probably you'd never have married Mom, gotten saddled with three daughters," Cass teased.

"Nothing could have kept me from that," he said. "But you'd have grown up in Tahiti."

Josie was braiding Cass's hair. The first braid hung off-center, just behind Cass's ear, in crooked steps.

"Very pretty, Deb," her father said, pointing. He nodded enthusiastically at Josie. Josie concentrated, her tongue between her teeth, beginning a second braid. She smiled at her grandfather, happy to have an audience.

"She is a little heartbreaker," he said. "Going to drive the boys crazy, just like her mother."

"Thanks, Dad," Cass said wryly, remembering their first conversation about Josie.

"You're still mad at what I said before, aren't you?" he asked, amazing Cass. Her father hardly ever admitted he was wrong.

"Sort of. More hurt, I guess."

"Well, I'm sorry. You're a wonderful mother."

"Thanks," Cass said. Then a silence fell; she didn't know how to respond to an apology from her father. He looked very serious.

"You've been doing a terrific job all along."

"Two compliments in a row?" she asked. "What have I done to deserve it?"

He stared at his hands on the desk, first the backs, gnarled and veined, then the palms, surprisingly smooth for a man who made his living by the sea.

"I've asked Willis to come down, take a look at these tax records," he said bluntly.

"Willis?"

"He's a real estate expert. He seemed like the best person for me to talk to."

"What do you need with a real estate expert?" Cass asked.

Her father looked at her dead-on, and she knew she was going to hear bad news. "I think we ought to develop the wharf," he said.

She wasn't sure she'd heard clearly. She stared dumbly at her father, watching his face while Josie rebraided her hair.

"I said I think we ought to develop the wharf," he said, a defensive note in his voice. "It's prime waterfront. We can get plenty for it. You throw in this warehouse and Lobsterville . . . what are you smiling about?"

Cass grinned as if her father had just told the joke of the century. "And we'll all be rich with nothing to do," she said.

"I don't see what's so funny about it," he said, scowling.

"I think it's hilarious," she said. "You're going to sell our land so someone can build brick condos? We'll have places called Whale Cove and Lobster Pot Way sitting right here, instead of the warehouse. Don't you think that's funny?"

"No."

"Wonder what they'll do with Lobsterville? Probably rip it down and build a nice high-rise with a view out to Block Island."

"I never thought it would come to this, but we can't afford not to sell, if you think about it," he said. "Just look at the waterfront, up and down the bay. No shortage of people wanting to live by the water. We can't afford to hold on."

She stared at him, the smile dissolving from her face. "Are you really serious?"

"Yes." Her father stared angrily at his hands.

"You can't be."

"You'll be glad to get your share of the money," her father said bitterly. "Just wait till Billy hits a dry spell, and the income isn't rolling in so steady. You've got three educations to pay for. I wonder if Billy thought of *that* before he bought that southern tub."

"Are you doing this out of spite?" Cass asked, her voice rising. "Because Billy got his own boat?"

"You'll be glad for the money," her father repeated.

"That's crazy," Cass said. "I don't want the money. I want us to keep the wharf. Not just for us — me, Bonnie, and Nora. For our kids, too."

"The fishing business isn't what it used to be, and it's only going to get worse. You don't see that, do you?"

"I know we'll get by."

"You and Billy had it too easy," he said. "I've always said so. Sure, you've had a setback or two, but you don't know what it's like to struggle. Your mother and I, we lived through the Depression. We don't look at this world through rose-colored glasses."

"Maybe not," Cass said, thinking how rare and bizarre it felt these days for someone to say she had it too easy. "But I still don't see us developing the wharf. I love it here, Dad."

"I love it, too. But I want to do what's best for the family, even if it means changing things. Your mother feels the same way."

"Mom knows about this?" Cass asked, feeling even more frightened.

"Sure she does."

"You'll wreck it," she said. "Everything we grew up believing in." Cass didn't know many people her age who had stayed so close to home. She and Billy were the only high-school sweethearts she knew who were still together; she and her sisters had stayed in Mount Hope, working for the family business. Aside from John Barnard, most of their childhood friends had scattered.

Ignoring her, her father examined documents in the manila folder.

"Did you hear me?" she asked, her voice shaking. It seemed impossible, that this place could cease to exist.

"I'm talking about a tough choice," her father said. "I'm not out to wreck anything."

"But that'll happen," Cass said, wishing Billy were there.

She checked the clock: time to go home. Josie, still playing hairdresser, had unbraided Cass's hair and was now brushing it.

"Come on, Deb," she said to Josie. "Let's go."

"Mrs. Clay, you forgot to pay me."

Her father chuckled. Cass glanced at him, startled. "She is definitely one of ours," he said.

Cass pulled some change from her pocket and handed it to Josie. "Is that enough?"

Josie nodded.

Cass and Josie went to kiss Jimmy Keating goodbye. Josie slung her thin arms around his neck and gave him a hard hug. When Cass leaned over, he looked up, directly into her eyes.

"Don't do this," she said.

"Drive safely," he said. "They're calling for freezing rain."

"I'm definitely supposed to go to Florida," Alison said miserably, huddled against T.J. in the school bus.

"For Christmas?"

"Yeah. And *she's* definitely going to be there."

"That sucks."

Alison nodded, her head pressed into his shoulder.

"Maybe your mom could tell your dad she needs you here. You know, the first Christmas since the separation, and all."

Alison made a sound T.J. had never before heard come out of her: something between a snort and a guffaw. That such a delicate girl could make such an embarrassing sound made him love her even more. He gave her a squeeze.

"My mom *wants* me to go," she said. "She can't wait. She has a new boyfriend, and they're going to go skiing in Colorado. No one in my family's upset about the divorce."

"Except you."

"Yeah."

T.J. held her tight, smelling her beautiful perfumy hair. He wanted the bus ride to last forever, till way after dark. You could tell it was going to snow any day now; he imagined a wicked snowstorm with drifts as tall as buildings, so the school bus would get marooned, and the temperature would drop and Alison would have to press close to him just to stay alive.

"I can't believe I'm grounded," he said. "It's lousy not seeing you after school."

"You can manage," she said in that sharp, borderline-mean voice that always shocked T.J.

"Maybe I can sneak out today. Depends on

if my mom works late or not."

"Oh, I can't today," she said, lifting her head.

"Why not?" T.J. asked, jealous of whatever could keep Alison from seeing him if he were to risk everything by sneaking out.

"My mom's making me go shopping." She stuck out her tongue.

"Oh," T.J. said, a little confused. Personally, he hated shopping, but he thought all girls loved it. Perfecto and Emma did, and so did his mom, and even Josie.

"Shit," he said, as the bus air-braked. His stop. "I'll call you later? When my mom's busy."

"We won't be home from shopping till late," she whispered, tilting her face up for his kiss.

He was still tasting her strawberry lip gloss when he stepped off the bus. Walking along, watching the bus turn onto Beacon Street, trying for one last glimpse of Alison, he hardly noticed Sean walking beside him. Belinda, even lugging her schoolbooks, was way ahead.

"Hey, man," T.J. said. He'd been ignoring Sean for a while, ever since he'd started going out with Alison, and it made him feel kind of guilty. Sean needed a lot of attention; he didn't have any self-confidence, and he was really porking out, on the way to being as big as Aunt Bonnie.

"Hey, man," Sean said. "What'd you get grounded for?"

"Driving my old man's truck."

"Yeah?" Sean asked, sounding psyched.

When they reached Sean's corner, T.J. could tell that Sean really wanted to talk to him, because he didn't say goodbye or turn toward home. He had this twisted expression on his face, like he had to go to the bathroom really bad. T.J. figured that Sean wanted to ask him about buying condoms or something else embarrassing.

"So, how's Alison?" Sean asked.

"She's great."

Sean didn't say anything for a minute, and T.J. was getting cold, just standing there. "You still into Satan?" T.J. asked, because he couldn't really think of anything else to say.

"Yeah, I'm thinking of stealing Jesus out of the manger when they put up the Christmas stuff."

"Sean, don't do that," T.J. said. The idea of Sean ripping off Jesus made him feel totally depressed. Ever since they were little kids their mothers had taken them to see the crèche at Our Lady of Mount Hope, and even though T.J. had outgrown it, he wanted it there for other little kids. Like Josie.

"Maybe I won't," Sean said. "I haven't re-

379

ally decided yet. You think I shouldn't?"

"You shouldn't."

"Yeah, I probably won't."

T.J. nodded. It depressed him even further that just by showing a little disapproval, he'd talked Sean out of his plan. He didn't like having that kind of influence over someone. He started edging down the street. Maybe Sean would take the hint and go home. "So, see you tomorrow?" T.J. said, walking backward.

"Listen, man," Sean said, spit flying out of his mouth. He looked all red, like he'd just cut a big fart in public. "It's probably a lie, I don't know, but I heard Emma telling Belinda she heard Alison is kinda going out with a senior. Or she likes him, or something. But they're, like, seeing each other. I'm only telling you what I heard on account of how much you're in love, all that shit. But it's probably a lie."

"Emma told you that?"

"She told Belinda, and I heard her. It's probably a lie."

"It's a definite fucking lie," T.J. said. He didn't know who he wanted to kill more, Emma or Belinda. He tore ass down Coleridge, without even saying goodbye to Sean. He slipped on a grease spot in his driveway, went down on his knees, and pounded up the back steps. Belinda was just taking off her jacket.

She looked up, surprised to see him. She took a step back and held her arm out, as if she could feel his anger and wanted to protect herself.

"Hey!" she said, frowning.

"What's this big lie Emma's spreading around?" T.J. asked, stepping forward menacingly.

Belinda dropped her arm. She gave him a long look, like she actually pitied him. That look scared T.J. so much, he couldn't speak. He ran upstairs, dialed Alison's number. He looked at his watch: she should be home. If she'd gone straight home, if she wasn't meeting someone else, she should answer the phone now.

"Hello?" she said.

"Alison," T.J. said, his relief so great he sat down hard on his bed.

"T.J., I thought you were going to call me later," she whispered. He wondered if she could hear his heart pounding.

"I just had to tell you . . . I love you," he said.

She giggled. "That's so sweet. Me, too."

He held the receiver so hard, he could just about feel his fingers denting the plastic. He wanted to tell her what he'd heard, but he couldn't. She'll think I don't trust her, he told himself.

"T.J., I have to get ready to go shopping," Alison said. "My mom's waiting."

"What time'll you be home?" he asked.

"Oh, late. When the mall closes."

"Have fun," T.J. said.

"I will," she whispered.

But as he hung up, T.J. admitted to himself the real reason for not telling Alison what he'd heard. It wasn't that he feared she'd think he didn't trust her; it was that he was afraid she wouldn't deny she was seeing someone else.

Later, T.J. tried to concentrate on his math homework, but all he could do was doodle "Alison" in his notebook. He lay on his back, listening to Guns 'n Roses, trying to take a deep breath. There's no way Alison would do that to you, he said to himself. I'm all she has, she's all I have.

"Alison," he said out loud, just before he lifted the receiver. Belinda was on the extension.

"T.J., that you?" Belinda asked. Shit, she was probably going to give him away to their mother.

"Yeah," he said.

"Go ahead, use the phone," she said quickly. "Let me know when you're done."

"Hi, T.J.," came Emma's voice.

"Hi," T.J. said, amazed when the girls instantly hung up instead of prolonging his agony.

His heart racing, he dialed Alison's number.

"Hello?" Alison's mother answered.

"Uh, hi, may I speak with Alison?" T.J. asked.

"She's not home. She's out for the evening," Mrs. McCabe said breezily, seeming not to recognize T.J.'s voice, even though he'd called a hundred times. T.J. heard a man in the background calling her. "Come on, Shirley," he said.

"Is there a message?" Mrs. McCabe asked, her voice laughing now, soft as a girl's.

"No message," T.J. said, hanging up.

"In my opinion, she is the lowest person in school," Emma said hotly.

"Poor T.J. I know he knows," Belinda said, sitting at the kitchen table. She should have been in bed by now, but this was an important call. "He came down for dinner and asked right away if he could be excused. My mom thinks he's sick."

"Did he talk to Alison? Not that she'd even admit it. T.J. is so much cuter than Martin. She probably only likes Martin because he's a senior."

"Are you positive about Alison?"

"One-hundred percent. I saw them, for one thing. Practically making out near the gym. And, Bel? They weren't a bit tragic. She was giggling her head off in that sickeningly cute happy-flirtass way she used to have before she and T.J. got together."

"I can't believe you saw them," Belinda said, even though Emma had told her the story sixteen times today.

"I saw them, all right. Plus, Chris Taylor told me she saw them on the bus home from the game. God, Martin Scoleri! He is such a jock!"

"Gross me out royal," Belinda said.

"You should have seen her letting him tickle her. 'Oh, Martin,' " Emma said, imitating Alison's breathless little voice. " 'You're so big and I'm so teensy. You could just break me in two.' "

"I wish he would," Belinda said. She had hated that look in T.J.'s eyes when he'd asked to be excused from dinner. She couldn't believe Alison McCabe had the power to do that to her older brother: squash him like a bug.

"Maybe it's for the best," Emma said. "Alison did bring out the down side of T.J."

"Yeah, but seeing him tonight, I think it's worse than ever."

"He'll get over it. Don't you know love hurts? God, Belinda! What radio station do you listen to, anyway?"

Belinda heard Emma cover the mouthpiece, some muffled conversation in the background, and then Emma's voice again. "Bel? My mother wants to talk to your mother. Mother-daughter phone relay. See you tomorrow."

"See you, Em. Mom! Telephone!"

"Did you get the call?" Bonnie asked.

"What call?"

"From Dad. About the wharf."

Cass frowned at the phone. "He actually called you? I heard it in person, this morning."

"Well, thanks for telling me!" Bonnie sounded irate, unlike herself.

"Do you think he's serious?" Cass asked.

"He sounded serious to me," Bonnie said. "He had Willis down, and they were figuring out the price per square foot."

Cass rested her hand on the top of her head. This was news she didn't want to hear. "Oh, God. Have you called Nora?"

"I tried before, but she wasn't home."

"I'll try now," Cass said.

After saying goodnight to Bonnie, she dialed Nora's number. Willis answered.

"Hello, dear," Willis said in his friendly southern drawl, recognizing her voice right away.

"Hi, Willis," Cass said, prickling. She

wanted to come straight out and accuse him of encouraging her father to sell the wharf. But she started off easy: "I hear you saw my father today."

"Yes. He told me you were pretty upset about his plan."

"He has a plan?" Cass asked, her heart falling.

"Well, not exactly. But he's heard about people selling these old wharves and making a bundle, and he has it in mind to leave you girls with a nice nest egg."

"I don't want a nest egg!"

"Cass, I don't know you very well yet, but that's basically what I told him you'd say. You and Bonnie. I knew how Nora felt, of course. Completely, one-hundred-percent against it."

"Is he serious?"

"Hard to say. He's thought it over, I'll tell you that. I stopped him a little short, telling him about a complex I'm building just up the bay from here. I paid big money to a guy whose family had owned the land for a hundred years, and now his salt-water farm's going to be called Salt Marsh Village. Your father got a funny smile on his face, said you'd been teasing him about Keating's Wharf being called Lobster Way."

"I wasn't teasing. I was pissed," Cass said, frowning. "I still am."

"He's a sentimental man. He likes to hide it, though."

"You see right through him," Cass said, nodding. "Not many people do. I know Billy and Gavin were pretty intimidated at first."

"A different situation, Cass," Willis said. "They were a lot younger than I am. Plus, you have to remember that I deal with guys like your father all the time. People get older, and they think about letting go. They want to leave some money for their kids, or they need to make a change in their lives, so they think about selling the family spread. Sometimes a drastic change is the easiest kind to make. You know when I acquire most of my property? When a person retires or has to face a nursing home."

"Oh," Cass said, realizing she liked Willis. Because he had obviously caught on to her difficult father, she felt reassured. A little, anyway.

"You want to talk to Nora?" Willis asked. "She's right down the hall."

"No thanks," Cass said. "Just kiss her good-night for me."

"I'll do that with pleasure," Willis said.

Still uneasy, she hung up. She turned off the light and walked to the window.

You couldn't see the harbor from here, but the Minturn Ledge Light beacon traced an arc over Alewives Park. Billy would have passed ten, maybe fifteen lighthouses on his way to the fishing grounds. All the old seaports with their lighthouses, fish piers, cobbled wharves, white steeples, sea captain's houses. Billy, her sea captain. Cass thought of all the fishermen sailing a hundred miles out, returning time after time to the same old seaport.

Cass watched the beacon pass five more times, and then she turned away from the window. Billy and all the other Mount Hope fishermen. They needed to follow the same lights, set a course by the same markers. Cass had grown up believing that was how the world worked, and it was too late to change things now.

22

Billy returned from the first trip on his new boat ready to make a quick turnaround and head straight out again. This four-day voyage had been a tryout, a chance for him to test her in the open sea. She'd proved to be solid and responsive, and Billy felt exhilarated. As often as he'd imagined owning his own boat, he'd never expected to love her this much.

Billy told his crew to report back to the *Cassandra* the next day, in time to catch the 2:30 tide. Usually he'd allow more time between trips, but now that he'd seen what the boat could handle, he couldn't wait to go fishing. He just had to load up with bait, fresh water, and diesel, and they'd be off.

Arriving at home that afternoon, he found Cass standing in the laundry room, pouring detergent into the washing machine. She didn't see him right away. Clicking the dial, she moved as if in a daze. She looked straight at him, seeming not to see him. Then, suddenly, she laughed and came toward him.

"I'm so glad you're home!" she said, kissing him. "How did she run?"

"Great," he said. "Unbelievably fantastic. Like a dream."

"Careful, or I'll get jealous."

Still high with excitement, Billy pushed Cass backward, against the machine. He gave her a long kiss, feeling the machine hum behind her.

"What were you thinking before, when I first came in?" Billy asked, stroking her back. He felt so happy, so turned on at seeing her, and she had appeared so distracted, he imagined she'd been thinking about him, lost in her own wild fantasies.

"You won't believe it," she said.

"Try me."

"Dad's planning to develop the wharf."

Billy's hand stopped moving. He forgot about his boat and about making love to Cass. Suddenly he saw the pain in his wife's eyes.

"He'll never do it," Billy said, partly to comfort her and partly out of his own disbelief.

"Willis thinks he might."

It was too bizarre to fathom, the possibility of Keating selling the wharf. Guiltily, Billy wondered if maybe he, by leaving the Keating fleet for his own boat, had somehow precipitated this. Billy held Cass tight.

"Maybe nothing will come of it," she said

after a minute. "I can drive myself crazy, thinking about it. Condos? On our wharf! Dad's got it all figured out."

Billy shook his head. "We can't blame it on senility — he's not there yet."

"At first, I wanted to blame it on Willis. But I think it's actually all Dad's idea." She paused, calming herself down. "Probably nothing will come of it. I mean, he does have a tendency to . . . make grand gestures. He can't just retire, like a normal old guy. He has to erase every trace of himself from the waterfront."

Billy laughed. "Right, that's probably it. Your father *is* the waterfront."

"It's been really hard, not having you to talk to about it."

"I know what that's like," Billy said. Away for weeks at a time, he would sometimes feel so lonely for Cass, he'd think he couldn't stand it.

"I'm just glad you're here," she said.

Billy knew this was the time to tell her that he wouldn't be here for long, that he planned to leave tomorrow for a long trip, but he couldn't make himself do it. Not right now, not when she needed his comfort. Instead, he held her, touching her face, listening to her tell him how much she needed him.

★ ★ ★

Cass let Billy sleep late. She fixed hot cereal for the kids, got T.J. and Belinda out the door, and helped Josie dress herself. Maybe later she and Billy could drive down to the wharf, have a talk with her father. But right now, she had her mind on something else. She moved quietly, not wanting to awaken Billy. She had an ulterior motive: Zach was coming, and she didn't want Billy to leave before he arrived.

When Zach pulled up, Cass met him at the door. "Hey, is that your husband's truck?" he asked, pointing.

"Yes," Cass said.

"You know, I've never met him," Zach said.

"This'll be your chance."

Cass watched Zach and Josie sign "hello" to each other. The three of them sat at the kitchen table. While Cass sipped coffee and watched, Zach and Josie worked on the alphabet. Within twenty minutes, she heard Billy's footsteps upstairs.

"Whew," he said. "Thanks for letting me sleep." He entered the kitchen, tucking his shirt into his jeans.

"Billy, this is Zach," Cass said.

Billy looked startled, but he put out his hand. "I've heard a lot about you," he said.

392

"Nice to meet you, Mr. Medieros," Zach said.

"Daddy!" Josie squealed, reaching up so Billy would bend over to kiss her.

"Morning, Josie," Billy said. Josie couldn't hear him, and she couldn't see his lips, which were kissing the top of her head. Cass watched Zach, to see how he would react. Funny, she thought, how Zach felt like an ally now. Zach understood deaf children, and Billy did not. Cass hoped that somehow Zach could help.

"What do we have here?" Billy asked, shuffling the flashcards. "ABC's."

Josie signed, "A-B-C-D-E-F . . ." But Billy turned away, to pour a cup of coffee, before she got to "G." Cass watched Josie's face fall. Josie pouted, her lower lip sticking out.

"Zach, can I get you some coffee?" Billy asked.

"No thanks."

"Billy," Cass said, "Josie was showing you her ABC's."

"Oh, sorry," Billy said. He reddened slightly, glancing at Zach. "I'm not used to this. I don't know how to read sign language."

"That's understandable," Zach said.

"I sit in every day," Cass said, "and Josie's way ahead of me." She wanted to reassure Billy, but she could tell by his expression that he still felt uncomfortable.

"We're never going to catch up," Billy said, a little sharply. "How are we going to know what she's saying?"

"All parents of deaf kids worry about that," Zach said. "At North Point they have support groups, seminars, classes to help you deal with it. They'll tell you about it when you visit."

"Visit?" Billy asked, looking confused.

"We have an appointment at North Point," Cass said. "Just to check the place out."

"When?"

"The Monday before Thanksgiving. A week from today."

"I won't be back by then," he said. "I'll be fishing."

"When are you leaving?" Cass asked, getting that sinking feeling in the pit of her stomach.

Billy stared into his coffee, stirring it slowly. "This afternoon," he said.

A tense silence fell over the table. Sensing it, Josie stopped signing. She looked from her mother to her father.

"Come on, Josie," Zach said. "Let's go to our classroom." He meant the sun porch, where he and Josie did most of their work.

"They're mad," Josie said, following him reluctantly.

"I didn't tell you last night," Billy said to

Cass, "because you seemed so upset about your father."

"Shit, Billy," Cass said. A wave of disappointment washed over her. She realized how much she had been counting on him — to help her know how serious her father was, to talk to Jimmy himself, to visit North Point with her.

"I have four guys showing up this afternoon," Billy said regretfully, as if he expected her to believe he was going out strictly for the well-being of four fishermen.

"You're the skipper," Cass said. "Send them home."

"They're counting on this trip, to get their cuts. With the holidays coming . . ."

"What about me? Can't I count on you?"

Billy gave her a long, serious stare. "You're not being fair. This is what I do for a living."

"I don't want you to go," she said. "I know it's unreasonable, but it's how I feel. I've been doing too much alone for too long. I don't want to visit North Point without you."

"You can reschedule the appointment."

Something about his tone made Cass look at him more carefully. "What?" she asked.

"This North Point place is a lousy idea," he said. "I've told you all along — that signing business will isolate her."

"She can't hear, Billy. That's what isolates her."

"She has a loving family, she's healthy. Why do you want to shut her off in a place like that?"

"She's not going to live there! And how do you know what it's like? 'A place like that.' Like what?"

"They'll cut her off, Cass. She'll be totally separate from us. She doesn't need that."

"You're not here enough to know what she needs," Cass said, suddenly overcome by a red fury.

Billy walked to the sink, sloshed water in his coffee cup, left it on the drainboard. He turned toward Cass, his back against the sink. "Are we going to do this now? Have a big fight when I have to leave for ten days?"

Cass took a deep breath, then shook her head.

"Maybe I'm wrong," he conceded.

She could see the confusion in his eyes. The whole thing was painful, and nothing about whether to enroll Josie in North Point seemed clear-cut.

"Shit," Billy said. "Now I wish I hadn't told the crew we were going out."

Cass tried to smile. "At least admit you're dying to go. I know you, Billy. You can't wait to go fishing in your new boat." A pause. "I don't even blame you," she said reluctantly.

"You don't?"

"Not really."

"Come here," he said, holding out his arms.

She leaned into his body, closing her eyes to make the time stretch out. A ten-day trip, coming right after four days out. Billy had been away for longer. She felt like being sarcastic, asking if he planned to make an appearance on Thanksgiving. But she held back. Billy hugged her, swaying slightly, saying nothing. She had the feeling that anything she said would be dangerous right now, and she'd have ten long days to regret it.

Late Tuesday morning, right after her hair appointment, Mary Keating stopped at the warehouse, to meet Jimmy for lunch. She said hello to everyone working in the tank room.

"Jim took the truck down to Old Lyme," Jack Doherty called.

"Standing me up, is he?" Mary said, pretending to be angry. She loved ribbing the guys.

"No, just delivering fish to the Inn. He said he'd be back by noon."

"Well, he'd better be. I'll just wait up in the office," Mary said. Climbing the steep wooden stairs, she paused twice, to catch her breath. One of these days, she was going to quit smoking. Inside the office she found Cass hard at work, filling orders.

"Hello, sweetheart," Mary said.

"Hi, Mom," Cass said. She cleared a stack of magazines off the chair beside her, and Mary sat down. "Your hair looks nice."

"She permed it too tight," Mary said, instinctively touching her hair. Nancy, her regular hairdresser, was out on maternity leave, and the new girl had left the solution on too long.

"Don't worry, Mom. It's really pretty."

Mary smiled, almost believing her. "Where's the little one?"

"Zach took her on a field trip," Cass said. "To the science museum."

"Oh, what fun," Mary said. She hadn't met Zach, but she knew he was doing wonders for Josie. Josie seemed less frustrated, less irritable and angry. And Mary could hardly contain her relief that Cass was finally considering North Point. Mary had heard such fine things about the place. And it would take some of the load off Cass.

"Mom," Cass said, wheeling her chair around to face Mary head-on. "Will you tell me what's going on?"

"Oh. You mean about your father." Mary sighed. She snapped open her purse to find her cigarettes. This was never easy, explaining Jim to his own daughters. The man was a bundle of contradictions: simultaneously generous and miserly, outgoing and suspicious.

"Is he really going ahead? With his big plan?"

"He says so."

Cass stared, unblinking. "Is he serious?"

Mary struggled, trying to find the best answer. She knew, had always known, how to read Jim. Always full of pomp and circumstance, he was occasionally full of wind. But explaining that to Cass, regardless of the fact that she had children of her own, felt wrong to Mary. She believed that a daughter, no matter what her age, needed to respect her father.

"Is he?" Cass pressed.

"I wouldn't worry too much," Mary said. Cass searched her eyes. Very slightly, Cass's shoulders relaxed.

"Is he scared of retiring?"

"Terrified," Mary said, exhaling smoke. She felt lucky to have such a perceptive daughter.

"Why can't he just go on the way he has? Spending a few hours here when he feels like it? It's not as if . . ."

Mary imagined Cass was going to say that it wasn't as if Jim ran the place anymore, and she felt glad Cass had stopped herself. "You know your father," Mary said. "He likes to do things in a big way. He'll go out with a bang."

"Why don't we just throw him a great party, all his friends and a Dixieland band?" Cass asked. "He can pretend to retire, and we can keep the wharf."

"Everyone wants to feel needed," Mary said. She knew this better than anyone. All through their marriage, Jim would forge ahead, damn the torpedoes, never asking Mary for her advice or opinion. He was the great independent, running the whole show; women fell in love with him and business competitors hated him. Often Mary had wondered whether he needed her at all, whether he would miss her if she were gone.

Ashamed to admit it, she felt strangely grateful to hear Jim worrying about retiring. Last night, in the middle of a bad dream, he had cried out. Mary had shaken him awake, as she always did. But this time Jim had turned to her. He'd slipped his arms around her, pulled her close, and, after a while, fallen back to sleep without moving away.

"Your father will be fine," Mary said, in response to a question Cass hadn't asked.

"He can't sell this place," Cass said. "There's too much of him in it."

Mary nodded. She had to agree with that.

T.J. had always expected a breakup to be eventful. He'd see girls in high school crying with their friends, guys punching out their own lockers. But this breakup seemed to happen without him. Alison just stopped sitting with him on the bus. Ever since he'd called her house that night, she wouldn't talk to him. Now when he'd call, the answering machine or her mother would pick up. Either way, T.J. would get the same message: Alison's not home. He thought he was going crazy.

She moved everywhere surrounded by her friends, like a squadron of strawberry-scented blond bodyguards. T.J. would sit in his usual bus seat, staring at the back of her head. She moved as if nothing were wrong, as if she had nothing on her mind but getting to school. Sometimes she wouldn't be on the bus at all, and he'd know she was getting a ride with someone who had a license.

Four days after she stopped talking to him, he waited near her locker until she came down the hall alone. He knew her schedule; she had just come from biology lab, and now she had a free period.

"Hi," he said.

"Oh, hi," she said, as if he were just any kid. It killed him that she could look so normal when he felt like he was dying.

"So, what's up?"

"The sky, the moon, the ceiling . . ." She giggled.

"You seem happy," he said.

"I'm okay. You?" She turned toward him, her arms full of books, and suddenly T.J. thought he was going to lose it. Just the way she said, "You?" As if she couldn't care less, just wanted to be polite so he'd leave faster.

"Not so good," he said.

"Well, you'd better get over that. We have exams this week. And Thanksgiving next Thursday."

"What happened?" T.J. asked in a voice so low he didn't know if she could hear him.

She tossed her head, impatient. "I just think we should break up."

"I figured that."

She stood there, the silence between them growing.

"Because of Martin, right?" T.J. asked.

She shrugged. "Not only."

"Then what?"

For a second, T.J. could swear she had a tear in her eye. This was the Alison he loved, whose feelings were all over her face, making her voice quaver, her hands tremble. The Alison from a broken family, with parents who didn't understand her or love her enough; the Alison that only T.J. could comfort.

"What?" he said again.

"I just can't take it anymore," she said. Her voice quavered, but from something hot, like

402

anger. Her brows scrunched into a frown. She looked at him straight on.

I can be different, T.J. wanted to say. I can change. Let me take care of you. But his voice wouldn't work.

"It's too intense, okay? Last week I thought I was pregnant. I'm not," she said hurriedly, probably frightened by the sight of his face.

"I wish you were," T.J. said. He didn't care if they were only fifteen. He loved her so much, he'd marry her tomorrow. He'd fish on his father's boat and support Alison and the baby, find them a little place where they'd all love one another.

"God, that's sick!" she said, looking disgusted. "When you talk like that, T.J., I don't know what to say. Don't love people so much; you scare them."

"You can't just decide to love someone less," T.J. said. He had to hold himself back from pleading with her. The effort caused him actual, nauseating pain.

"I just can't take it," she said. "We were getting too serious. Even my mother noticed it."

"I thought your mother didn't care."

"I just want to see other people for a while," she said.

"Martin," T.J. said.

"He's another person." Alison stood there,

her chest pushed forward and her nose turned up. T.J. stared at her, as if he were memorizing her features, trying to figure out how so many beautiful parts could make a girl look so cold and snotty. He started walking away.

"We can be friends," she called after him.

T.J. walked past room 301, where he was already missing English class, down the north stairs, out the north door, and across the football field. Snow flurries swirled in the wind. He'd left without his jacket or his books, and he just kept walking. He couldn't have said exactly why, whether he wanted to scare Alison or prove to her how completely desperate he felt, or whether he just wanted to show her he wasn't a run-of-the-mill wimp lovesick sucker, but T.J. was on his way home to get the gun.

Marriage agreed with Nora; she never would have believed how much she loved it. She felt utterly transformed, like one of those women in a magazine makeover who start out drab and listless and, three pages later, turn out to be beautiful. Her parts were all the same, but suddenly her eyes sparkled, her hair had a sheen, her skin glowed. Nora felt as new as her name: Nora Randecker. She couldn't wait until after Thanksgiving, to send out boxes of Christmas cards imprinted with the message: "A Happy Holiday Season from Mr. & Mrs. Willis Randecker." Yesterday their new checks had arrived, printed with both their names, and Nora kept peeking at them, as if she couldn't quite believe they were real.

Since their marriage, she'd changed her hours. She worked lunch and early dinner, and she left the restaurant in time to fix dinner for Willis at home. An hour before lunch one cold November day, as she gazed out Lobsterville's picture windows, wondering what Willis was doing, she saw Bonnie's station wagon weaving backward down the wharf, Bonnie at the wheel. Bonnie backed right up to the warehouse loading dock.

Nora pulled on her long black alpaca coat and headed into the wind. By the time she reached the warehouse, Cass was on the loading dock, too, pushing a tire. The Keating girls stored their snow tires in the warehouse from April till November every year. At the first hint of snow, they would switch their tires. Nora glowed; just this morning Willis had taken her tires from the warehouse, driven her 280Z down to Ledoux's Garage to have them mounted and balanced.

"They're forecasting six inches," Nora called.

"Wouldn't you know it?" Bonnie moaned.

"My first gig's in Newport this afternoon, and we're having a blizzard."

"It's not a blizzard," Cass said, shoving the second tire across Bonnie's tailgate.

"What gig?" Nora asked.

"It's a quilt expo," Bonnie said. She was bundled warmly in a scarlet mackinaw that made her look like a magnificent red bell pepper. "I'm selling my brownies at the food table."

Nora peered into the front seat and saw an enormous basket covered with a linen towel. Bonnie whipped off the cloth. She'd wrapped each brownie in cellophane and attached a hand-lettered sticker. Nora read the labels: Mocha Toffee Crunch, Fudge Lava Whirl, Peanut Butter Sticky.

"Do you think the names are stupid?" Bonnie asked, her brow tight with seriousness.

"They are delicious names," Cass called from the loading dock. Nora was thinking she might have toned them down, but Cass threw her a warning look.

"I'd buy one," Nora said.

"Get moving," Cass said to Bonnie. "There's going to be a tire line at Ledoux's, and you want to hit the road before the snow starts."

"You can take mine if it's ready first," Nora said.

"Thanks!" Bonnie called. Cass and Nora waved as she pulled away.

"Where's Josie?" Nora asked, glancing around.

"With Belinda. Belinda stayed home from school today."

"Oh, is she sick?"

"A bad case of VR. Can you believe it?"

"Belinda has her period already?" Nora asked.

"She's thirteen," Cass said. "She told me she'd spent the night curled in a ball, wishing she'd been born a boy. Also, she has three tests tomorrow. That might have something to do with it. My good student."

"Doesn't take after her mother, that's for sure," Nora said fondly.

"I saw Willis this morning," Cass said, crouching on the loading dock so her head was level with Nora's.

"It's the little things about marriage," Nora said. "I never imagined how it would feel to have my husband tell me to sleep late while he had my snow tires put on."

"I haven't experienced that, exactly," Cass said. "Billy's always fishing at the first snow. I'm quitting work in an hour or so; I'll get mine put on then. Dad's been hounding me all morning. Just cause he's so efficient and thought of it last night."

"I love being taken care of," Nora said. She had the feeling she'd said the wrong thing; she wondered if maybe Cass and Billy had had a fight. Nora had always wondered what their fights were like, whether they had knockdown-dragouts, like thunderstorms, to counterbalance the steady pull of electricity between them.

"Willis is being really patient with Dad," Cass said.

"Isn't he?" Nora said, thrilled that Cass would notice. "He drives down almost every day to talk to him."

"Are you as upset as I am?"

"About Dad?"

"About him wanting to sell out."

"Well, I would be, if I thought he'd actually go through with it."

"You don't think he will?"

Nora shook her head. "Let's face it. Dad loves his big ideas. But how often . . ."

"Does he actually go through with them?" Cass said, nodding her agreement.

"I think Willis is helping him."

"Dad loves talking real estate, and Willis is a great listener. I just stay in the background, trying to keep my mouth shut. Dad's determined to leave us all 'set for life.' "

"I know. Willis has to break it to him gently that selling the wharf isn't exactly like winning

408

the jackpot. After taxes and everything, there wouldn't be all that much left."

"I can see how Dad feels," Cass said, squinting as she looked over the harbor. "We love this place so much, we feel like someone would *have* to pay us a fortune to get it away from us."

Suddenly Cass's gaze traveled down the pier, and Nora looked over her shoulder. Here came Al Sweet, dressed for the North Atlantic, running at full tilt.

"Oh, great. My old flame," Nora said before she could stop herself. Al had a very sarcastic way of calling her "Mrs. Randecker" every time he saw her.

"Slow down, Al," Cass called. "The fish'll wait for you."

"Nah," Al said, skidding to a stop. "I hear Billy Medieros is catching them all, cleaning the banks right out. The big shot, with his own boat."

"*My* big shot," Cass said, rocking on her heels.

"Hey, Mrs. Randecker," Al said, kissing the back of Nora's hand. "How's married life treating you?"

"Fine," Nora said crisply. As if she'd ever discuss her marriage with Al. His big mustache drooped, and he looked hurt.

"You know I want the best for you, Nora.

You've gotta know that."

Cass raised her eyebrows, urging Nora to be nice.

"Okay," Nora said, smiling at Al. "Thank you. Sincerely."

"You're sincerely welcome," Al said. He continued down the dock and began throwing his gear into the *Aurora*'s cockpit.

"You can afford to be big about it," Cass whispered, squeezing Nora's arm. "He'll never have anyone like you again. You've gotta know that."

Nora laughed. "I do, don't I?" On top of everything else, marriage to Willis had given her a sense of humor.

His fourth day at sea on his new boat, with black ice coating the deck and turning the rigging silver, while Cass and her sister stood laughing on Keating's Wharf, Billy Medieros made his first call to the Coast Guard.

"Mayday, mayday," he said into the microphone. "This is fishing vessel *Cassandra*. We need assistance."

"Coast Guard station Nantucket, we read you *Cassandra*. What is your position?"

Billy leaned across the chart table, peered at the log. He'd taken a loran reading two minutes earlier, just after the accident, but now he couldn't read his own writing, his hand had been shaking so badly. Fumbling to draw the book closer, he knocked over the sleek black flashlight Cass had stuck in his stocking last Christmas.

He read the coordinates to the Coast Guard operator. "One hundred twenty miles south-southeast of Sankaty Head," Billy said. "We're taking on water." He paused, catching his breath. "And we've lost two men." He blinked, seeing Frank Santos and Jesse Gabriel slide down the stern, through the trawl door, into the bottle-green wash. No more than five minutes had passed since it had happened.

"Dispatching rescue vessels," the operator said.

"It's an emergency," Billy said, and the words sounded hollow. Why else would he be calling the Coast Guard? At first he'd thought they'd caught a sea monster — its slimy black head rose up above the surface, with the *Cassandra*'s dark nets cascading like a mourning veil, trapping it. Then the water parted, and the dark hull of a submarine glistened, hovering on the surface. They'd trapped its periscope.

"Cut loose!" Frank had yelled, heading for the starboard winch.

But it wasn't a submarine; it was a sea monster after all. They'd snagged a humpback whale, its tail thrashing in the nets, trying to free itself. It breached, shooting straight out of the sea like a missile from hell, its entire sixty-foot body clearing the water, its tense white flukes just missing the transom. Crashing into the sea, it displaced a wall of water that washed over *Cassandra*'s decks, draining in a sheet through the trawl doors.

Billy had held the wheel, feeling his boat cant backward, the stern tipping under. In that instant he'd been sure they'd all drown, be dragged straight to the sea bottom. Tony Domingus, his first mate, grabbed the rifle.

At the helm, feeling his boat pull backward as he drove forward, Billy knew a shot would be futile. Tony would have to hit the brain on the first shot to kill the whale. Even dead, the creature's sheer weight would drag them under. But before Tony could clear the cockpit, the whale sounded.

"We're sinking!" Jesse shouted. The whale swam straight down, a torpedo to the center of the earth, its great white flukes disappearing in the murk. Billy felt his boat lurch beneath his feet, tipping so the bow arched toward the sky and the stern went under. The cockpit's rear wall became the floor, and Billy stared through the glass beneath his feet to see Frank and Jesse drop into the sea, their fingers scrabbling across the icy deck, their screams howling through the wind as they vanished.

Then, suddenly, as if there had been no whale, the Cassandra righted herself. She rode with grace, rolling across the rhythmic waves of a stormless sea. Billy and Tony moved cautiously at first, inching their way out the cockpit door, across the deck. Then they ran for the stern, to look for Frank and Jesse. Tony threw two life rings into the empty current.

"It freed itself," Billy said. Two hundred yards off the port quarter he saw the whale blow, arch its massive black back, and dive.

"What the fuck happened?" Paul Skillin, who'd been off watch, sleeping down below, clambered onto the deck.

"We snagged a whale," Tony said, his teeth chattering. "Frank and Jesse. Shit —"

"What are you talking about?" Paul asked, following Tony's gaze. Then, "In the water? They went over?"

"Just look," Billy said. "Keep looking."

"Water's pouring in," Paul said, gesturing at the companion ladder, leading below. "It's bad. The fucker pulled some fittings loose."

"They just went over," Tony said, scanning the surface. "It happened so fast."

"Go down and start the hand pump," Billy directed Paul. "We've got maybe five minutes to get those guys onboard."

"They're finished," Tony said fiercely. "They're frozen."

Billy saw something bright just below the surface. He grabbed the boat hook, plunged it into the sea, and caught Frank's crimson watch cap. It dangled off the long hook; Billy tried to pull it onboard, but the wind grabbed it away.

"Haul in the nets," Billy yelled to Tony. He sprinted to the cockpit, worked the engine through its paces; it didn't seem to be damaged. Once Tony got the nets onboard, Billy would beat in widening circles until he found the men. They would have cut their boots off; maybe they'd grabbed onto the life rings and could see *Cassandra* even now, a little distant to hear their calls, but not so far off they'd have lost hope.

"Hang on, hang on," Billy said, more to himself, searching the waves with binoculars. He shivered in his warm jacket, his hands numb in their black leather mittens. Icicle daggers hung everywhere, sharks' teeth in the rigging.

The winches groaned, hauling in the heavy nets. They had just started dragging a new area, just before they'd caught the whale. Billy turned away, to check his loran position. At that instant, the framed photo of Cass and the kids caught his eye. He focused on Cass, her soft blue eyes telling him to stay steady, not to panic, to keep his head.

"Cass," he said, for luck.

Tony shouted for help, and the words trailed into a high, bloodcurdling scream taken by the wind. Billy turned to run toward him, but what he saw stopped him cold. There, tangled in the nets, were the lifeless bodies of Frank Santos and Jesse Gabriel. Billy stared for perhaps thirty seconds. He turned away, caught sight of Cass's picture again. His stomach pitched, thinking of the danger they were in. He made a second call to the Coast Guard.

"Mayday," he said into the microphone, his voice shaking. "This is the *Cassandra* again. . . ."

"*Cassandra*, we are on the way," came the voice over the radio.

23

Josie didn't know how to tell time, but she knew T.J. shouldn't be home from school yet. She sat in the TV room watching cartoons while Belinda slept on the sofa, and she saw T.J. walk down the hall. He had rosy cheeks; he shivered like he'd gone outside without his jacket. Josie sneaked into the hall. She wanted to talk to him, but she was afraid he would be mad. He'd seemed mad ever since she'd had her accident.

No T.J. in the hall, but the cellar door was open. Josie peeked down the scary stairs into the dark cellar. T.J. had said there was danger down here. She took one step at a time, down all the stairs. She couldn't hear anything, but she saw a light in the Ping-Pong room.

T.J. had his head in the danger cupboard. Josie stayed far back, watching him. He took something out and pointed it like a gun at the wall. It *was* a gun! Maybe he was so mad, he was going to shoot it at Josie. Josie remembered once Mommy had told her never to let someone go away mad. Maybe if you let them, they would come back madder, with a gun.

She stood against the wall, watching him. He pointed the gun at his own head, then tried to stick it in his pocket. It looked just like the guns in cartoons, a big long kill gun. But no matter how scary T.J. looked holding the gun in the shadowy Ping-Pong room, Josie knew he wouldn't hurt her.

"Put that down," she said very loudly.

T.J. jumped. He hunched over, hiding the gun behind him. "That you, Josie?" he asked, frowning the way he did when he couldn't understand her. Now he was talking; she wished she could hear everything he was saying, but it had to do with "Bob," "work," "cold."

"Don't be mad," she said. She tried to speak and sign at the same time.

"I'm not mad at you."

Backing up, she bumped her wrist. Her cast had been off for more than a week, but her wrist still felt weak and wobbly. Holding it with her good hand, she stopped signing for a moment.

T.J. shook his head. He put the gun on the floor and took Josie in his arms. She pressed her hands on both sides of his face. "You cold!" she said.

"I'm okay," he said, hugging her. "I'm not

mad at you." Then he said something Josie didn't get. If he hadn't been holding her tight to prove he still loved her, Josie would have thought he was saying that he *used* to love a little girl, but then he got mad and now he hated her. It made her so frustrated, she felt like squirming out of his hug and running in big circles around the cellar. She hated when people, especially T.J., said things she couldn't understand.

Josie wriggled away and stared straight at his mouth. "Say again?" she said, trying to stay calm.

"Alison doesn't love me anymore," he said slowly.

"She doesn't?"

T.J. shook his head.

"Are you going to shoot her?"

T.J.'s eyes dropped to the gun, as if he'd forgotten about it. "No," he said.

"Not kill the girl?"

"No." Tears ran down her brother's cheeks, and he wiped them away. Josie could tell by his quick fingers — wipe, wipe — that he didn't want Josie to see him crying.

Josie signed, "I love you, T.J."

"I don't understand, Josie," T.J. said.

Josie nodded. She made the sign again. Then she kissed the back of T.J.'s hand. She didn't let go of his hand right away; he let her hold it. With his other hand, he wiped away more tears. They stood there, looking down at the gun. It was as big as T.J.'s foot.

Like quicksilver, Josie bent down. She picked up the gun. She wished there were a secret trap door that she could throw it down. She wanted it to sail down a chute into the ground, into a secret pit for bad, scary things, which could never get out to hurt you because they would be trapped forever. She wanted to throw all guns, knives, snakes, sharks, and eels into the trap door and lock them away.

But there wasn't a trap door. She looked around. She knew a place. The suds hole! She bolted away from T.J. before he could catch her. She carried the gun — she couldn't believe how heavy, heavier than a puppy — to the place. She heard a sound, loud, that might have been T.J. yelling her name. But she wouldn't stop. He'd said he wouldn't kill the girl, but she'd seen him put the gun to his own head, and it might have shot him, and Josie couldn't imagine how someone with a shot head would look.

The big washing machine, the clothes dryer. Josie knew a place, the scariest place in the house. When her mother washed their clothes, Josie used to hold on to her leg, never daring to let go, because snakes or a ghost might come out of the deep hole where the soapy water went.

The light from the Ping-Pong room didn't go this far, and Josie didn't know if she could make herself go near the washing machine. But if she didn't, T.J. would get the gun back, and that thought made her more afraid than the suds hole. So she kept running, the gun out in front, so heavy to hold up, but this way it would get to the hole before she did.

She knew the spot. Even in the dark she could see the hole's black mouth, blacker than the dark, wide open and waiting to eat anything that fell inside it. She held out the gun, running fast, and she dropped it into the hole. Then she jumped back.

T.J. was right behind her. She stood still, waiting for him to say mad things to her.

"Was a *bad gun,*" she said in her mad voice, because Josie was at least as mad as T.J.

He pulled her into the light. She could see his face clearly, and it looked very, very mad. Something else, too — scared, maybe? He had his hands tight on both her arms. He wanted her to see his mouth, because he was going to say something important.

"You could have gotten *killed,*" he said to her, giving her a hard, angry shake. He stared at the hole, frowning.

"You, too!" she said, outraged.

"That was really stupid, Josie." Then his eyes went up, to the stairs, and Belinda came flying down, her mouth open in a terrible panic. Josie had never seen her sister so upset, crying so hard her face was bright red.

Belinda said something that made T.J. drop Josie's arms and stand up straight. Belinda's mouth was moving so fast, then T.J.'s, that Josie couldn't understand. Belinda was grabbing T.J.'s arm, jumping up and down. Josie knew something horrible was happening.

"What say?" she asked, feeling terrified inside.

They just kept talking, faster than ever, not even looking at her. She could only make out one word: Bob. Josie jumped up and down, to make them tell her. She clutched Belinda's hand, yanking it hard. Belinda had a red face and terrible fear in her eyes.

"Bob?" Josie asked. "Bob okay?"

"It's *Daddy*," Belinda said, shaking off Josie's hand. Belinda said some other words, then "boats," to T.J.

T.J. looked calm, like everything was going to be all right. He said something to Belinda, then he leaned over to kiss Josie. "Be good," he said.

Josie watched him run up the stairs. She looked up at Belinda. She felt a storm in her tummy, and she knew if someone didn't help her understand she would have a bad fit and she wouldn't be able to stop. She could taste the fit on the back of her tongue.

All of a sudden, Belinda began to pay attention. She kneeled down in front of Josie. She signed "Daddy."

"Daddy," Josie signed back.

"T.J. going to Daddy," Belinda signed. "Why?"

"To save him," Belinda said out loud, wiping tears from her eyes.

She looked into Josie's eyes without saying another word. Josie didn't know exactly what was happening, but she could tell from Belinda's expression that it was very scary. Maybe T.J. should have taken the gun.

Cass had to wait forever to have her snow tires put on. Half the town had come to Ledoux's Garage, just because a little snow was forecast. Well, six inches. But it did seem people couldn't handle snow anymore. School would be called off before two inches lay on the ground; people drove off the road as if they'd never learned to steer out of a skid. She and Billy had loved to skip school on snowy days. They'd drive out to Minturn Ledge, walk down the rocks, and watch snowflakes fizz as they hit the dark silver water.

Sitting in the garage waiting room, she enjoyed the sense of being out of touch. No one knew where to find her. Usually she was surrounded by her sisters, her children, her parents; and as much as she loved her life, it felt good to get away. She opened a magazine but didn't read it.

Rachel Barnard walked in with Maura Santos. Rachel wore a stylish snow-bunny outfit and a fur-trimmed suede hat. She looked great. Cass felt the old rivalry with Rachel flaring. She compensated for it by over-complimenting Rachel, acting as klutzy as possible.

"Wow," Cass said, eyeing Rachel's outfit. "I believe you forgot to turn left for St. Moritz, dear. This is the Shell station. Hi, Maura."

"Isn't it a knockout?" Maura asked. Maura, a comfortable, bosomy blond, was one of Cass's favorite fishing wives. Unfortunately, they saw each other only at PTA meetings, Holy Ghost Society dances, and Ledoux's Garage.

"Rachel, when you walk in looking like Bergdorf Goodman, I realize it's time I hang up the L. L. Bean twenty-four-hour hotline," Cass said, wishing she could just shut up. She would never in a million years dress like Rachel; Rachel's tight ski pants would look cute on Belinda and Emma, but they made you think Rachel was trying to recapture her non-existent pinup years.

"Not Bergdorf's," Rachel said without any irony. "Boston Downhill."

"Oh," Cass said, trying not to meet Maura's eyes. Maura winked and looked away.

"Hey, Frank's fishing with Billy," Maura said. "The maiden fishing trip."

"Must be nice, having a boat named after you," Rachel said.

"News travels fast," Cass said, thrilled.

"John leaves tomorrow for a week. He'll be gone for Thanksgiving," Rachel said wistfully, making Cass feel sorry for her.

"I hate when they miss holidays," Cass said. "Billy missed Christmas one year — that was awful."

"That would be the worst," Rachel and Maura agreed.

"You make more money, fishing this time of year," Maura said. "Not as many boats going out."

"John said the *Aurora*'s a nice boat," Rachel said. "One of the best in your father's fleet."

Cass wondered if John had told her about all the ways her father saved money, and she felt a little breath of relief knowing her father would retire soon. Her father bragged that he had the safest fleet in Mount Hope, but Cass would make it even safer. She figured a fisherman's wife would run the safest fleet in the world.

"It is," Cass said. "The *Aurora* is a very good boat. Do you have plans for Thanksgiving?" She was thinking of her own plans: every year Lobsterville served Thanksgiving dinner from three till eight. The Keatings themselves ate at twelve o'clock, sitting at one long table in the Captain Ed Room, with all the traditional dishes Sheila and Eddie had eaten at their own first Thanksgiving.

"I guess the kids and I will have dinner with John's mother in Jamestown," Rachel said, not sounding quite so forlorn.

"We'll be at Lobsterville," Maura said. "Five o'clock, same as ever. Frank's parents love it. It's always a combination Thanksgiving–farewell dinner. They leave the next day for Florida."

"Oh, where in Florida?" Cass asked.

"Naples," Maura said. "On the Gulf Coast."

"My father's been talking about retiring," Cass said.

"Jimmy Keating retire?" Maura said, laughing.

"That's a hot one," Rachel said.

Burton Ledoux, the garage owner, came into the waiting room. He was swarthy, with a pencil-thin mustache and a mysterious manner. He stood in the doorway, waiting for the three women to stop talking and notice him. He eyed them, one at a time, as if he were

425

trying to decide whom he wanted first. With his Grecian Formula black hair, Burton looked more like an international jewel thief than the owner of a gas station. Cass always expected him to speak with a French accent. But when he opened his mouth, the cadence of Mount Hope rolled out.

"Cass, you're all set," he said, squinting through the smoke of his cigarette as if it were a Gauloise instead of a Camel.

"*Merci,* Burton," she said.

Burton had driven her newly shod Volvo wagon into the parking lot. She checked in back to make sure he'd remembered to send her home with her summer tires, and she pulled on her rag-wool mittens. As she shifted into first, she spied her father's truck pulling in. She rolled down her window.

"Hey, I thought you already had yours put on," she called. Her father climbed out of his truck and walked to her car. He opened the door and made her get out. She stood in Ledoux's parking lot, suddenly knowing this was bad.

"Oh, my God," she said before he spoke. He had a grave expression on his face, and he crushed her roughly against him. Her heart was pounding, her face pressed into his old wool coat. She smelled fish and mothballs.

"Who is it?" she asked.

"Billy," he said.

"Is he . . . ?" She didn't know how to finish the sentence.

"Coast Guard got a call. He's taking on water. They've sent out a spotter plane, and they have boats on the way. The whole Mount Hope fleet is heading out."

Cass couldn't speak. There's a storm coming, she thought.

"They'll bring him home," her father said. "They'll have him safe aboard a Coast Guard boat by dark tonight."

Cass sank to the ground, hugging her knees. Her father crouched beside her. "When?" she asked.

"Tonight," her father said. "They'll have him home in no time."

"No, I mean when did it happen?" she asked, wondering what she had been doing at the exact moment Billy had started having trouble. She tried to think back, through the day. But her mind was stuck.

"I don't know. Come on," her father said, sliding his arm around her shoulder.

"He's sinking, right?" Cass asked. "That's what they mean, 'taking on water.' "

"Don't think like that," her father said harshly. He gave her a little shake.

People walked through the parking lot,

wondering what Cass and her father were doing, sitting on the ground. Cass wanted to leave, but she didn't think she could move.

"Come on," her father said again. "Let's get to a phone."

She nodded, pushing herself up. Her father held on tight, leading her to his truck. He opened her door, and she stopped halfway in. "Dad, they have to bring him home," she said, tears choking her throat.

"They will, Cass," he said. He stared into her eyes, strong and steady. Then he went to find Maura Santos, to tell her that Billy's boat, with her husband aboard, was in danger.

Both bad news and rumors traveled fast in Mount Hope, and often it was difficult to tell them apart. By the time Cass and her father reached Keating's Wharf, people were saying that Billy and his crew had been rescued by a Liberian tanker, that flares were still being sighted, that after that first call there'd been no word or sign.

Sitting in her father's truck, Cass stared dumbly at the harbor. There, she thought, staring at Billy's empty mooring. Right there. Right there. As if by picturing his boat — her gleaming white hull, the bold red trim — she could make it appear. The polished brass, the sooty exhaust pipe, the nets wound onto a spindle, Billy at the helm. Right there.

"What could have happened?" she heard herself ask.

"We don't know," her father said sternly. "So don't panic. He called the Coast Guard, that's all we know. But if he had time to use the radio, he's going to be fine."

"How could the boat be taking on water? It's completely solid, tight as a drum. He saw to it himself."

Her father didn't reply.

Nora and Bonnie came toward the truck. "What's Bonnie doing here?" Cass asked, frowning. "She went to Newport."

"We couldn't find you when the news first came through, and your mother thought you might have gone to the fair with Bonnie. We tracked her down."

Cass couldn't quite look at her sisters. They stood outside the truck, their hair tossing in the wind, watching Cass. She knew that once she stepped out, let them hug her, she would enter a stage of waiting that she didn't know if she could endure. They would usher her into some warm place where behind her back people would whisper the terrible possibilities and to her face would assure her that Billy would be home soon. She remembered sitting with Joan Cardinale the night Ralph's boat sank. The memory terrified her.

She took a breath and stepped out of the truck. Nora gave her a quick hug, and Bonnie, obviously trying to hold back tears, crushed her to her bosom. Cass gave her a long hard look.

"Don't start," Cass said.

Bonnie nodded.

"Any more news?" their father asked.

"Not yet," Nora said.

"I'm going to call the Coast Guard," their father said.

"Good," Cass said, watching him head for the warehouse. The Coast Guard operator was her closest link to Billy, but she knew the operator would be reporting thirdhand what the radio person aboard some cutter had been told to say. She wanted to be there, at sea herself, searching for Billy.

"Boats are going out. To look for him," she said.

"Everyone wants to help," Nora said.

"Cass, sweetheart," their mother called, running across the parking lot. Her little feet in their red high heels kicked out as she came, making Cass think crazily of a young girl running the fifty-yard dash.

"I'm fine, Mom. I'm fine," Cass said as her mother rammed her full force. "Why didn't you put on a coat? It's freezing out."

"My little Cass," Mary said, tears streaming

down her wrinkled cheeks.

Cass let her mother hang on, sobbing; Cass looked across her mother's curls at her sisters. Bonnie and Nora exchanged glances.

"Come on, Mother," Nora said. "Let's get you inside."

"We're all going inside," Mary said, sniffling. "We're going to sit at the picture window and watch for that boat to come around the breakwater. We'll say our prayers."

"Has anyone told the kids?" Cass asked.

"I'm afraid I did," Mary said. "I was frantic, looking for you, and I got Belinda on the phone."

"I'd better go home," Cass said. "I left my car at Ledoux's, though."

"I'll drive you," Bonnie said.

"We should all be together," Mary said. "We need each other now. Don't pull that strong business, Cass. I see it written all over your face. You are not made of granite, you know."

"Well, maybe pink granite," Bonnie said, and Cass gave her a smile.

"She's being a rock," Mary said, getting cross. "Pink or not. A pink rock isn't any softer than a gray one. Don't give me that. I just want you to know, Cass, that we love you." She took Cass's hands. "We've seen this happen to other families, and we've always thanked God it wasn't us. Well, now it is. Now it is."

Cass squeezed her mother's tough hands. She didn't trust herself to speak. Just holding her mother's hands, thinking of Billy, made Cass tighten her muscles from head to toe.

Cass and Bonnie headed toward Bonnie's car. As Bonnie was backing out, Cass spotted T.J. on his bike, wheeling into the parking lot in a wide, furious arc. While Bonnie's car was still moving, Cass tried to open her door. She struggled to undo her seat belt. T.J. let his bike clatter to the pavement, and she saw him tear around the warehouse.

Cass ran after him. He stood on the wharf, dressed in his warmest winter jacket, a knapsack slung over his shoulder.

"Is Dad okay?" he asked, his eyes wide when he saw Cass.

"He called the Coast Guard," she said, managing to steady her voice. "And they've sent boats and a plane to rescue him."

"Who from here's going out?" T.J. asked, gesturing at the trawlers lashed to the dock.

Cass's eyes traveled the dock's length. At that moment Manny Oliviera's boat pulled away. There were the *Aurora*, *Norboca*, and *Stephanie P.*, all teeming with activity. Fishermen ran down the dock, jumping onboard.

"I'm going out," T.J. said. "Whoever'll take

432

me, I'm going." He spoke defiantly, his chin thrust forward, his black eyes flashing. At fifteen, he had the barest hint of a mustache. He expected his mother to fight him, to hold him down if necessary.

She nodded. "I think you should," she said.

"You do?" he asked, surprised.

"I do," she said, surprising herself.

"I thought you'd be mad," he said as they hurried down the dock.

"I'd go if I could." Cass thought of it; she could jump on a boat right now. Her sisters would take care of Josie and Belinda. She ached to search for Billy. She felt him pulling her to him now, as if he held the other end of a long cord. But she knew she had to be home. Belinda could manage without her, but Josie couldn't. Cass felt the pull from both directions: Billy at sea, Josie at home. She understood why T.J. needed to go.

"John!" she called, approaching the *Aurora*. At the sound of her voice, John bounded onto the dock. He gave her a quick hug.

"We'll find him," he said.

"I want you to take T.J.," Cass said.

John frowned, looking from Cass to T.J. and back again. "I don't think that's a good idea, Cass," he said. "I mean, there's a winter storm coming, and T.J.'s a good sailor, but things can get a little hairy."

Cass knew he was trying to soft-pedal the danger, deflect their awareness from the fact that Billy was in trouble out there with a storm closing in, that T.J. was too young. It terrified her, the thought of her son going to sea right now. But she knew as clear as morning that T.J. needed to go.

T.J. stood between them, his fists clenched. His posture was tense as the arrow in its bow. "You have to let me," he said to John.

John searched Cass's face, giving her the chance to change her mind.

"Please," she said.

"Okay. Get aboard. We leave now," John said abruptly. He hopped onto the deck and gave orders for his crew to shove off.

T.J.'s eyes glittered with excitement. Cass knew how he must feel: the relief to be doing something instead of just waiting for news.

"T.J., listen to John," she said. "You know it could be dangerous, don't you? John's a good captain, and I happen to know firsthand the *Aurora*'s a good boat. But anything can happen."

"Why are you letting me go?" T.J. asked.

She thought long and hard, looking into his eyes. Black eyes, just like Billy's. Right now she knew he was impatient to get going. But behind the impatience was a fear as deep as Cass's own.

"Because I want your father to come home," she said.

"Aboard!" John shouted, revving the big Cat diesel.

Cass managed only the quickest kiss as T.J. leapt off the wharf onto the *Aurora*.

The sea and sky were white as pearls, waiting for snow. Cass could barely make out the line that separated them. She listened to the trawler engines, watched the *Aurora* pull away from the dock. The harbor was flat calm, but Cass could feel the storm coming. It tugged something inside of her, and she imagined it pulling the slats beneath her feet: the pilings, the entire wharf on which Keating & Daughters sat.

T.J. stood on deck, waiting to be told what to do. John threw him a line to coil. Cass shivered, standing in the spot where she'd kissed him goodbye. She watched the green boat glide across the smooth white surface, its engine thrumming steadily. Just before it rounded Minturn Ledge, T.J. turned. He seemed to scan the town. Cass waved hard, and he waved back. Right then, sending her only son to search for her husband at sea, Cass felt something let go, and she started to sob.

24

As darkness fell that November night, Billy Medieros, far from his home port, steered his damaged boat through the North Atlantic. The hole was small. The whale had pulled out two fastenings that Billy should have been able to fix. But when he'd probed the area with his pocketknife, he'd found dry rot that neither he nor the marine surveyor nor the boatyard had suspected. Water was pouring in. The electricity flashed on and off. Even with Tony and Paul pumping nonstop, they were losing their battle against the sea.

Back on deck, Billy figured it was about time to abandon ship. The ice-coated riggings were silver ladders to a vault of stars, but before it had turned dark, he'd seen storm clouds on the horizon. The swells were growing. Billy's hands, mitted in black leather, clung to the wheel as if frozen there. His lungs ached. Holding the wheel, he felt his boat riding lower in the water and it felt heavy. The boat didn't respond to the wheel. It was sinking.

Overhead, the aurora borealis shimmered. Billy, like most New England fishermen, had seen it before — the pipes of green, gold, and rose in the northern sky. It was a sight he'd always wanted to show Cass. Now he fantasized driving his boat with one arm around his girl, the northern lights illuminating their path across the sea. Screws turning, the boat throbbed beneath his feet, and he closed his eyes to see Cass.

When Cass fell in love with him, Billy couldn't believe it. She had skin like an angel's, those deep and mysterious blue eyes that promised secrets, and long, beautiful legs. He wished he could hold her now.

From the beginning, Billy had thought Cass was too good for him. Not that he'd ever let her know. He used to have nightmares that she'd realize how much better she could do than him. He'd act cocky, trying to impress her. Once, dropping her off at home, he'd peeled out in his Camaro, laying rubber all the way down Billow Road. But then some neighbor kid came whipping around the corner on her bike, Billy slammed on his brakes to avoid her, and he gashed his eye on the rear-view mirror. Big shot. Still had the scar.

To impress Cass, Billy used to do the sort of stuff he'd ground T.J. for now. He thought of his kids, wondered how much Cass had told them about this. The Coast Guard had promised to call her, and it gave him weird comfort to imagine Cass thinking of him, maybe picturing him at his wheel the way he was picturing her . . . where? He had to get it fixed in his mind. He closed his eyes, saw her at the kitchen table, with T.J. and Belinda doing their homework, Josie sitting on Cass's lap.

Connecting with Cass made him feel better. She was thinking about him so hard, he could feel it. She wouldn't stop until he came home. He knew it, as sure as if he'd just heard her whisper a promise in his ear.

Suddenly Billy saw a drop of water fall on the windshield, then another. He jumped with fright. Glancing up, he saw rain coming down. But no — it was the ice melting; things were warming up. He unzipped his parka and found he'd been sweating under all the layers of cotton and wool. His fingers, which had been frozen numb, suddenly prickled with feeling.

Tony and Paul came on deck. They were sweating.

"We're going down," Tony said.

"Let's get the life raft," Billy said. He swallowed hard.

"What's happening?" Paul asked, looking around.

"We've crossed into the Gulf Stream," Billy said. The northern lights still flickered overhead, but frost smoke wisped out of the sea. Cold air was hitting warm water that flashed with the golden fire of bioluminescence. A big fish, trailing phosphorescence, swam alongside them. A minke whale, Billy thought, or even another humpback. They were heading south for the winter-mating migration; maybe Billy should have foreseen it, chosen other grounds to fish.

"Get on your survival suits," Billy said. The men went below one last time, to gather what they could. Billy lifted the mike to call the Coast Guard once more. The breeze felt as balmy as Mount Hope in June. He took a deep breath and smelled flowers. Something green flashed by his cheek, then again. He ducked, holding his arms around his head, surrounded by wings beating and a murderous clacking. He looked up.

Parrots. Hundreds of parrots, emerald-green with orange throats, filled the rigging. They clung to shrouds and halyards with scarlet claws, chattering in a language Billy didn't understand. He made out the words "Havana" and *"isola."* They'd ridden the tropical air currents northward from Cuba and come to rest on Billy's boat. More and more settled on the mast, the radar scanner.

Billy opened his mouth, to yell for Tony and Paul. There were hundreds of parrots roosting in his rigging, and he wanted them to see. But before he could make any sound, all at once, in a clamorous green cloud, the parrots flew away.

For a moment Billy blinked, wondered if it could all be a dream. But there was the mike in his hand, the speaker crackling back at him, "We read you, *Cassandra*."

"We're abandoning ship," Billy said into the mike, reporting their loran position. "We have survival suits and a life raft, flares. . . ."

"Our plane is closing in on your area," the voice said. "They'll spot your flares. Hang tight, Billy. We're on the way."

Billy didn't want the transmission to stop. He didn't want to lose touch with dry land. He gripped the mike, afraid to hang up.

"How much longer?" he asked.

"The plane will get there within the hour. Keep your eyes peeled."

"I think we're in the Gulf Stream," Billy said, to keep her on the phone. Tony and Paul were on deck now, looking stocky and fore-shortened in their orange survival suits. They reminded Billy of his kids in their snowsuits when they were little, like Michelin men.

"I'll report that to the plane," the voice said through static. The cockpit lights flickered. Billy knew they were losing power.

"You're fading," the voice said. Billy could

tell she was speaking loudly. "Is there anything else?"

"Yes," he said. "Call my wife. Cass. Call Cass and tell her I love her. Over and out," Billy said as the mike went dead. Then he took the framed picture of Cass and the kids, stuck it under his arm, and went out to put on his survival suit. To abandon his ship.

"It's not fair T.J. got to go," Belinda said. "I wanted to, but I was stuck here. Someone had to stay with her." She flung her hand in Josie's direction.

"Thank you for staying," Cass said. "I know it's frustrating." She sat at the kitchen table, Josie on her lap. Belinda had schoolbooks open in front of her, but she wasn't reading.

"How am I supposed to take a stupid test tomorrow?" she asked, whining in a voice Cass hadn't heard since Belinda was a baby.

"You don't have to," Cass said. "The teacher will understand."

"Daddy's really missing?"

The word "missing" made Cass's heart skitter. She nodded. "He called in his position to the Coast Guard, so they'll head straight out. He knows where he is, or was, but we don't, exactly. But he's going to come home safe."

"Do you actually believe T.J. is helping?

441

I mean, what chance does a Mount Hope fishing boat have of finding Daddy?"

"The more boats looking, the better," Cass said. She was thinking of the plane; the Coast Guard had said it was in Billy's area. Any second the telephone would ring, and it would be Billy, being patched through from the rescue ship.

"I can't stand waiting," Belinda said, exploding out of her seat.

"What doin'?" Josie asked, frowning.

"Shut up!" Belinda screeched.

Josie's lower lip stuck out, but she didn't cry. Her eyes met Cass's, and Cass shrugged. "Leave her alone," she said to Josie.

"Me and Bob," Josie said quietly, snuggling her bottom deeper into Cass's lap. Cass felt amazed by Josie's behavior. Josie understood that everyone was worried about Billy, that he was in danger, but somehow she had decided to comfort Cass, to stay close and very calm. Cass gave her a long hug.

"Mom," Belinda said, bursting back into the room. "I need to get on a boat. I can't stand being here for one more second."

"All the boats have left," Cass said. "You can help Daddy a lot more by staying with me."

Belinda just stared angrily. "I hate this. Why did he get a new boat, anyway? Is

Daddy going to die?"

Cass had been asking herself the same questions, with the same level of fury and panic. But one thing about having children, it forced you to keep your head.

"Daddy is not going to die," Cass said.

"Why'd he get a new boat? I'd like to kill that old fart Mr. Magnano. Something was probably wrong with it, and he sold it to Daddy anyway."

"Mr. Magnano would never, never do that," Cass said sternly, hiding the fact that she had been entertaining homicidal thoughts of George herself.

"Can I call Emma?"

"Belinda, you know we have to keep the phone open. But I'll tell you what. Would you like to sleep over there?"

"At Emma's?"

"Yes. I'm sure Bonnie would pick you up."

Belinda's expression turned doubtful, guilty. "I shouldn't leave you with Josie."

"Josie and I will be fine," Cass said. But already she was dreading the moment when Josie would fall asleep. She didn't want to be alone, unable to call her sisters, listening for the phone. She shivered, knowing she couldn't go to bed that night.

"If you're sure," Belinda said, watching Cass's face with skepticism.

Cass nodded. She grabbed the receiver, speed-dialed Bonnie's number.

"Bon, can you pick up Belinda so she can sleep over? Thanks, bye."

"That was the fastest I've ever heard you talk," Belinda said admiringly. "There's no way you missed a call."

Cass just smiled, feeling exhausted. Belinda went upstairs to pack. When she came down, she kissed Josie sweetly. She signed a quick message, and Josie signed back. Cass listened for the phone and for Bonnie's car.

Moments later she heard Bonnie drive up. Going to the door, she saw that snow had started to fall. Fine flakes, slanting from the north, glowed like a golden mist in the porch light.

"Any news?" Bonnie asked, coming to the door.

Cass shook her head.

"Would you like Belinda to stay? Emma could sleep here instead. We all could."

"I don't think so. But thanks."

"Nora has her hands full with Mom," Bonnie said. "Mom wants to pack up Dad and Granny and move right in here. She tried to recruit Nora and Willis, me and the kids."

"Gavin's not home?"

"He's out looking," Bonnie said. "On board Derek's boat. Did you think he wouldn't be?"

"Of course he would be," Cass said, hugging herself. Snow gusted through the open door.

"Hi, Aunt Bonnie," Belinda said. "Night, Mom. Call me? If there's anything?"

"I promise. You'll be the first person I call," Cass said. She kissed her daughter goodnight, and Belinda ran ahead to the car.

"How are you holding up?" Bonnie asked.

"Okay."

"Call if you want me here."

Bonnie backed out the driveway. Inside the kitchen, Cass listened to her drive away, down Coleridge Avenue. Then she turned her attention to the phone. The plane had to be over Billy; the phone would ring any second. Now. It will ring now.

It didn't. The phone didn't ring then, and it didn't ring all night.

Sheila held on to her glass locket and thought of her boys. She considered her granddaughters' husbands to be her boys as much as Jimmy and Ward, her own sons. She thought of the girls — the women — in her family. Everyone imagined girls needed protecting, extra care, shielding from danger, while boys just skated along, thin ice or not, ready for anything.

But Sheila knew that Ward, hardly twenty

years old, hadn't been ready to go down in flames. And Billy wasn't ready to die at sea. The old grandfather clock across the room ticked along, every second bringing Billy closer to death. Sheila stared at it, the brass pendulum swinging blurrily.

She would never forget the day she heard about Ward. Such a sunny day, quiet in the garden, with just a few sea gulls crying overhead. She had been on edge ever since Ward had gone overseas, constantly uneasy, praying for his safety. But there was something about that day — the peace, the bright sky — that had reassured her.

She'd been planting the window boxes. She could see the flowers now: red geraniums, white petunias. She could smell the damp loam, feel the warmth of it as she buried the roots. Then the doorbell rang. In her haste to answer it, she knocked over a geranium, breaking its thick stem.

The mail woman, her buttons gleaming. Sheila couldn't see her face now, she wasn't their usual mail woman, but she could picture those brass buttons. The raised eagles, polished to catch the sunlight. Sheila had stared at those buttons, accepting the telegram. Still, she hadn't believed it. The sunlight, the sea gulls. The dirt under her fingernails.

Sheila had read the message.

"I'm sorry," the woman had said. "So sorry."

Sheila had sat down in the dark living room, the curtains drawn to keep the bright sun from fading the slipcovers. She had held the telegram in her hand, and then smoothed it over her knee. She had gotten dirt on it. She had tried to brush it off, but it stayed dirty. She had stared at it, trying to figure how long it had taken to reach her. She had held it on her lap, wondering what she had been doing at the exact minute her son had been shot down. She had wondered how she could have lived her life, enjoying the sunshine, not knowing her son was dead.

That was the difference between Ward and Billy. All the family, everyone who loved him, was watching the clock tick by, imagining his terror, helpless to save him. Sheila knew how his own parents would feel, if they had still been alive. She thought of Cass, her favorite granddaughter; Sheila would give her own life if it would save Billy.

Now her eyes traveled to Ward's painting, behind which she kept all the important family documents. She took a deep breath and forced herself out of her chair. She held on to the chair arms for a minute, getting her balance. Her chest felt tight.

She eased the picture off the wall and opened

the envelope taped to its back. With her fingers shaking, she took out the telegram. It was still smudged with dirt from the window boxes after all these years.

She blinked. For a second, she thought she saw Eddie. Lately he had been haunting this corner of her room where Ward's painting hung. She squinted, trying to make Eddie come into focus.

"I'd do it, Eddie. If it would bring Billy home. He can't die, Eddie. He can't leave Cass alone."

"The way I left you?"

Had she really heard it? She was wide awake, and she was sure she had heard Eddie's voice. She felt so shocked, she sat back down in her chair.

"Yes, the way you left me," she said. "Cass isn't ready."

She sat very still, listening. But Eddie didn't reply. Sheila shook her locket, watching the pearl rattle. In her other hand she held the telegram. She prayed for Billy, and she prayed to fall asleep. Sleep was the only sure way she'd see Eddie again.

Every wave was a mountain. You'd ride up one side, then fall off the other. Ride up, fall off. Ride up, fall off. You couldn't see anything, the night was so black and the snow so thick.

"This is crazy," some smelly fat guy said to John. "You can't see nothin'."

"Watch for flares," John said, staring straight ahead. He gripped the wheel.

"Crazy," the fat guy said again.

T.J. had his corner of the wheelhouse. John had assigned him one area of sea to watch, from nine to twelve o'clock. T.J.'s eyes roved the quadrant, ticking back and forth. He concentrated on not throwing up.

"We're not there yet," John said. "You won't see him for a while. But look anyway."

T.J. kept watching.

"You hear me?" John asked.

"Huh? Me?" T.J. said, so surprised, he turned toward John for one second.

"Yeah, you."

"I hear you."

"We'll find your father. Boats go down all the time. We haven't lost a Mount Hope guy in years."

"Mac Pearson," the fat guy said.

"Explosions at the dock are different. They're always killers," John said.

"Boats go down all the time?" T.J. asked. "And the guys are okay?"

"Sure," John said. "Especially someone as smart as your father. He and I sank one time."

"You did?"

"Yeah. Off Block Island. We got rescued

ten minutes after shooting off the first flare."

"Block Island's not like this," T.J. said as the boat pitched off another wave. This was way out, and T.J. knew that the farther offshore a boat sank, the worse the chances. He'd heard his father say that.

"I've been in bigger storms than this off Block Island," John said.

"What did you mean before, when you said we're not there yet?" T.J. asked, his eyes covering his area. "You sound like you know where we're going. Even the Coast Guard doesn't know, and my dad called them."

T.J. had been listening when John radioed the Coast Guard. The Coast Guard lady had sounded royally pissed to hear that John was joining the search. "Next we'll be searching for you," she'd said in a really snide tone.

"You never know with the Coast Guard," John said, his eyes focused dead ahead. "With all their classes and training you'd expect them to be smarter than they usually are. It proves one of my favorite points."

"What?"

"Put brass and a uniform on a guy and watch him go brain-dead."

"So what makes you think you know where my dad is?"

"Because your dad and I have fished together, and I know his spots. I know exactly where he was when he bailed out, and I know his raft is setting for Bermuda. Here — take the wheel." He walked to the chart table; T.J. just stood there.

"You want us to roll over?" John asked sharply. "Take the wheel."

T.J. left his post. He'd steered his father's boat plenty of times, but not in waves like this. Clamping his hands on the wheel, he felt it try to twist his arms off.

"Steer for a compass heading of ninety-six," John ordered. He flipped on a greenish light that cast reflections on all the wheelhouse windows, and he began reading the chart.

"John, man," the fat guy said, "I'm losing it. I need an hour to sleep."

"Okay, Sid," John said without looking up. "We'll call you when we get close."

No one spoke for a while. T.J. fought the wheel. First he turned it way to the left, and just as the bow seemed to be heading straight for ninety-six, the compass swung past, and he had to pull right. Finally he got the boat on course. Waves continued to pound the hull.

T.J.'s eyes felt tired. He tried to fight back his fear. The timbers moaned and creaked with every wave; it seemed like the ocean had teeth and claws and was trying to tear their boat apart. T.J. pictured great white sharks following them, down below where everything was pitch-black and calm, their dead eyes and sonar tracking a boat full of shark bait.

"Do you get scared, John?" he asked before he could help himself.

"You get used to it, T.J.," John said. "But this is a bad storm."

T.J. couldn't imagine getting used to this. He had to fight just to stay on his feet. The ocean was everywhere: waves battered the windows, and if T.J. hadn't had the compass to refer to, he wouldn't have known which way was up. He glanced at the compass, a black globe illuminated in a brass binnacle. His eyes fell upon markings in the wood. Carved in the mahogany on which the binnacle was mounted was the name "Cass." The letters were scored deep, blackened by salt.

His father had skippered this boat before John. T.J. imagined his dad on a boring night, when the sea was calm and he didn't have to fight every wave, whipping out his pocket-knife, carving his mom's name. So that on nights like this, when he felt afraid, she would be right there with him. On the opposite side, someone had carved "Rachel." The letters were just as deep, but white, as if they'd been carved recently.

"Rachel's your wife," T.J. said to John.

"Yeah," John replied.

Staring at the names felt much better than

thinking of his father in a raft trying to ride waves like this, with snow turning him into a white island. T.J. narrowed his eyes, watching through the eerie green glass for flares. But all he could see were waves.

"Nantucket waters are tricky," John said. "Shallow where you'd expect no bottom at all."

"Do you think he went aground?" T.J. asked.

"Nah. Your father can navigate anything. Something must've happened to his boat."

"Like what?" T.J. asked.

"I don't know."

"How can the planes fly in this?"

"What planes?"

"The ones looking for my dad."

"There aren't any planes out here," John said, not looking up. "Maybe there were before, but not now. They're safe in a hangar somewhere." He continued studying the chart.

The raft bucked the white waves. Up became down, and Billy was drowning in snow, clawing downward toward the sea. Every swell took them to the edge, promised to flip them over. A thousand times, every time a wave hit, they'd thought they would turn over. Tony couldn't take it anymore. He cried through the night, until the screaming wind and his sobs became the same. Billy and Paul actually watched him lose his mind. They tried to talk to him, but it seemed he didn't know they were there. All of a sudden, he grasped the lifeline, crossed himself, and climbed over the side.

Billy lunged toward him, but Tony had disappeared into the sea. "Oh, my God," Billy said.

"He's gone," Paul said, his teeth chattering.

The night suddenly seemed horribly quiet.

An hour went by. At first Billy thought about Tony's wife and two sons, wondering what he was going to say to them. But after a while, the cold blocked out everything.

Billy didn't think of the storm, the sea, the falling snow, the ice in his eyes. He'd stopped listening for engines, stopped thinking about the raft pitching over, stopped beating his arms against his chest to stay warm. He just lay in the bottom of the raft, curled on his side, looking at the back of Paul's head. He had a hood on. Monk. Kid in a snowsuit. Billy blinked, staring at the stiff orange fabric.

The raft danced over the mountains. Some sharply peaked, craggy like the Rockies. Crevasses, ravines, ledges, jagged river valleys piercing the evil rocks. Some smoothed into hills, like the ancient mountains in Ireland, worn down by the storms of a million years, rounded as a woman's breasts.

Cass's breasts. Where did that come from? The thought stirred Billy so, he almost rose on his elbow. A hard object dug into his side. He did not recognize it as his family's picture in its frame. Billy stopped thinking of the mountains he rode over, stopped feeling every descent in his throat. He stared at the back of Paul's head. He tried to push himself up, but he couldn't. He was a block of ice.

25

Cass hadn't slept or talked to anyone all night. As the sun rose her heart lurched, because the snow had stopped. She sat at the window, watching pink light spread across the pillowy drifts. The Coast Guard planes would be flying by now, crisscrossing the North Atlantic, searching the sea.

She searched her mind for Billy and found him alive. Yes, she knew with certainty he was. She'd discovered during the night a thrilling ability to zoom in on him. She picked up messages from him. But she couldn't rush them; she had to let her mind drift: the falling snow, Josie sucking her thumb, the recipe for cranberry bread. Then, pow!

She'd get a flash of Billy.

As long as they kept coming, she knew he was alive.

The day began. Josie awakened, asking for Daddy. Cass told her he was on his boat, still waiting for help. Josie seemed cranky. She sat at the kitchen table, dressed in her yellow flannel nightgown, whimpering because her hearing aids itched. Cass made pancakes to keep busy and tried to cajole Josie with blueberry jam instead of the usual maple syrup. But Josie wouldn't eat.

Cass dressed herself and Josie in jeans and turtlenecks. Josie wanted to play in the snow. But Cass couldn't leave the phone. She scooped snow off the top step, made a big pile on the back porch. She buckled on Josie's snow boots, zipped up Josie's ski jacket. Then she hooked the porch door and let Josie pretend she was outside.

She heard a car drive up, and Josie squealed with pleasure.

Cass's heart pounded; she ran through the house. Would he really surprise her like this, just show up without calling? For one second she felt angry, that he would have let her worry all these hours, when he could have called her ship-to-shore, from the Coast Guard station, from a hundred points along the way. But then Josie called, "Gampy!"

Cass caught her breath. She met her father, with Josie riding his boot like a pony, in the back hall. He gave Cass a hug, and Josie scampered back to her snow pile.

"Want some coffee?" she asked. "It'll just take me a minute."

"No thanks," her father said, and Cass realized he was pushing her into a chair.

"What?"

"The Coast Guard has called off the search," her father said.

"No," Cass said stupidly.

"Yes."

"They can't. Look at the day! The planes can fly today."

"They don't believe he could have survived the storm."

Her father watched her gravely, letting his words hang in the air. But Cass wouldn't accept them.

"He's alive," she said.

Her father tried to take her hand, but she pulled it back. She popped out of her seat, paced around the kitchen. Her father was watching her, pity knotting his brow.

"I know what you're thinking," she said, gulping air as she'd done in childbirth. She thought she might hyperventilate. "That I'm crazy, that I can't accept this."

"None of us . . ."

"I know he's alive," she said. "I know it. They have to keep looking."

"They found his boat. The wreckage, I should say," her father said, making the word sound unnecessarily harsh, as if he were trying to make her face a terrible fact.

"You know people in the Coast Guard,"

Cass said. "You have to make them keep going."

Her father stared at his hands, then looked up. "I've called everyone I can think of. Your mother's been hounding me since six this morning to get on the phone."

"How long have you known about this?" Cass exploded. "It's ten now."

"We didn't know anything. Now just hold your horses," he said gruffly. "I've been through this before, you know. Not with family, but I've lost boats. I watched the weather last night, and I knew the Coast Guard would be thinking they couldn't have made it."

"What do *you* think?" Cass asked, knowing that if her father gave the wrong answer, she'd kick him out of her house.

He sat silent. He looked everywhere but at Cass. "Say it," she said.

"I think it's unlikely," he said, "that they are alive."

Cass tried to breathe. She wanted to scream at him, tell him to leave her alone. She wanted to attack him with her fists and her fingernails. But she couldn't move.

"All the captains have the news. Most of them are coming home."

"The Mount Hope guys?" Cass asked, sitting down.

"Most."

Cass stared at the flowers embroidered on her tablecloth. Her grandmother had made it herself, given it to Cass and Billy for their third anniversary. It was the kind of thing people set aside to pass on to their children. Tablecloths like this were usually found in trunks, perfectly pressed and white, wrapped in tissue paper. But this one had grape-jelly stains, coffee-cup rings, the ghostly remains of a ketchup spill.

"Who's not coming home?" she asked.

"John Barnard," her father said. "Al Sweet. David Griswold and Kelly Dellerba. Dave and his crew."

"Did you talk to John yourself?"

"Yes. T.J. is fine."

Cass nodded. No matter what the Coast Guard said, what her father believed, Billy had to be alive. She felt him so strongly, he couldn't be gone. He must have been scared last night, frozen stiff, maybe delirious. But she thought of the sun rising, throwing what warmth it could, the hope it must have brought to Billy and his men.

"Dad," Cass said, reaching for his hand. "Don't believe Billy is dead. You can't believe it yet."

He didn't reply.

"Call the Coast Guard. Do it for me. Please, Dad. Make them keep searching. Even for a few hours. Just for today. Please?"

He hesitated, tracing the embroidered flowers with his index finger. Without saying a word to Cass, he pushed himself up and lifted the telephone receiver. He dialed a number he knew by heart.

"Governor Malloy, please," he said. "James Keating calling."

Cass couldn't look. She stared at the tablecloth, pictured her grandmother's fingers pushing the needle.

"Mike, I need a favor," her father said. He laid out the scenario, talking without interruption for three or four minutes. From the passion in his voice, you'd believe he knew beyond any shadow of a doubt that Billy was alive, that his survival depended on the Coast Guard finding him within the next few hours. When he hung up the phone, he walked around the table and grasped Cass's shoulders with both hands. "They'll keep at it till sunset tonight."

The bright-red raft bobbed in the sparkling blue sea. The two men lay still, past shivering. Sunlight reflected off the flat ocean like a mirror. No mountains today, no caverns. A little to the north, a jet flew over. Ten minutes later, it flew over again. Ten minutes after that, it flew closer. A chart in the cockpit showed the

461

pilot his pattern. A spotter with binoculars watched the water.

"After last night? No way," the pilot said.

"I doubt it," the spotter said. It was hard to keep the binoculars steady. He put them down, scanned with his bare eyes. Something dark flashed just below the surface. "What's that?" the spotter asked, slapping the binoculars to his eyes.

The pilot flew down for a closer look. The dark spot rose to the surface and a fountain spouted.

"A whale," the spotter said, laughing. "Boy, they're pretty."

"They sure are," the pilot said.

"There!" the spotter said sharply. "That's no whale."

The pilot peered down. "No, it isn't." He radioed to shore.

"Go ahead," the operator said.

"I believe we've spotted one of them," the pilot said. "We'll guide the cutter out."

"One of the men?" the operator asked.

"A body," the pilot said.

In the bright-red raft, just half a mile from where the plane had spotted, one of the men stirred. He licked his lips, which were cracked and swollen. He heard something far off that throbbed like an engine. He tried to lift his head, but he couldn't seem to move. Then the sound faded, and his dreams took him back.

Or maybe it was the other way around.

The hours went by so fast. Sitting in her kitchen, Cass couldn't stop watching the clock. Eleven, noon, one. Time for Josie's nap. Two, two-thirty. She pictured the planes, buzzing like bees across a clover patch, doing their work. She pictured T.J. watching the horizon, John driving them closer to Billy. They still had hours of daylight left, but, in a way, Cass was waiting for dark.

Flares.

Last night the visibility had been too poor, the snow driving in sheets, the waves so big. No one could have seen Billy's flares. But tonight the sky would be clear. A flare in this wintery sky would blaze like a rocket, like fireworks on the Fourth.

How did you define sunset, anyway? The planes were supposed to fly till sunset, but did anyone expect the pilot to check the almanac, to land at the exact published moment? No. They would fly until it was too dark to see. And just before they turned for home, they'd see Billy's flares.

Three o'clock, three-thirty. Cass sat still, keeping track of Billy in her mind. There he is. Yes, there. Still alive. Billy.

She stayed in the same place, in her chair at the kitchen table. When Josie woke up from her nap, she was in a better mood. She wanted to play in the snow again. The sun had melted the snow closest to the house, so Cass had to venture farther into the yard to rebuild Josie's pile. She made sure to leave the door open, so she could hear the phone.

Belinda called.

"I'm sorry, I know I shouldn't call you. Any news?"

"No," Cass said. "They're still looking."

"Mommy, I'm so scared," she said, her voice thin and high.

"I know, honey."

They hung up. Three-forty-five, four o'clock, four-thirty; getting dark.

Belinda walked through the door. "I had to come home," she said, burying her face in Cass's shoulder. Bonnie walked through the door, her face blank.

"Is it okay that I'm here?" Bonnie asked. Cass nodded.

"Where's Josie?" Belinda asked. "I want to see her."

"On the porch," Cass said, realizing she'd lost track for a moment. Josie would be freezing, she'd been so intent playing in her snow pile. "Will you get her to come in, honey?"

"Sure," Belinda said.

Bonnie just stared at Cass, as if she were waiting for something. She had the most terrible expression of fear in her eyes. "What's wrong?" Cass asked.

"The time," Bonnie said gently, stepping closer. "It's getting dark out. It's sunset."

Cass went to the window. Do it, Billy, she said to herself. You went down on the boat you named after me. I can't live with that. I need you back so I can tell you I love you. Cass clenched her fists, closed her eyes, concentrated with all her might. Do it, she thought. Send a flare. Send it now. Now. Now.

"It's over," Sid said. The sun's last rays lit the western sky, settling across the water in silvery lilac ripples. "They're quitting."

The plane's engine chopped overhead, louder and louder, as it beat a path homeward. T.J. watched it come, its lights unbelievably bright. He'd been watching the plane all day. First he'd hear it, then it would appear, then it would be gone. But it always came back. It had comforted and excited T.J., both at the same time. Once it had flown in circles, and all the boats had driven over.

All the boats but John's. John knew where he was going.

"Whatever they're spotting, it isn't Billy," John had said. "Billy's in the current by now."

"The current?" T.J. had asked.

"The Gulf Stream. Good thing we have such a big motherfucking diesel, because he's drifting fast."

John had said the planes were looking in the wrong place, but T.J. didn't care. At least they were looking.

"Shit," Sid said, watching the plane.

"Now's when they'd do some good," John said, peering up through the wheelhouse window. "Now's when they'd spot a flare."

"They can't quit," T.J. said. They needed the planes: John, Sid, and T.J., the other guys on the other boats, and the pilots were part of a team, out to save his father.

"They have orders to quit," John said.

"So what? They can keep looking if they want to," T.J. said, positive they would want to.

Sid made a gross laughing snort. "Son, the name of the game is moola. Costs a fortune to run a rescue operation. Fifty, a hundred grand, who the hell knows?" Now he made a disgusted snort. "Men's lives are at stake, and the Coast Guard worries about its bottom line."

T.J. couldn't believe it. The plane flew overhead and didn't turn around. It just kept flying.

"He can't quit!" T.J. yelled.

"Come on, Billy," John said. "Come on, man."

"What?" Sid asked.

"One flare, Billy," John said. "It's dark now."

T.J. ran out of the wheelhouse. "Poor kid," he heard Sid say softly. T.J. tore across the deck, to the life raft. John had shown it to him the day before, when it looked as if the weather was getting really bad. "Just in case," John had said. At the time all T.J. had been able to do was stare, thinking, My dad's in this storm in one of those?

He dove into the raft, rummaged around, found the flare gun. It weighed a ton, much more than the pistol Josie had thrown in the suds hole. What an asshole he'd been, pointing it at his own head. Alison seemed like a million years ago.

He lifted the flare gun, pointed it straight up. Except for Venus and the plane's lights, moving away fast, the sky was totally dark. T.J. shot off the flare.

It zipped through the sky, a red dot. Then it exploded into a fireball, red sparkles flying everywhere. He shot again.

"*What the fuck?*" John yelled, racing across the deck. He yanked the flare gun out of T.J.'s hand. T.J. glanced at the wheelhouse, saw Sid frowning at the helm. He felt the engines slow.

"If they see flares they have to keep searching," T.J. said, shoving John back.

"You little shit, you don't know anything. It's already gone, T.J. The plane is gone. Messing with my flares, you could have set my fucking boat on fire."

But T.J. had his eyes on the sky. Here it came. The plane had turned around, was coming this way.

"I'll be damned," John said.

T.J. just watched the lights getting bigger, drawing nearer.

"This is the wrong place," John said. "They're going to be searching the wrong place."

"At least they're still searching," T.J. said, watching the horizon.

With the sun gone, the cold came back. The man arched his back. He tried to touch the other man, but he couldn't reach. He knew there was something he should remember. He knew there was something he should do. Shoot, he told himself. Shoot. He heard himself laugh, and he wondered what was so funny. Then it came to him: how was he supposed to shoot when he couldn't even move? But the word locked in his mind, so he could hear the sound, like a whistle, and see the letters. *Shoot.* Then it was gone.

After the sun had been down for an hour and the phone hadn't rung, Cass lowered her head to the table and started to cry. Belinda, Josie, and Bonnie stood there watching her, but Cass felt she was alone. She heard her own sobs ringing in her ears, and she couldn't stop.

"They're going to stop looking now, aren't they?" Belinda asked, her voice high and thin. "They said they'd look till the sun set, and now it's set. Are they going to stop?"

"Yes, dear," Bonnie said.

Belinda burst into tears.

"Bob?" Josie asked, her voice anxious, tapping Cass's hand. "Bob?"

When Cass didn't look up, Josie began to fret. "Eh, eh, eh," she started. But Cass no longer heard her own daughter. She no longer heard Bonnie, trying to calm Josie, trying to comfort Belinda. She didn't hear Bonnie, her own sister, whisper in her ear, "Cass, don't give up. John's still looking. Other boats are, too."

Cass didn't hear, and she didn't care that the Coast Guard had stopped looking. She didn't care whether the planes had flown home. She wouldn't have cared if someone had told her John and T.J. had turned around, abandoning the search.

Cass didn't hear her own daughters crying,

and she didn't care that the search had been called off. She only cared about one thing, and it wasn't there. Cass could no longer feel Billy.

Sheila held on tight to her locket. She sensed Eddie's presence as strongly as she had on their wedding day. The sun had gone down, and streetlights smoothed all the room's edges into gentle shadows. The grandfather clock ticked along, its pendulum flashing as it caught the light. She could hear Mary and Jimmy talking in their bedroom, their low tones interrupted by Mary's sudden sobs. A cold wind knifed past a loose windowpane, moving the white curtain. Sheila's pulse raced with alarm and excitement.

"Eddie, are you there?" she asked.

One of the shadows stirred. "I'm here," he said.

"I'm so scared for Cass," Sheila said. "When I lost you, I thought I'd lost everything. Cass and Billy have every bit as much as we did. I can't bear to think of her."

Sheila sat still, her heart pounding, waiting for Eddie to come toward her. She peered at every shadow. Her room held an army of shadows, crouched by her night table, the armchair, the tall clock, her bureau.

"Eddie," she pleaded, "are you there? I

need to know you're waiting for me."

But all Sheila heard was a branch scraping her window.

The morning after he'd shot the flares, the third day of the search, T.J. heard John call his name. T.J. had been asleep for two hours, and he felt good. The sun was just coming up, but the air felt warm, like springtime. He grabbed his jacket, from habit, but he didn't need it. When he stepped outside, his mouth dropped open. He couldn't believe his eyes.

T.J. stepped into a cloud of parrots. Thousands of bright-green parrots, the kind you'd see in a pet store, fluttered overhead, landing on every surface. They perched in John's rigging, on the cabin top, on Sid's head. They crapped all over. First thing T.J. did was yank his Red Sox cap out of his pocket, jam it on his head. He wondered if he was still dreaming.

"What the hell's going on?" he asked John.

"We're in the Gulf Stream," John said, his shirt unbuttoned. "And we have company."

"Uh, does this happen all the time out here?" T.J. asked, watching the parrots.

"Not to me," John said.

It felt unbelievably warm. John had an even more serious air about him than T.J. had seen so far on this trip. He squinted right into the sun, unsmiling, like a gunfighter.

"Are the planes still searching?" T.J. asked.

John gestured over his shoulder. "They're back there. We left them behind a while ago."

"Oh," T.J. said, wondering if they should stay with the planes.

"Start looking," John said, "and don't even blink. This is where we'll find your father."

"How do you know?" T.J. asked, already scanning.

"Like I said, I know where your dad fishes, and I know how tides and currents work. They're not magical. You just need to factor in the wind. You use your math." John craned his neck, looking overhead. "I need you up high. You can scope out a bigger field that way. Can you shinny up the mast?"

"Yeah, I can," T.J. said.

"Get yourself secure in the rigging." He handed T.J. a pair of massive binoculars and a red web strap to hold them around his neck.

T.J. waved his arms to scatter the parrots. They didn't scare easy; they hopped along the yardarm, shifted their claw holds, flapped their wings. T.J. climbed the mast, hanging tight with his left arm. He braced his feet against the nylon lines John had coiled on hooks.

T.J. felt like a whaler in a crow's-nest. You could see forever from up here, twice as far

472

as from the deck. He wasn't more than twelve feet up; he imagined how far the planes could see, and he wished one would fly over. That would make him more secure about John's determination to search the Gulf Stream. It felt so warm, he thought they could be in Florida by now.

The parrots were squawking. T.J. tried to shoo them, but they only moved closer to him. He didn't want to be distracted from his lookout. Mainly he roved with his naked eyes, from nine o'clock to twelve o'clock, from twelve o'clock to three o'clock, then back again. Tick, tock. He felt like the black-cat clock in Dr. Malone's office, whose eyes and tail clicked back and forth every second.

He wished he'd see something besides water. A log, some fish jumping, another boat: anything to interrupt the endless stretch of sea. He began to believe there *was* nothing else. He turned his cap around, peak to the back, so it wouldn't interfere with the binoculars. Not that anything needed a closer look. At least when the planes were around you knew you were going to see something else. You knew that within a few minutes there'd be something other than water. It might not be the raft yet, but it gave you hope.

Sunlight glared, skittering off the water's surface. Every so often it caught his eye —

at ten o'clock, say, when his eyes had ticked over to one. He'd look back fast, afraid he'd missed something. But it would only be sparkles dancing on a wave in the east.

As the sun moved higher, closer to noon, the sparkles spread out. They were everywhere. T.J. couldn't keep up his rhythm. Over there! He'd jerk his head, but it would just be sparkles. There! More sparkles. They began to seem alive and mischievous. The sparkles started to scare him; they gave him a headache and made him think he was seeing things. He worried that one would distract him in the single split second his father's raft was visible. With John and Sid in the wheelhouse, T.J. began to feel like he was the only person onboard. He began to appreciate the parrots.

Their squawks sounded like words, kind of nasal, like Josie. That thought made him laugh a little, picturing a little tiny Josie-bird, all green and serious, sitting on his shoulder. Then he worried he was going crazy. Weren't there a million sea legends about guys going crazy on voyages?

Old salts who lusted after walruses, thinking they were hot babe mermaids? Sailors who heard their mothers calling their name, only their mothers had been dead twenty years, and it was just the wind? Peg-leg dudes who chased whales around the world. You saw it in the movies all the time. But most of the guys were old, T.J. told himself. Not teenagers.

The sun burned his face. Sparkles covered every surface of the sea, three-hundred-sixty degrees of them. T.J. couldn't shake this sick feeling that the sun sparkles were evil. They reminded him of devils dancing on white-hot coals. There: one of them burned up.

A devil on fire. Or dying in a pool of blood. T.J. stared at the little red patch. He lifted the glasses, tried to fit the lenses to his eyes as the boat pitched. The bloody sparkle danced in and out of his sight; the other sparkles wanted to hide it, bury it before T.J. could see.

T.J. adjusted the binoculars, fiddling with the wheel. John was steaming ahead too fast. T.J. had to curve his body around the mast to get a better look. He craned, held his body rigid, so he could focus. Hidden in the waves' trough, then a flash, and finally a wave held it up, like an offering, just long enough for T.J. to get one clear look.

"The raft!" T.J. shouted. "John, my father's raft! Eight o'clock!"

John brought the boat around. He opened the throttle as far as it would go, but it took forever to cross the water. T.J. stayed in the rigging, the binoculars pressed to his eyes.

Now that he'd seen the raft, had it in his sight, it wasn't enough. He wanted to see his father. He wanted to see his father jumping up and down, waving like crazy, yelling for help. He didn't see anyone.

Just the raft, a big red rubber circle, high and rounded; at first T.J. couldn't tell if it was right-side up or upside down. But as they got closer he saw small dark shadows defining the center hollow, and now T.J. felt glad for the sun, because the shadows meant the raft hadn't flipped over.

They were close enough so that T.J. didn't need the binoculars. He stayed on the mast, watching for someone to move. Surely his dad would hear the engine by now. Even if he'd been asleep, he'd hear the noisy pulse and wake up. Or one of the other guys. His father had a crew of four; T.J. didn't see how they could all fit on that little raft, much less stay so still. T.J. didn't know what he was thinking, but suddenly his heart felt like it would pound out of his chest.

"Get down here, T.J.," John called. "I need your help."

T.J. used a couple of hooks as toeholds, then jumped to the deck. His arms and legs felt rubbery, and he fell down, scrambling a few steps like a crab. He ran to John, who stood at the port rail. Sid had the wheel.

"We're going to come around, and I'll grab a line with the boat hook," John said, a grim frown on his face.

"It's good, we found it," T.J. said. It was so fucking unbelievable, if you thought about it. He hadn't let himself see it that way, all during the search: What were the odds of anyone finding this little red blob? He should be congratulating John: Wow, man, how did you know? You're a genius, an amazing sailor. T.J. should have been excited out of his mind, but he wasn't. T.J. had a terrible, sick feeling deep inside.

No one on the raft was moving.

It was close enough to see. Some bogus red rubber cover had blown half off, and you could see legs. Two pairs of legs. T.J. recognized his father's legs right away: they were covered by safety-patrol orange leggings, but T.J. knew them. He stared at them, wishing that they would twitch.

"Almost there," John said. Sid pulled way back on the throttle, circling around, the boat's wake making the red raft bob.

T.J. stared, and he had the weirdest memory. His mom was pregnant with Josie at the same time as Rory, their old Scottie. One day Rory disappeared, and when she came home, you could tell she'd had the litter. Her big belly was gone. Everyone was psyched about locating the puppies. They followed Rory everywhere that first morning, all excited about finding a bunch of squirmy, hairless Scotties.

T.J. and his dad found them, under the Camarras' back-porch stairs, and just before T.J. could reach in, his dad grabbed his hand. "They're dead, Teej." All five puppies, stillborn. T.J. had nightmares about it.

John reached for the raft with the boat hook, caught an eye of nylon line. He pulled the raft alongside, and then paused. You could tell he didn't want to go aboard.

"I'll go," T.J. said.

John reached out, to grab T.J.'s hand, exactly the way his dad had done with the puppies.

"No," John said. He lowered himself carefully over the side, his toe flapping in the air, trying to make gentle contact with the raft. T.J. couldn't watch. He held his stomach with both arms. He walked across the deck to the starboard rail. Something burned in his throat. He spit to get rid of it, then spit again.

"Get over here," John called, and T.J. came running. He leaned over the port rail. John had thrown back the cover, and he stood over two men. T.J. stared at his father, curved around the other man's back. They weren't moving, and you couldn't see their faces for

the orange hoods. T.J. clutched the coaming.

"They're alive!" John said.

T.J.'s knees buckled; he snapped his head down, blinking to hold back the tears.

"They're in shock, but they're alive! Call for help!" John shouted, even though T.J. and Sid were standing right there.

T.J. leapt aboard the raft while Sid radioed the Coast Guard. John knelt there, beaming. He slapped T.J. on the back. "We did it!" John said. T.J. smiled, clasping John's arm with one hand, wiping away hot tears with the other. "I'll get some blankets," John said, hoisting himself onto the boat.

Gently, T.J. rolled his father over. He felt like dead weight. For a second T.J.'s heart thumped, wondering if John had made a mistake. The other man — T.J. didn't even know who it was — just lay there beside them.

T.J.'s fingers fumbled for the cord that puckered the hood around his father's face, and managed to untie it. Salt water had gotten inside; his father's lips were cracked and bloody, his eyes swollen shut. T.J. groped behind his father's ear, down the side of his neck.

A pulse.

"Dad," T.J. said. "Dad."

He felt himself grinning like an idiot, holding his father's head. His father looked terrible, like a mountain man. Black whiskers all over his face, sour yellow bruises, dried blood. A muscle in his cheek started to twitch, vibrating nonstop. It bothered T.J. when embarrassing things happened to sleeping people. So he put his index finger on the tic, and his father opened one eye.

"T.J.," his father said. He gazed at T.J. through the narrowest possible slit. "T.J.," he said again, more like a croak.

"We found you, Dad," T.J. said. It was beginning to hit him: he and John had actually done it. Sid, too. They'd found the raft; they'd saved his father's life.

His father kind of smiled, then his eye fluttered back down. John stood over them, leaning over the rail. "He was awake?" John asked.

"Yeah," T.J. said, nodding. "He looked straight at me."

"There's someone on the radio who wants to talk to you," John said. "Want to come up?"

T.J. sat still, cradling his father's head. "You come down first. I don't want to leave him alone."

John clambered over the rail, big woolly blankets under one arm. T.J. watched him tuck the bright blue one around his father — even under his feet, right up to his chin. Then T.J. climbed up on deck. As he did, the first

480

Coast Guard plane arrived. It flew in a wide circle over the *Aurora* and the raft, and it continued to circle, marking their position for the cutter. All the parrots dove for cover, roosting amid nets and fishing gear.

Sid sat in the wheelhouse. He rose when T.J. walked in, gave him a monster hug and smile, and handed him the microphone. "Press this button when you want to talk, let go when you want to listen."

"I know how," T.J. said.

"Why aren't I surprised?" Sid asked, ambling out of the wheelhouse.

"Hello," T.J. said into the chrome mike.

"T.J., is that you?"

"Mom! We found him. He talked to me. He knew who I was, right away. He's alive, Mom. Dad's alive. We found him!" The words poured out, so fast T.J. almost forgot to let go of the button.

"I'm so proud of you, T.J.," his mom said, and you could tell she was crying. "Thank you, honey. Thank you, T.J. Is he really okay? You're positive? You were with him? You saw?"

"Yes, I was with him. He opened his eyes and everything. The Coast Guard's on its way out now. I kept the planes looking, Mom. I shot off flares so they wouldn't call off the search."

"You did?" she asked, sounding amazed.

"Yeah," T.J. said proudly.

"The other men? Are they with your father?"

"Only one, Mom."

"The others?" she asked in a tiny voice.

"They're not here."

Suddenly a strange thudding noise filled the air. T.J. looked outside and saw a big white helicopter, coming fast. "A helicopter's coming to get Dad," he said, excited. "They wouldn't have gotten here so fast if they'd called off the search, would they?"

"No, they wouldn't," his mom said, her voice still full of tears. "But you found him. You're bringing him home."

"I'd better go," T.J. said, one hand over his ear. The helicopter was coming down, unbelievably loud.

"Tell him I love him," his mom yelled over the racket. "Did you hear me? T.J.?"

"I heard you, Mom," T.J. yelled back. He clicked off the radio, and he hurried to give his father a message from home.

Cass ran out to the car, then realized she had forgotten the keys. No, she had them in her hand. She'd left her purse in the house. Hating to waste the time, she started to run back, then realized she had fifteen dollars,

482

enough for an emergency, in her pocket. Since talking to T.J., she'd waited an hour for more news. At first they told her they were taking Billy to Hyannis, then Boston. She called the Coast Guard three times, and each time she got a different story. Finally the official call came: they had taken Billy to Providence General Hospital. Belinda said she would stay with Josie.

She fumbled the key, trying to fit it into the ignition.

"Come on, come on," she said, when the car wouldn't start.

Brakes squealed; she looked over her shoulder. Nora parked her car in the street, and she and Bonnie jumped out.

"We heard," Bonnie said, running to Cass. She and Nora pulled Cass out of the car, and the three sisters grabbed each other. Cass kissed the tears off Bonnie's cheeks.

"He's in Providence," Cass said. "I have to go to him."

Bonnie held her hands. "You can't drive," she said. "You're shaking."

"We'll drive you," Nora said, her arm tight around Cass's shoulders.

"We can't all fit," Cass said dumbly, looking at Nora's sports car.

"Not that one, honey," Bonnie said. "We'll take your station wagon."

483

Cass let Bonnie take the wheel. Belinda and Josie stood in the front window, grinning and waving like mad. Cass rolled down her window, and she waved back until Bonnie sped them out of sight.

"Tell us everything," Nora said, leaning over from the back seat, her head between Cass's and Bonnie's.

"They found him," Cass said. "He's alive."

She didn't have many details; anyway, those were the only things that mattered. Her sisters talked on, filling the car with ecstatic reports of rumors they'd heard about the search, news Jimmy had picked up from the Coast Guard. Cass listened, her heart racing as they neared Providence.

Bonnie kept left on the highway, flashing her brights at the rear mirrors of anything in the way. Forty minutes after leaving Mount Hope, she sped down the exit ramp, into Benefit Street, veering past a rosy blur of colonial brick. At Providence General, Bonnie screeched to the curb. Cass leapt out of the car, her sisters right behind her.

Inside the hospital, Cass stopped dead, looking around, disoriented.

"Patient information," Nora said. "Over there."

"William Medieros," Cass said to the salmon-pink-smocked volunteer. The woman checked her computer. "He's in 653N," she said, giving Cass a casual smile.

Starting for the elevator, Cass turned to her sisters, who were holding back.

"Hurry," she said. "Let's go."

Bonnie shook her head, smiling. "No," she said.

"You go," Nora said, squeezing Cass's arm. "We'll be here when you need us."

Cass nodded, stepping backward. Then she turned and ran for the elevator.

Sixth floor, north wing. Signs directed her down a maze of gleaming white corridors. Cass raced past the solarium, the nurses' station, the laundry cart, rows of patient rooms: 656, 655, 654 . . .

Room 653. Cass stopped, out of breath. The door was ajar. She reached for the handle, almost afraid to push it open. Hr fingers closed around the polished stainless-steel knob, and the big door squeaked on its hinges.

Billy. He lay on his side, facing away from her, his black hair curling on the pillow. Cass heard a sharp intake of breath: her own. She moved to the bed. IV lines ran to Billy from bottles of clear fluid hanging overhead. Cass stared at him, taking everything in. She touched his shoulder, so lightly she didn't know if he'd feel it. Billy turned around.

"Cass," he said.

"Oh, my God," she said at the sight of his bruised and swollen eyes.

They stared at each other, then Billy pulled her down hard. He kissed her roughly, holding her close; she lay across his chest, half in and half out of the bed. Cass ran her hands through his hair, across his face, down his arms, as if she wanted to reassure herself that he was really there.

"I thought I'd never see you again," she said, tears streaming down her cheeks.

"Me, too," Billy said, unwilling to let her go. He clutched her shoulders, gently kissing her collarbone.

"Tell me everything," she said, after a long while.

"I didn't think I'd come back. We lost Jesse and Frank," he said. "And Tony."

"I know," Cass said, her fingers brushing his forehead. She wanted him to tell her what had happened, but his silence was brutal and absolute.

"The Coast Guard said that if you hadn't been in the Gulf Stream, you would have frozen to death," Cass said. "You almost did, anyway."

"I don't remember much," he said. "Getting into the life raft. I guess we lost consciousness. The next thing I remember is seeing T.J. I didn't know where I was."

"I can't believe any of it," Cass said, shaking her head. "That you sank, that they found you. None of it. I can't believe John knew where to look."

Billy half smiled. "When he heard I went down off Nantucket, he knew I'd been dragging a little trench we'd found together. I don't fish it that often, but in those waters, John knew that's where I'd be."

"Still, Billy. Even if he knew the exact spot on the chart where you'd been fishing, three days went by."

"He's a smart sailor," Billy said, really smiling now. "And T.J. Wow."

"I'm so proud of him," Cass said, choking up as she thought of her son, now on his way home from sea with John. She made slow circles on Billy's palm with her finger. "Were you afraid?"

"I was afraid when the whale first got tangled. Once I knew what was happening. And when I saw Jesse and Frank go overboard."

Billy frowned; Cass could see him reliving the scene. He closed his eyes.

"You couldn't have done anything," she said.

But he went on as if he hadn't heard her. "I was mostly afraid that last time I called the operator, when I realized we were going down. The lights were flashing, and it meant we were about to lose power. I had to give her our position first, whatever information I could, so she could tell the rescue boat. But I was afraid that . . ."

Cass just stroked his hand, waiting.

"That we'd lose power before I had the chance to tell her to call you. To tell you I love you. I didn't think I'd ever have the chance to do it myself."

Cass held his hand, silent for a long minute. She pictured the whale ripping his boat apart, the men drowning, Billy afraid that he was going to die. She blinked, to get the images out of her mind.

"But, Cass?" he said.

"Yes?"

"Here's my chance."

She leaned closer to his mouth, to listen.

"I love you," he said.

26

"Oh, God, I feel so important he's my cousin," Emma said, slouched down in her chair in the school auditorium.

"I know," Belinda said, feeling a major adrenaline rush. Any second now the principal was going to introduce T.J., and the entire student body would rise as one and salute him. It was the day before Thanksgiving. "Just check out Alison. This is going to be great."

"That slut," Emma said, popping gum. "Look at her, on the edge of her seat."

Alison had a fourth-row center-aisle seat. As close to the stage as she'd dare sit without sacrificing coolness, but so incredibly obvious. She perched there, her knees together, tilting into the aisle, her fawn suede mini hiked up to *there*, her expertly blushed cheeks glowing, her doe eyes batting a mile a minute, waiting for T.J. to appear.

"He can't miss her, that's for sure," Emma said. "I'll kill him if he even looks at her. She does not deserve the time of day."

"I notice she's left Martin high and dry."

"That seems to be her big talent, dropping guys."

"T.J. survived," Belinda said. She hadn't told anyone, not even Emma, about Josie's revelation. After T.J. had left to search for their father, Josie had told Belinda about the gun. Belinda hadn't believed her at first. Why should she have? Josie had kept saying "shoot head," "shoot head," only her funny pronunciation made it sound like "shoe Ed."

"What shoe? Who's Ed?" Belinda had asked, until Josie flew into a rage, pulled Belinda right down to the cellar, showed her the suds hole, too deep to see anything, and the cupboard, full of bullets, where T.J. had found the gun.

Belinda watched Alison now. Alison was gazing adoringly at the stage curtain, and T.J. wasn't even there yet. Her friends, taking up the rows around her, buzzed with anticipation.

"You're going to get arrested," Emma said.

"For what?"

"Assault with attempt to shave. You're giving her razor looks. Quit staring at her and have some gum." Emma offered her a stick. Cinnamon.

"Hey, dudettes." Sean porked his way past some kids to nab the empty seat in front of Belinda and Emma.

"Hey, pudge," Emma said. Belinda felt glad Emma was taking it easy on Sean.

Suddenly Mrs. Foster, the principal, walked across the stage. She clasped the podium, and almost before anyone had noticed her, she was introducing T.J.

". . . what the Coast Guard could not accomplish. Against terrible odds, through one of the worst storms of this decade, through the blackness of night . . ."

"Is she introducing a mailman?" Emma whispered.

"Shush!" Belinda said, even more on the edge of her seat than Alison.

". . . love for his father. Something we all have, but often don't admit until it's too late. Three men lost their lives — men whose children some of you know. Today, many of your parents will attend their funeral. Many of your fathers fish for a living, and many of you will carry on that tradition.

"All through those terrible days, when we didn't know the *Cassandra*'s fate, we pulled together as a school. Some of us prayed. Some of us kept busy, trying to keep from watching the hours tick by. But one thing united us all: our deep concern and admiration for your classmate, Tom Medieros. He's a real hero."

"I can't believe she called him 'Tom'!"

Belinda squealed, her eyes closed.

"T.J.!" Emma yelled. "Yo, Teej!"

Then the whole assembly, everyone from middle school to high school, got going: "T.J., T.J."

Finally, the curtain opened and T.J. stepped out. Belinda leapt to her feet, clapping till her hands hurt. T.J. looked so cute, all sunburned and tall, as if he'd grown six inches on the trip. Or maybe it was just because he was onstage. Belinda didn't care. Just looking at her brother, knowing he'd rescued their father, made her so proud.

T.J. stared at Alison for a minute, but he didn't smile. He looked up. Cleared his throat.

"Thanks for thinking about me while I was out there," he said, still not smiling. "I was really scared, and I know your thoughts, or whatever, helped. All of you whose fathers fish probably know how I felt. You would have done the same. Or you would have wanted to do the same. But maybe your moms wouldn't let you. Maybe you wouldn't have made it to the dock on time to jump onboard a boat. Maybe you would have had to stay home with your little sister."

He cleared his throat, seeming nervous. He scanned the crowd, and this time he found Belinda. Her eyes glittered, and she gave him her biggest smile, glad because he'd looked at her for courage. He didn't look away.

"In a way, it's probably harder staying home, waiting while someone else looks," he said. "So that's why I want to thank my sister, Belinda. She wanted to be searching just as much as I did."

Suddenly the whole school was yelling her name, clapping their hands, and Emma pulled Belinda to her feet. Emma and Sean pushed her into the aisle, so Belinda didn't have any choice.

"Way to go, Bel!" Emma called.

Belinda walked down the aisle, feeling small as she passed rows of standing freshmen, sophomores, even juniors and seniors, all clapping and watching her. She climbed the steps to the stage, feeling like she'd never get to the top. But she did, and there was T.J., clapping as hard as everyone else, grinning from ear to ear.

"Bel from hell," he said.

"Tom Medieros."

She waved to Emma, then she and T.J. walked off the stage. Belinda thought she'd explode, she felt so happy. She hurried down the aisle, noticing that Alison barely looked at them. Sean and Emma gave her high-fives. The bell rang: only two more periods, and then the school day would be over and it would be Thanksgiving break.

Josie was going to stay with Zach while her parents went to the men's funeral. She played in her room, waiting for him to come.

Josie loved her parrot. T.J. had brought it home for her. He told her it had flown onto his boat with all its friends and family, and when they all flew away, her parrot stayed. Josie named him Ken.

Ken lived in a cage that Josie's grandmother used to keep in the cellar. Josie had wanted to get in the cage herself, it was so beautiful and fancy, and nearly big enough for a girl. White wire with swings and platforms. But her mother had said no, it was Ken's home.

Josie kept Ken in her room. At night her mother showed her how to put a sheet over his cage. In the morning Josie gave Ken water and birdseed. Ken liked to hop around, looking for food. Sometimes T.J. came into her room, and they'd close Josie's door and let Ken fly free.

T.J. and Belinda talked to Ken, and Ken talked back. To Josie, Ken's words sounded just like noise, but Belinda said they were words. She promised she would teach Ken how to say Josie's name. Josie stared at Ken, wishing she could hear him talk. Zach had taught her how to sign "Ken," and Josie tried it now.

Her father walked into her room. He knelt beside Ken's cage, so he was closer to Josie's height. Josie was so happy to have him home from the hospital, but right now she felt sad, because she couldn't hear Ken. She raised up her arms, so her father would hug her.

"How's Ken?" he asked.

"He's good."

Ken must have been talking, because suddenly her father laughed. "That's a smart bird," he said.

"Why?" Josie asked.

"Because he can talk."

Josie pushed away from her father. Her face felt hot and she was embarrassed. Ken could probably talk better than Josie did. Her father didn't think Josie was as smart as her parrot.

"What's wrong?" he asked.

Josie shook her head. She wished he would go away. She felt very mad at her father, and very sad, both at the same time.

"Please tell me, Josie," he said.

Tears pushed out of her eyes, and she felt like hitting him. "It's because you think I'm stupid," she yelled.

"No, I don't think that!" Her father tried to hug her, but she squirmed away.

Josie hid her face, so she wouldn't be able to see his mouth. "I can't hear you," she signed. "I'm not listening to you."

Her father waited for her to look up.

"I think you're very smart," he said, when she did.

She shook her head, because she didn't believe him.

"Yes," he said.

"Not as smart as Ken," she said.

"Much smarter," he said. "Smarter than me, and I'm your father."

Josie began to smile, but she felt suspicious. How could her father say she was smarter than him?

"You're learning a whole new language," he said. "Zach says you're the fastest learner he's ever taught."

Josie smiled wide, in spite of herself. Zach had told her that, too. But she hadn't thought her father would think it was a big deal.

"Zach likes me," Josie said.

"I know he does. Next week he's going to take me and Mommy to visit a school. Where you might go next year."

"North Point," Josie said, signing the words as she said them. She felt very scared, thinking about kindergarten. At first she'd been afraid because she didn't want to be with other kids who would make fun of her. But Zach had told her about North Point, where all the kids were deaf. Kindergarten still scared her, but not as much.

Mommy came into the room. "Hi, Josie," she signed.

"Hi, Mom," Josie signed back.

"Zach is here," Mommy signed.

Josie gave her father a quick kiss and ran out of her room, down the hall to the sun porch, where she knew Zach would be waiting.

James Keating thought of Jesse's and Frank's and Tony's families, having to have their funeral the day before Thanksgiving. And he felt guilty as hell, because he had so much to feel thankful for.

He stood at one of Lobsterville's big picture windows, surveying the harbor while he waited for Mary. His gaze kept returning to the *Aurora*, tied to the dock. Her evergreen hull, the white trim — a good, solid boat. For all the Keatings, a good-luck boat: it had brought Billy home alive.

Jimmy had never in his wildest dreams thought it would happen. Many boats sank and many fishermen were rescued, but not a hundred miles off Nantucket in a November gale. He had given Billy up for dead. His worst thoughts over that last day had been for Cass and the kids.

"Hi, love," Mary said. She sneaked up behind him, put her arms around his waist. "A

497

penny for your thoughts."

"Just looking at the *Aurora*," he said. "Who'd have thought it?"

"Must fill you with pride," Mary said.

"It's not like I was there," Jimmy said, wishing he had been in on the rescue.

"Just wipe that frown off your face and feel a little pleasure, for heaven's sake. Will you please lose the hair shirt?"

Jimmy gave her a little squeeze.

"After all, you called the governor. The search would have ended an entire day earlier. You've really got clout, Jimmy."

"Know when to quit, Mary," Jimmy said, but he smiled.

"What a Thanksgiving."

"Yes, I was just thinking that myself."

With his arm around Mary, as he looked across from Lobsterville to the warehouse, something rang clear as a bell. There were the *Aurora* and the *Norboca*. When Billy was ready to come back, while he looked for a boat to replace the *Cassandra*, the *Norboca* was waiting. Jimmy owned the fleet, the wharf, the warehouse, and the best restaurant in Rhode Island, and he had a family who loved each other. He might retire, but he wasn't getting rid of any of it.

"Christmas in Florida," he said, trying it out.

"We'd miss the festivities up here."

"That's true," he said. "But wouldn't some warm weather be nice?"

"We could go in January, after New Year's," Mary suggested.

"That's a thought," Jimmy said.

"Just for a month, to see how we like it," Mary said.

Jimmy smiled, nodding. They stood together, their arms around each other's waist, gazing at the harbor.

Jimmy saw a mooring that needed checking, a hull that needed caulking. A couple of wharf pilings needed replacing. Icicles hung from the warehouse roof, weakening the gutters. Then his gaze lighted on the *Aurora*. Solid, lucky boat. A muscle twitched, lifting the left corner of his mouth.

But now it was time to leave for the church. He took a deep breath, and he and Mary headed for their car.

Sheila said her Thanksgiving prayers and waited. And waited. She began to feel cross, he was taking so long. She fell asleep, woke up, fell back to sleep in her chair.

"Eddie," she muttered, waking herself up.

And then, there he was. Standing right in front of her. The sight of her husband was enough to make Sheila's eyes glitter with tears.

For this wasn't the man who had died of a stroke at the age of sixty-seven; this was Eddie aged twenty-seven, dressed for the Blue Moon in a white flannel suit and a straw boater, still the handsomest man Sheila had ever laid eyes on.

"You've come!" she said, struggling to stand up.

"Shee, you're a sight for sore eyes," he said, smiling.

"The boy's fine," Sheila said, leaning back in her chair for just a minute, smiling back at Eddie.

"You said Cass couldn't let him go."

"Let me show you something," Sheila said. Her throat had that choked-up, out-of-breath feeling as she pushed herself out of her chair. She crossed the room to Ward's painting.

"That's my girl," Eddie said, wearing an amazed expression, as if he were proud watching her just walk.

"Could you give me a hand?" Sheila asked. "It's behind that painting Ward did. Isn't that a work of art?"

"What a talented son he was. Weren't we lucky to have two such talented sons? Who would have thought Jimmy would run the wharf with such good sense?" Eddie asked, but he made no move to lift the painting from its nail.

"Eddie? Could you pass it over to me? I want to show you something."

"You know I can't, Sheila." He checked his pocket watch, a heavy gold one that had been Sheila's father's.

"Then what about that?" she asked, gesturing.

"Like they say, you can't take it with you," he said. "But you do find what you love on the other side. Now come on — you'd better get a move on. We're stepping out."

"Out? You and me?" Sheila asked, her heart fluttering.

"That's right. You and me."

"Oh, I'd better hurry," Sheila said. She stood on her tiptoes to reach the painting. She'd shrunk since the last time she'd taken it down; she had to stretch much farther.

"That's it," Eddie said encouragingly.

This was her time? Sheila could hardly believe what Eddie was saying to her. Would he take her away and not bring her back? Would Eddie, dapper and fine, escort her to the other side as she was now, with white hair and cataracts, and could she expect to keep him?

"Eddie, tell me straight out," she said, blinking at him, trying to clear her blurry vision. "Are you here to tell me I'm going to die?"

501

He nodded his head. He seemed hardly able to contain his happiness. "Yes. Don't be afraid."

"Will you be with me?"

"Forever."

"Then I'm not afraid." Sheila sat in her chair and removed from its envelope the telegram informing them of Ward's death.

"The worst news we ever got," Eddie said, his voice thick.

Sheila sighed, handing the paper to Eddie. "I couldn't protect Ward, but I helped Billy. I did that for Cass."

Eddie read what she had written on the telegram, and then Sheila put it away. She held on to her pearl, in its tiny globe dangling from the chain around her neck, as tight as she could.

"I'm ready," she said again.

"We're going to the Blue Moon, my darling," Eddie said, his voice becoming clearer with every word. "Put on your white dress and that beautiful big hat. You'll see Patrick and Doreen, and, yes, Sheila, you'll see Ward. Bring a shawl — the wind's blowing from the east."

"I'm coming, Eddie," Sheila whispered.

The bells of Mount Hope rang when wars were won, when sons and daughters of the town married, when children were born.

Sometimes the bells were rung for joy. Other times, the bells of Mount Hope rang with sorrow: when fishermen drowned, when hope was lost.

Cass and Billy stood in the sun-porch door, watching Zach teach Josie some new signs. Suddenly Billy's eyes looked over their heads, toward the window. He caught Cass's eye, to see if she'd heard it, too. The Portuguese church bell. It started to ring, and then the bell at Our Lady of Mount Hope started, then the deeper bell at St. Matthew's Episcopal, until all the bells in town were ringing, drowning out the foghorn at Minturn Ledge.

"It's time," Cass said.

"Bye, Zach," Billy said. He and Cass kissed Josie goodbye, as the bells grew louder.

"I wish I could say something," Zach said, shrugging. "I'm sorry about the men."

"Thanks," Billy said.

"Thanks for staying with Josie," Cass said.

She and Billy got their dark coats and headed outside. In the driveway, approaching the car, Billy stopped short. He looked at Cass, helplessly.

"I couldn't even bring their bodies home," Billy said. He reached for her; they held each other close. There in the driveway, they stood still, pressed together, listening to the funeral bells. Then they got in their car, and Billy drove toward the harbor.

Suddenly, Cass became aware of an unusual brightness in the sky. She leaned forward to see where it came from. The air seemed awash with particles of gold burnishing the mid-morning blue sky.

"What's that light?" Cass asked.

"I don't know," Billy said. "Reminds me of skies I've seen offshore. Sunset skies." But it was nine-thirty in the morning.

Billy rounded the corner for Minturn Ledge Light. To Cass, the light was nothing like a sunset. It wasn't a bank of golden clouds or a streak of orange in the western sky. It was diffused through the entire sky, the air itself, and the golden light grew more concentrated as they neared her parents' house.

Just as Cass and Billy approached the Keatings', Cass caught sight of a young couple leaving her parents' house.

"Who are they?" Billy asked.

"Stop the car!" Cass said.

"We'll be late," he said, glancing at his watch.

"Please," Cass said. "We have half an hour."

The couple was dressed all in white, he in a flannel suit and she in a beautiful dress flowing to her ankles. They wore straw hats with blue ribbons around the crowns, and she carried an umbrella. They skipped down the steps, as if they were in a hurry to get somewhere, laughing with pleasure. They looked familiar; the woman had features that closely resembled Cass's own. Yet they seemed old-fashioned, otherworldly, like a modern couple got up like John Singer Sargent portraits for a costume ball.

"Hello," Cass called to them, climbing out of the car. "Hello!"

At the sound of her voice, they stopped short. Their smiles vanished for a moment. They seemed ready to bolt. But they turned around and walked toward Cass and Billy.

"May I help you?" Cass asked, her voice quavering.

"Isn't she lovely?" the young man asked. "She was just a girl when I last saw her."

"You should see *her* daughters," the young woman said. "Beauties, both of them. And a handsome son."

By the voice, Cass knew. "Granny?" she asked.

The young woman nodded, giving Cass a beautiful smile. She had sparkling, even teeth. All of them. She wore the pearl globe, dangling from its dainty chain.

"I don't understand," Cass said.

Sheila nodded. She made a move to touch Cass's cheek, but stopped herself. "We're off to the Blue Moon; we can't be late. Say hello to your grandfather." She turned to her companion. "And this is Billy."

"Hello," Billy said.

"Our Billy," the young woman said. "Home safe."

It seemed strange, calling this handsome young man "Grandpa," but Cass did it. "Hello, Grandpa."

The two couples stood there, gazing at each other. Cass, in her funeral black, smiled at her grandmother, radiant as a bride in white.

"We really must be going, Sheila," Eddie said gently, cupping Sheila's elbow with his strong hand.

Sheila stood very close to Cass and studied the expression in her eyes. "Don't be sad," she said. "Promise?"

Cass wanted to promise, but she found she could not.

"And whatever happens, remember I did what I thought was best. I did what I needed to do. I love you very much. Thanksgiving, Cass," she said.

A sob caught in Cass's throat. She knew that this was goodbye.

"We musn't stay," Sheila said. Then, in one quick motion, she pulled her crystal globe, breaking the chain, and thrust it into Cass's hand. Then she and Eddie ran off. Cass stood watching them until they disappeared — not around the corner, but into a shimmering haze of golden light.

"Billy," she said, afraid to move.

"Let's go inside," he said, his hand cupping her elbow, just as Eddie's had Sheila's.

They made their way up the front steps, into her parents' house. Once inside, with the memory of what she had just seen burning in her mind, she ran up the stairs to her grandmother's room.

"Oh, Granny," she said. Her grandmother sat slumped forward in the rocking chair. Cass touched her cold wrist, fumbled for a pulse.

The clock ticked loudly. Cass sat on the floor beside her grandmother's body, sensing the light fade outside. The room seemed dim and cold. Cass noticed Ward's painting lying on the floor. She stared at it for a minute, the two boys clamming at low tide. She recognized Easton's Beach and the boardwalk in the background. She recognized which boy was her father: the one with the cowlick, the devilish smile, his skinny long legs. Slowly she stood, then replaced the painting on the wall.

She returned to her grandmother's body. She had the urge to cover it with a blanket. She didn't want to see her grandmother's eyes. But she had to check, she had to know — the necklace. She felt for it and finally tipped her grandmother's head back so she could see. But, of course, it wasn't there; Cass held the pearl globe and its broken chain in the palm of her left hand. At that instant, she noticed that her grandmother was clutching a piece of paper. Easing it out of her stiff grasp, Cass began to read.

"It's the telegram," Cass said. "Telling them Ward had been killed."

"There's something on the back," Billy said.

Cass turned it over. She and Billy huddled close, trying to read. Sheila had written something in a frail, spidery hand.

"Keep Billy safe," it said, "and let me go in his place."

"Oh," Cass said, holding Billy.

They stood together, looking down at Sheila. Tears ran down Cass's cheeks, and she read the message over.

"Is it possible? Do you think?" she asked.

Billy nodded. "It was a miracle," he said. "I shouldn't have come home. I knew that from the first night. I hoped — I hoped like hell. But to be rescued like that . . ."

"By T.J."

"By my own son."

Cass slowly opened her hand. There was the pearl, safe in its glass locket. She clasped it in her palm, thinking of what her grandmother had said: Thanksgiving. She kissed her grandmother's forehead, and then she slipped her hand into Billy's.

"It's Thanksgiving," she said out loud. Outside, the funeral bells, the bells of Mount Hope, rang and rang.

The employees of THORNDIKE PRESS hope you have enjoyed this Large Print book. All our Large Print books are designed for easy reading — and they're made to last.

Other Thorndike Large Print books are available at your library, through selected bookstores, or directly from us. Suggestions for books you would like to see in Large Print are always welcome.

For more information about current and upcoming titles, please call or mail your name and address to:

THORNDIKE PRESS
PO Box 159
Thorndike, Maine 04986
800/223-6121
207/948-2962